THE DREAM LOVER

THE DREAM LOVER

SHORT STORIES

WILLIAM BOYD

BLOOMSBURY

Some of these stories were first published by Hamish Hamilton in 1981
under the title *On the Yankee Station*, and appeared in the following
publications: *London Magazine, Mayfair, Punch, Isis, Literary Review*, BBC
Radio 4's *Morning Story, Company* and *New Stories 6*. Others were first
published by Sinclair-Stevenson in 1995 under the title *The Destiny of
Nathalie 'X'* and four of the stories ('The Destiny of Nathalie "X"', 'Cork',
'Transfigured Night' and 'Alpes Maritimes') have been published in *Granta*.
'The Dream Lover' was published in *London Magazine*, 'Hôtel des
Voyagers' in the *Daily Telegraph* and 'N is for N' appeared in *Hockney's
Alphabet* (Faber and Faber, 1993). 'Extracts from the Journal of Flying
Officer J.' was first published in *Shakespeare Stories* edited by Giles Gordon,
first published by Hamish Hamilton in 1982. 'The Care and Attention of
Swimming Pools' was first published in the *New Statesman* in 1981.

Bloomsbury Publishing Plc, 36 Soho Square, London W1D 3QY

A CIP catalogue record for this book is available from the British Library

ISBN 978 0 7475 9229 7

10 9 8 7 6 5 4 3

Typeset by Hewer Text UK Ltd, Edinburgh
Printed in Great Britain by Clays Ltd, St Ives plc

Bloomsbury Publishing, London, New York and Berlin

All papers used by Bloomsbury Publishing are natural, recyclable products
made from wood grown in well-managed forests. The manufacturing
processes conform to the environmental regulations of the country of origin

www.bloomsbury.com/williamboyd

For Susan

Contents

Introduction	1
Killing Lizards	9
Not Yet, Jayette	19
Bizarre Situations	27
Hardly Ever	38
The Care and Attention of Swimming Pools	62
Next Boat from Douala	74
Gifts	83
My Girl in Skin-Tight Jeans	102
Histoire Vache	110
On the Yankee Station	123
Bat-Girl!	148
Love Hurts	157
Extracts from the Journal of Flying Officer J.	169
The Coup	179
Long Story Short	202
The Destiny of Nathalie 'X'	210
Transfigured Night	244
Hôtel des Voyageurs	261
Never Saw Brazil	268
The Dream Lover	286

Alpes Maritimes	303
N is for N	319
The Persistence of Vision	321
Cork	335

Introduction

The first genuine, proper piece of fiction I wrote was a short story. It was in 1971, I was nineteen years old, and it was called 'Reveries of an Early Morning Riser'. The story was transparently autobiographical in nature – a somewhat elegiac account of a relationship I had had with a German girl in the previous spring and summer while I was studying at the University of Nice[1]. I wrote it specifically for a competition run by the English Literature department of Glasgow University where I had just begun my MA degree. Most unusually for the time, the university had appointed a resident creative writer, an elderly poet called George Bruce[2], and the short-story competition was his idea, a competition open to all the undergraduates reading first-year Eng. Lit. (a large number, several hundred strong). I wrote my story, submitted it and to my delight and astonishment won first prize – a £10 book token. I still have the typescript of

1 That year (1971) at the University of Nice provided the backdrop for other, later short stories: in this volume they are 'Gifts', 'Alpes Maritimes' and 'The Dream Lover'.
2 I remember George Bruce but I remember his successor in the post, William Price Turner, better. Both were amiable and supportive: these were the first writers I ever met.

'Reveries of an Early Morning Riser' and the manuscript of another short story I wrote a little later but it seems that after this initial spurt my taste for writing short stories lapsed, rather. However, I wrote a great deal at Glasgow University (1971–75): much journalism – I was the film and theatre critic for the university newspaper – a play about my schooldays (submitted unsuccessfully for a playwriting competition), quite a lot of pseudonymous poetry and a novel called *Is That All There Is?* The title came from a great Peggy Lee song and the story was once again set in the south of France on the Côte d'Azur and, yet again, was unabashedly all about me (though I called my fictional alter-ego 'Henry Rush'). My formative year in Nice was proving a fertile mulch for my embryonic fiction-writing imagination.

Looking back now I can see that I was writing in the way many young writers begin: using my own life experiences as raw material – changing the odd name here and there, introducing the odd wish-fulfilling narrative swerve (the boy *gets* the girl) – but basically relying on the simple authenticity of the experience (which I could certainly vouch for) as the motor for the narrative and its characters. It's a phase most young writers go through – only a very few brilliant exceptions produce work of any value, let alone of lasting value – and I can see that the fiction I wrote while at Glasgow University represents a working-through of the autobiographical mode. Very soon afterwards I stopped writing about myself and my life and have never really started again.

In 1975 I left Glasgow and went to Oxford University to do a post-graduate degree – I was working on a D.Phil thesis earnestly entitled 'Philosophical Influences on the Poetry and Prose of P.B. Shelley' (another substantial piece of unpublished writing) – and it was at Oxford that the short story came back into favour. Once again the catalyst was competitions. The university magazine, *Isis*, diligently and civilly exploited the fact that many distinguished writers lived in and around the city and, every term or so, invited one or other of them to judge a short-story competition. In 1976 I wrote a short story called 'The Laubnitsch Upright' and entered it for an *Isis* competition judged by Iris Murdoch and John Bayley. 'The Laubnitsch Upright' was inspired by a poem, 'Sunday Morning' by Wallace Stevens, and was set in a provincial American city, telling the story of two removal men who, one Sunday morning, try effortfully to manoeuvre a huge rare piano (the 'upright' of the title) into the house of a rather attractive older woman. For me this story is significant in that it was about people, a world and an idiom I had never encountered (I hadn't been to the USA at that stage of my life). I was going against the received wisdom handed down to young writers – 'write about what you know' – and was deliberately writing about something I knew nothing about. I was obliged, in other words, to use my imagination. I don't know if Iris Murdoch and John Bayley picked up the complex skein of allusions to Stevens' poem running through the story but they liked it sufficiently to award it second prize in the competition (and another book token duly came my way). Over the next year or so I entered other *Isis* short-story competitions. One was judged by Roald Dahl and he bestowed third prize on me for a story I wrote called 'Patience at Spinoza's'; another was a science-fiction story for a competition judged by Brian Aldiss[3] in which I wasn't placed at all. The downward curve was plain to see – it seemed it was time to stop entering short-story competitions.

And so I went to the wider world and started sending out my short stories to magazines – literary magazines, humorous

3 In 1979, Brian Aldiss became a near neighbour in Oxford – and a firm and lasting friendship ensued (no mention was ever made of his oversight in the competition).

magazines, women's magazines – anywhere that published short stories, in fact. I reworked 'Patience at Spinoza's' and sent it off to *London Magazine*, a legendary small literary journal edited by Alan Ross with a reputation for discovering new writers and poets. Alan Ross[4] wrote back remarkably quickly: yes, he would take the story and would pay me £15 but I had to change the title – 'Patience at Spinoza's' simply wouldn't do. I concurred – it was a terrible title – and immediately changed it to 'Next Boat to Douala'. It was published in the August 1978 issue of the magazine.

More significances accrue here: 'Next Boat from Douala' was not only the first story of mine to be professionally published – and it's included in this collection – but it also launched my career as a novelist. The story relates an unhappy sexual misadventure in the life of a young, overweight, often drunk British diplomat living in West Africa named Morgan Leafy. Inspired by my success with Alan Ross and *London Magazine* I wrote another story about Morgan Leafy, 'The Coup' (also published in this collection), that was taken by *Mayfair* magazine. This time the cheque was in three figures and there was a commissioned illustration – I seemed to be on a roll. And in a sense I was: my scatter-gun submission programme drew its fair share of rejections but I began to place more and more stories – *Punch*, *Company*, the *Literary Review*, the BBC's *Morning Story* among others – over the next few months and soon, it seemed to me, I had the makings of a small collection.

However, during this time (1976–9 approximately) I was also, amongst other things, writing novels. I wrote a novel called

---

4 Alan Ross became, therefore, the first person to publish me, picking my work out from the dozens of unsolicited stories routinely submitted to his magazine, and was an influential figure in my literary life and someone for whom I continued to write up until his death. My memories of Alan and *London Magazine* can be found in my book of collected non-fiction, *Bamboo* (Penguin, 2006), page 547.

Against the Day about the Nigerian civil war, the Biafran war, that I had witnessed at close-ish hand while I had been living in Nigeria during the late 1960s. This was somewhat self-consciously experimental – a kind of collage-novel made up of scraps: newspaper articles, letters, diary extracts and so on. Alan Ross said he liked it but I think I knew in my heart it was not fully achieved. Moving from the post-modern to the commercial I wrote another novel, a thriller about a poet (if that's not too grotesque an oxymoron) called *Truelove at 29*[5], but I never offered it to a publisher as by then I had formulated another plan.

By the summer of 1979 my short-story success rate was looking fairly impressive. In two years or so I had managed to place eight stories in different magazines and on BBC radio. I calculated that I would have a better chance submitting a collection of these stories to publishing houses rather than one or other of the two novels I had written (*Is That All There Is?* had been permanently bottom-drawered). So I chose two publishers who had a reputation for publishing short-story collections – Hamish Hamilton and Jonathan Cape – and simultaneously sent my stories off to them, addressed to the managing director of each firm. I added as a postscript to my covering letter – and I'm not sure why I did so – that I had also written a novel featuring the character 'Morgan Leafy' who appeared in two of the stories. This was pure fantasy: I had a pretty clear idea of a novel featuring Morgan Leafy in my head but not a word of it had been written down.

5 I did, however, pinch the name – 'Neil Truelove' – of my eponymous poet/hero for the lead character in my second film, *Dutch Girls*, where he was played by the very young Colin Firth. Also, a lot of thinking about war and human conflict in *Against the Day* went into my second novel *An Ice-Cream War*. Writers recycle avidly: nothing is wasted.

With unheard-of speed – again in a couple of weeks – I received a letter from Hamish Hamilton (I never had a reply from Cape). It was signed by Christopher Sinclair-Stevenson, the managing director, and it said that he was interested in the stories but would like to see my synopsis of the 'Morgan Leafy' novel before he came to any decision. The novel in my head swiftly became a five-page outline, swiftly despatched. Christopher Sinclair-Stevenson wrote back (and I remember this vividly, the ultimate red-letter day): yes, he would like to publish my short-story collection but with one proviso – the 'Morgan Leafy' novel, which I had by now entitled *A Good Man in Africa*, would have to be published first.

Slight problem: massive euphoria clouded by the need for a potent white lie. So I lied – I needed to do some work on the manuscript, I said, some re-writing, re-typing, re-organizing, a matter of a few weeks only. Luckily my wife, Susan, was by now working for Oxford University Press, so there was one salary coming into the household. With the aid of the Hamish Hamilton offer now official – on paper – I managed to secure an Arts Council grant (£900 I think). By then I was a jobbing college lecturer at Oxford (also teaching English to foreign students) – and all this work would have to be temporarily dropped as I hastily wrote my 'already-completed' novel – bills would still have to be paid. Money secured, I sat down at the kitchen table in Oxford and wrote *A Good Man in Africa* in a white-heat of passion, febrile excitement and total conviction. Three months later the novel was delivered: Christopher Sinclair-Stevenson[6] had no idea what demonic energies he had provoked.

6 Christopher Sinclair-Stevenson therefore joins Alan Ross as my other key literary mentor. Christopher remained my editor until he left publishing to become a literary agent. The two collections of stories that make up this volume were published under his aegis, as were my first six novels. He has known the true story for many years now.

So my short stories led to my first novel and the purpose behind all this reminiscing is to illustrate just how intertwined the two forms have been in my own beginnings as a writer and in my ongoing development. I've always written short stories alongside my novels and the essential reason is, I believe, that the short story offers a different aesthetic experience, both in the writing and in the reading. For the novelist it is more akin to changing art form – as when one leaves the novel to write a play or a film or a poem. Different mental gears are engaged, different pleasures are experienced – and, crucially, more risks can be taken.

A few years ago I wrote a long piece for the *Guardian*[7] newspaper in which I came up with an unofficial taxonomy of the short-story form. There were, I claimed, basically seven types of short story – and I duly defined them. Looking at the stories collected here I think I have written stories in five of the seven categories that I cited and I think this variety tells me, and tells readers, perhaps, a great deal about why I write short stories. It is a question, finally, of freedom: freedom to change habits, to experiment, to take risks, to try out different voices, to fracture narrative – freedom to do things in your writing life that the novel doesn't allow for the simple reason that it takes so long to write a novel. Fiction, for me, is all about liberating my imagination: and that liberation seems to function particularly appealingly in the short-story form.

This new omnibus volume of stories, *The Dream Lover*, gathers together the stories in my first two collections: *On the Yankee*

7 I seem to have written a fair bit of theory about the short story recently. The *Guardian* essay on the seven types of short story is in *Bamboo* (page 237). There is another essay called 'A Short History of the Short Story' that I wrote for *Prospect* magazine and which can be read on my website (in the 'Journalism' section on the Media page) at www.williamboyd.co.uk.

Station (1981) and *The Destiny of Nathalie 'X'* (1995) representing approximately a decade and a half of my short fiction. All the stories are published in the same order I originally devised for the collections – and they are loosely chronological. My third collection, *Fascination* (Penguin, 2004), is still in print and my fourth is taking shape with three new stories, post-*Fascination*, having already seen the light of day in other publications and formats. The practice is well established: I write novels but I will also always continue to write short stories, I'm sure, for the reasons listed above. However, there seems something faintly valedictory about this new collection – an oddly baleful sense of 'setting one's house in order'. But this kind of re-arranging and re-assessing is also squarely within the tradition of the short story: a story's first appearance in a newspaper or a magazine or broadcast on the radio has an impact but, inevitably, it is an ephemeral one. So the writer collects the disparate stories he has written between hard covers in a slimmish volume and christens them with a general title as a way of making their ephemeral life a little more permanent. However, with a very few exceptions, the shelf life of a short-story collection is not the same as that of a novel – though this is nothing new: Chekhov was acutely aware of this phenomenon in the 1890s and assiduously republished his early volumes. Thus, for writers, the urge remains a powerful one – to gather their stories together and lead them into the embracing fold of the *oeuvre* and keep them there, safely. The stories in *The Dream Lover* are as much a part of my writing life – and help explain who I am as a writer of fiction – as my novels.

William Boyd
London, 2007

Killing Lizards

Gavin squatted beside Israel, the cook's teenage son, on the narrow verandah of the servants' quarters. Israel was making Gavin a new catapult. He bound the thick rubber thongs to the wooden Y with string, tying the final knot tight and nipping off the loose ends with his teeth. Gavin took the proffered catapult and tried a practice shot. He fired at a small grove of banana trees by the kitchen garden. The pebble thunked into a fibrous bole with reassuring force.

'Great!' Gavin said admiringly, then 'hey!' as Israel snatched the catapult back. He dangled the weapon alluringly out of Gavin's reach and grinned as the small twelve-year-old boy leapt angrily for it.

'Cig'rette. Give me cig'rette,' Israel demanded, laughing in his high wheezy way.

'Oh all right,' Gavin grudgingly replied, handing over the packet he had stolen from his mother's handbag the day before. Israel promptly lit one up and confidently puffed smoke up into the washed-out blue of the African sky.

Gavin walked back up the garden to the house. He was a thin dark boy with a slightly pinched face and unusually thick eyebrows that made his face seem older than it was. He went through the kitchen and into the cool spacious living room with its rugs and tiled floor, where two roof fans energetically beat the hot afternoon air into motion.

The room was empty and Gavin walked along the verandah past his bedroom and that of his older sister. His sister, Amanda, was at boarding school in England; Gavin was going to join her there next year. He used to like his sister but since her fifteenth birthday she had changed. When she had come out on holiday last Christmas she had hardly played with him at all. She was bored with him; she preferred going shopping with her mother. A conspiracy of sorts seemed to have sprung up between the women of the family from which Gavin and his father were excluded.

When he thought of his sister now, he felt that he hated her. Sometimes he wished the plane that was bringing her out to Africa would crash and she would be killed. Then there would only be Gavin, he would be the only child. As he passed her bedroom he was reminded of his fantasy and despite himself he paused, thinking about it again, trying to imagine what life would be like – how it would be different. As he did so the other dream began to edge itself into his mind, like an insistent hand signalling at the back of a classroom drawing attention to itself. He had this dream quite a lot these days and it made him feel peculiar: he knew it was bad, a wrong thing to do, and sometimes he forced himself not to think about it. But it never worked, for it always came faltering back with its strange imaginative allure, and he would find himself lost in it, savouring its pleasures, indulging in its sweet illicit sensations.

It was a variation on the theme of his sister's death, but this time it also included his father. His father and sister had died in a car crash and Gavin had to break the news to his mother. As she sobbed with grief she clung to him for support. Gavin would soothe her, stroking her hair as he'd seen done on TV in England, whispering words of comfort.

In the dream Gavin's mother never remarried, and she and Gavin returned to England to live. People would look at them in the street, the tall elegant widow in black and her son, growing tall and more mature himself, being brave and good by her side. People around them seemed to whisper, 'I don't know what she would have done without him' and 'Yes, he's been a marvel' and 'They're so close now'.

Gavin shook his head, blushing guiltily. He didn't hate his father – he just got angry with him sometimes – and it made him feel bad and upset that he kept on imagining him dead. But the dream insistently repeated itself, and it continued to expand; the narrative furnished itself with more and more precise details; the funeral scene was added, the cottage Gavin and his mother took near Canterbury, the plans they made for the school holidays. It grew steadily more real and credible – it was like discovering a new world – but as it did, so Gavin found himself more and more frustrated and oppressed by the truth, more dissatisfied with the way things were.

Gavin slowly pushed open the door of his parents' bedroom. Sometimes he knocked, but his mother had laughed and told him not to be silly. Still, he was cautious as he had once been horribly embarrassed to find them both asleep, naked and sprawled on the rumpled double bed. But today he knew his father was at work in his chemistry lab. Only his mother would be having a siesta.

But Gavin's mother was sitting in front of her dressing table brushing her short but thick reddish auburn hair. She was wearing only a black bra and pants that contrasted strongly with the pale freckly tan of her firm body. A cigarette burned in an ashtray. She brushed methodically and absentmindedly, her

shining hair crackling under the brush. She seemed quite unaware of Gavin standing behind her, looking on. Then he
coughed.

'Yes, darling, what is it?' she said without looking round.

Gavin sensed rather than appreciated that his mother was a
beautiful woman. He did not realize that she was prevented from
achieving it fully by a sulky turn to her lips and a hardness in her
pale eyes. She stood up and stretched languidly, walking bare-
footed over to the wardrobe where she selected a cotton dress.

'Where are you going?' Gavin asked without thinking.

'Rehearsal, dear. For the play,' his mother replied.

'Oh. Well, I'm going out too.' He left it at that. Just to see if
she'd say anything this time, but she seemed not to have heard.
So he added, 'I'm going with Laurence and David. To kill
lizards.'

'Yes, darling,' his mother said, intently examining the dress she
had chosen. 'Do try not to touch the lizards, they're nasty things,
there's a good boy.' She held the dress up in front of her and
looked at her reflection critically in the mirror. She laid the dress
on the bed, sat down again and began to apply some lipstick.
Gavin looked at her rich red hair and the curve of her spine in her
creamy back, broken by the dark strap of her bra, and the three
moles on the curve of her haunch where it was taughtened by
the elastic of her pants. Gavin swallowed. His mother's presence
in his life loomed like a huge wall at whose foot his needs
cowered like beggars at a city gate. He wished she bothered
about him more, did things with him as she did with Amanda.
He felt strange and uneasy about her, proud and uncomfortable.
He had been pleased last Saturday when she took him to the pool
in town, but then she had worn a small bikini and the Syrian men
round the bar had stared at her. David's mother always wore a
swimsuit of a prickly material with stiff bones in it. When he

went out of the room she was brushing her hair again and he didn't bother to say good-bye.

Gavin walked down the road. He was wearing a striped T-shirt, white shorts and Clarks sandals without socks. The early afternoon sun beat down on his head and the heat vibrated up from the tarmac. On either side of him were the low senior-staff bungalows, shadowy beneath their wide eaves, and which seemed to be pressed down into the earth as if the blazing sun bore down with intolerable weight. The coruscating scarlet dazzle of flamboyant trees that lined the road danced spottily in his eyes.

The university campus was a large one but Gavin had come to know it intimately in the two years since his parents had moved to Africa. In Canterbury his father had only been a lecturer but here he was a professor in the Chemistry Department. Gavin loved to go down to the labs with their curious ammoniacal smells, brilliant fluids and mad-scientist constructions of phials, test-tubes and rubber pipes. He thought he might pay his father a surprise visit that afternoon as their lizard hunt should take them in that direction.

Gavin and his two friends had been shooting lizards with their catapults for the three weeks of the Easter holidays and had so far accounted for one hundred and forty-three. They killed mainly the male and female of one species that seemed to populate every group of boulders or area of concrete in the country. The lizards were large, sometimes growing to eighteen inches in length. The females were slightly smaller than the males and were a dirty speckled khaki colour. The males were more resplendent, with brilliant orange-red heads, pale grey bodies and black-barred feet and tails. They did no one any harm; just basked in the sun doing a curious bobbing press-up motion. At first they were ludicrously easy to kill. The boys could creep up to within three or four feet and with one well-placed stone reduce the basking complacent lizard to a writhing knot, its feet clawing at a buckled spine or shattered head. A slight guilt had soon grown up among the boys and they accordingly convinced themselves that the lizards were pests and that, rather like rats, they spread diseases.

But the lizards, like any threatened species, grew wise to the hunters and now scurried off at the merest hint of approach, and the boys had to range wider and wider through the campus to find zones where the word had not spread and where the lizards still clung unconcernedly to walls, like dozing sunbathers unaware of the looming thunderclouds.

Gavin met his friends at the pre-arranged corner. Today they were heading for the university staff's preparatory school at a far edge of the campus. There was an expansive outcrop of boulders there with a sizeable lizard community that they had been evaluating for some time, and this afternoon they planned a blitz.

They walked down the road firing stones at trees and clumps of bushes. Gavin teased Laurence about his bandy legs and then joined forces with him to mock David about his spots and his hugely fat sister until he threatened to go home. Gavin felt tense and malicious, and lied easily to them about how he had fashioned his own catapult, which was far superior to their clumsier home-made efforts. He was glad when they rounded a corner and came in sight of the long simple buildings of the chemistry labs.

'Let's go and see my Dad,' he suggested.

Gavin's father was marking exam papers in an empty lab when the three boys arrived. He was tall and thin with sparse black hair brushed across his balding head. Gavin possessed his similar tentative smile. They chatted for a while, then Gavin's father showed them some frozen nitrogen. He picked a red hibiscus bloom off a hedge outside and dipped it in the container of fuming liquid. Then he dropped the flower on the floor and it shattered to pieces like fine china.

'Where are you off to?' he asked as the boys made ready to leave.

'Down to the school to get lizards,' Gavin replied.

'There's a monster one down there,' said David. 'I've seen it.'

'I hope you don't leave them lying around,' Gavin's father said. 'Things rot in this sun very quickly.'

'It's okay,' Gavin affirmed brightly. 'The hawks soon get them.'

Gavin's father looked thoughtful. 'What's your mother doing?' he asked his son. 'Left her on her own, have you?'

'Israel's there,' Gavin replied sullenly. 'But anyway she's going to her play rehearsal or something. Drama, drama, you know.'

'Today? Are you sure?' his father asked, seemingly surprised.

'That's what she said. Bye Dad, see you tonight.'

The school lay on a small plateau overlooking a teak forest and the jungle that stretched away beyond it. The outcrop of rocks was poised on the edge of the plateau and it ran down in pale pinkish slabs to the beginning of the teak trees.

The boys killed four female lizards almost at once but the others had rushed into crevices and stayed there. Gavin caught a glimpse of a large red-head as it scuttled off and the three of them pelted the deep niche it hid in and prodded at it with sticks, but it was just not coming out.

Then Gavin and Laurence thought they saw a fruit bat in a palm tree, but David couldn't see it and soon lost interest. They patrolled the deserted school buildings for a while and then hung, bat-like themselves, on the Jungle-Jim in the playground. David, who had perched on the top, heard the sound of a car as it negotiated a bumpy rutted track that led into the jungle and which ran for a while along the base of the plateau. He soon saw a Volkswagen van lurching along. A man was driving and a woman sat beside him.

'Hey, Gavin,' David said without thinking. 'Isn't that your mother?'

Gavin climbed quickly up beside him and looked.

'No,' he said. 'Nope. Definitely.'

They resumed their play but the implication hung in the air like a threat, despite their suddenly earnest jocularity. In the unspoken way in which these things arrange themselves, David and Laurence soon announced that they had to go home. Gavin said that he would stay on a bit. He wanted to see if he could get that big lizard.

Laurence and David wandered off with many a backward shouted message about where they would meet tomorrow and what they would do. Then Gavin clambered about half-heartedly on the Jungle-Jim before he walked down the slope to the track which he followed into the teak forest. There was still heat in the afternoon sun and the trees and bushes looked tired from a day's exposure. The big soup-plate leaves of the teak trees hung limply in the damp dusty atmosphere.

Gavin heard his mother's laugh before he saw the van. He moved off the track and followed the curve of a bend until he saw the van through the leaves. It was pulled up on the other side of the mud road. The large sliding door was thrown back and Gavin could see that the bunk bed inside had been folded down. His mother was sitting on the edge of the bunk, laughing. A man without a shirt was struggling to zip up her dress. She laughed again, showing her teeth and throwing back her head, joyously shaking her thick red hair. Gavin knew the man: he was called

Ian Swan and sometimes came to the house. He had a neat black beard and curling black hair all over his chest.

Gavin stood motionless behind the thick screen of leaves and watched his mother and the man. He knew at once what they had been doing. He watched them caper and kiss and laugh. Finally Gavin's mother tugged herself free and scrambled round the van and into the front seat. Gavin saw a pair of sunglasses drop from her open handbag. She didn't notice they had fallen. Swan put on his shirt and joined her in the front of the van.

As they backed and turned the van Gavin held his breath in an agony of tension in case they should run over the glasses. When they had gone he stood for a while before walking over and picking up the sunglasses. They were quite cheap; Gavin remembered she had bought them last leave in England. They were favourites. They had pale blue lenses and candy-pink frames. He held them carefully in the palm of his hand as if he were holding an injured bird.

MUMMY . . .

As he walked down the track to the school the numbness, the blank camera stare that had descended on him the moment he had heard his mother's high laugh, began to dissipate. A slow tingling charge of triumph and elation began to infuse his body.

OH MUMMY, I THINK . . .

He looked again at the sunglasses in his palm. Things would change now. Nothing would be the same after this secret. It seemed to him now as if he were carrying a ticking bomb.

OH MUMMY, I THINK I'VE FOUND YOUR SUN-GLASSES.

The lowering sun was striking the flat rocks of the outcrop full on and Gavin could feel the heat through the soles of his sandals as he walked up the slope. Then, ahead, facing away from him, he saw the lizard. It was catching the last warmth of the day, red head methodically bobbing, sleek torso and long tail motionless. Carefully Gavin set down the glasses and took his catapult and a pebble from his pocket. Stupid lizard, he thought, sunbathing, head bobbing like that, you never know who's around. He drew a bead on it, cautiously easing the thick rubber back to full stretch until his rigid left arm began to quiver from the tension.

He imagined the stone breaking the lizard's back, a pink welling tear in the pale scaly skin. The curious slow-motion way the mortally wounded creatures keeled over, sometimes a single leg twitching crazily like a spinning rear wheel on an upended crashed car.

The lizard basked on, unaware.

Gavin eased off the tension. Holding his breath with the effort, heart thumping in his ears. He stood for a few seconds letting himself calm down. His mother would be home now, he should have enough time before his father returned. He picked up the sunglasses and backed softly away and around, leaving the lizard undisturbed. Then, with his eyes alight and gleaming beneath his oddly heavy brows, he set off steadily for home.

Not Yet, Jayette

This happened to me in L.A. once. Honestly. I was standing at a hamburger kiosk on Echo Park eating a chilé-dog. This guy in a dark green Lincoln pulls up at the kerb in front of me and leans out of the window. 'Hey,' he asks me, 'do you know the way to San José?' Well, that threw me, I had to admit it. In fact I almost told him. Then I got wise. 'Don't tell me,' I says. 'Let me guess. You're going back to find some peace of mind.' I only tell you this to give you some idea of what the city is like. It's full of jokers. And that guy, even though I'd figured him, still bad-mouthed me before he drove away. That's the kind of place it is. I'm just telling you so's you know my day is for real.

Most mornings, early, I go down to the beach at Santa Monica to try and meet Christopher Isherwood. A guy I know told me he likes to walk his dog down there before the beach freaks and the surfers show up. I haven't seen him yet but I've grown to like my mornings on the beach. The sea has that oily sheen to it, like an empty swimming pool. The funny thing is, though, the Pacific Ocean nearly always looks cold. One morning someone was swinging on the bars, up and down, flinging himself about as if he was made of rubber. It was beautiful, and boy, was he built. It's wonderful to me what the human body can achieve if you treat it right. I like to keep in shape. I work out. So most days I hang around waiting to see if Christopher's going to show then I go jogging. I head south; down from the pier to Pacific Ocean Park. I've got to know some of the bums that live around the beach, the junkies and derelicts. 'Hi Charlie,' they shout when they see me jogging by.

There's a café in Venice where I eat breakfast. A girl works there most mornings, thin, bottle-blonde, kind of tired-looking. I'm pretty sure she's on something heavy. So that doesn't make her anything special but she can't be more than eighteen. She knows my name, I don't know how, I never told her. Anyway each morning when she brings me my coffee and doughnut she says 'Hi there, Charlie. Lucked-out yet?' I just smile and say 'Not yet, Jayette.' Jayette's the name she's got sewn across her left tit. I'm not sure I like the way she speaks to me – I don't exactly know what she's referring to. But seeing how she knows my name I think it must be my career she's talking about. Because I used to be a star, well, a TV star anyway. Between the ages of nine and eleven I earned twelve thousand dollars a week. Perhaps you remember the show, a TV soap opera called *The Scrantons*. I was the little brother, Chuck. For two years I was a star. I got the whole treatment: my own trailer, chauffeured limousines, private tutors. Trouble was my puberty came too early. Suddenly I was like a teenage gatecrasher at a kids' party. My voice went, I got zits all over my chin, fluff on my lip. It spoilt everything. Within a month the scenario for my contractual death was drawn up. I think it was pneumonia, or maybe an accident with the thresher. I can't really remember, I don't like to look back on those final days.

Though I must confess it was fun meeting all the stars. The big ones: Jeanne Lamont, Eddy Cornelle, Mary and Marvin Keen – you remember them. One of the most bizarre features of my life since I left the studio is that nowadays I never see stars any more. Isn't that ridiculous? Someone like me who worked with them, who practically lives in Hollywood? Somehow I never get to see the stars any more. I just miss them. 'Oh he left five minutes ago, bub,' or 'Oh no, I think she's on location in Europe, she hasn't been here for weeks.' The same old story.

I think that's what Jayette's referring to when she asks if I've lucked-out. She knows I'm still hanging in there, waiting. I mean, I've kept on my agent. The way I see it is that once you've been in front of the cameras something's going to keep driving you on until you get back. I know it'll happen to me again one day, I just have this feeling inside.

After breakfast I jog back up the beach to where I left the car. One morning I got to thinking about Jayette. What does she think when she sees me now and remembers me from the days of *The Scrantons*? It seems to me that everybody in their life is at least two people. Once when you're a child and once when you're an adult. It's the saddest thing. I don't just mean that you see things differently when you're a child – that's something else again – what's sad is that you can't seem to keep the personality. I know I'm not the same person any more as young Chuck Scranton was, and I find that depressing. I could meet little Charlie on the beach today and say 'Look, there goes a sharp kid.' And never recognize him, if you see what I mean. It's a shame.

I don't like the jog back so much, as all the people are coming out. Lying around, surfing, cruising, scoring, shooting up, tricking. Hell, the things I've seen on that sand, I could tell you a few stories. Sometimes I like to go down to El Segundo or Redondo beach just to feel normal.

I usually park the car on Santa Monica Pallisades. I tidy up, change into my clothes and shave. I have a small battery-powered electric razor that I use. Then I have a beer, wander around, buy a newspaper. Mostly I then drive north to Malibu. There's a place I know where you can get a fair view of a longish stretch of the beach. It's almost impossible to get down there in summer; they don't like strangers. So I pull off the highway and climb this small dune-hill. I have a pair of opera glasses of my aunt's that I use to see better – my eyesight's not too hot. I spotted Rod Steiger one day, and Jane Fonda I think but I can't be sure, the glasses tend to fuzz everything a bit over four hundred yards. Anyway I like the quiet on that dune, it's restful.

I have been down on to Malibu beach, but only in the winter season. The houses are all shut up but you can still get the feel of it. Some people were having a bar-b-q one day. It looked good. They had a fire going on a big porch that jutted out high over the sand. They waved and shouted when I went past.

Lunch is bad. The worst part of the day for me because I have to go home. I live with my aunt. I call her my aunt though I'm not related to her at all. She was my mother's companion – I believe that's the right word – until my mother stuffed her face with a gross of Seconal one afternoon in a motel at Corona del Mar. I was fifteen then and Vanessa – my 'aunt' – became some kind of legal guardian to me and had control of all the money I'd made from *The Scrantons*. Well, she bought an apartment in Beverly Glen because she liked the address. Man, was she swallowed by the realtor. They build these tiny apartment blocks on cliff-faces up the asshole of the big-name canyons just so you can say you live off Mulholland Drive or in Bel Air. It's a load. I'd rather live in Watts or on Imperial Highway. I practically have to rope-up and wear crampons to get to my front door. And it is mine. I paid for it.

Maybe that's why Vanessa never leaves her bed. It's just too much effort getting in and out of the house. She just stays in bed all day and eats, watches TV and feeds her two dogs. I only go in there for lunch; it's my only 'family' ritual. I take a glass of milk and a salad sandwich but she phones out for pizza and enchiladas and burgers – any kind of crap she can smear over her face and down her front. She's really grown fat in the ten years since my mother bombed out. But she still sits up in bed with those hairy yipping dogs under her armpits, and she's got her top and bottom false eyelashes, her hairpiece and purple lipstick on. I say nothing usually. For someone who never gets out she sure can talk a lot. She wears these tacky satin and lace peignoirs, shows half her chest. Her breasts look like a couple of Indian clubs rolling around under the shimmer. It's unfair I suppose, but when I drive back into the foothills I like to think I'm going to have a luncheon date with . . . with someone like Grace Kelly – as was – or maybe Alexis Smith. I don't know. I wouldn't mind a meal and a civilized conversation with some nice people like that. But lunch with Vanessa? Thanks for nothing, pal. God, you can keep it. She's a real klutz. I'm sure Grace and Alexis would never let themselves get that way – you know, like Vanessa's always dropping tacos down her cleavage or smearing mustard on her chins.

I always get depressed after lunch. It figures, I hear you say. I go to my room and sometimes I have a drink (I don't smoke, so dope's out). Other days I play my guitar or else work on my screenplay. It's called *Walk. Don't Walk*. I get a lot of good ideas after lunch for some reason. That's when I got the idea for my screenplay. It just came to me. I remembered how I'd been stuck one day at the corner of Arteria Boulevard and Normandie Avenue. There was a pile of traffic and the pedestrian signs were going berserk. 'Walk' would come on so I'd start across. Two seconds later 'Don't Walk' so I go back. Then on comes 'Walk' again. This went on for ten minutes: 'Walk. Don't Walk. Walk.

Don't Walk.' I was practically out of my box. But what really stunned me was the way I just stayed there and obeyed the goddam machine for so long – I never even thought about going it alone. Then one afternoon after lunch it came to me that it was a neat image for life; just the right kind of metaphor for the whole can of worms. The final scene of this movie is going to be a slow crane shot away from this malfunctioning traffic sign going 'Walk. Don't Walk.' Then the camera pulls further up and away in a helicopter and you see that in fact the whole city is fouled up because of this one sign flashing. They don't know what to do; the programming's gone wrong. It's a great final scene. Only problem is I'm having some difficulty writing my way towards it. Still, it'll come, I guess.

In the late afternoon I go to work. I work at the Beverly Hills Hotel. Vanessa's brother-in-law got me the job. I park cars. I keep hoping I'm going to park the car of someone really important. Frank – that's Vanessa's brother-in-law – will say to me 'Give this one a shine-up, Charlie, it belongs to so and so, he produced this film,' or 'That guy's the money behind X's new movie,' or 'Look out, he's Senior Vice-President of Something incorporated.' I say big deal. These guys hand me the keys – they all look like bank clerks. If that's the movies nowadays I'm not so sure I want back in.

Afternoons are quiet at the hotel so I catch up on my reading. I'm reading Camus at the moment but I think I've learnt all I can from him so I'm going on to Jung. I don't know too much about Jung but I'm told he was really into astrology which has always been a pet interest of mine. One thing I will say for quitting the movies when I did means that I didn't miss out on my education. I hear that some of these stars today are really dumb; you know, they've got their brains in their neck and points south.

After work I drive back down to the Santa Monica pier and think about what I'm going to do all night. The Santa Monica pier is a kind of special place for me: it's the last place I saw my wife and son. I got married at seventeen and was divorced by twenty-two, though we were apart for a couple of years before that. Her name was Harriet. It was okay for a while but I don't think she liked Vanessa. Anyway, get this. She left me for a guy who was the assistant manager in the credit collection department of a large mail order firm. I couldn't believe it when she told me. I said to her when she moved out that it had to be the world's most boring job and did she know what she was getting into? I mean, what sort of person do you have to be to take on that kind of work? The bad thing was she took my son Skiff with her. It's a dumb name I know, but at the time he was born all the kids were being called things like Sky and Saffron and Powie, and I was really sold on sailing. I hope he doesn't hold it against me.

The divorce was messy and she got custody, though I'll never understand why. She had left some clothes at the house and wanted them back so she suggested we meet at the end of the Santa Monica pier for some reason. I didn't mind, it was the impetuous side to her nature that first attracted me. I handed the clothes over. She was a bit tense. Skiff was running about; he didn't seem to know who I was. She was smoking a lot; those long thin menthol cigarettes. I really didn't say anything much at all, asked her how she was, what school Skiff was going to. Then she just burst out, 'Take a good look, Charlie, then don't come near us ever again!' Her exact words. Then they went away.

So I go down to the end of the pier most nights and look out at the ocean and count the planes going in to land at L. A. International and try to work things out. Just the other evening I wandered up the beach a way and this thin-faced man with short grey hair came up to me and said 'Jordan, is that you?' And when he saw he'd made a mistake he smiled a nice smile, apologized and walked off. It was only this morning that I thought it might have been Christopher Isherwood himself. The more I think about it the more convinced I become. What a perfect opportunity and I had to go and miss it. As I say: 'Walk. Don't Walk.' That's the bottom line.

I suppose I must have been preoccupied. The pier brings back all these memories like some private video-loop, and my head gets to feel like it's full of birds all flapping around trying to get out. And also things haven't been so good lately. On Friday Frank told me not to bother showing up at the hotel next week, I can't seem to make any headway with the screenplay and for the last three nights Vanessa's tried to climb into my bed.

Well, tonight I think I'll drive to this small bar I know on Sunset. Nothing too great, a little dark. They do a nice white wine with peach slices in it, and there's some topless, some go-go, and I hear tell that Bobby de Niro sometimes shows up for a drink.

Bizarre Situations

Before we start, something from this book I'm reading, called *Truth, Falsehood and Philosophy*:

> It occasionally happens that a situation is so new and unusual that no speaker of the language is equipped to say what words are appropriate for it. We shall call such situations *bizarre*.

That's what the book says, and I think it's quite interesting and fairly relevant. But, how to begin? Perhaps:

> I shall never forget the sight of Joan's crumpled body, her head clumsily de-topped like a fractious child's attempt to open a boiled egg; as if some giant's teaspoon had levered and battered its way to Joan's decidedly average brain.

Or maybe:

> I am here in Paris, Monday night, Bar Cercle, Rue Christine – well into my third Pernod – looking for Kramer. Kramer who came to stay and allowed his wife to suicide in my guest

bedroom. Suicide? No chance. Kramer murdered her and I have the proof. I think.

Or possibly:

To cure some chronic cases of epilepsy surgeons sometimes resort to a severance of the *corpus callosum*, the substance that holds together – and forms a crucial link between – the two hemispheres of the brain. The cure is radical, as is all brain surgery, but on the whole completely successful. Except, that is, for some very unusual side effects.

Into which we shall go later – my own epilepsy has been cured in this way. But, to return, the problem now is that all the beginnings are very apt, very apt indeed. Three of them though: three routes leading God knows where. And then, endings too are equally important, for – really – what I'm after is the truth. Or even TRUTH. A very elusive character. As elusive as bloody Kramer, sod him.

My preoccupation with truth arises from the division of my *corpus callosum* and explains why I am reading this book called *Truth, Falsehood and Philosophy*. I open at random. Chapter Two: Expressing Beliefs in Sentences. 'Beliefs are hard to study directly and many sentences do not naturally state beliefs . . .' My eyes dart impatiently down the page, '. . . although truth does *not* have degrees it *does* have many borderline cases.' At last something pertinent. For someone with my unique problems these donnish evasions and qualifications are incredibly frustrating. So, 'truth has borderline cases'. Good, I'm glad to find the academics admit this much, especially as since my operation the whole world has become a borderline case for me.

★   ★   ★

Kramer was at school with me. To be candid I admired him greatly and he casually exploited my admiration. In fact you could say that I loved Kramer – in a brotherly sort of way – to such an extent that, had he bothered to ask, I would have laid down my life for him. It sounds absurd to admit this now, but there was something almost noble about Kramer's disregard for everyone except himself. You know these selfish people whose selfishness seems quite reasonable, admirable, really, in its refusal to compromise. Kramer was like that: intelligent, mysterious and self-absorbed.

We were at university together for a while, but he was scandalously sent down and went off to America where he duly made something of a name for himself as a sort of hoodlum art critic; a cultural vigilante with no respect for reputations. I often saw shadowy photographs of him in fashionable glossy magazines, and it was in one of them that I learned of his marriage – after ten years of rampant bachelorhood – to one Joan Aslinger, heiress to a West Coast fast-food chain.

Kramer and I had grown to become close friends of a sort and I continued to write to him regularly. I'm happy to report that he kept in touch: the odd letter, kitsch postcards from Hammamet or Tijuana. He used to come and stay as well – with his current girlfriend, whoever that might be – in my quiet Devon cottage for a boisterous weekend every two years or so.

I remember he was surprisingly solicitous when he heard about my operation and in an uncharacteristic gesture of largesse sent a hundred white roses to the clinic where I was convalescing. He promised shortly to visit me with his new wife Joan.

It was during one of my periodic sojourns in the Sanatorium that I experienced the particularly acute and destructive epileptic attack which prompted the doctors to recommend the severing of my *corpus callosum*. The operation was a complete success. I remember only waking up as bald as a football with a thin livid stripe of lacing running fore and aft along my skull.

The surgeon – a Mr Berkeley, a genial elderly Irishman – did mention the unusual side effects I would have as a result of the *coupage* but dismissed them with a benign smile as being 'metaphysical' in character and quite unlikely to impair the quality of my daily life. Foolishly, I accepted his assurances.

Kramer and his wife came to stay as promised. Joan was a fairly attractive girl; she had delightful honey-blonde hair – always so clean – bright blue eyes and a loose generous mouth. She chatted and laughed in what was clearly an attempt at sophisticated animation, but it was immediately obvious to me that she was hopelessly neurotic and quite unsuited to be Kramer's wife. When they were together the tension that crackled between them was unbearable. On the first night they stayed I overheard a savage teeth-clenched row in the guest bedroom.

It was the effect on Kramer that I found most depressing. He was drawn and cowed, like a cornered beaten man. His brilliant wit was reduced to glum monosyllables or fervent contradictions of any opinion Joan ventured to express. Irritation and despair were lodged in every feature of his face.

It didn't surprise me greatly when, three strained days later, Kramer announced that he had to go to London on business and Joan and I found ourselves with a lot of time on our hands. She tried hard, I have to admit, but I found her tedious and dull, as most obsessively introspective people tend to be. She came slightly more alive when she drank, which was frequently, and our preprandial lunch-time session swiftly advanced to elevenses.

I soon got the full story of Kramer's constant bastardy of course: a tearful, finger-knotting account leaden with self-pity that went on well into the night. Other women apparently, from the word go. Things had become dramatically worse because now, it seemed, there was one in particular; one Erica – said with much venom – an old flame. As Erica's description emerged I realized to my surprise that I knew her. She had figured in two of Kramer's visits before his marriage to Joan. Erica was a tall intelligent red-head, strong-shouldered and of arresting appearance and with a calm and confident personality. I had liked her a lot. Naturally I didn't tell any of this to Joan whom – as Kramer predictably rang from London announcing successive delays – I was beginning to find increasingly tiresome; she was getting on my nerves.

Take her reaction to my own particular case, for example. When I explained my unique problems caused by the side effects of my operation, she didn't believe me. She laughed, said I must be joking, claimed that such things could never happen. I admitted such cases were exceptionally rare but affirmed it as documented medical fact.

I now know, thanks to this book I'm reading, the correct academic term for my 'ailment'. I am a 'bizarre situation'. Reading on I find this conclusion:

> Our language is not sufficiently articulated to cope with such rare and unusual circumstances. Many philosophers and lo-gicians are deeply unhappy about 'bizarre situations'.

So, even the philosophers have to admit it. In my case there is no hope of ever reaching the truth. I find the concession reassuring somehow – but I still feel that I have to see Kramer again.

Indeed, my condition is truly bizarre. Since the link between my cerebral hemispheres was severed my brain now functions as two discrete halves. The only bodily function that this affects is perception, and the essence of the problem is this. If I see, for example, a cat in my *left*-side area of vision and I am asked to write down what I have seen with my *right* hand – I am right-handed – I cannot. I cannot write down what I have seen because the right half of my brain no longer registers what occurred in my left-hand area of vision. This is because the hemispherical division in your brain extends, so to speak, the length of your body. Right hemisphere controls right side, left hemisphere left side. Normally the information from both sides has free passage from one hemisphere to the other – linking the two halves into one unified whole. But now that this route – the *corpus callosum* – has gone, only *half* my brain has seen the cat, the right hemisphere knows nothing about it so it can hardly tell my right hand what to note down.

This is what the surgeon meant by 'metaphysical' side effects, and he was right to say my day-to-day existence would be untroubled by them, but consider the radical consequences of this on my phenomenological world. It is now nothing but a sequence of *half* truths. What, for me, is really true? How can I be sure if something that happens in my left-side area of vision really took place, if in one half of my body there is *absolutely no record of it ever having occurred*?

I spend befuddled hours wrestling with these arcane episte-mological riddles. Doubt is underwritten; it comes to occupy a superior position to truth and falsehood. I am a genuine, physiologically real sceptic – medically consigned to this fate by the surgeon's knife. Uncertainty is the only thing I can really be sure of.

You see what this means, of course. In my world truth is exactly what I want to believe.

★   ★   ★

I came to this book hoping for some sort of guidance, but it can only bumble on about the 'insufficient articulation of our language', which is absolutely no help at all, however accurate it may be. For example, the door of this café I'm sitting in is on my left-hand side. I clearly see in my left field of vision a tall woman in black come through it and advance towards the bar. I take a pen from my pocket and intend to write down what I saw in the margin of my book. I say to myself: 'Write down what you saw coming through the door.' I cannot do it, of course. As far as the right-hand side of my body is concerned the lady in black does not exist. So which hemisphere of my brain do I trust, then? Which version of the truth do I accept, lady or no lady?

They are both true as far as I am concerned, and whatever I decide one half of my body will back my judgement to the death.

Of course there is a simple way out: I can turn round, bring her into my right field of vision, firmly establish her existence. But that's entirely up to me. Oh yes. Unlike the rest of you, verification is a gift I can bestow or withdraw at will.

I turn. I see her. She is tall, with curly reddish auburn hair. Our eyes meet, part, meet again. Recognition flares. It is Erica.

It was I who discovered Joan's body on the floor of the guest bedroom. (One shot: my father's old Smith & Wesson pressed against her soft palate. I use the revolver – fully licensed of course – to blast at the rooks which sometimes wheel and caw round the house. Indeed, Joan and I spent a tipsy afternoon engaged in this sport. I couldn't have known . . .)

Kramer was still in London. I had gone out to a dinner party leaving Joan curled up with a whisky bottle – she had muttered something about a migraine. Naturally, I phoned the police at once.

Kramer arrived on the first train from London the next morning, numbed and shattered by the news.

At the inquest – a formality – it came out that Joan had attempted suicide a few months earlier and Kramer admitted to the rockiness of their marriage. He stayed with me until it was all over. They were stressful edgy days. Kramer was taciturn and preoccupied which, under the circumstances, wasn't surprising. He did tell me, though, that he hadn't been continually in London but in fact had spent some days in Paris with Erica where some sort of emotional crisis had ensued. He had only been back thirty-six hours when the police phoned his London hotel with the news of Joan's death.

And now Erica herself sits opposite me. Her face has very little make-up on and she looks tense and worried. After the initial pleasantries we both blurt out, 'What are you doing here?' and both realize simultaneously that we are here for the same reason. Looking for Kramer.

When Kramer left after the inquest he told me he was going to Paris to rejoin Erica and make a film on De Chirico for French TV. Apparently unperturbed he had continued to sleep in the guest bedroom but it was several days before I could bring myself to go in and clean it out. In the waste-paper basket I found several magazines, a map of Paris, a crumpled napkin from the Bar Cercle with the message 'Monday, Rue Christine' scrawled on it and, to my alarm and intense consternation, a semi-transparent credit card receipt slip from a filling station on the M4 at a place no more than an hour's drive from the house. This unsettled me. As far as I knew Kramer had no car. And, what was more disturbing, the date on the receipt slip was the same as the night Joan died.

*   *   *

34

Erica is distinctly on edge. She says she has arranged to meet Kramer here tonight as she has something to tell him. She picks at her lower lip distractedly.

'But anyway,' she says with vague annoyance, 'what do you want him for?'

I shrug my shoulders. 'I have to see him as well,' I say. 'There's something I have to clear up.'

'What is it?'

I almost tell her. I almost say, I want the truth. I want to know if he killed his wife. If he hired a car, drove to the house, found her alone and insensibly drunk, typed the note, put the pistol in her lolling mouth and blew the top of her head off.

But I don't. I say it's just a personal matter.

There is a pause in our conversation. I say to Erica, who nervously lights a cigarette, 'Look, I think I should talk to him first.'

'No!' she replies instantly. 'I must speak to him.' Speak to him about what? I wonder. It irritates me. Is Kramer to be hounded perpetually by these neurotic harpies? What has the man done to deserve this?

We see Kramer the same time as he sees us. He strides over to our table. He stares angrily at me.

'What the hell are you doing here?' he demands in tones of real astonishment.

'I'm sorry,' I say, nervousness making my voice tremble. 'But I have to speak to you.' It's like being back at school.

Erica crushes out her cigarette and jumps to her feet. I can see she is blinking back tears.

'I have news for you,' she says, fighting to keep her voice strong. 'Important news.'

Kramer grips her by the elbows. 'Come back,' he says softly, pleadingly.

I am impatient with whatever lovelorn drama it is that they are enacting, and also obscurely angered by this demeaning display of reliance. Raising my voice I flourish the credit card receipt. 'Kramer,' I say, 'I want to know about this.'

He ignores me. He does not take his eyes from Erica. 'Erica, please,' he entreats.

She lowers her head and looks down at her shaking hands.

'No,' she says desperately. 'I can't. I'm marrying Jean-Louis. I said I would tell you tonight. Please let me go.' She shakes herself free of his arms and brushes past him out into the night. I am glad to see her go.

I have never seen a man look so abject. Kramer stands with his head bowed in defeat, his jaw muscles bulging, his eyes fixed – as if he's just witnessed some dreadful atrocity. I despise him like this, so impoverished and vulnerable, nothing like the Kramer I knew.

I lean forward. 'Kramer,' I say softly, confidingly. 'You can tell me now. You did it, didn't you? You came back that night while I was away.' I spread the slip of transparent paper on the table. 'You see I have the facts here.' I keep my voice low. 'But don't worry, it's between you and me. I just need to know the truth.'

Kramer sits down unsteadily. He examines the receipt. Then he looks up at me as if I'm quite mad.

'Of course I came back,' he whispers bitterly. 'I drove back that night to tell Joan I was leaving her, that I wanted Erica.' He shakes his head in grim irony. 'Instead I saw everything. From the garden. I saw you sitting in your study. You had a kind of bandage round your head. It covered one eye.' He points to my right eye. 'You were typing with one hand. Your left hand. You only used one hand. All the time. I saw you take the gun from the drawer with your left hand.' He paused. 'I knew what you were going to do. I didn't want to stop you.' He stands up. 'You are a sick man,' he says, 'with your sick worries. You can delude yourself perhaps, but nobody else.' He looks at me as if he can taste vomit in his mouth. 'I stood there and listened for the shot. I went along with the game. I share the guilt. But it was you who did it.' He turns and walks out of the café.

KRAMER IS LYING. It is a lie. The sort of mad impossible fantastic lie a desperate man would dream up. I know he is lying because I know the truth. It's locked in my brain. It is inviolate. I have my body's authority for it.

Still, there is a problem now with this lie he's set loose. Mendacity is a tenacious beast. If it's not nipped in the bud it's soon indistinguishable from the truth. I told him he didn't need to worry. But now . . .

He is bound to return to this melancholy bar before long. I know the banal nostalgia of such disappointed men – haunting the sites of their defeats – and the powerful impulses of un-requited love. I will have to see Kramer again; sort things out once and for all.

I signal the waiter for my bill. As I close my book a sentence at the bottom of the page catches my eye:

Many logicians and philosophers are deeply unhappy about bizarre situations.

A curse on them all I say.

Hardly Ever

'Think of it,' Holland said. 'The sex.'

'Sex.' Panton repeated. 'God . . . Sex.'

Niles shook his head. 'Are you sure?' he asked. 'I mean, can you guarantee it? The sex, that is. I don't want to waste time farting around singing.'

'Waste bloody time? Are you mad?' Holland said. 'It only happens every two years. You can't afford to miss the opportunity. Unless you're suffering from second thoughts.'

'What, *me*?' Niles tried to laugh. He looked at Holland's blue eyes. They always seemed to know. 'You must be bloody kidding, mate. Jesus, if you think . . . God!' he snorted.

'All right, all right,' Holland said. 'We agreed, remember? It's got to be all of us.'

Niles had never asked for this last fact to be explained. Why – if, as Holland attested – the sex was freely available, on a plate so to speak, why did they all have to participate at the feast? Holland made out it was part of his naturally generous personality. It was more fun if you all had a go.

'Let's get on with it,' Panton said.

They walked over to the noticeboard. Holland pushed some juniors out of the way. Prothero, the music master, had written

38

on the top of a sheet of paper: GILBERT AND SULLIVAN OPERA – HMS PINAFORE – CHORUS: BASSES AND TENORS WANTED, SIGN BELOW. Half a dozen names had been scrawled down.

'Cretins,' Holland said. 'No competition.' He wrote his name down. Panton followed suit.

Niles took a biro from his blazer pocket. He paused.

'But how can you be so sure? That's what I want to know. How can you tell that the girls just won't be – well – music-lovers?'

'Because I know,' Holland said patiently. 'Every Gilbert and Sullivan it's the same. Borthwick told me. He was in the last one. He said the girls only come for one thing. I mean, it stands to reason. What sort of girl's going to want to be in some pissing bloody operetta. Ask yourself. Shitty orchestra, home-made costumes, people who can't sing to save their life. I tell you, Nilo, they're doing it for the same reason as us. They're fed up with the local yobs. They want a nice public-school boy. Christ, you must have heard. It's a cert. Leave it to Pete.'

Niles screwed up his eyes. What the hell, he thought, it's time I tried. He signed his name. Q. Niles.

'Good old Quentin,' Panton roared. 'Wor! Think of it waiting.' He forced his features into a semblance of noble suffering, wrapped his arms around himself as if riven with acute internal pain and lurched drunkenly about, groaning in simulated ecstasy.

Holland grabbed Niles by the arm. 'The shafting, Nilo my man,' he said intensely. 'The royal bloody shafting we're going to do.'

Niles felt his chest expand with sudden exhilaration. Holland's fierce enthusiasm always affected him more than Panton's most baroque histrionics.

'Bloody right, Pete,' he said. 'Too bloody right. I'm getting desperate already.'

Niles sat in his small box-like study and stared out at the relentless rain falling on the gentle Scottish hills. From his study window he could see a corner of the dormitory wing of his own house, an expanse of gravel with the housemaster's car parked on it and fifty yards of the drive leading down to the main school house a mile or so away. On the desk in front of him lay a half-completed team list for the inter-house rugby leagues and an open notepad. On the notepad he had written: *The Rape of the Lock*, and below that '*The Rape of the Lock* is a mock heroic poem. What do you understand by this term? Illustrate with examples.' It was an essay which he was due to hand in tomorrow. He had no idea what to say. He gazed dully out at the rain, idly noting some boys coming out of the woods. They must be desperate, he thought, if they have to go out for a smoke in this weather. He returned to his more immediate problem. Who was going to play scrum-half now that Damianos had a sick-chit? He considered the pool of players he could draw on: asthmatics, fatsos, spastics every one. To hell with it. He wrote down Grover's name. They had no chance of winning anyway. He opened his desk cupboard and removed a packet of Jaffa Cakes and a large bottle of Coca-Cola. He gulped thirstily from the bottle and ate a few biscuits. *The Rape of the Lock*. What could he say about it? He didn't mind the poem. He thought of Belinda:

'On her white breast a sparkling cross she wore,' . . . He found her far and away the most alluring of the fictional heroines he had yet encountered in his brief acquaintance with English Literature. He read the opening of the poem again. He saw her lying in a huge rumpled bed, a lace peignoir barely covering two breasts as firm and symmetrical as halved grapefruits. He had had a bonkon all the English lesson. It hadn't happened to him since they'd read *Great Expectations*. What was her name? Estella. God, yes. She was almost as good as Belinda. He thought about his essay again. He liked English Literature. He wondered if he would be able to do it at university – if he could get to university at all. His father had not been at all pleased when he had announced that he wanted to do English A-level. 'What's the use of that?' he had shouted. 'How's English Literature going to help you sell machine tools?' Niles sighed. There was an opening for him in Gerald Niles (Engineering) Ltd. His father knew nothing of his plans for university.

Niles ran his hands through his thick wiry hair and rubbed his eyes. He picked up his pen. 'Alexander Pope,' he wrote, 'was a major poet of the Augustan period. *The Rape of the Lock* was his most celebrated poem.' He sensed it was a bad beginning – uninspired, boring – but sometimes if you started by writing down what you knew, you occasionally got a few ideas. He scanned Canto One. 'Soft bosoms', he saw. Then 'Belinda still her downy pillow prest'. He felt himself quicken. Pope knew what he was doing, all right. The associations: bosom and pillow, prest and breast. Niles shut his eyes. He was weighing Belinda's perfect breasts in his hands, massaging her awake as she lay in her tousled noonday bed. He imagined her hair spread over her face, full lips, heavy sleep-bruised eyes. He imagined a slim forearm raised to ward off Sol's tim'rous ray, Belinda turning on to her back, stretching. Jesus. Would she have hairy armpits? he wondered, swallowing. Did they shave their armpits in the eighteenth century? Would it be like that French woman he'd seen on a campsite near Limoges last summer? In the camp super-market, wearing only a bikini, reaching up for a tin on a high shelf and exposing a great hank of armpit hair. Niles groaned. He leant forward and rested his head on his open book. 'Belinda,' he whispered, 'Belinda.'

'Everything okay, Quentin?'

He sat up abruptly, banging his knees sharply on the bottom of his desk. It was Bowler, his housemaster, his round bespectacled face peering at him concernedly, his body canted into the study, pipe clenched between his brown teeth. Why couldn't the bastard knock? Niles swore.

'Trying to write an essay, sir,' he said.

'Not that difficult, is it?' Bowler laughed. 'Got the team for the league?'

Niles handed it over. Bowler studied it, puffing on his pipe, frowning. Niles looked at the sour blue smoke gathering on the ceiling. Typical bloody Bowler.

'This the best we can do? Are you sure about Grover at scrum-half? Crucial position, I would have thought.'

'I think he needs to be pressured a bit, sir.'

'Right-ho. You're the boss. See you're down for *Pinafore*.'

'Sorry, sir?'

'*Pinafore*. HMS. The opera. Didn't know you sang, Quentin? Shouldn't have thought it was your line really.'

'Thought I'd give it a go, sir.'

Bowler left and Niles thought about the opera. Holland had said it was a sure thing with the girls: they only came because they wanted to get off with boys. Niles wondered what they'd be like. Scottish girls from the local grammar school. He'd seen them in town often. Dark blue uniforms, felt hats, long hair, mini-skirts. They all looked older than him – more mature. He experienced a sudden moment of panic. What in God's name would he do? Holland and Panton would be there, everyone would see him. He felt his heart beat with unreasonable speed. It was a kind of proof. There was no chance of lying or evading the issue. It would be all too public.

★　　★　　★

They gathered in the music room behind the new chapel for the first mixed rehearsal. There had been three weeks of tedious afternoon practices during which some semblance of singing ability had been forcibly extracted from them by the efforts of Prothero, the music master. Now Prothero watched the boys enter with a tired and cynical smile. This was his seventh Gilbert and Sullivan since coming to the school, his third *HMS Pinafore*. Two sets of forms faced each other at one end of the long room. The boys sat down on one set staring at the empty seats opposite as if they were already occupied.

'Now, gentlemen,' Prothero began. 'The ladies will be here soon. I don't propose to lecture you any more on the subject. I count on your innate good manners and sense of decorum.'

Niles, Holland and Panton sat together. Whispered conversations were going on all around. Niles felt his lungs press against his rib cage. The tension was acute, he felt faint with unfamiliar stress. What if not one of them spoke to him? This was dreadful, he thought, and the girls weren't even here. He looked at the fellow members of the chorus. There were some authentic tenors and basses from the school choir but the rest of them were made up of self-appointed lads, frustrates and sexual braggarts. He could sense their crude desire thrumming through the group as if the forms they were sitting on were charged with a low electric current. He looked at the bright-eyed, snouty expectant faces, heard whispered obscenities and saw the international language of sexual gesticulation being covertly practised as if they were a gathering of randy deaf-mutes. He felt vaguely soiled to be counted among them. Beside him Holland leaned forward and tapped the shoulder of a boy in front.

'Bloody Mobo,' he said quietly and venomously. 'Didn't you get the message? No queers allowed. What are you bloody doing here? It's girls we're singing with. Not lushmen, Mobo, no little lushmen.'

'Frig off, Holland,' the boy said tonelessly. 'I'm in the choir, aren't I?'

'Bloody choir,' Holland repeated, his face ugly with illogical aggression. 'Bloody frigging choir.'

Then the girls came in.

No one had heard the bus from town arriving and the room, to Niles' startled eyes, seemed suddenly to be filled with chattering uniformed females. He heard laughter and giggles, caught flashing glimpses of cheeks and red mouths, hair and knees as the other half of the chorus sat itself down opposite. The boys fired nervous exploratory glances across the two yards of floor between them. Niles studied his score with commendable intensity. He noticed Holland brazenly scrutinizing the girls. Cautiously, Niles raised his eyes and looked over. They seemed very ordinary, was his first reflection. Dark blue blazers, short skirts, some black tights. There was one tall girl with a severe, rather thin face. Her hair was tied up in an elaborate twisted bun and at first he thought she was a mistress, but then he saw her uniform. He scanned the features of the others but their faces refused to register any individuality – he might have been staring at a Chinese football team.

Holland bowed his head.

'Mm-mm. I've seen mine,' he said in a low voice. 'The blonde in front.' He gave a whimper of suppressed desire. Some boys looked round and smiled, complicity springing up instantly, like recognition.

'Right, everybody,' Prothero shouted, banging out a chord on the piano. 'Page twenty-three please.'

'And I'm never ever sick at sea,' Prothero sang.

'What *never*?' boomed the chorus of sailors.

'No never,' replied Prothero.

'What never?' the chorus sceptically inquired again.

'Hardly ever,' Prothero admitted.

'He's hardly ever sick at sea . . .'

'Fine,' Prothero called. 'Good, that'll do for today. Thank you, ladies. Your bus should be outside. Scores on the end of the piano as you go out, please.'

The bus was late and the girls had to wait for five minutes outside the chapel. Niles took his time finding his coat in the vestibule and when he went outside Holland and Panton were already talking to four girls. 'Niles, Niles,' they shouted as he emerged into the watery sunlight of a February afternoon. 'Over here.' He walked over, the blood pounding in his ears like surf. Holland stood behind a slim blonde girl with moles on her face, Panton by a cheery-looking redhead. Niles approached. One of the two remaining girls was the tall sharp-faced one he'd seen earlier. The other was small with wispy fair hair and spectacles.

'This is Quentin,' Holland said. 'Hero of the rugby field, captain of the squash team. Master flogger extraordinaire.'

'Shut up!' Niles exclaimed, appalled at this slander. 'You bastard.'

'What's a flogger?' Holland's girl asked. Panton was doubled up with mirth. The tall girl looked on expressionlessly.

'Never mind,' Holland said. 'Sorry, Quent. Little joke. Now, this is Joyce,' he indicated Panton's girl. 'This is Helen,' pointing to his own. 'And,' he looked at the tall girl, 'Alison? Yes, Alison. And, um . . .'

'Frances,' said the small girl.

Niles had moved round to stand beside Alison. Frances was clearly on her own. She stood undecidedly for a moment before wandering off without a further word.

Holland and Panton had instinctively sensed out the kind of girl they were after. Innuendoes were already being exchanged with a wanton suggestiveness. Niles looked at Alison. She was tall. In her high heels slightly taller than him. She appeared older, in her twenties almost, but the severity of her face was partly an illusion caused by her schoolmarmy bun. Her skirt was not as short as Helen's or Joyce's; it stopped two inches above her knees. Her legs were long and shapely. On the lapel of her blazer were numerous badges: three Robertson's gollies, a small Canadian maple leaf, a yellow square, and a blue rectangular one with 'monitor' written on it in plain silver letters. She wore a white shirt, and a tie with the smallest knot in it Niles had ever seen.

He had to say something. He cleared his throat. 'Campaign medals?' he said, pointing to the badges. He realized his finger was two inches from her right breast and he snatched his hand away. He thought she gave the thinnest of smiles in response but he couldn't be sure.

'Cold though,' he said, huffing and puffing into his cupped hands.

She rummaged in her blazer pockets. 'Cigarette?' she asked taking out a packet and offering it to him.

Niles was taken aback by this unselfconsciously adult gesture. 'Christ no,' he said hurriedly. 'I mean, we're not allowed.'

But she was already offering them to Joyce and Helen. Alison took out a box of matches and lit the others' cigarettes. For some reason Niles was impressed by the capable way she did this – she obviously smoked a lot. Meanwhile Holland and Panton aped nicotine starvation. When Joyce and Helen exhaled they chased the clouds of smoke about, beating it into their gaping mouths with their hands as if it were vital oxygen. The girls laughed delightedly.

'What I'd give for a fag,' said Holland through gritted teeth.

'Oh yeah?' said lissom Helen.

'Now see what you've done,' Niles said to Alison with more accusation in his voice than he'd meant.

Alison laughed briefly.

Niles brushed his teeth, alone at the row of basins. He rinsed his mouth out and went to stand in front of the large mirror by the urinals. He looked at his square face. He rubbed his jaw. He'd need to shave tomorrow. He had to shave every two days now. Somebody shouted 'virile!' through the washroom door. Niles whirled round but he didn't see who it was. When he turned back to the mirror his face was red.

He thought about Alison. Everything about her was maddeningly indistinct and ambiguous. All he'd heard her say was 'cigarette?' and 'bye'. It wasn't much to build a relationship on. He had an image of the back of her long legs in their tan tights as she'd climbed on to the bus. He wondered what her breasts were like. Her 'soft bosoms'.

He sighed and belted his dressing gown tighter around him. He walked through the quiet empty house towards his dormitory. A junior came padding down the corridor in pyjamas.

'Where are you going, Payne?' Niles said tiredly.

'For a slash, Niles.'

'Where's your bloody slippers and dressing gown then?'

'Oh Niles,' Payne moaned.

'Get back and bloody put them on.'

'Oh God, Niles, *please*, I just want a pee. I'll only be a second.'

'Go on, you little shit,' Niles raised his hand menacingly. Payne turned and ran back up the corridor.

Niles walked on towards his dormitory. It was a small one, only eight beds. He opened the door quietly. It was well past lights out. The long room was quite dark. He closed the door softly behind him.

'Okay, folks,' came a voice. 'Stop flogging, here's Niles.'

'Shut up, Fillery,' Niles said. Fillery was fat and wicked. His mother was an actress who lived in Cannes.

'What's she like then, Niles?' Fillery said.

'Who?'

'Who? The bloody bird of course, that's who. *Pinafore*. What's your one like?'

'Yeah, go on, Niles,' said another voice. 'Tell us, what's she like?'

'Shut up. I'm warning you lot.'

'Come on, Niles,' Fillery said wheedlingly. 'I bet she's all right. I bet you got a good one.'

Niles got into bed. He lay down and put his hands behind his neck. 'She's okay,' he said grudgingly. 'I'm not complaining.' There were soft groans of envy at this. 'Not bad, I suppose,' he went on. 'She's got nice long legs.'

'What's her name?'

'Alison.'

'Oh Alison, Alison.' People tried out the name on their tongues as if it were a foreign word.

'Tits?' Fillery asked.

'You filthy bugger,' Niles said. 'Trust bloody Fillery.' But Niles felt the lie rise unprompted in his throat. 'They're nice if you must know,' he said. 'Average size. Sort of pointy, if you know what I mean.' There was a chorus of groans at this, deep and despairing. Someone jiggled furiously up and down on his bed causing the springs to creak and complain.

'Shut up,' Niles hissed angrily. 'That's your lot. Now get to sleep.'

★   ★   ★

He saw Alison at the next rehearsal a week later. Already people had paired off, Helen and Joyce making straight for Holland and Panton at the first break.

'Fifteen minutes, ladies and gentlemen,' Prothero called.

Niles wandered over to Alison. Again he was impressed by her mature looks.

'Hi there,' he said, as casually as he could.

'Oh . . . hello.' She smiled. 'It's, um, Quentin, isn't it?'

Niles hated his name. ' 'Fraid so,' he said.

'Phew,' she said. 'Any chance of us having a quiet smoke somewhere?'

They picked their way through the small wood at the back of the chapel. It had rained heavily that morning and the stark trunks of the beech and ash trees were wet and shiny. Alison puffed aggressively at her cigarette. Niles had declined again. He turned up the collar of his blazer and remarked on the inclemency of the season. Alison looked suspiciously at him, as if he were making a joke. Her hair was mid-brown and her skin was very white. She had a thin mouth but her lips were well formed, there was a deep and pronounced dip to her cupid's bow. Niles found this detail endearing, as if somehow this validated his choice of her. His heart seemed to swell with emotion. Their elbows touched as the path narrowed. Niles checked his watch.

'Better not go too far,' he said, then paused before adding, 'they might get suspicious . . .'

'Sure,' Alison said, flicking her cigarette away. 'Smoking like a chimney. I've got Highers in a few months.'

'Mmmm,' Niles sympathized. 'I've got my A's,' he said. 'Then Oxbridge.'

'Are you going to Oxford?' Alison asked. She had a mild Scottish accent, she pronounced the 'r' in Oxford.

'Yes,' he said. 'Well, that's the general idea.' He wondered why he'd lied.

'I'm going to Aberdeen,' she said.

'Ah.'

They walked slowly back to the music room. They were the last to arrive. Holland and Panton looked up admiringly at him as he regained his seat.

'Quent,' Holland whispered. 'You bloody sex-maniac.'

'Shagger,' Panton accused. 'Bloody old shagger, Quent.'

'Quiet please,' Prothero called. 'If you're quite ready, Niles. Now can we have the ensemble? Jolly tars, female relatives and Josephine: "Oh joy oh rapture unforeseen, for now the sky is all serene," right? Two, three.'

'What happened next?' Fillery prompted.

Niles lay in bed. He could sense the entire dormitory waiting in quiet expectancy. Hands on their cocks, he thought.

'We went round the back of the chapel,' he continued. 'Walked into the wood a bit. We sat down on a log. Chatted a bit . . . I could feel the atmosphere between us just building up. We were talking about work, but not talking about it, if you know what I mean. It was more just something to say.'

'Who made the first move?' Fillery asked.

'I did of course. I was talking. Then I stopped, and looked up. She was looking at me . . . in that sort of way.'

'Oh God.'

'She was looking at me, as if to say . . . and we just sort of moved close together and kissed.'

There was a pause.

'Get your tongue down?'

'*Jesus*, Fillery. One track bloody mind . . . Yeah, yeah, if you must know every detail. Not at first – the third or fourth kiss. But it got pretty passionate. Frenching just about all the time.'

'Stop it! Stop it!' somebody called. 'I can't stand it any more.'

'What else happened,' Fillery implored. 'Did you . . . you know?'

'We kissed mainly. Hell, we didn't have much time. She was just sort of running her hand through my hair. I got a bit of a feel but not much. I'll have to wait until next week.'

Fillery was quiet. 'God you bastard, Niles,' he said. 'You lucky bastard.'

On Saturday, after lunch, Holland and Panton bicycled the three miles to the coast. Helen's family kept a caravan on the caravan site by the beach. Helen and Joyce had arranged to meet the boys there. Niles was playing in a first XV rugby match. He heard all about their exploits later in the afternoon. He was in his study changing out of his rugby kit – the school had lost and he thought he'd pulled a muscle in his thigh – when Holland and Panton burst in.

'Oh my God, Quent,' Holland crowed. 'I don't believe it. It was incredible. They had booze too. I'm pissed.' He held up his middle finger. 'Sticky finger, Quent. First time.'

Niles plucked at his laces. An irrational hatred and resentment for Holland and Panton festered inside him. Holland he didn't mind. Pete was screwing all the time by all accounts. But Panton? He was short-arsed and had spots. Why should he have any luck?

'Get your rocks off then?' he asked without looking up.

'Not this time. They wouldn't let us. But, my God, Nilo, we could, you know, we could. We've got to fix something up.'

Niles felt a vast relief. Just feel-ups then. Big bloody deal.

'Here,' Holland said. 'Almost forgot. A message from Alison. Wey-hey!' With a flourish he handed over a lilac envelope. Niles felt his throat contract. He opened it carefully.

'Any clippings?' Holland asked with a snigger.

'Hardly,' Niles said. Holland had a French girlfriend who used to send him cuttings of her pubic hair. They were cherished and passed round like sacred relics. This fact had single-handedly boosted Holland's reputation to near-legendary heights.

'Dear Quentin,' Niles read. 'I was wondering if by any chance you would like to come and have tea tomorrow (Sunday). I realize this is short notice but if I don't hear from you I'll expect you at four. I hope you can make it. Sincerely, Alison.'

Niles felt his pulled muscle twitch spasmodically in his thigh. 'I hope you can make it.' That was good. But 'sincerely'? really!

'What is it, for Christ's sake?' Panton asked.

'Tea,' Niles said. 'Tomorrow afternoon.'

Holland shook his head admiringly. 'You got it made, Quent boy. You are home and dry . . . We must get something fixed up though. For all of us. After the last performance maybe. Jesus, the bloody show's over in a couple of weeks.'

Alison's house was a grey sandstone bungalow at the better end of the small Scottish county town near the school. Niles cycled the six miles there through a fine rainy mist and arrived damp and chilled. He met Alison's parents – Mr and Mrs McCullen – and her fourteen-year-old sister Diane. They sat in a warm immaculate sitting room and ate scones and pancakes. The family were kind and genial and Niles relaxed almost immediately and made them laugh with anecdotes of school life. He was a great success with Diane. Alison sat quietly for most of the time, occasionally passing round plates or pouring out more tea. She was wearing jeans and a tight pale blue sweater that gave her a firm breasty look. It was the first time he'd seen her out of uniform and the first time he'd seen her with her hair down. It was long and wavy, dull and thick. It made her look less severe. He felt buoyant with lust and desire, as if he were over-inflated, as if his lungs were crammed with extra capacity of air. He had a sherry before remounting his bike for the long ride back. He reached the school in time for supper.

'I undressed her very slowly,' he told the dormitory. 'As if she was, sort of fragile, or very weak. I unfastened her bra and I kissed her breasts gently. Then . . . then I pulled down her pants and I told her to stand there while I looked at her. She was very slim. Her breasts were firm with almost perfectly round nipples . . .' He swallowed, gazing up unblinkingly at the ceiling as he elaborated his fiction. Even Fillery was silent. 'Then I undressed and we got into bed. I ran my hands all over her body. I wanted to make love but, well, we couldn't because I . . . I didn't have a johnny.'

'I've got dozens,' Fillery said. 'If you'd only asked me.'

'How was I meant to know it would happen?' Niles protested. 'That her parents weren't going to be in? I thought it was just an invitation for tea, for God's sake.'

Niles, Holland and Panton stood at the back of the assembly hall. They were wearing cadet force naval bell-bottoms rolled up to mid calf, singlets and red-spotted neckerchiefs. In front of the stage Prothero was trying to get the school orchestra into tune. On stage Mr Mulcaster, the art teacher, was applying final touches to his backdrop depicting the poop deck of HMS *Pinafore*. Mulcaster's initials were T. A. M., Thomas Anthony Mulcaster. He was known as Tampax Tony.

'Christ almighty, look at Tampax,' Panton said scornfully. 'It's pathetic. I think he's actually painting in a seagull.'

'Ah, now that's an original touch,' Holland confessed. 'Almost as good as his rigging and halliards.'

'A seagull,' Niles said. 'What's it supposed to be doing? Hovering in one spot for the entire course of the play?'

'Oh no. He's painting in a ship on the horizon. A three-master me hearties, ar.'

'We've got to work something out,' Holland said seriously. 'We must have something arranged for after the cast party. Think of something for Christ's sake.'

'I've already told you,' Panton said. 'It's got to be the squash courts. They're ideal.'

'Not a chance, mate,' Niles said. 'Do you know what would happen to me if we got caught?'

'Yes. You'd lose your squash colours,' Panton said with heavy sarcasm.

'Jesus, Nilo,' Holland pleaded. 'You're captain of squash. You've got the keys. We can lock the doors behind us. No one'll know.'

'It's all very well for you. I'll get the bloody boot.'

'Come on, Quentin. Think of the orgy we can have. I've got blankets, booze. Look, I promised the girls we'd have a party. They're expecting one. We haven't got much time. It'll all be over after Saturday night. Gone. Finished.'

Niles was pondering Holland's use of the word 'orgy'.

'Okay,' he said. 'I'll think about it. But I'm not promising anything, mind.'

Alison wore a long flouncy dress that looked as if it were made out of mattress ticking, and a bonnet. Niles stood beside her in the wings. He could hear the audience taking their seats.

'Like the costume,' he said. 'Nervous?'

Alison cocked her head. 'No, I don't think I am actually.' Niles looked more closely at her. She grew daily more inscrutable. They had seen more of each other during the final run-up to the play but he felt that the bizarre intimacy of their first encounter had never been approached. The prospect of inviting her to the party seemed an awesome task.

'Listen,' he began. 'Some of us are having a little "do" after the cast party on Saturday night. Wondered if you'd fancy coming. You know, select little gathering.'

'Saturday night? After the cast party? Yes, okay.'

'And I want you lot to think about me this time tomorrow night,' Niles told his cowed and quiescent dormitory, 'because,' he paused, exultation setting up a tremor in his voice, 'because this time tomorrow night I shall be making love. Got that? Making love to a real girl.'

Niles gazed transfixed across the stage at Alison. The final performance of *HMS Pinafore* was almost over. Mr Booth, the physics master, as Captain Corcoran sang to Buttercup – a pre-pubescent boy called Martin – that wherever she might go he would never be untrue to her.

'What, never?' Niles and Alison and the company wanted to know.

'No, never,' asserted Captain Corcoran.

'What . . . *never*?' the cast repeated.

'Well . . .' ad-libbed the Captain. 'Hardly ever.'

'Hardly ever be untrue to thee-ee-ee . . .' the cast echoed at full volume.

'I mean, be honest,' Holland said to assorted members of the cast. 'It's pretty bloody really. I mean, how these people turn up year in year out and pay good money to see that crap I'll never know.' He ate some more of his cream bun and put his arm round Helen. 'Ah, Quentin, old son,' he said as Niles came into the dressing room with a paper cup of Coke for Alison. 'A word in your ear.' Niles came over. 'I think we can make our move now.

Discreetly though. See you outside the squash courts in five minutes.'

'Be careful,' Niles said to Alison. He held her arm supportively. 'Watch out for these paving stones.' Alison's high heels seemed to ring out with unpropitious clarity as they walked across the courtyard to the squash courts. It was cold and dark and their breath hung in the air long enough for them to walk through the thin clouds before they dispersed. Alison's hair was down and Niles thought she had never looked so beautiful. Her proximity to him and the thought of what was waiting suddenly seemed to make the simple act of walking hideously complicated. He felt as if a sob were lodged in the back of his throat ready to spring from his mouth at any moment.

'I'm okay,' Alison said, and he released her arm.

Holland and Panton were already there with Helen and Joyce. 'At last,' Holland said. 'What've you two been up to? Couldn't wait, eh?' Everyone giggled. Niles bent his head more than he needed to unlock the door into the squash courts.

Inside number three court they spread rugs on the boards and sat in a circle round a solitary candle placed in a jam jar. Holland unpacked the picnic. There was some Gouda and Ryvita, a piece of Stilton, slices of salami, gherkins and two long, knobbled Polish sausages. From his coat pockets Panton produced a bottle of South African sherry and half a bottle of gin. Paper cups were distributed and the drinks passed around.

Niles drank some neat gin. 'To Gilbert and Sullivan,' he toasted the company.

'Ssh,' Holland said. 'Keep it down, Quentin. Your voice I mean.' There were sniggers at this. Niles didn't dare look at Alison's shadowy face.

They ate their meal with a certain urgent decorum, conscious of the fact that it had to be got out of the way – but in no unseemly rush – before the night's real business could commence. Eventually, after a pre-arranged nod from Holland, Panton said, 'Quiet. I think I can hear someone outside.' Then he leant forward and blew out the candle. This act was followed by a muffled squeal from Joyce and a flurry of whispered instructions, scuffles and collisions as Holland and Panton, Joyce and Helen, gathered up rugs and paper cups and groped their way out of the door to their respective squash courts, leaving number three to Alison and Niles.

Niles sat in a darkness so total it seemed solid and shifting, like deep water. He realized he was holding his breath and let it out slowly. He peered intensely in front of him, a screen of blasting mental supernova and arcing tracer bullets exploding before his eyes, brightening the absence of vision. Only the unyielding firmness of the court floor beneath his buttocks anchored him to the dimensional world.

He heard Alison move. How close was she?

'Are you all right?' he whispered. He stretched out his hand, encountering nothing.

'Yes,' she said. 'Is there anyone?'

'I don't think so. False alarm. Just Panton panicking.' His hand touched her shoulder. 'Sorry. Can't see a thing.'

'I'm here.'

'Oh.' The darkness began to retreat. He sensed rather than saw Alison. He moved across the rug, closer to her.

'Bloody dark.'

'Yes.'

He moved his head towards hers, gently, almost blindly, like two docking space craft. After some soft bumps and readjustments, their lips connected tenuously, then sealed. Niles felt his heart swell to inflate his chest as he felt her thin cool lips beneath his.

This was the fifth girl he had kissed properly. It remained as thrilling and exciting as the first time. He wondered if he would always feel this way. With little grunts and discreet pressures he managed to lie Alison down on the rug. Her long hair caught across his face, strands filling his mouth which he had to pull free with his fingers. They kissed again. Niles felt enormously humble and reverential. The accumulated sensations of triumph and release in a kiss were almost enough for him really, but he promptly banished such heretical thoughts from his mind. He managed to get both his arms round Alison and he felt her hands move on his back. His head was resting comfortably on his own left shoulder, Alison's head nestled in the crook of his left elbow. Their knees were touching, her face was perhaps three inches away from his. Some faint source of light picked out a curve on a cheekbone, a glimmer in an eye. The warm breath of her exhalations grazed his cheek. What should he do now, he wondered? Had he much time? What would she like him to do? What was she expecting? Perhaps she wanted to make love too? The novelty of this last idea came to him as rather a shock. He felt suddenly vulnerable and insecure: he sensed the alien presence of her femininity descend on and enfold him. He became immediately aware of his vast ignorance about Alison – the person, the girl – separating him ineluctably from her. Despite the fact that they were lying in each other's arms they might have been facing each other across some great river estuary. The figure on the far bank was a girl's, yes, but that was all he knew.

He felt a gentle shaking. He woke up with a start. His eyes were open but he saw nothing. He sat up. His left arm was dead. It flopped lifelessly at his side.

'You've been asleep,' Alison said. 'I've got to go.'

'What?'

'It's just gone eleven. I've got to get the last bus.'

'Jesus. Asleep? You mean I . . . How long was . . .?'

'You just drifted off. You've been sleeping about half an hour. I didn't want to wake you.'

Niles felt shame and disgrace cause tears to prickle at the corner of his eyes. He picked up his left hand and started to massage it. In the darkness it was like holding an amputated limb. To his right hand his nerveless left felt rough and calloused, like a stranger's.

'Can you find the door?'

They went outside. Alison wondered about the remains of the picnic. Niles told her he'd clean up in the morning before anyone came.

He was about to lock the door. 'What about the others?' he asked, fighting to keep the bitterness from his voice.

'They left about ten minutes ago. I heard them going.'

Niles locked the squash court door. He gazed bleakly around him. Alison stood patiently, knotting her scarf at her throat. It was a sharp, frosty night. The school buildings loomed on either side, dark and unpeopled.

'I'd better go, Quentin,' Alison said.

'I'll come with you to the bus stop.'

They set out together, Niles looking nervously back over his shoulder. He was taking a calculated risk. The bus stop lay half a mile beyond the school gates. If he was caught out of bounds with a girl at this time of night he would be in serious trouble. But equally he felt that whatever happened nothing should prevent him from being with Alison at this moment. They walked on in silence. Niles' mind was a tangle of conflicting emotions. Sentences formed in his head only to split into whirling separate words like some modish animated film. He felt he should say something, explain that he hadn't meant to fall asleep, allude to his romantic plans, but his tongue and his mind refused to co-ordinate. His brain seemed to lock into an imbecilic stupidity. He couldn't do anything right.

At the school gates he let Alison stride confidently through and go a little way down the road before he snaked beneath the lodge windows, squirmed through the side gate and made a sequence of zig-zag dashes from bush to tree trunk, like a commando behind enemy lines, before he caught up with her.

Alison stood in the middle of the road waiting for him. 'That's a bit dramatic, isn't it?'

'I'm out of bounds, you see. If I get caught . . .'

'I don't want you to get into trouble, Quentin.'

'Forget it, really. I don't care.' He took her hand. There was a small shelter by the bus stop . . . 'Come on, let's go.' They walked briskly down the road.

The shelter was empty. A nearby street light threw the graffiti carved on its green wooden bench into high relief. Small drifts of cigarette packs, soft drink cans and wrappers were banked beneath it.

'Alison,' Niles began. 'Listen. I have to say this, I don't want you to think that . . .'

'Here it comes,' cried Alison, as the bus appeared round the corner. 'That was lucky.'

The bus stopped. She gave him a swift kiss on the cheek, so swift it was almost a clash of heads, and got on. Niles looked at the single decker bus. Inside it was soft yellow and smoky. A couple of old women looked curiously back at him. On the rear seats some louts drank beer from cans. Alison stood at the top of the steps, her back to him, buying her ticket from the driver. Her long legs seemed twin symbols of rebuke.

'I'll phone,' he shouted, louder than he meant. It sounded like a grievance, a threat. She turned, smiled, and walked down the bus to take her seat. Niles saw her thick dark hair on her blazer, saw her head toss as she sat down. She waved. The bus drove off. He didn't wave back.

Niles walked morosely up the drive. He walked on the verge, ready to duck behind one of the beech trees that lined the road should a car come by. He stumbled over a root, stopped, turned and kicked savagely at it. In a sombre mood of reassessment he cursed his school, the closed society he was compelled to live in, his demanding, predatory, so-called friends. 'Women,' his father had once patronizingly told him, 'are a lifetime's study.' He was off to a late start then, he observed grimly, and wondered if he would ever catch up. He felt suddenly exhausted by the daily, monotonous absorption with sex, disgusted by the lonely idolatry of masturbation. He felt that his sexual nature, whatever it might be, was irretrievably corrupted.

He paused and took a few deep breaths, trying to shake the mood from him. At this point the drive curved gently to the right, back towards main school. On his left and ahead of him lay a wide flat expanse of playing fields, fixed and still under a faint starlight. His house lay in that direction. It would be quicker, but he wondered if he dared expose himself on the open space. He made up his mind. He set off, breaking into a steady jog, feeling the frost cracking under his feet, puffing his condensed breath ahead of him like a steam engine. He loped silently and strongly across the pitches. He felt that he could run for ever. He would be back in the dorm before twelve. They would all be waiting for him. Fillery had said they'd stay up specially. They wanted to know everything, Fillery had said, every little detail. The bastards, Niles said to himself, smiling. His mind began to work. He'd give them a good story tonight, all right. They wouldn't forget this one in a long time. He ran on, a strange jubilation lengthening his stride.

The Care and Attention of Swimming Pools

Listen to this. Read it to yourself. Out loud. Read it slow and think about it.

A swimming pool is like a child,
Leave it alone and it will surely run wild.

Who said that? Answer: Me. I did.

Wintering

'Can I swim?' says Noelle-Joy. 'It's a fantastic pool.'

Much as I would like to see her jugs in a swimsuit, I have to say no.

'Aw. Pretty please? Why not?'

'I'm afraid the pool is wintering.'

Noelle-Joy squints sceptically up at the clear blue sky. There's not even any smog today. She exposes the palms of her hands to the sun's powerful rays.

'But it's *hot*, man. Anyways, we don't get no winter in L.A.,' she argues.

Patiently I explain that, four seasons or no, every pool has to winter. A period of rest. What you might call a pool-sabbath. I've lowered the water level below the skimmers, superchlorinated and washed out my cartridge filter. A pool, as I explain several times a day to my clients, is not just a hole in the ground filled with water. Wintering removes constant wear and tear, rests the incessantly churning pump machinery, allows essential repairs and maintenance, permits cleansing of the canals, filter system and heating units. You can't do all that if you're splashing around in the goddam thing. Most people realize I'm talking sense.

We walk around my pool. It's small but it's got everything. No-skid surrounds, terrace lights, skimmers, springboard, all-weather poolside furniture and a bamboo cocktail bar plus hibachi. I've got to admit it looks kind of peculiar stuck in my little backyard. (In this part of the city it's the only private pool for seventeen blocks.) But so what! I busted my balls for that little baby. I got me a new vacuum sweep last month. I'm aiming for a sand filter now, to replace my old cartridge model.

I stand proudly behind the bar and pour Noelle-Joy a drink. She's wearing a yellow halter-neck and tight purple shorts. Maybe if she were a little thinner they'd look a bit better on her . . . I don't know. If you got it, flaunt it, I guess. Her legs are kind of short and her thighs have got that strange rumpled look. She stacks her red hair high on top of her head to compensate. She lights a Kool, sips her drink, sighs and hugs herself. Then she sees my hibachi and screams. I drop my cocktail shaker.

'My God! A Hibachi. Permanent as well. Hey, can we barbecue? Please? Don't tell me that's wintering too.'

I ignore her sarcasm. 'Sure,' I say, picking up ice cubes. 'Come by tomorrow.'

I work for AA1 Pools (Maintenance) Inc. We've also been ABC Pools and Aardvark Pools. I tell my boss, Sol Yorty, that we should call ourselves something like Azure Dreams, Paradise Pools, Still Waters – that kind of name. Yorty laughs and says it's better to be at the head of the line in the Yellow Pages than sitting on our butts, poor, with some wise-ass, no-account trademark. The man has no pride in his work. If I wasn't up to my ears in hock to him I'd quit and set up on my own. Tropical Lagoons, Blue Diamond Pools . . . I haven't settled on a name yet. The name is important.

Green Water

Down Glendale Boulevard, Hollywood Freeway, on to Santa Monica Freeway. Got the ocean coming up. Left into Brent-wood. Client lives off Mandeville Canyon. My God, the houses in Brentwood. The *pools* in Brentwood. You've never seen swimming pools like them. All sizes, all shapes, all eras. But nobody looks after them. I tell you, if pools were animate, Brentwood would be a national scandal.

The old Dodge van stalls on the turn up into the driveway. Yorty's got to get a new van soon, for Christ's sake. I leave it there.

The house stands at the top of a green ramp of lawn behind a thick laurel hedge. It's a big house, Spanish colonial revival style with half-timbered English Tudor extension. A Hispanic man-servant takes me down to the pool. 'You wait here,' he says. Greaser. I don't like his tone. One thing I've noticed about this job, people think a pool cleaner is lower than a snake's belly. They look right through you. I was cleaning a pool up on Palos Verdes once. This couple started balling right in front of me. No kidding.

The pool. Thirty yards by fifteen. Grecian pillared pool house and changing rooms. Marble-topped bar. Planted around with oleanders. I feel the usual sob build up in my throat. It's quiet.

There's a small breeze blowing. I dip my hand in the water and shake it around some. The sun starts dancing on the ripples, wobbling lozenges of light, wavy chicken-wire shadows on the blue tiles. What is it about swimming pools? Just sit beside one, with a cold beer in your hand, and you feel happy. It's like some kind of mesmeric influence. A trance. I said to Yorty once: 'Give everybody their own pool to sit beside and there'd be no more trouble in this world.' The fat moron practically bust a gut.

I myself think it's something to do with the colour of the water. That blue. I always say that they should call that blue swimming pool blue. Try it on your friends. Say swimming pool blue to them. They know what you mean right off. It's a special colour. The colour of tranquillity. Got it! Tranquillity Pools . . . Yeah, that's it. Fuck Yorty.

But the only trouble with this particular pool is it's *green*. The man's got green water.

'Hey!' I hear a voice. 'You come for the pool?'

I'm only wearing coveralls with AA1 Pools written across the back in red letters. This guy's real sharp. He comes down the steps from the house, his joint just about covered with a minute black satin triangle. He's swinging a bullworker in one hand. Yeah, he's big. Shoulders like medicine balls, bulging overhang of pectorals. His chest is shiny and completely hairless, with tiny brown nipples almost a yard apart. But his eyes are set close together. I guess he's been using the bullworker on his brain too. I've seen him on the TV. Biff Ruggiero, ex-pro football star.

'Mr Ruggiero?'

'Yeah, that's me. What's wrong wit da pool?'

'You got green water. Your filtration's gone for sure. You got a build-up of algae. When was the last time you had things checked out?'

He ignored my question. 'Green water? Shit, I got friends coming to stay tomorrow. Can you fix it?'

'Can you brush your teeth? Sure I can fix it. But you'd better not plan on swimming for a week.'

'. . . and this stupid asshole, Biff Ruggiero – you know, pro footballer – he hangs around all day asking dumb questions. "Whatcha need all dat acid for?" So there I am, I'm washing out his friggin' cartridges with phosphate tri-soda, and all this crap's like coming out. "Holy Jesus," says Mr Nobel Prize winner, "where's all dat shit come from?" Jesus.' I laugh quietly to myself. 'He's so dumb he thinks Fucking is a city in China.'

I watch Noelle-Joy get out of bed. She stands for a while rubbing her temples.

'I'm going to take a shower,' she says.

I follow her through to the bathroom.

'It just shows you,' I shout over the noise of the water. 'Those cartridge filters may be cheap but they can be a real pain in the nuts. I told him to put in a sand filter like the one I'm getting. Six-way valve, automatic rinsage . . .'

Noelle-Joy bursts out of the closet, her little stacked body all pink from the shower. She heads back into the bedroom, towels off and starts to dress.

'Hey, baby,' I say. 'Listen. I thought of a great name. Tranquillity Pools.' I block out the letters in the air. 'Trang. Quill. It. Tee. Tranquillity Pools. What do you think?'

'Look,' she says, her gaze flinging around the room. 'Ah. I gotta, um, do some shopping. I'll catch up with you later, okay?'

Noelle-Joy moves in. Boy, dames sure own a lot of garbage. She works as a stapler in a luggage factory. We get on fine. But already she's bugging me to get a car. She doesn't like to be seen in the Dodge van. She's a sweet girl, but there are only two things Noelle-Joy thinks about. Money and more money. She says I should ask Yorty for a raise. I say how am I going to do that seeing I'm already in to him for a $5,000 sand filter. She says she wouldn't give the steam off her shit for a sand filter. She's a strong-minded woman but her heart's in the right place. She loves the pool.

'You look after this pool great, you know,' Ruggiero says. I'm de-ringing the sides with an acid wash. We cleaned up the green water weeks ago but we've got a regular maintenance contract with him now.

'I never realized, like, they was so complicated.'

I shoot him my rhyme.

'That's good,' Ruggiero says, scratching his chin. 'Say, you wanna work for me, full-time?'

I tell him about my plans. Tranquillity Pools, the new sand filter, Noelle-Joy.

I come home early. An old lady called up from out in Pacific Palisades. She said her dog had fallen into her pool in the night. She said she was too upset to touch it. I had to fish it out with the long-handled pool sieve. It was one of those tiny hairy dogs. It had sunk to the bottom. I dragged it out and threw it in the garbage can.

'No poolside light, lady,' I said. 'You don't light the way, no wonder your dog fell in. If that'd got sucked into the skimmers you'd have scarfed up your entire filter system. Bust valves, who knows?'

Wow, did she take a giant shit on me. Called Yorty, the works. I had to get the mutt's body out of the trash can, wash it, lay it out on a cushion . . . No wonder I'm red-assed when I get home.

Noelle-Joy's out by the pool working on her tan. Fruit punch, shades, orange bikini, pushed-up breasts. There's a big puddle of water underneath the sun-lounger.

'Hi, honey,' she calls, stretching. 'This is the life, yeah?'

I go mad. 'You been in the water?' I yell.

'What? . . . Yeah. So I had a little swim. So big deal.'

'How many times I got to tell you. The pool's wintering.'

'The pool's been wintering for *three fuckin' months*!' she screams.

But I'm not listening. I run into the pool-house. Switch on the filters to full power. I grab three pellets of chlorine – no, four – and throw them in. Then I get the sack of soda ash, tip in a couple of spadefuls just to be sure.

I stand at the pool edge, panting.

'What do you think you're doing?' she accuses.

'Superchlorination,' I say. 'You swam in stagnant water. Who knows what you could've brought in.'

Now she goes mad. She stomps up to me. 'I just *swam* in your fuckin' pool, turd-bird! I didn't piss in it or nothing!'

I've got her there. 'I know you didn't,' I yell in triumph. ''Cause I can tell. I got me a secret chemical in that water. *Secret*. Anybody pisses in my pool it turns *black*!'

We made up, of course. 'A lovers' tiff' is the expression, I believe. I explain why I was so fired up. Noelle-Joy is all quiet and thoughtful for an hour or two. Then she asks me a favour. Can she have a housewarming party for all her friends? There's no way I can refuse. I say yes. We are real close that night.

OTO

OTO. I don't know how we ever got by without OTO, or orthotolodine, to give its full name. We use it in the Aquality

Duo Test. That's how we check the correct levels of chlorination and acidity (pH) in a pool. If you don't get it right you'd be safer swimming in a cesspit.

I'm doing an OTO test for Ruggiero. He's standing there crushing a tennis ball in each hand. His pool is looking beautiful. He's got some guests around it – lean, tanned people. Red umbrellas above the tables. Rock music playing from the speakers. Light from the water winking at you. That chlorine smell. That fresh coolness you get around pools.

One thing I will say for Ruggiero, he doesn't treat me like some sidewalk steamer. And the man seems to be interested in what's going on.

I show him the two little test tubes lined up against the colour scales.

'Like I said, Mr Ruggiero, it's perfect. OTO never lets you down. You always know how your pool's feeling.'

'Hell,' Ruggiero says, 'looks like you got to be a chemist to run a pool. Am I right or am I right?' He laughs at his joke.

I smile politely and step back from the pool edge, watch the water dance.

'A thing of beauty, Mr Ruggiero, is a joy forever. Know who said that? An English poet. I don't need to run no OTO test. I been around pools so long I got an instinct about them. I know how they feel. Little too much acid, bit of algae, wrong chlorine levels . . . I see them, Mr Ruggiero, and they tell me.'

'Come on,' Ruggiero says, a big smile on his face. 'Let me buy you a drink.'

Sol Yorty looks like an ageing country-and-western star. He's bald on top but he's let his grey hair grow over his ears. He lives in dead-end East Hollywood. I walk down the path in his back garden with him. Yorty's carrying a bag of charcoal briquettes. His fat gut stretches his lime-green sports shirt skintight. He and his wife, Dolores, are the fattest people I know. Between them they weigh as much as a small car. The funny thing about Yorty is that even though he owns a pool company he doesn't own a pool.

He tips the briquettes into his barbecue as I explain that I'm going to have to hold back on the sand filter for a month or two. This party of Noelle-Joy's is going to make it hard for me to meet the deposit.

'No problem,' Yorty says. 'Glad to see you're making a home at last. She's a . . . She seems like a fine girl.' He lays out four huge steaks on the grill.

'Oh, sorry, Sol,' I say. 'I didn't know you had company. I wouldn't have disturbed you.'

'Nah,' he says. 'Just me and Dolores.' He looks up as Dolores waddles down the garden in a pair of flaming-orange Bermudas and the biggest bikini top I've ever seen.

'Hey, sweetie,' he shouts. 'Look who's here.'

Dolores carries a plastic bucket full of rice salad. 'Well, hi, stranger. Wanna eat lunch with us? There's plenty more in the fridge.'

I say I've got to get back.

It looks like Noelle-Joy's invited just about the entire workforce from the luggage factory. Mainly guys, too, a few blacks and Hispanics. The house is crammed with guests. You can't move in the yard. This morning I vacuum-swept the pool, topped up the water level, got the filters going well and threw in an extra pellet of chlorine. You can't be too sure. Some of Noelle-Joy's friends don't seem too concerned about personal hygiene. Everybody, though, is being real nice to me. Noelle-Joy and I stand at the door greeting the guests. Noelle-Joy makes the introductions. Everyone smiles broadly and we shake hands.

I feel on edge as the first guests dive into the pool. I watch the water slosh over the sides, darkening the No-Skid surrounds. I hear the skimmer valves clacking madly.

Noelle-Joy squeezes my hand. She's been very affectionate these last few days. Now every few minutes she comes on over from talking to her friends and asks me if I'm feeling fine. She keeps smiling and looking at me. But it's what I call her lemon smile – like she's only smiling with her lips. Maybe she's nervous, too, I think, wondering what her friends from the luggage factory will make of me.

I have to say I'm not too disappointed though when I'm called away by the phone. It's from Mr Ruggiero's house. Something's gone wrong; there's some sort of sediment in the water. I think fast. I say it could be a precipitation of calcium salts and I'll be there right away.

I clap my hands for silence at the poolside. Everyone stops talking.

'I'm sorry, folks,' I say. 'I have to leave you for a while. I got an emergency on. You all just keep right on having a good time. I'll be back as soon as I can. Bye now.'

Traffic's heavy at this time of the day. We've got a gridlock at Western Avenue and Sunset. I detour around on the Ventura Freeway, out down through Beverly Glen, back on to Sunset and on into Brentwood.

I run down the back lawn to the pool. I can see Ruggiero and some of his friends splashing around in the water. Stupid fools. The Hispanic manservant tries to stop me but I just lower my shoulder and bulldoze through him.

'Hey!' I shout. 'Get the fuck out of that water! Don't you know it's dangerous? Get out, everybody, get out!'

Ruggiero's muscles launch him out of the pool like a dolphin.

'What's goin' on?' He looks angry and puzzled. 'You ain't a million laughs, you know, man.'

I'm on my knees peering at the water. The other guests have clambered out and are looking around nervously. They think of plagues and pollution.

In front of my nose the perfect translucent water bobs and shimmies; nets of light wink and flash in my eyes.

'The sediment,' I say. 'The calcium salts . . . didn't somebody phone . . .?'

By the time I get back I've been away for nearly an hour and a half. She worked fast, I have to admit. Cleaned out everything. She and her friends – they had it all planned. I'd been deep-sixed for sure.

There was a note. YOU MAY NO A LOT A BOUT POOLS BUT YOU DONT NO SHIT A BOUT PEPLE.

I don't want to go out to the yard but I know I have to. I walk through the empty house like I'm walking knee-deep in wax. The yard is empty. I can see they threw everything in the pool – the loungers, the tables, the bamboo cocktail bar, bobbing around like the remains from a shipwreck. Then all of them standing in a circle around the side, laughing, having their joke.

I walk slowly up to the edge and look down. I can see my reflection. The water's like black coffee.

Yorba Linda. It's just off the Riverside Expressway. I'm working as a cleaner at the public swimming pool. Open-air, Olympic-sized.

Yorty had to fire me after what he heard from Ruggiero. Sol said he had no choice. He was sorry but he would 'have to let me go'.

I sold up and moved out after the party. That pool could never be the same after what they had done in it. I don't know – it had lost its innocence, I guess.

Funny thing happened. I was standing on Sunset and a van halted at an intersection. It was a Ford, I think. It was blue. I didn't get a look at the driver, but on the side, in white letters, was TRANQUILLITY POOLS. The van drove off before I could get to it. I'm going to file a complaint. Somebody's stolen my name.

Next Boat from Douala

Then the brothel was raided. Christ, he'd only gone down to Spinoza's to confront Patience with her handiwork. She hadn't been free when Morgan first arrived, so he had chatted to the owner, Baruch – as his better-read clients whimsically dubbed the diminutive Levantine pimp – for half an hour or so, and watched the girls dancing listlessly under the roof fans. His anger had subsided a bit but he managed to stoke up a rage when he was eventually ushered into Patience's cubicle. 'Hey!' he had roared, lowering his greyish Y-fronts. 'Bloody look at this mess!' But then his tirade had been cut short by the whistles and stompings of Sgt Mbele and his vice squad.

The day had started badly. Morgan woke, hot and sweaty, his sheets damp binding-cloths. Three things presented themselves to his mind almost simultaneously: it was Christmas Eve, in four days he would be catching the next boat home from Douala and he had a dull ache in his groin. He eased his seventeen-and-a-half stone out of bed and started for the bathroom. There, a hesitant diagnosis set off by the unfamiliar pain was horrifyingly confirmed by the sight of his opaque, forked and purulent urine.

He dropped off at the local clinic before going into the office. Inside it was cool and air-conditioned. Outside, in the shade cast by the wide eaves, mothers and children sprawled. And inside he ruefully confessed to a Calvinistic Scottish doctor, young and unrelentingly professional, of his weekly visits to Patience at Spinoza's. Then a plump black sister led him to an ante-room where, retreating coyly behind a screen, he delivered up a urine sample. The clear tinkle of his stream on the thin glass of the bottle seemed to rebound deafeningly from the tiled walls. With a cursoriness teetering on the edge of contempt the doctor told him that the result of the test would be available tomorrow.

He vented his embarrassment and mounting anger at his office, Nkongsamba's Deputy High Commission, turning down all that day's applications for visas out of hand, vetoing the recommendations of senior missionaries for candidates in the next birthday honours and, exquisite zenith of the day's attack of spleen, peremptorily sacking a filing clerk for eating fu-fu while handling correspondence. He began to feel a little better, the fear of some hideous social disease retreating as time interposed itself between now and his visit to the clinic.

After lunch his air-conditioner broke down. Morgan detested the sun and because of his corpulence his three years in Nkong-samba had been three years of seemingly constant perspiration, virulent rashes and general discomfort. He had accepted the posting gladly, proud to tell family and friends he was in the Diplomatic Service, and had enthusiastically read the literature of West Africa, searching, with increasing despair, first in Joyce Cary then through Graham Greene right down to Gerald Durrell and Conrad, for any experience that vaguely corres-ponded with his own. When the cream tropical suit he had so keenly bought began to grow mould in the armpits – a creeping greenish hue eventually encroaching on the button-down flap of a breast pocket – he had forthwith abandoned it, and with it all hopes of injecting a literary frisson into his dull and routine life. But, thank God, he was leaving it all soon, next boat from Douala, leaving the steaming forest, the truculent natives, the tiny black flies that raised florin-sized bites. What would he miss? The beer, strong and cold, and, of course, Patience, with her lordotic posture, pragmatic sex and her smooth black body smelling strangely of 'Amby', a skin lightening agent that sold very well in these parts.

Morgan came home after work. There had been an unexpected fall of rain during the afternoon. The air was heavy and damp, great ranges of purple cumulus loomed in the sky. He climbed up the steps to his stoop shouting for Pious his houseboy to bring beer. There on the stoop table lay his copy of Keats, sole heritage of his years at his plate-glass university. He had come across it while packing and had glanced through it, with nostalgic affection, at breakfast. Now, carelessly left out in the rain, it sat there swollen, and steaming slightly it seemed, in the late afternoon heat – a grotesque papier mâché brick. He picked it up and bellowed for Pious.

He stood under the cold shower allowing the stream of water to course down his face plastering his thinning hair to his forehead. A startled Pious had received the sodden complete works full in the face and when he scrabbled to pick it up Morgan had booted him viciously in the arse. He smiled, then frowned. The sudden movement, though producing a satisfying yelp from Pious, had done some damage. Pain pulsed like a Belisha beacon from his testicles, now, he was convinced, grown palpably larger. He counted slowly from one to ten. Things were ganging up on him, he was beginning to feel insecure, hunted almost. Only three days to the boat, then away, thank Christ, for good.

An obsequious, chastened Pious brought him the gin on the stoop. Morgan poured two inches into a glass full of ice, added some bitters and a dash of water. He hated the drink but it seemed the apt thing to do; end of a tropical day, sundowners and all that. It was dark now and unbearably humid. There would be a storm tonight. Fat sausage flies brought out by the rain whirled and battered about him. Ungainly on their wings one landed in his gin and drowned there, straddled on the cubes. His shirt stuck to his back, the minatory hum of a mosquito was in his ear. Crickets chirped moronically in the garden. He would go and sort out that Patience.

In Sgt Mbele's fetid detention hall Morgan had two hours in which to repent that decision. Finally he managed to impress Mbele, a grinning stubborn man, with, also, the help of a thirty-bob bribe, that as he was First Secretary at the Commission he possessed diplomatic immunity, and that he would take it as a personal favour if the sergeant wouldn't mention him in his report. H. E., though profligate himself, admired a sense of decorum in his subordinates.

Leaving the police station Morgan decided there and then to abandon his car at Spinoza's and instead go to the club – a ten-minute walk – and get drunk. The Recreation Club, as it was inspiringly named, had been built for the expatriate population of Nkongsamba in the heady days of the Empire. A long rambling high-ceilinged building, surrounded by a piebald golf-course and tennis courts, it preserved, with its uniformed servants and airmail copies of British newspapers, something of the ease and tenor of those times. As Morgan approached it became evident that quiet inebriation was out of the question. Gerry and the Pacemakers boomed from the ballroom, coloured lights and streamers were festooned everywhere. It was the

Christmas Party. Morgan, scowling and black-humoured, brutally shouldered his way through the crowd around the bar and
drank three large gins very quickly. Then, moderately composed,
he sat on a bar stool and surveyed the scene. The men wore
white dinner jackets or tropical suits and looked hot and
apoplectic. The women sported the fashions of a decade ago
and appeared strained and ill-at-ease. There were few young
people; young people did not come to the tropics from choice,
only if they were sent, like Morgan.

'Um, excuse me,' a tap on his elbow, 'it is Mr Morgan, isn't it?'

He looked round. 'Yes. Hello. Mrs . . . Brinkit, yes? Erm, let
me see. Queen's Birthday, High Commission last year?'

'That's right.' She seemed overjoyed that he had remembered.
She was tall and thin and just missed being attractive. Thirtyish,
late, probably. She wore a strapless evening gown that exposed a
lot of bony chest and shoulder. Her nose was red, she was a bit
drunk, but then so was Morgan.

'Doreen,' she said.

'Sorry?'

'Doreen. My name.'

'Christ yes. So sorry. And your husband, ah, George, how's
he?'

'It's Brian actually. He would be here but Tom, our dachshund, ran away and Brian's been out all night looking for him.
Doesn't want him to catch rabies.'

'*A la recherche du Tom perdu*, eh?' Morgan laughed at his
joke.

'Pardon?' said Doreen Brinkit smiling blankly and swaying
gently up against him.

Morgan drank a lot more and danced with Doreen. They
became very friendly, more by force of circumstance – they were
both alone, unattractive and needing to forget it – than by desire.

At midnight they kissed and she stuck her tongue in his ear. There was no sign of Brian. Morgan remembered them now from the cocktail party at the Commission. Brinkit small bald and shy. Doreen six inches taller than him. Brinkit telling him of his desire to leave Africa and become a vet in Devon. Wanted kids, nothing quite like family life. No place for children Africa, very risky, healthwise. No place for you either, Morgan had thought, as he looked at the man's little eyes and his frail earnest features.

Some time later in a dark corner of the ballroom Doreen squirmed and hissed 'No! Morgan! Stop it . . . honestly, not *here*.' Then more suggestively, 'Look, why don't I give you a run home. I've got the van outside.'

Breathless with excitement and lust Morgan excused himself for a moment. On his way to the lavatory he reflected that possibly it hadn't been such a bad day after all. God. A real white woman.

But then a five-minute session of searing agony in the gent's toilet brought home to him – with an awful clarity – the nightmarish significance of the lyrics in Jerry Lee Lewis' 'Great Balls of Fire'. He reeled out of the toilet, eyes streaming, teeth clenched, and collided with a small firm object. Through the mists of tears the prim features of his doctor shimmered and formed, mouth like a recently sutured wound.

'Oh! Morgan, it's you. Well, I won't waste any words. Save you a trip tomorrow. Bad news I'm afraid. You've got gonorrhoea.' As if he didn't know.

The VW bus was parked up a track off the main road some miles out of town. The jungle reared up on all sides. Heavy rain beat down remorselessly. Inside, lit by the inadequate glow of a map light, Morgan and Doreen Brinkit lay in the back, spacious with the seats folded down. Doreen moaned unconvincingly as

Morgan nuzzled her neck. His heart wasn't in it. His mind was obsessed with a single image, rooted there since he'd heard the appalling news, of a rancid gherkin astride two suppurating black olives. With a shudder he broke off and took great pulls at the gin bottle he'd purchased before leaving the club. His brain seemed to cartwheel crazily in his skull. Bloody country! he screamed inwardly. Bloody filthy Patience! Three rotting years just to end up with the clap. He drank deep, awash with self-pity. A tense frustrated rage mounted within him. Distractedly he looked round. Doreen was tugging at the bodice of her skirt, all tulle and taffeta, reinforced with bakelite and whalebone. She pulled it down revealing an absurd cut-away bra that offered her nipples like canapés on a cocktail tray. Morgan's rage was replaced by a spasm of equally intense lust. What the hell, he was on the next boat from Douala, clearing out. She was desperate for it. He reached up and switched out the map light.

But then somewhere in the prolonged pre-coital tussle, Doreen's dress concertina-ed at her waist, Morgan's trousers at his knees, the rain drumming on the tin roof, the air soupy with sweat and deep breathing, Morgan took stock. Perhaps it was when, spliced between Doreen's pale shanks, she breathed 'come on Morgan, it's okay, it's okay, it's the safe time of the month' and Morgan looked up at the windscreen awash with water and images began to zig-zag through his mind, like bats in a room seeking an open window. He thought of his testicles effervescing with bacilli, he thought of pathetic Brian Brinkit searching for his fucking dachshund in a downpour, then he thought of impregnating Doreen, his putrid seed in her womb, Brian's innocent alarm at the diseased monster he'd inadvertently produced. He thought of Brian diseased too, a loathsome spiral of infection, a little septic carbuncle festering in Africa behind him. And he realized as Doreen's grunts began to reach a crescendo beneath him that, no, in spite of everything – Patience, Keats, Pious, Mbele, the stinking heat and the clap – it just wasn't on.

He withdrew and sat up breathing heavily.

'What is it, Morgan?' Surprised, a tint of anger colouring her voice.

What the hell could he say? 'I'm sorry, Doreen,' he began pathetically, desperately running through plausible reasons. 'But . . . it's just, um . . . well I don't think this is fair to Brian. I mean . . . he is out looking for Tom, in this rain.' Then, despite himself, he laughed, a half-suppressed derisive snort, and Doreen abruptly burst into tears, sobbing as she tried to cover herself up. Morgan sat and finished the gin.

'*Get out!*' Morgan looked round in alarm. Doreen, hair all over the place, face tracked with mascara, shrieking at him. 'Fucking get *out*! How *dare* you treat me like this? You filth, you fat sodding bastard!' She started to pummel him with her fists, pushing him towards the back of the van with surprising strength. Somehow the door sprang open.

'Hang on, Doreen! It's pouring. Let's talk about it.' She was hitting him about the head and shoulders with the empty gin bottle, screaming obscenities all the while. Morgan fell out of the back of the van. He scampered out of the way seconds later as she reversed violently down the road. Morgan sat on the verge, the jungle at his back, rain soaking him completely. 'Jesus,' he said. He wiped his wet hair from his forehead. For some curious reason he felt light-headed, suddenly hugely relieved. He got to his feet noticing unconcernedly that his trousers were covered in mud. Then, for a brief tranquil moment, the rain beating down on his head, he felt intensely exhilaratingly happy. Why? He couldn't really be sure. Still . . . He set off down the track, a bulky dripping figure, humming quietly to himself at first, and then, spontaneously, filling his lungs and breaking into a booming cockney basso profundo that spilled out into the dark and over the trees.

'Hyme a si-i-inging in a ryne, hyme a singin' in a ryne.'

Cicadas trilled in his path.

Gifts

We land in Nice. Pan Am. I go through customs without much trouble and stand around the arrivals hall wondering what to do next – if there's a bus into town; whether I should get a taxi. I see a man – black hair, white face, blue suit – looking curiously at me. I decide to ignore him.

He comes over, though.

'Tupperware?' he asks unctuously. He pronounces it tooper-wère.

'Sorry?' I say.

'Ah, English,' he says with some satisfaction, as if he's done something clever. 'Mr Simpson.' He picks up my suitcase, it's heavier than he expects. He has tinted spectacles and his black hair is getting thin at the front. He looks about forty.

'No,' I say. I tell him my name.

He puts my suitcase down. He looks around the arrivals hall at the few remaining passengers. I am the only one not being met.

'*Merde*,' he swears softly. He shrugs his shoulders. 'Do you want a ride into town?'

We go outside to his car. It's a big Citroën. The back is filled with plastic beakers, freezer boxes, salad crispers and such like. He puts my case in the boot. He shovels stacks of pamphlets off the front seat before he lets me into his car. He explains that he has been sent to meet his English opposite number from Tupperware UK. He says he assumed I was English from my clothes. In fact he goes on to claim that he can guess any European's nationality from the kind of clothes he or she is wearing. I ask him if he can distinguish Norwegians from Danes and for some reason he seems to find this very funny.

We drive off smartly, following the signs for Nice *centre ville*. I can't think of anything to say as my French isn't good enough and somehow I don't like the idea of talking to this man in English. He sits very close to the steering wheel and whistles softly through his teeth, occasionally raising one hand in rebuke at any car that cuts in too abruptly on him. He asks me, in French, how old I am and I tell him I'm eighteen. He says I look older than that.

After a while he reaches into the glove compartment and takes out some photographs. He passes them over to me.

'You like?' he says in English.

They are pictures of him on a beach standing by some rocks. He is absolutely naked. He looks in good shape for a forty-year-old man. In one picture I see he's squatting down and some trick of the sun and shadow makes his cock seem enormously long.

'Very nice,' I say, handing them back, 'but *non merci*.'

He drops me in the middle of the Promenade des Anglais. We shake hands and he drives off. I stand for a while looking down on the small strip of pebble beach. It's January and the beach is empty. The sky is packed with grey clouds and the sea looks an unpleasant blue-green. For some reason I was expecting sunshine and parasols. I let my eyes follow the gentle curve of the Baie des Anges. I start at the airport and travel along the sweep of the coast. The palm trees, the neat little Los Angeleno-style hotels with their clipped poplars and fancy wrought ironwork, along past the first of the apartment blocks, blind and drab with their shutters firmly down, past the Negresco with its pink sugary domes, past the Palais de la Méditérranée, along over the old Port, completing the slow arc at the promontary of Cap St Jean, surmounted by its impossible villa. I see the ferry from Corsica steaming gamely into harbour. I stand looking for a while until I begin to feel a bit cold.

It's Sunday so I can't enrol for my courses at the university until the next day. I carry my case across the Promenade des Anglais, go up one street and book into the first hotel I see. It's called the Hotel Astoria. I go down some steps into a dim foyer. An old man gives me a room.

I sit in my room reading for most of the evening. At about half past nine I go out for a coffee. Coming back to the hotel I notice several young girls standing in front of brightly lit shop windows in the Rue de France. Despite the time of year they are wearing boots and hot pants. They all carry umbrellas (unopened) and swing bunches of keys. I walk past them two or three times but they don't pay much attention. I observe that some of them are astoundingly pretty. Every now and then a car stops, there is a brief conversation, one of the girls gets in and is driven away.

Later that night as I am sitting on my bed reading there is a knock on my door. It turns out to be the fat daughter of the hotel manager. He has told her I am English and she asks if I will help her do a translation that she's been set for homework.

I enrol at the university. This takes place at a building called the Centre Universitaire Méditérranéan or CUM as it's generally known (the French pronounce it 'cume'). The building is on the Promenade des Anglais and looks like a small exclusive art gallery. Inside there is a huge lecture room with a dull mytho-logical mural on three walls. This morning I am the first to arrive and there is a hushed marmoreal stillness in the place. In a small office I enrol and pay my fees. I decide to postpone my first class until the next day as I have to find somewhere to live. A secretary gives me a list of addresses where I can rent a room. I look for the cheapest. Mme D'Amico, it says at the bottom of the list, 4 Rue Dante. I like the address.

As I leave the Centre I see some of my fellow students for the first time. They all seem to be foreign – in the sense that not many are French. I notice a tall American girl surrounded by chattering Nigerians. There are some Arabs. Some very blonde girls whom I take to be Scandinavian. Soon the capacious marble-floored entrance hall begins to fill up as more and more people arrive for their classes. I hear the pop-pop of a motor bike in the small courtyard at the front. Two young guys with long hair come in talking English. Everyone seems happy and friendly. I leave.

Rue Dante is not far from the Centre. Number four is a tall old apartment block with bleached shutters and crumbling stone-work. On the ground floor is a café. CAVE DANTE it says in plastic letters. I ask the concierge for Mme D'Amico and am directed up three flights of stairs to the top floor. I ring the bell, mentally running through the phrases I have prepared. '*Mme D'Amico? Je suis étudiant anglais. Je cherche une chambre. On m'a donné votre nom au Centre Universitaire Méditérranéan.*' I ring the bell again and hear vague stirrings from the flat. I sense I am being stared at through the peep-hole set in the solid wooden door. After a lengthy time of appraisal, it opens.

Mme D'Amico is very small – well under five feet. She has a pale thin wrinkled face and grey hair. She is dressed in black. On her feet she is wearing carpet slippers which seem preposterously large, more suitable for a thirteen-stone man. I learn later that this is because sometimes her feet swell up like balloons. Her eyes are brown and, though a little rheumy, are bright with candid suspicion. However, she seems to understand my French and asks me to come in.

Her flat is unnervingly dark. This is because use of the electric lights is forbidden during hours of daylight. We stand in a long gloomy hallway off which several doors lead. I sense shapes – a wardrobe, a hatstand, a chest, even what I take to be a gas cooker, but I assume my eyes are not yet accustomed to the murk. Mme D'Amico shows me into the first room on the left. She opens shutters. I see a bed, a table, a chair, a wardrobe. The floor is made of loose red hexagonal tiles that click beneath my feet as I walk across to look out of the window. I peer down into the apartment building's central courtyard. Far below the concierge's alsatian is scratching itself. From my window I can see into at least five other apartments. I decide to stay here.

Turning round I observe the room's smaller details. The table is covered with a red and brown checked oilcloth on which sits a tin ashtray with 'SUZE' printed on it. On one wall Mme D'Amico has affixed two posters. One is of Mont Blanc. The other is an SNCF poster of Biarritz. The sun has faded all the bright colours to grey and blue. Biarritz looks as cold and unwelcoming as the Alps.

I am not the only lodger at Mme D'Amico's. There is a muscle-bound taciturn engineer called Hugues. His room is separated from mine by the WC. He is married and goes home every weekend to his wife and family in Grenoble. Two days after I arrive the phone rings while I am alone in the flat. It is Hugues' wife and she sounds nervous and excited. I somehow manage to inform her that Hugues is out. After some moments of incomprehension I eventually gather that it is imperative for Hugues to phone her when he comes in. I say I will give him the message. I sweat blood over that message. I get my grammar book and dictionary out and go through at least a dozen drafts. Finally I prop it by the phone. It was worth the effort. Hugues is very grateful and from that day more forthcoming, and Mme D'Amico makes a point of congratulating me on my French. She seems more impressed by my error-free and correctly accented prose than by anything else about me. So much so that she asks me if I want to watch TV with her tonight. I sense that this is something of a breakthrough: Hugues doesn't watch her TV. But then maybe he has better things to do.

Almost without any exertion on my part, my days take on a pattern. I go to the Centre in the morning and afternoon for my courses. At lunch and in the evening I eat at the enormous university cafeteria up by the Law faculty. I return home, have a cup of coffee in the Cave Dante, then pass the rest of the evening watching TV with Mme D'Amico and a neighbour – a fat jolly woman to whom I have never been introduced but whose name, I know, is Mme Franchot.

Mme D'Amico and Mme Franchot sit in armchairs. I bring a wooden chair in from the hall and sit behind them looking at the screen between their heads. While the TV is on all other source of illumination is switched off and we sit and watch in a spectral grey light. Mme D'Amico reads out loud every piece of writing that appears on the screen – the titles of programmes, the entire list of credits, the names and endorsements of products being advertised. At first I find this intensely irritating and the persistent commentary almost insupportable. But she speaks fairly softly and after a while I get used to her voice.

We watch TV in Mme D'Amico's bedroom. She has no sitting room as such. I think that used to be the function of my room. Hugues sleeps in what was the kitchen. He has a sink unit at the foot of his bed. Mme D'Amico cooks in the hall (I was right: it was a cooker) and washes up in the tiny bathroom. This contains only a basin and a bidet and there are knives and forks laid out alongside toothbrushes and flannels on a glass shelf. There is no bath, which proved something of a problem to me at the outset as I'm quite a clean person. So every two or three days I go to the municipal swimming baths at the Place Magnan. Formal, cheerless, cold, with pale green tiles everywhere, but it stops me from smelling.

The fourth room in the flat is a dining room, though it's never used for this purpose as this is where Mme D'Amico works. She works for her son, who is something – a shipper I think – in the wine trade. Her job is to attach string to a label illustrating the region the wine comes from and then to tie the completed label round the neck of a wine bottle. The room is piled high with crates of wine, which she sometimes calls on me to shift. Most days when I come back I see her sitting there, patiently tying labels round the necks of the wine bottles. It must be an incredibly boring job. I've no idea how much her son pays her but I suspect it's very little. But Mme D'Amico is methodical and busy. She works like hell. People are always coming to take away the completed crates. I like to think she's really stinging her son.

There are lots of girls I'd like to fuck who do courses with me at the Centre. Lots. I sit there in the class with them and think about it, unable to concentrate on my studies. I've spoken to a few people but I can't as yet call any of them friends. I know a Spanish girl and an English girl but they both live outside Nice with their parents. The English girl is called Victoria and is chased all day by a Tunisian called Rida. Victoria's father was a group-captain in the RAF and has retired to live in Grasse. 'Out to Grasse' Victoria calls it. Somehow I don't think the group-captain would like Rida. Victoria is a small, bland blonde. Not very attractive at all, but Rida is determined. You've got to admire his persistence. He doesn't try anything on, is just courteous and helpful, tries to make Victoria laugh. He never leaves her side all day. I'm sure if he perseveres his luck will turn. Victoria seems untroubled by his constant presence, but I can't see anything in Rida that would make him attractive to a girl. He is of average height, wears bright-coloured, cheap-looking clothes. His hair has a semi-negroid kink in it which he tries to hide by ruthlessly brushing it flat against his head. But his hair is too long for this style to be effective and it sticks out at the sides and the back like a helmet or an ill-fitting wavy cap.

There are genuine pleasures to be derived from having a room of one's own. Sometimes at night I fling back the covers and masturbate dreamily about the girls at the Centre. There is a Swedish girl called Danni whom I like very much. She has big breasts and long white-blond hair. Is very laughing and friendly. The only trouble is that one of her legs is considerably thinner than the other. I believe she had polio when young. I think about going to bed with her and wonder if this defect would put me off.

My relationship with Mme D'Amico is very formal and correct. We converse in polite phrases that would not disgrace a Victorian drawing room. She asks me, one day, to fill out a white *fiche* for the police – something, she assures me hastily, every resident must do. She notices my age on the card and raises her eyebrows in mild surprise. She says she hadn't supposed me to be so young. Then one morning, apropos of nothing, she explains why she reads everything that appears on TV. It seems that Mme Franchot is illiterate. If Mme D'Amico didn't relate them to her, she would never even know the names of the old films we watch nightly on Monte Carlo TV. I find I am surprisingly touched by this confidence.

One evening I go to a café with Rida after our courses and meet up with some of his Tunisian friends. They are all enrolled at one educational institution or another for the sake of the *carte d'étudiant*. They tell me it's very valuable, that they would not be allowed to stay in France if they didn't possess one. Rida, it has to be said, is one of the few who actually tries to learn something. He shares a room with a man called Ali who is very tall and dapper. Ali wears a blazer with brass buttons that has a pseudo-English crest on the breast pocket. Ali says he bought it off a tourist. The English style is *très chic* this year. We drink some beer. Rida tells me how he and Ali recently met a Swiss girl who was hitch-hiking around Europe. They took her back to their room and kept her there. They locked her in during the day. Rida lowers his voice. '*On l'a baissé,*' he tells me conspiratorially. '*Baisser. Tu comprends?*' He says he's sure she was on drugs as she didn't seem to mind, didn't object at all. She escaped one afternoon and stole all their stuff.

The café is small, every shiny surface lined with grease. It gets hot as the evening progresses. There is one very hard-faced blonde woman who works the cash register behind the bar, otherwise we are all men.

I drink too much beer. I watch the the Tunisians sodomize the pinball machine, banging and humping their pelvises against the flat end. The four legs squeal their outrage angrily on the tiled floor. At the end of the evening I lend Rida and Ali twenty francs each.

Another phone call when I'm alone in the flat. It's from a doctor. He says to tell Mme D'Amico that it is all right for her to visit her husband on Saturday. I am a little surprised. I never imagined Mme D'Amico had a husband – because she always wears black I suppose. I pass on the message and she explains that her husband lives in a sanatorium. He has a disease. She starts trembling and twitching all over in graphic illustration.

'Oh,' I say. 'Parkinson's disease.'

'*Oui*,' she acknowledges. '*C'est ça. Parkingsums.*'

This unsought for participation in Mme D'Amico's life removes another barrier. From this day on she uses my first name – always prefixed, however, by 'Monsieur'. 'Monsieur Edward,' she calls me. I begin to feel more at home.

I see that it was a misplaced act of generosity on my part to lend Rida and Ali that money as I am now beginning to run short myself. There is a postal strike in Britain which is lasting far longer than I expected. It is quite impossible to get any money out. Foolishly I expected the strike to be short-lived. I calculate that if I radically trim my budget I can last for another three weeks, or perhaps a little longer. Assuming, that is, that Rida and Ali pay me back.

When there is nothing worth watching on television I sit at the window of my room – with the lights off – and watch the life going on in the apartments round the courtyard. I can see Lucien, the *patron* of the Cave Dante, sitting at a table reading a newspaper. Lucien and his wife share their apartment with Lucien's brother and his wife. They all work in the café. Lucien is a gentle bald man with a high voice. His wife has a moustache and old-fashioned, black-framed, almond-shaped spectacles. Lucien's brother is a big hairy fellow called Jean-Louis, who cooks in the café's small kitchen. His wife is a strapping blonde who reminds me vaguely of Simone Signoret. One night she didn't draw the curtains in her bedroom properly and I had quite a good view of her undressing.

I am now running so low on money that I limit myself to one cup of coffee a day. I eat apples all morning and afternoon until it is time for my solitary meal in the university restaurant up by the *fac du droit*. I wait until the end because then they give away free second helpings of rice and pasta if they have any left over. Often I am the only person in the shining well-lit hall. I sit eating bowl after bowl of rice and pasta while the floors are swabbed around me and I am gradually hemmed in by chairs being set on the tables. After that I wander around the centre of town for a while. At half nine I make my way back to the flat. The whores all come out at half nine precisely. It's quite amazing. Suddenly they're everywhere. Rue Dante, it so happens, is right in the middle of the red-light district. Sometimes on my way back the girls solicit me. I laugh in a carefree manner, shrug my shoulders and tell them I'm an impoverished student. I have this fantasy that one night one of the girls will offer to do it free but so far I've had no success.

If I've saved up my cup of coffee for the evening my day ends at the Cave Dante. I sit up at the zinc bar. Lucien knows my order by now and he sets about making up a *grande crème* as soon as I come in the door. On the top of the bar are baskets for brioches, croissants and pizza. Sometimes there are a few left over from breakfast and lunch. One night I have a handful of spare centimes and I ask Lucien how much the remaining bit of pizza costs. To my embarrassment I still don't have enough to buy it. I mutter something about not being hungry and say I've changed my mind. Lucien looks at me for a moment and tells me to help myself. Now every night I go in and finish off what's left. Each time I feel a flood of maudlin sentiment for the man but he seems uneasy when I try to express my gratitude.

One of the problems about being poor is that I can't afford to send my clothes to the '*pressings*' any more. And Mme D'Amico won't allow washing in the flat. Dirty shirts mount up on the back of my single chair like so many soiled antimacassars. In a corner of the wardrobe I keep dirty socks and underpants. I occasionally spray the damp heap with my aerosol deodorant as if I were some fastidious pest controller. When all my shirts are dirty I evolve a complicated rota for wearing them. The idea is that I wear them each for one day, trying to allow a week between subsequent wears in the faint hope that the delay will somehow have rendered them cleaner. At least it will take longer for them to get *really* dirty. At the weekend I surreptitiously wash a pair of socks and underpants and sneak them out of the house. I go down to an isolated part of the beach and spread them on the pebbles where a watery February sun does a reasonable job of drying them out.

One Saturday afternoon I am sitting on the shingle beach employed in just such a way. I wonder sadly if this will be my last weekend in Nice. The postal strike wears on, I have forty-two francs and a plane ticket to London. Small breakers nudge and rearrange the pebbles at the water's edge. This afternoon the sea is filled with weed and faeces from an untreated sewage outlet a little way up the coast. Freak tides have swept the effluence into the Baie des Anges. The sun shines, but it is a cool and uncongenial day.

The thought of leaving Nice fills me with an intolerable frustration. Nice has a job to do for me, a function to fulfil and it hasn't even begun to discharge its responsibility.

I hear steps crunching on the stones, coming towards me. I look round. It is Rida with a girl I don't recognize. Frantically I stuff my washing into its plastic bag.

'*Salut*,' Rida says.

'*Ça va?*' I reply nonchalantly.

'What are you doing here?' Rida asks.

'Oh . . . nothing particular.'

We exchange a few words. I look carefully at the girl. She is wearing jeans and a tie-dyed T-shirt. She has reddish–blonde medium length hair and a flat freckly face. It is not unattractive though. Her eyebrows are plucked away to thin lines and her nose is small and sharp. She seems confident and relaxed. To my surprise Rida tells me she's English.

'English?' I say.

'Hi,' she says. 'My name's Jackie.'

Rida has literally just picked her up on the Promenade. I don't know how he singles them out. I think he feels he has another Swiss girl here. He saw me sitting on the beach and told Jackie he knew an English guy he would like her to meet.

We sit around for a bit. I talk in English to Jackie. We swop backgrounds. She comes from Cheshire and has been living in Nice for the last four months. Latterly she has worked as au pair to a black American family. The father is a professional basketball player, one of several who play in the French leagues now that they're too old or too unfit to make the grade in the US.

With all this English being spoken Rida is beginning to feel left out of it, and is impatiently throwing pebbles into the sea. However, he knows that the only way for him to get this girl is through me and so he suggests we all go to a disco. I like the sound of this because I sense by now that Jackie is not totally indifferent to me herself. She suggests we go to the 'Psyché', a rather exclusive disco on the Promenade des Anglais. I try to disguise my disappointment. The 'Psyché' costs eighteen francs to get in. Then I remember that Rida still owes me twenty francs. I remind him of this fact. I'll go, I say, as long as he pays me in. Reluctantly he agrees.

We meet at nine outside the 'Psyché'. Jackie is wearing white jeans and a scoop-necked sequinned T-shirt. She has pink shiny lipstick and her hair looks clean and freshly brushed. Rida is wearing black flared trousers and a black lacy see-through shirt unbuttoned down the front. Round his neck he has hung a heavy gold medallion. I'm glad he's changed. As we go in he touches me on the elbow.

'She's mine, okay?' he says, smiling.

'Ah-ha,' I counter. 'I think we should rather leave that up to Jackie, don't you?'

It is my bad luck that Jackie likes to dance what the French call *le Swing* but which the English know as the jive. I find this dance quite impossible to master. Rida, on the other hand, is something of an expert. I sit in a dark rounded alcove with a whisky and coke (a free drink comes with the entry fee) and nervously bide my time.

Rida and Jackie come and sit down. I see small beads of sweat on Jackie's face. Rida's lace shirt is pasted to his back. We talk. A slow record comes on and I ask Jackie to dance. We sway easily to the music. Her body is hot against mine. Her clean hair is dark and damp at her temples. As if it is the most natural thing in the world I rest my lips on the base of her neck. It is damp too, from her recent exertions in *le Swing*. Her hand moves half an inch on my back. I kiss her cheek, then her mouth. She won't use her tongue. She puts her arms round my neck. I break off for a few seconds and glance over at Rida. He is looking at us. He lights a cigarette and scrutinizes its glowing end.

To my astonishment when we sit down Jackie immediately asks Rida if he'd like to dance again as another *Swing* record has come on. She dances with him for a while, Rida spinning her expertly around. I sip my whisky and coke – which is fizzless by now – and wonder what Jackie is up to. She's a curious girl. When they come off the dance floor Rida announces he has to go. We express our disappointment. As he shakes my hand he gives me a wink. No hard feelings I think he wants to say.

We go, some time later, to another club called Go-Go. Jackie pays for me to get in. Inside we meet one of Jackie's basketballers. He is very black – almost Nubian in appearance – and un-believably tall and thin. He is clearly something of a sporting celebrity in Nice as we get a continuous supply of free drinks while sitting at his table. I drink a lot more whisky and coke. Presently we are joined by three more black basketball players. I become very subdued. The blacks are friendly and extrovert. They wear a lot of very expensive-looking jewellery. Jackie dances with them all, flirts harmlessly, sits on their knees and shrieks with laughter at their jokes. All the French in the club seem to adore them. People keep coming over to our table to ask for autographs. I feel small and anaemic beside them. My personality seems lamentably pretentious and unformed. I think of my poverty, my dirty clothes, my shabby room and I ache with an alien's self-pity, sense a refugee's angst in my bones.

Then Jackie says to me, 'Shall we go?' and suddenly I feel restored. We walk through quiet empty streets, the only sound the rush of water in gutters as they are automatically swilled clean. We pass a café with three tarts inside waiting for their pimp. They chatter away exuberantly.

Jackie shivers and I obligingly put my arm around her. She rests her head on my shoulder and in this fashion we awkwardly make our way to her flat. 'Shh,' Jackie cautions as we open the front door, 'be careful you don't wake them up.' I feel a rising pressure in my throat, and I wonder if the bed has squeaky springs.

We sit in the small kitchen on hard modern chairs. My buttocks feel numb and strangely cold. The fluorescent light, I'm sure, can't be flattering if its unkind effects on Jackie's pale face are anything to go by. Slowly I sense a leaden despair settle on me as we sit in this cheerless efficient module in this expensive apartment block. *Immeuble de très grand standing* the agent's advertisement says outside. We have kissed from time to time and I have felt both her small pointed breasts through her T-shirt. Her lips are thin and provide no soft cushion for my own. We talk now in a listless desultory fashion.

Jackie tells me she's leaving Nice next week to return to England. She wants to be a stewardess she says, but only on domestic flights. Intercontinental ones, it seems, play hell with your complexion and menstrual cycle. Half-heartedly I offer the opinion that it might be amusing if, say, one day I should find myself flying on the very plane in which she was serving. Jackie's face becomes surprisingly animated at this notion. It seems an appropriate time to exchange addresses, which we do. I notice she spells her name 'Jacqui'.

This talk of parting brings with it a small cargo of emotion.

We kiss again and I slip my hand inside her T-shirt.

'No,' she says gently but with redoubtable firmness.

'Please, Jackie,' I say. 'You're going soon.' I suddenly feel very tired. 'Well at least let me see them then,' I say with petulant audacity. Jackie pauses for a moment, her head cocked to one side as if she can hear someone calling her name in the distance.

'Okay then,' she says. 'If that's what you want. If that's all.'

She stands up, pulls off her T-shirt and slips down the straps of her bra so that the cups fall free. Her breasts cast no shadow in the unreal glare of the strip-light. The nipples are very small, her breasts are pale and conical and seem almost to point upward. She exposes them for five seconds or so, not looking at me, looking down at her breasts as if she's seeing them for the first time. Then she resnuggles them in her bra and puts her T-shirt back on. She makes no comment at all. It's as if she's been showing me her appendix scar.

'Look,' she says unconcernedly at the door, 'I'll give you a ring before I leave. Perhaps we could get together.'

'Yes,' I say. 'Do. That would be nice.'

Outside it is light. I check my watch. It's half past five. It's cold and the sky is packed with grey clouds. I walk slowly back to Mme D'Amico's through a sharp-focused, scathing dawn light. Some of the cafés are open already. Drowsy *patrons* sweep the pavements. I feel grimy and hungover. I plod up the stairs to Mme D'Amico's. My room, it seems to me, has a distinct fusty, purulent odour; the atmosphere has a stale recycled quality, all the more acute after the uncompromising air of the morning. I strip off my clothes. I add my unnaturally soft shirt to the pile on the back of the chair. I knot my socks and ball my underpants – as if to trap their smells within their folds – and flip them into the corner of the wardrobe. I lie naked between the sheets. Itches start up all over my body. I finger myself experimentally but I'm too tired and too sad to be bothered.

I wake up to a tremulous knocking on my door. I feel dreadful. I squint at my watch. It's seven o'clock. I can't have been asleep for more than an hour.

'*Monsieur Edward? C'est moi, Madame D'Amico.*'

I say come in, but no sound issues from my mouth. I cough and run my tongue over my teeth, swallowing energetically.

'*Entrez, Madame,*' I whisper.

Mme D'Amico comes in. Her hair is pinned up carelessly and her old face is shiny with tears. She sits down on the bed and immediately begins to sob quietly, her thin shoulders shaking beneath her black cardigan.

'Oh Madame,' I say, alarmed. 'What is it?' I find it distressing to see Mme D'Amico, normally so correct and so formal, displaying such unabashed human weakness. I am also − inappropriately − very aware of my nakedness beneath the sheets.

'*C'est mon mari,*' she cries. '*Il est mort.*'

Gradually the story comes out. Apparently Monsieur D'Amico, sufferer from Parkinson's disease, was having a final cigarette in his room in the sanatorium before the nurse came to put him to bed. He lit his cigarette and then tried to shake the match out. But his affliction instead made the match spin from his trembling fingers and fall down the side of the plastic armchair upon which he was sitting. The chair was blazing within seconds, Monsieur D'Amico's pyjamas and dressing gown caught fire and although he managed to wriggle himself onto the floor his screams were not sufficiently loud to attract the attention of the nurses immediately. He was severely burned. The shock was too much for his frail body and he died in the early hours of the morning.

I try to arrange my sleepy unresponsive senses into some sort of order, try to summon the full extent of my French vocabulary.

Mme D'Amico looks at me pitifully. '*Oh Monsieur Edward,*' she whimpers, her lips quivering.

'*Madame,*' I reply helplessly. '*C'est une vraie tragédie.*' It seems grossly inept, under the circumstances, almost flippant, my thick early-morning tongue removing any vestige of sincerity from the words. But it seems to mean something to Mme D'Amico, who bows her head and starts to cry with light high-pitched sobs. I reach out an arm from beneath the sheets and gently pat her shoulder.

'There, there, Madame,' I say. 'It will be all right.'

As I lean forward I notice that in her hands there is a crumpled letter. Peering closer I still can't make out the name but I do see that the stamp is British. It is surely for me. The postal strike, I realize with a start, must now be over. Suddenly I know that I can stay. I think at once about Jackie and our bizarre and unsatisfactory evening. But I don't really care any more. My spirits begin to stir and lift. I get a brief mental flash of Monsieur D'Amico in his blazing armchair and I hear the quiet sobs of his wife beside me. But it doesn't really impede the revelation that slowly overtakes me. People, it seems, want to give me things – for some reason known only to them. No matter what I do or how I behave, unprompted and unsought the gifts come. And they will keep on coming. Naked photos, cold pizza, their girls, their wives, their breasts to see, even their grief. I feel a growing confidence about my stay in Nice. It will be all right now, I feel sure. It will work out. I think about all the gifts that lie waiting for me. I think about the Swedish girls at the Centre. I think about spring and the days when the sun will be out . . .

The bed continues to shudder gently from Mme D'Amico's sobbing. I smile benignly at her bowed head.

'There, there, Madame,' I say again. 'Don't worry. Everything will be okay. You'll see. Everything will be fine, I promise you.'

My Girl in Skin-Tight Jeans

I would like to make one thing clear before I tell my story. I don't want you to think that because I have never married that there is any kind of . . . of a problem between me and the female sex. I could in fact have married any number of girls had I so chosen – but I didn't choose to, so there it is. It was a question of my health, you see. I do not have a strong constitution and largely for that reason I decided, once my dear mother had died, to remain a bachelor.

My mother left me a small legacy along with the house. I live quietly and economically there. I have several projects with which I am currently occupied and they take up a fair amount of my time. I am a great reader too, and one of the luxuries of not having to work for a living is that I can indulge to the full my passion for reading. Lately, however, I have grown rather tired of books and for the last year or so have read only magazines. I have subscriptions to thirty-eight and buy many others on a casual, sporadic basis. I read all kinds except the political ones; I like the bright, happy illustrations and I have been progressively coming round to the opinion that magazines are, indeed, more imaginative than many novels. The world of the glossy magazine holds more allure for me than the grimy realistic tragedies that pass for literature these days.

Every winter I leave the house, board it up and switch off the water and electricity. I spend the winter months in a small resort town a few miles up the coast from San Luis Obispo in northern California. I get all my magazine subscriptions forwarded there. It's a quiet life, but cheap and necessary for my health. Over the years I've got to know most of the inhabitants, but they're not very sociable folk and I find that few of them have much to say for themselves.

This last winter had been a bad one for me. My budget, due to the failure of one of my projects, was lower than ever and my life-style was correspondingly reduced. I had been chronically depressed through most of January and February and if it hadn't been for the regular arrival of my magazines with their laughing happy people in their primary-coloured world I'm sure I would have done something drastic. However, as spring approached my spirits rallied and I began to feel a little better.

Then she arrived – a modern primavera – and the sleepy resort town seemed to respond to her exciting presence. I began to think of her possessively as 'my girl'. She was definitely my kind of girl. My girl in skin-tight jeans, I called her. It was merely a fancy of mine, I never actually plucked up the courage to introduce myself. I saw her regularly every day from my room and soon grew to feel that somehow I had come to know her, got to grips with what I believe is a rare, remarkable personality.

She's beautiful too. Shaggy, clean blonde hair, a short, crisp white T-shirt leaving a gap of navel-dimpled caramel belly between its hem and her dark tight navy jeans. Those long-legged, tapered blue-jeans.

It makes me feel good to think of her as my girl. For some reason she always wears the same outfit every day – but it's always fresh and well-laundered. She's the most truly at-ease person I've ever come across: there's an astonishing serenity which beams out of her eyes. I have noticed too, that she never wears a brassière, and the thin material of her T-shirt is moulded closely to her breasts.

My room is small but I keep it tidy. There's an electric ring and a sink in the corner but I don't do much cooking because I hate the smell it leaves. My room is on the top floor of an old building on the sea front. It has two windows and from one of them I can get a good view of the ocean and the coast. In this town only two cafés stay open through the winter season and I divide my meals more or less equally between them; I don't wish to seem particular and have no desire to give offence. In fact I prefer the Del Mar, but I don't want to alienate old Luke who runs Luke 'n' Loretta's. He's nearly blind, but we talk a lot and I kind of like the old guy. I'm unwilling to tell him but, as his sight's got worse, so has his place. Nowadays he leaves nearly everything up to his sister Loretta. She's an overweight, red-rinsed whore who lives in a camping truck out the back. For five dollars she'll give you a quick time out there. Believe me, it isn't worth it. For some reason though, she's taken a shine to me – asked me round for a drink after closing a couple of times. But since the girl in skin-tight jeans arrived I've stayed away. Then Loretta cut me dead in the street yesterday so I thought I'd better go back, just to keep the peace.

There was the first spring-quickening in the air this morning as I walked to Luke's for breakfast. A watery sun warmed the sea breeze, the day was mild with a light blue sky up above. However, any elation I felt was dissipated when I got to Luke's. There was no sign of the old man and the place was a real toilet. I sat at my usual table and waited for Loretta to come and clear it up. It was swimming with spilt coffee, the ashtray was full of butts and someone had ground out a cigar in a half-eaten plate of pancakes and syrup. Loretta wore a loose Hawaiian blouse and stretch slacks in honour of the clement weather. She sat down and chatted and offered me one of the menthol cigarettes she chain smokes so I guessed I must have been forgiven. Then she leant right over in front of me while she cleared the table so I could get a good look down her front at her heavy breasts. I ordered a hot tea, no milk, with a slice of lemon.

It may have been warmer outside but Loretta wasn't taking any chances. All the windows were tight shut and their film of condensation and grease obscured any view of the beach.

I heard a car pull up. I wiped the window and peered out. It was a battered convertible and there were three guys inside. They got out and stretched, rubbing their buttocks and looking around. They were young; two whites and a Hispanic. There was a thin one with a pimp's moustachio and a thick-lipped, black-haired guy with oddly white tattooed arms. They were wearing worn-out sharpie clothes.

This is a quiet little town we live in and I hoped they'd just move on through. But just then the sun came out from behind some clouds and, in the corner of my eye, I caught its flash on the girl's white T-shirt. It was the first time I'd seen her that day and I wiped the window some more to get a better look. But they saw her too and they glanced at each other and laughed in that shifty teeth-baring way men in a group have. One of them bent his arm and did something with his fingers while the thick-lipped guy cupped his hands over his crotch and groaned. They all laughed again.

I felt my face flush and a pulse beat at my temples. When I put my cup down in its saucer there was a rattle of china. They disgust me, this kind of filth. City scum degenerates, just drifting up the coast in a hot car looking for cheap kicks.

★   ★   ★

I spent the rest of the day in my room reading my magazines. Later I tried to sleep but I had developed a bad headache. In the afternoon I had a long shower. That made me feel a little better.

At dusk I went to a small supermarket that I sometimes buy provisions at when I don't feel like going out to eat. I was reaching for a tin of clam chowder when I saw the girl through the window. I was a little surprised. Usually I never managed to see her this late and I always wondered where she went. But tonight it was obvious; her eyes were gazing out to sea, her easy stride would carry her determinedly down to the beach.

The clam chowder tasted like earth. I couldn't clear my mouth of it so I drank a glass or two of rye. I opened the window that gives me a sea view and sat on the sill looking out at the darkening waters. Quite a way along the beach I could see the glimmer of a campfire burning and I knew at once that was where the girl would be – out there alone. Maybe she had cooked something and was enjoying the peace and absolute solitude. Then I could imagine her stripping off her clothes, her tan body with white bikini patches maybe, paler in the gloom, the breeze tensing her nut-brown nipples, the cool of the water as the waves broke against her golden thighs . . .

But then I was distracted by the noise of raucous laughter in the street below. The three youths, half bombed, spilling out of the liquor store clutching six-packs and a bottle of wine. With a bizarre sense of mounting premonition I watched them laughing and joshing for a while in the street. Then one of them said, 'Hey, look. A fire.' And with whistles and whoops they went running down the boardwalk, all heroic with beer, jumping gleefully onto the sand and heading up the beach towards my girl.

*   *   *

For an instant I heard my heart booming in my skull and my eyeballs seemed to bulge rhythmically to its beat. With a forefinger I wiped beads of perspiration from my upper lip. *Bastards!* SCUM TRASH BASTARDS! I saw stubby stained fingers fondling corn-yellow hair, spectral tattooed arms circling her slim brown body, probing tongue between thick dabbing lips, young beards on soft skin. She'd come dripping from the surf, wading quietly out of the green sea, her body dim and mysterious, to find a leering drunken horror waiting round her fire.

I felt the sharp taste of vomit in my throat for I was almost sick with a desperate fear and anxiety as I rummaged in my bureau for my gun, an old police special. I was sick with insane visions of the fabulous lusts of nightmare hooligans, terrible images of deviant sex-dreams being foully realized out there on the lonely coast.

I came up behind them through the dunes, my feet silent on the sand. The three of them sat around the fire drunk. One of them was singing quietly to himself. Discarded beer cans lay like shell cases round a gun emplacement. There was no sign of the girl.

They heard the sound of my feet as I crossed the strip of pebbles that lay above the high-tide mark.

'Hey, man,' the thick-lipped one said. 'Whatcha doin'? Have a drink. Luis, give . . .'

Then he saw the gun. His jaw slackened as his beer-numbed brain tried to cope with what was happening.

'C'mon, what gives?' There was a smile of disbelief on his face. The other two began to edge away from me.

'Where is she?' I said, my voice shaking with rage and disgust. I raised my eyes looking for signs of a shallow grave, half expecting to see her violated body cast up on the beach by the waves.

'What have you filth done with her? Where is she? Where have you put her?'

He stood up shakily, an uncertain smile on his face. He looked round at his friends for support. 'Who, man?' he said, shrugging his shoulders. 'For chrissake, who?'

'*My girl!*' I screamed at him, maddened by his feeble attempts to protest his innocence. 'My sweet girl, you bastard!'

'We ain't seen no friggin girl, man,' he shouted back, arcs of spittle flying from his lips.

The waves seemed to be crashing and breaking in my head as I levelled the gun at his denimmed groin and pulled the trigger. I missed, but the bullet tore off a chunk of his thigh which splashed a bright red in the firelight. He screamed with the pain and went down.

When the sound of the waves and the echoes of the shot had diminished I heard the rattle of pebbles as his two friends ran off.

Thick-lips was crawling painfully down the sand towards the sea. One leg of his jeans was damp and left a trail like a slug. He was making little whimpering noises.

'I'll give you one last chance,' I shouted after him. 'Tell me where she is.'

He said nothing.

I pocketed the gun and picked up a piece of driftwood about the size of a baseball bat. I weighed it in my hand, swishing it gently through the air to get my grip right. Then I walked down the beach to thick-lips and with five or six firm strokes battered his head into the wet sand at the surf edge. The foam went pink like a milk shake.

When it was over I pushed him well out into the breakers. The tide was ebbing and it would be a couple of days before he washed up again.

Then I stood on the beach and shouted out into the waves just in case she was out there. 'It's okay,' I shouted. 'You can come out. They've gone.'

But she never appeared.

When I woke up the next morning I knew instinctively she had gone forever and for a moment I felt the sadness of her passing intensely.

I went to the window and opened it and took a few deep breaths. Across the street a man was working on the billboard. Distracted, I began to admire the way he handled the huge cumbersome folds of paper, his dexterity in spreading the sheets so accurately and with such little fuss, the precision with which he manipulated the long sopping brush. And, as the new advertisement took shape, I found I was forgetting about the girl as she disappeared, with her impossibly white T-shirt and her ludicrously skin-tight jeans.

I stood there at the window a while, just looking.

Yes, I thought to myself. Yes. Definitely my kind of drink. Mellow, with the real tawny glow . . .

Histoire Vache

'So you are still a virgin,' Pierre-Etienne said triumphantly, stubbing out his cigarette.

It had to come out, Eric thought. They had been talking earnestly about sex all afternoon. Under cross-examination Eric had mentioned an older girl-cousin called Jean and suggestively introduced the notion of a seaside holiday and a sand dune picnic *à deux*. He had tried to keep the details vague but conversations of this sort remorselessly turned towards the specific and Pierre-Etienne and Momo (Maurice) had been unsparing in their search for the truth. They had really pinned him down this time. Yes or no, they demanded; did you or didn't you.

'I don't believe it,' Momo said. 'You never?'

Eric shook his head, trying to smile away his blush. They were sitting at a café in the main square of Villers-Bocage. It was market day and the place was full of livestock and people. Momentarily Eric's attention was distracted by the sight of a red-faced farmer in the typical knee-length Normandy blouson, energetically tugging on the tail of a cow as if he was trying to wrench it out by the roots. Eric winced.

He looked back at his two companions. Pierre-Etienne was the same age as him; last Easter he'd spent two weeks in England at Eric's home. Momo was Pierre-Etienne's brother, a little older – nearly seventeen, plump and trying to grow a moustache. Eric didn't like him that much; his air of amused tolerance towards the two younger boys was extremely irritating. Momo had a girl friend of sorts, Eric knew, but he'd never seen Pierre-Etienne with one.

Eric sipped his Diabolo-menthe. He adored the chill green drink, clear and clinking with ice cubes. It was the best thing about France he decided. He'd never learn the language, he was sure, and as far as he was concerned it wasn't worth the last two weeks of his summer holiday. Pierre-Etienne's father was the director of the Villers-Bocage abattoir, and as a result of his job the family ate meat for every meal; every sort and cut imaginable: pork, veal, beef, kidneys, heart, brains, revolting spongy tripe, lamb, ox-tails, trotters, fatty purple sausages, all of it pink and undercooked and oozing with blood. Eric was returning directly to school in three days and he sometimes found himself longing for shepherd's pie or a thick Bisto stew.

'But surely you're one – a virgin – too?' he said to Pierre-Etienne in half-hearted counter-attack.

'Of course not.' Pierre-Etienne looked offended.

'But you don't have a girl friend,' Eric said. 'How could you?'

'No,' Momo said, 'he don' have a girl friend, but he has Marguerite.'

'And who's she?'

Marguerite Grosjean shouted good-bye to her mother and eased her bulk into her tiny 2-CV. As usual her mother didn't reply. Marguerite lit her fifth Gauloise of the day, She sat for a moment in her car. It was only half past five and Villers-Bocage was just ten minutes away through the early morning mist. She puffed on her cigarette and scratched her thigh. Her mother leaned out of the upstairs window and shouted at her. It was just a noise. Her mother ran out to the car screaming abuse. Marguerite flipped down the window. Arcs of spittle from her mother's mouth spattered on the glass. Marguerite let it go on a few seconds. It was like this every morning. Then she started the engine and drove off leaving the small dishevelled figure still shaking with rage alone in the yard.

She arrived at the abattoir a little early so she went to the nearby bar and ordered a café-calva. The waiter brought her the drink. He was new to the café. He smiled and said good morning but Marguerite appeared not to notice him. He found this somewhat unusual as he had taken her against the wall at the back of the café only three nights ago when she came off night shift. He said good morning again but she didn't reply. He shrugged his shoulders and walked off, but he kept the tab. It wasn't much but it was something. One of the butchers who worked in the abattoir had told him about Marguerite and all the butchers, farm hands, meat packers and lorry drivers. You just need to ask, the man had said, that's all, a simple request, and he had tapped his temple with a forefinger. The waiter had met her on her way back from the toilet. The butcher had been right.

He thought of asking her again, just now, to see if it was really true, but the clear morning light was unkind to the fat woman so he went on wiping the tables.

Eric, Pierre-Etienne and Momo stood at the back of the abattoir looking over a wall at the stream of departing workers from the morning shift.

'Which one is she?' Eric asked.

'That one there, the big one, going in the car.'

Eric saw lots of cars and quite a few large women.

'Which car?' he asked.

'That one,' Momo said, pointing to an old 2-CV being driven away. Eric couldn't really see the driver, just a white face and black hair.

He felt a thump of excited pressure in his chest. 'What do I have to do?' he asked.

'You just go and tell her what you want,' Pierre-Etienne said.

'Is that *all*? Just ask?'

'Yes, it's all.'

'But why does she do it? Do . . . do I have to pay her or anything?'

The two French boys laughed delightedly. 'No, no,' Momo said. 'She do it for nothing. She likes it.'

'Oh,' said Eric knowledgeably, 'a nympho. But are you sure? You're not lying? She does it just like that?'

'Everybody is going to Marguerite,' Momo said with emphasis. '*We* have gone.'

'Bloody hell. Did *you*?' Eric asked Pierre-Etienne.

'Of course,' he replied. 'I have been three times. It is easy.'

'God,' said Eric quietly. The ease of the whole venture astonished him. It really was going to happen. 'But I still don't understand *why*. What for? Why does she do it?'

Marguerite parked her car at the back of the abattoir near the packed cattle pens full of grunting and shifting beasts. As she walked into the room where she worked the familiar pungent ammoniacal smell of guts and excrement tickled her nostrils. She took her plastic overall off the peg and buttoned it tightly across her massive chest. She stepped into her gum boots and pulled the white cap over her wiry black hair just beginning to be streaked with grey.

She heard the men arrive, the jokes and the early morning banter. A few stepped in for a moment and said hello. She stood looking at the huge stainless steel basins. She leant back against the mangle. She wasn't thinking about anything, just waiting for Marcel to wheel in the first shivering gelid tub of brown and purple guts.

Then she heard the familiar sound of the slaughter begin. The compressed air phut of the humane killer as the retractable six-inch spike was driven into the animal's skull. The clang as the side of the pen fell away to let the beast tumble down the concrete incline, the rattle of its hooves on the cement. Then there was the whirr of the hoist as the carcase was lifted up by a rear leg and almost simultaneously the splash as the blood poured from twin slits made in the throat. It took barely a minute for the skin to be removed before the buzzing circular saw carved down the length of the suspended body opening it wide. The first today was a cow, she recognized the second splash – this time of milk – as the udder was halved by the whining blade. Then there was the slithering slopping waterfall as the insides fell out. The moan of the overhead rails – as the carcase was swung down the line to the butchers and the cavernous refrigerating plant – was punctuated by the thumps and splashings of the second animal being killed.

Eight cows later Marcel wheeled in the first of the buckets. He was simple and had a hare lip. He never spoke much. He turned on the hoses and water sprays and plunged his bare hands into the gelatinous mass of entrails and heaved great piles into the brimming sinks. There were arm-length, rubber gloves for this purpose but Marcel maintained that they only made his job harder.

Marguerite stood above the overflowing steaming basins and quickly sorted the larger pieces of offal from the long strings of intestines. She flung the stomachs onto a recessed tray which Marcel later took through to the tripe room. Her overalls were soon covered by a green slime of blood and feculence. She took a bucket of the washed viscera over to the mangle and forced an end of gut between the rollers. She grunted slightly as she turned the handle to run them through. Green and purple efflux plopped and spouted from the other end, splashing onto her boots and the floor where it was hosed into the drains by Marcel.

Pale emptied ropes of intestine were collected in a zinc bucket on the other side of the mangle. Marguerite gave them a final wash through with a high-pressure hose to remove all remaining particles before Marcel took them to be prepared for tripe. She worked on this way until lunchtime, pausing occasionally to smoke a cigarette or take a drink from a bottle of Calvados she kept on a window ledge.

That night Eric lay in bed thinking about the next day. It was all arranged for lunchtime. Apparently Marguerite always ate lunch in her car. Momo was going to write a note for him to give to her. That was all he had to do.

Eric wondered what it would be like. What it would feel like. He wondered what Morton and Haines would say when he told them back at school. Was it going to be any different from when he did it himself? He slipped his hand into his pyjama trousers and touched himself, ran his fingers over his neat bush of public hair. He couldn't imagine it at all. It seemed so easy. What if something went wrong?

The three boys were waiting at the back of the abattoir by 11 o'clock. Eric kept clearing his throat and his palms were wet with perspiration even though it was a cool morning. Momo had written out the brief note; he was being especially nice that day. 'What is it I have to say?' Eric asked for the tenth time.

'Just say "*Vous êtes Madame Marguerite?*" and give her the note.'

'*Vous êtes Madame Marguerite?*'

'Good,' Momo said, '*Très bien,*' and handed him the piece of paper. Eric unfolded it. Momo had printed in block letters '*JE VOUDRAIS TE SAUTER GROSSE TRUIE*'.

'What does it mean?' Eric asked Pierre-Etienne.

'It means "I want to make love with you, you lovely woman." '

Eric frowned. 'Are you sure? I always thought *sauter* meant to jump.'

'Oh it's an expression you can use,' Pierre-Etienne said quickly, glancing at Momo who added,

'It's a more agreeable way to say it.'

'Ah. I see. Okay.'

When Marguerite appeared Eric was surprised at how big she was. When she climbed into her car it tossed on its springs like a boat in a storm. At once a blind funk seized him and he felt convinced that he wouldn't be able to go through with it. But Momo and Pierre-Etienne were urging him on relentlessly as if they were aware of the weight of self-doubt building up in his mind. The consequences of backing out at this stage were too severe to be contemplated; the immense agonies of shame and abuse that would have to be endured. It was too late for second thoughts now. In any case he felt strangely cushioned from events and embarrassment by the barrier of language; it was like watching yourself on a home-movie. Besides if she swore at him or called the police he just wouldn't understand and, anyway, he was going home tomorrow.

However, as he crunched across the gravel of the car park he felt very lonely and exposed. He looked back at Pierre-Etienne and Momo who eagerly waved him on. They had made it sound like the most natural thing in the world, something any youth in

Villers-Bocage did as a matter of course – an easy initiation. There had been disparaging remarks about the effeminate, gelded sissies who balked at the opportunity. '*Ils sont vraiment les gonzesses, les tantouzes.*' Eric asked what they were. '*Les pédés, homosexuels,*' plump Momo said, his voice hoarse with disdain. Now as he walked across the car park he felt the gaze of the two boys at his back like a goad.

Marguerite sat in the passenger seat of her small car which listed heavily. She had finished her sandwich. Eric looked at her forearm which rested on the sill. It was very white, white as a fridge, and large and soft. There was a dark shadow of hairs running down it. Her fingernails were rimmed with what looked like brown ink.

Eric cleared his throat. '*Etes-vous Madame Marguerite?*' he asked, holding out the note.

'*Etes-vous Madame Marguerite?*'

Marguerite looked round. The boy was standing against the light and at first she couldn't really see him. She took the note he was holding but he didn't go away. She opened it up and read the message. She felt her face grow hot with anger and her mouth tightened. To her surprise the boy remained standing; she had expected to see him scampering off laughing delightedly at his filthy joke. But he was not even smiling; he seemed a little nervous.

Marguerite opened the door of the car and got out. She folded her arms across her bosom and glared at the boy. He was tall and slender with straight blond hair that fell across his forehead. His face was awkward and uneven with adolescence as if he'd borrowed some features from a larger person. He had small pink spots at the corners of his mouth and on his chin.

'*Ah, bon,*' she said, her anger making her voice tremble. '*Tu veux m'sauter.*'

'Um . . . ah, *pardon?*' the boy said.

She heard his accent. Her anger began to fade. It never lasted long anyway. The joke was on him. *'Anglais?'* she asked.

He nodded. Marguerite looked around for his friends, the ones who had played the joke, but she couldn't see anyone. She flourished the note.

'C'est ordurier ça.' But he didn't understand her. His quick smile was nervous and uncertain and she suddenly felt sorry for him. She breathed out slowly and looked at him again. The anger had barely rippled the placid lake of her total indifference. She seldom let her mind contribute anything to the flow of experience. It had only brought her anguish and difficulty. So now she passively received the sensations it threw at her. She had no doubts and she had no complaints.

'OK,' she said and beckoned him to follow. She led him out of the car park and round a corner to a cluster of outbuildings, garages and store rooms. She opened a wooden door at the back of a garage and showed him in. A shelf of sunlight on the wall from a high window illuminated some old packing cases and cardboard boxes. In the corner was a bed of sorts; a mattress and a blanket. There was a grimy sink and a table and a chair. Some newspapers and magazines lay on the table. The room was used by the security guards; somewhere to go if the rain was heavy, a place for an undisturbed smoke and a chat, somewhere to take Marguerite.

She came up behind the boy who was looking around him uncomfortably. She touched his hair; it was very clean and shiny. He was surprised and looked round quickly, automatically raising a hand to the back of his head. Marguerite smiled at him, enjoying his youth and his reticence.

'Vas y,' she said, pointing to the mattress. The boy started to unbutton his shirt and slipped it off his shoulders. He kicked off

his shoes. Marguerite was surprised; no man had ever bothered to undress for her before – at the most trousers were lowered to the knees – and she only removed what was essential.

The boy stood there in his underpants, uneasy in the intensity of her gaze. With a start she realized he was waiting for her to undress. She looked at his hairless body, the slim legs, the shadows of his ribs, the lean jut of his pelvis, and he seemed to her almost painfully beautiful. As she fumbled with the buttons on her dress she felt a strange thick sensation in her throat and for a brief moment the utter grief of her life cut like a razor and her eyes spangled with tears.

Eric lay still in Marguerite's arms. She was holding him tight running her hands up and down his body, muttering soft phrases that he couldn't understand. Eric was aware of an unfamiliar tiredness and now that it was all over he longed to be away from this small room and this large white woman with her curious smell. At the beginning he had been numbed and filled with nervousness when she had taken off her clothes and lain down beside him on the mattress. What struck him was not the heavy flat breasts with their stark brown nipples, the bushy armpits or the overhanging belly, but the shocking nude whiteness of the woman. She was so white she was almost grey, as he remembered his arm had once been when it was removed from a plaster cast.

The brief unsatisfactory coupling was completed within seconds, or so it seemed to Eric, who now ran through his past sensations like a clerk at a filing cabinet, seeking for something that was memorable, that retained traces of excitement. She had kissed his face and rolled him on top of her, manipulating and pushing him around like a worker he'd once seen operating a die stamper. But now it was over she just seemed to want to hold him and Eric didn't know what to do. And there was the smell. At first he thought it came from the mattress but then he realized it rose from her skin, a thin acidic smell, almost organic and living.

Eric was confused about his role; it had not been like the books he'd read or the stories he'd heard. He had been passive, merely fulfilling a function. He hadn't felt anything. Once, when waiting for the school train, Haines had pointed to a group of women in black overalls carrying long brushes who were heading up the platform towards the sidings. The women who cleaned the carriages, Haines said, were notorious. They'd do it for ten bob, anywhere, with anyone.

Tentatively Eric brought his hand up from the mattress and touched Marguerite's breast. The nipple was coarse and thick like a small brown raspberry. His palm cautiously inched up the slack bulge of her breast. He gently touched the nipple and let his fingers trickle over it. As he touched it she said something and hugged him close to her with a strength he found surprising, so that he felt in a moment of panic that the viscid-white flesh might envelop him, lapping round his body like mud. She reached down for him, her other hand pressing his face into her neck, and he could smell her, he could feel it filling his lungs like water.

With a wriggle he broke free and sat up. He pointed to his watch. 'I have to go,' he said, and quickly pulled on his clothes. Marguerite, alone on the mattress and suddenly aware of her nakedness, covered herself with her dress.

Eric crouched in the corner tying up his shoelaces, his face hot with embarrassment, unable to say a word, the silence heavy in the air like a threat. From the corner of his eye he saw her leg, the purple veined thigh with its furze of dark hairs and he felt his top lip twitch with distaste. He went over to her, carefully avoiding her gaze and breathing through his mouth.

Marguerite was very quiet. Eric reached into his pocket and withdrew two ten-franc notes. 'Here,' he held them out. '*Merci*,' he added feeling foolish. But she just curled his fingers back round them and pushed his hand away. For a moment his hand with the notes seemed to hover disconnectedly between them. Suddenly Eric wished she had taken the money. It would have been better.

'Well, good-bye,' he said. '*Au revoir*.'

Outside the air felt washed and fragrant. Eric took deep breaths and tried to lift the mood he sensed was descending on him as inevitably as night . . .

The afternoon sun beat down on him. It was that curious pause in the year: high summer slipping into autumn. Things started to decay then; wars began, dogs went mad. The green of the trees and the grass looked tired, old, and tramped on.

'How was it?' Pierre-Etienne asked when Eric caught up with them.

'Fantastic,' Eric lied automatically.

'You were a long time,' Momo said.

'Was I? Oh well, you know how it is.'

'Did you . . . really?' Pierre-Etienne asked.

Eric looked at him curiously. 'Yes. It went just like you said.' He shivered. 'She's big. Huge . . . you know.' He weighed two mammoth breasts in front of him.

Pierre-Etienne and Momo looked on with ill-concealed amazement. Eric said, '*Elle pue*,' and they both laughed uneasily. He touched his back pocket and heard the crinkle of notes. He turned and walked away from the abattoir back towards the market place. Pierre-Etienne and Momo followed behind deep in conversation.

'Come on,' Eric shouted, 'I'll buy you a Diabolo-menthe.'

★   ★   ★

Marcel looked up in surprise when Marguerite said good-bye. Normally they parted without a word. She went to the café and ordered a drink. The late afternoon sun cast long shadows across the street, a slight breeze shifted a scrap of paper on the pavement, amber light flashed momentarily from a chrome bumper. Some of the butchers from the day shift came into the café but she paid them no attention. She was thinking about clean shiny hair, smoothness, a touch.

She called for another calva. She would go home late tonight, maybe see a film or just sit on here in the café for a while. It was a pleasant evening; there was something solid and achieved about the depth of the shadows, it seemed to her; the kindness of the yellowy sun patches on the table tops pleased her obscurely. She took the last sip of calva. The English boy had been gentle and she had made him happy.

The waiter brought her new drink over. As he put it down he whispered his request in her ear. She looked round. The man leant confidentially over the table. She saw his oily hair, his silver tooth, his shiny watch.

'Well?' he asked, smiling, his eyebrows raised.

'No,' said Marguerite abruptly, before she had really even thought about it. 'No. Tomorrow perhaps, we'll see. But not today. Not today.'

On the Yankee Station

When Lt Larry Pfitz lost his Phantom on his first mission he decided, quite spontaneously and irrationally, to blame the Vietnamese people and Arthur Lydecker, a member of his ground crew.

Pfitz was a new pilot and his face was taut as he ran through the cockpit checks before being catapulted off the heaving deck of the USS *Chester B. Halsey*. The Phantom was heavy with four clusters of 500lb bombs and extra poundage of pressure was demanded from the old steam catapults. Pfitz was third in line and as the *Chester B.* heeled round into the wind the deck crew noticed the way his eyes continuously flicked from left to right at the rescue helicopters hovering alongside.

There had been a ragged jeer as Pfitz's plane dipped alarmingly on being hurled off the deck before the straining engines thrust him up in a steep climb to join the other two members of his flight. The fourth jet was ready on the second catapult when one of the fire guards shouted and pointed up. There, in the pale grey sky, Pfitz hung beneath his orange parachute. His plane flew on straight for a brief few seconds before tilting on one wing and curving elegantly down into the sea.

It was as well for Pfitz that, just before it smashed into the water, there was a muffled crack of explosion and a puff of smoke from the jets, otherwise the court of inquiry might have peremptorily dismissed his claim of a serious engine malfunction. Still, it left an uneasy aroma of doubt in the air. The Phantom had been new, flown over from Guam three days prior to Pfitz's arrival, and the loss of several million dollars of expensive equipment for no real and pressing reason was regarded – even in this most extravagantly wasteful of wars – as a fairly serious matter. Pfitz was reprimanded for over-hasty reactions, and as a measure of the Captain's disapproval was assigned to fly an old Ling-Temco-Vaught Crusader that was stored in the back of the below-deck hangar until a replacement Phantom arrived.

Pfitz's considerable self-esteem never recovered from this blow and his fellow pilots ribbed him unmercifully. He came to the conclusion that the loss of his Phantom was somehow symbolic of the animosity of the Vietnamese people to the American presence, and, more particularly, the direct result of some gross act of carelessness on the part of his ground crew. And it was Lydecker on whom his venom alighted.

Pfitz's maintenance crew consisted of five people. There was Dawson, a huge taciturn black; two Puerto Ricans called Pasquale and Huq; Lee Otis Cooper who came, like Pfitz, from Fayette County, Alabama; and there was Lydecker. There were good and sensible reasons for selecting Lydecker as scapegoat; Dawson was too big, Pasquale and Huq too united, and Cooper, well, he was a white man. So was Lydecker, for that matter, but of a particularly inferior, Yankee city-scum sort. Lydecker came from Sturgis, New Jersey; a mean smog-mantled town that seemed to have stamped its own harsh landscape on Lydecker's body and visage. He was small, dark and thin, with pale skin and permanently red-rimmed eyes. His face looked as if it had been compressed vertically in a vice, pursing his mouth and forcing his eyes close together.

Pfitz's resolute persecution came as no surprise to Lydecker: persecution of one form or another, whether from drunken father, bored teachers or cruel playmates, was the abiding feature of his memories. Questions of justice or injustice, of blame rightly apportioned had never carried much weight in his world. He never really stopped to consider how unfair it was, even though he had a good idea of who in fact was responsible. Lee Otis had been checking the engine casings of the Phantom's port jet the morning before Pfitz's doomed flight, and had borrowed Lydecker's own small monkey wrench to adjust what he thought was a loose faring deep in the complex mechanism. A mock fire drill had interrupted work on that shift, Lydecker remembered, and he recalled Lee Otis bolting down the inspection hatch immediately it was resumed. He never returned the monkey wrench either, and, when requested for it a few days after the accident, Lee Otis flushed momentarily before informing Lydecker that he 'Fuckn gave it you back, turdbird, so beat it, heah?'

Lydecker shrugged. Maybe he was wrong, so who gave a shit anyway? He merely tried to keep out of Pfitz's way as much as possible and on occasions when he was chewed out or put on a charge accepted the screaming flow of abuse with the practised, hang-dog, foot-shuffling resentment that he knew Pfitz's injured pride demanded. Lydecker never thought about trying to change things; experience had taught him to adapt to the world's crazy logic. It was a hostile alien terrain of unrelieved frustration and disappointment out there, and this was the only method of survival he had found. But at those times when its harsh realities inescapably obtruded into his consciousness he responded with a sullen, silent hatred. It was a comfort to him, his hatred; comforting because he came to realize that no matter what the world or people did to him they couldn't regulate his emotions, couldn't stop him hating, however they tried. After particularly bad days he would exult in his hatred at night, allowing the waves of his disdain and contempt to wash through his body with the potency of some magic serum, numbing and restoring, and letting him, when the sun rose, face once again whatever the world had to offer. Recipients of his hatred had in the past included his father, and Werbel, the manager of the filling station where he had worked before he was drafted. And now there was Pfitz.

Lydecker had expected the insults, the dirty jobs and the regular appearance on charge sheets to die down after Pfitz had flown a few more missions, but if anything they intensified. Soon Lydecker came to see that the old Crusader was acting as a catalyst; a regular reminder of Pfitz's shame. Every time the Crusader was towed out amongst the Phantoms and the Skyhawks Pfitz remembered all the details of that day: watching his new plane scythe cleanly into the waves, the hours of subjective time as he gently floated down into the sea, the rows of incredulous grinning faces as the rescue helicopter deposited him back on board, the sly jibes and quips of his fellow officers in the mess-rooms. And each time he climbed into the cockpit, saw the unfamiliar instrument layout and the dated mechanisms, the shame returned. And as he pulled away from the ship on a mission he imagined it brazenly echoing to the crews' gleeful laughter. And every time he took the Crusader up and landed Lydecker was there, the man who'd caused the foul-up, weaselly shit-face Lydecker, draining the fuel tanks or fitting the chocks to the wheels. And then Pfitz would claim his cannon misfired or the fuel-flow was imbalanced and he'd put him on a charge for slipshod work, or kick his narrow butt the length of the repair bay, or assign him to descale the afterburner all night.

For Lydecker the one benefit of the whole thing was the Crusader. His first posting had been to a 6th fleet carrier in the Mediterranean that still had a squadron of Crusaders in operation. He had grown familiar with the planes and had an affection for them that he did not bestow on the lean Phantoms or the dainty Skyhawks. The Crusader was a hefty rectangular machine, large for a single seater, with the crude geometry of a bus. Its single intake was set in the nose, like a gaping mouth beneath the matt black cone that housed the radar. It was like greeting an old friend when Pfitz's was wheeled out from storage and hoisted up to the deck. Its strong unambiguous profile seemed to render the other planes less significant and somehow pretentious. Pfitz was loudly derogatory, complaining that she was a pig to fly and sluggish to manoeuvre. But then he soon discovered in it other qualities which he employed in wreaking his revenge on the population of Vietnam.

The payload of the Crusader was prodigious; its sturdy frame could carry an anthology of destructive weaponry beneath its wings. Pfitz was highly satisfied with this aspect, soon indifferent to the absence of computer technology that precluded him from carrying laser or guided bombs like the Phantoms. And he was never happier than when he supervised his crew as they bolted the finless cigar-shaped canisters of napalm to the underwing pylons. Pasquale overheard him talking about a request he'd made to be excused the carrying of all other bomb loads and how he'd voluntarily restricted himself to napalm. He started to refer to his aircraft as the 'Rose Train' and had Huq, who was something of an artist, paint this below his cockpit.

'It's like roses in the jungle, man,' he would crow on returning from a mission. 'You see them cans tumblin' and whoomph, it's like a fuckin great flower bloomin in the trees – wham, pink an' orange roses. Beautiful man, just beautiful.' He made Huq keep a tally of missions by painting a red rose beneath the cockpit sill.

Lydecker thought he had gone mad, and so did many of the other pilots. Napalm had to be delivered from low level making the plane vulnerable to ground fire. With half-a-dozen canisters wobbling like overripe fruit beneath your wings you could be transformed into a comet of blazing petroleum jelly with one lucky shot. Lydecker sometimes thought about this as he patched bullet holes in the wings and tail.

Often at night Lydecker would leave the brightly lit crew quarters, where the air was thick with smoke, and bored sailors played cards or told obscene stories, and wander up to the dark cavern of the main hangar below the deck where the atmosphere had a tranquil metallic chill and the smell of oil and engine coolant clung to the air. He would go over to the Crusader, ponderously low-slung on its curious trolley undercarriage that jutted like spavined legs from the fuselage belly, and run his hands over the scarred and chipped aluminium, his fingers tracing and caressing the lines of rivet heads. Like the hated bullied schoolchild who tinkers with his bike all day Lydecker enjoyed the mute presence of his plane. It was like some gigantic familiar toy, stored in a cupboard with its wings folded and canopy up. He knew every square centimetre of the plane, from its gaping intake to the scorched jet at the rear. He had clambered all over its body, fuelling and rearming it, riveting patches of aluminium alloy over the puckered ulcers caused by random bullets. He had climbed into the dark ventral recesses of the undercarriage bay checking the hydraulic system, and had inched along its ribbed length replacing frayed control wires and realigning the armour plate. And he found himself, like an anxious mother, fretting for its return after long missions to Laos or Haiphong.

The war was a distant affair to the men on the 'Yankee Station' in the South China Sea. Just a green haze on the horizon sometimes. Even for the pilots who flew above it, dumping tons of high explosive on the jungle, the war and the enemy remained abstract and remote. To them it was a dangerous demanding job and only Pfitz openly expressed the requisite warlike antagonism; only he seemed to be exulted by the regular missions and the crop of red roses that grew on the side of the plane.

Then one late afternoon a seabird was sucked into the intake as the Crusader came in to land. The thump made Pfitz veer up and away and make his approach again. This caused a lot of hilarity amongst the deck crew and when Pfitz had landed safely someone shouted, 'Hey! Why din't ya eject Pfitz?' There was no real danger as, set about a metre and a half down the intake vent, was a fine wire mesh that protected the delicate compressor fans of the engine from such incidents.

Lydecker wheeled the light ladder against the fuselage as soon as the plane was towed to its bay on the deck. Pfitz took off his helmet, sweat shining in his crew-cut hair, his beefy face red with anger. As he climbed down Lydecker stepped back from the ladder and looked away, but Pfitz grabbed him by the arm, fingers biting cruelly into his bicep.

'Fuckin bumpy landing again, you fuckin shithead creep. How many times I told you to get those tyre pressures reduced? You're on a fuckin charge.'

That night Lydecker abandoned the letter he was trying to write to a cinema usherette he had known in Sturgis and made his way up to the hangar. He roved around the familiar contours of the plane noting, with a surge of anger, the bulge of the fat soft tyres on the steel floor. His brain hummed with an almost palpable hatred for Pfitz. His hands were raw and astringent from an evening spent cleaning latrines with coarse scouring powder as a result of the charge he'd been placed under. He leant up against the side of the Crusader and rested his hot cheeks on the cool metal, his eyes blank and tearless yet his mouth uncontrollably twisted in a rictus of sadness and utter frustration with his life. He forced himself to think of something else. He thought of the plane and the bird it had engulfed, how his heart had leapt in panic as it had jerked from its approach run. Without thinking he peered into the maw of the intake. In the gloom he could make out the detritus of feathers and expressed flesh stuck to the fine grille. He climbed into the intake, easily adapting the posture of his body to the narrowing curves of the interior, and began to pick the feathers and bones away from the wire mesh. He felt his spine moulded against the curve of polished metal and sensed all about him the complex terminals of controls and cables running from the cockpit above his head. The only sound was the noise of his breathing and the quiet pinging of his nails on the wires as he plucked the trapped feathers away.

When he heard the voices he suddenly realized he did not know how long he'd been hunched in the throat of the plane. With a chill of alarm he recognized Pfitz's oddly high laugh among them and hastily clambered out of the intake. He saw three officers sauntering towards the Crusader down the aisle of parked aircraft. Momentarily distracted he tried to slip round the plane out of sight but Pfitz had seen him and ran forward.

'Ho! You there, sailor, stop!'

Lydecker stood at attention, his face red with embarrassment, as if his mother had discovered him having sex or masturbating. As Pfitz approached the shame dissipated and fear suddenly gripped like a hand at his heart.

'Lydecker! This is off limits to you, man.' Pfitz was enraged, he clutched a beer can in his fist. 'What're you fuckin doing here, jerk-off?'

The other two officers stood back grinning. Pfitz was aware of their amused observation.

Lydecker held out his hand showing the ball of fluff and feathers by way of explanation.

'Uh, I was just clearing the intake, sir. The bird? You know, when you landed this afternoon . . .?'

The two officers snorted with laughter. Pfitz's eyes widened in fury. He cuffed at the feathers and the bundle exploded into a cloud of swooping fluff.

'Hey Larry,' one of the officers guffawed, 'it's a fuckin souvenir, man.'

Pfitz struck out blindly at Lydecker, punching him in the chest. Lydecker staggered backwards. Pfitz's voice rose to a shriek.

'You're fuckin finished you fuckin dipshit asshole! Get outa here an' don't come back or I'm gonna dump a giant shit on you, boy!'

Pfitz held the beer can up threateningly. Lydecker backed down the row of planes. Helpless with laughter the two officers tried to restrain Pfitz.

'You're getting transferred off of my crew. You ain't gonna mess around with me any more you bastard. Now git out!' His face rigid with fury Pfitz hurled the half-full beer can at the retreating Lydecker. It glanced off his forehead and went ringing along the steel deck. Lydecker turned and fled only to slip on a patch of oil. He skidded to the ground careening into the nose wheel of a Skyhawk. The beer can rested against the tyre. All Lydecker could hear was laughter, Pfitz's harsh triumphant laughter. He picked up the beer can, paused for an instant, then got to his feet and limped off, the can clutched to his chest with both hands.

Pfitz had Lydecker transferred from aircraft crew to catapult maintenance, one of the worst details on the ship. It meant hours on the exposed bow of the carrier as it steamed full speed into the wind for a mission launch. Lydecker's new job was to shackle the planes onto the towing block that protruded from the indented track of the catapult. He wore a huge goggled helmet with bulging ear protectors that made him look like some insect-headed alien or demented astronaut. It was a cheerless companionless job. The rush of wind made his bright nylon overalls crack like a pennant in a hurricane and conversation of any kind was impossible due to the shattering roar of jet engines driven at full thrust. As the plane was moved into take-off position Lydecker would run forward with the cumbersome steel-cable towing strop. He would secure each end of the strop to pinions in the undercarriage bay or just below the leading edge of the wings and slip the middle over the angled blade of the towing block. He then darted out from beneath the plane giving a thumbs-up to the catapult officer. If everything was in order the officer held five fingers up to the pilot of the plane who saluted his acknowledgement. Then like some ardent coach cheering on his team the catapult officer dropped to one knee, swept his arm forward and a seaman on a catwalk across the deck pressed the launch button. The catapult would be released hurling the plane, on full afterburn, along the narrow expanse of deck and into the air. The cable too would be flung out ahead of the carrier, dropping away from the climbing plane to splash forlornly into the sea in a tiny flurry of spray. The next plane was then towed into the take-off position, ghostly wreaths of steam hissing from the length of the catapult track.

Some strange impulse made Lydecker keep the beer can Pfitz had thrown at him. It stood on a small shelf above his bunk beside his electric razor and a creased Polaroid snapshot of the cinema usherette. For a week after the incident he had worn sticking plaster on his forehead, then the scab had sloughed off leaving a paler stripe on his already pale skin. Lydecker found that he unconsciously kept touching the thin scar, repeatedly running his forefinger gently over it, as if he had to keep reminding himself of its presence, like a teenager with his first moustache.

Denied the satisfaction of working on a plane Lydecker's life became one of routine mindless boredom. There were long periods of inactivity or futile chores. There was the deadening monotony of the catapult maintenance crew; the endless scurrying beneath screaming jets with the heavy cable, the grease thick on his gloves as he fought with recalcitrant pinions. Sometimes the frequent malfunctioning of the *Chester B.*'s old steam catapult brought tedious afternoons of stripping the mechanism down, searching for faults and elusive defects. The pressure that was required to fling tons of lethal weaponry into the air caused valves to blow back, bearings to jam and gauges to crack and leak. There were many accidents. Planes given insufficient lift from the catapult belly-landing in the sea; a tardily raised blast deflector had caused a parked helicopter to be flipped overboard; combat-dazed pilots had misjudged their landings and ploughed off the end of the carrier. Once a deck-tractor had momentarily stuck in reverse and backed a Skyhawk into the ocean – just like kicking a pebble off the quayside.

Throughout this time Lydecker appeased his tired and numb body by hating Pfitz. The man came to obsess him. His throat would be thick with emotion and fury as he forced the launching cable onto the Crusader's grips. Sometimes he would wander over to the plane when the crew were working on it, but he was invariably met with insults and told to stay away. Slowly he came to feel that Pfitz had deliberately set out to deprive his life of the little meaning and satisfaction it had, and for some reason the only solace he found, the only way he knew of combating this emptiness was to replace it with his hatred. The emotion gave his life a structure of sorts, it became something he could rely on, constant and unwavering, like a picture he had once seen of St Paul's Cathedral in the London blitz. Lydecker's hatred was a familiar comfort; it had done able service from his earliest days. It had sustained him as he had lain in bed and listened to his father batter his frail mother in a frenzy of crapulous rage. It had provided support when Werbel took him off cars and put him on the pumps and had then restricted him to cleaning the lavatories and sweeping the concrete forecourt. As he had freed plugged drains or picked sodden cigar butts from chill pools of lubricant, listening to the laughter and banter of the mechanics in the warm garage, all that had kept his mind from tilting over into twitching insanity was his passionate hatred. It was this and the knowledge that no matter what Werbel made him do, no matter how he was debased by him, the hate lived on – secretly firing and fuelling his spirit. He was grateful to the Navy for allowing the hate to subside for a while. He still had no friends, was still one of the few despised and ignored that figure in any large company, but his ability with machinery was recognized and his self-esteem inched up from ground zero. He found his reward in the perfect roar of an engine, the smooth retraction of an undercarriage, or the clean function of an aileron. Never having asked for much, he needed nothing more, and his life reached a plateau of tolerance which was as close as he'd come to happiness. Until Pfitz had lost his Phantom.

Working away from Pfitz's immediate sphere of influence Lydecker became more aware of the man's other obsession. Pfitz's fascination with napalm was the subject of bemused reflection among the members of the catapult maintenance crew. 'Hell, there goes Fireball Pfitz,' one of them would remark, and there would ensue some discussion about the 'poor fuckin gooks'. Lydecker didn't pay much attention at first. He had never been to Vietnam, even though he'd been on the

Yankee station for four months. The fleet made an endless patrol, usually just over the horizon from the coast, rarely steaming into sight unless cruisers or destroyers were called to bring their large guns into play. But gradually Lydecker came to see that Pfitz hated Vietnam as much as he loathed Lydecker himself; and he felt an involuntary sympathy start up in his body as Pfitz lovingly recounted the devastation eight canisters of napalm had wrought in a straw village to the wide-mouthed audience of his ground crew. 'The Rose Train' climbed the gradients into the sky weighted with seething latent fire like some modern archangelic predator. Lydecker would watch it go, his head a confused muddle of thoughts and sensations.

And each night, exhausted, he would gaze at the slightly buckled beer-can as if it were some ikon or idol of his hate. In the distorted planes of its surface he seemed to see a vague metallic template of Pfitz's bullish features. He would stroke the scar on his forehead and think about Pfitz and the men he had known like him – his father and Werbel – and the intensity of his hatred brought his flesh up in goose-pimples. He would clutch the sides of his bunk and screw his eyes tight shut as if in the grip of an acute migraine attack. Men like that shouldn't be allowed to go about unhindered, he would think distractedly, something should be done to them.

Then one day Pfitz had an engine cut-out as Lydecker was shackling the expendable wire bridle to the nose wheel of the Crusader. The air vibrated with the idling jets of planes waiting in line and the hot gases of the exhausts made the crowded deck of the carrier shimmer and dance in the haze. Pfitz had to be towed off line and there was some delay as Lydecker fought to free the cable from the stiff nose-wheel clamps. Pfitz had raised his cockpit canopy and as Lydecker stood up, the cable finally released, he saw Pfitz's purple enraged face screaming inaudible obscenities at him through arcs of spittle. It was as if Lydecker had been responsible for the cut-out, as if his particular touch on the nose wheel had mysteriously spooked the functioning of the jet. And in the waves of Pfitz's anger Lydecker was disturbed by the sudden realization that Pfitz was a hater too, that, like him, he needed his hate, needed his malice to beat the world.

That evening Lydecker applied for a long overdue spell of shore leave. The bizarre feeling of kinship had unsettled him. It appeared that Pfitz's plane would be out of action for a week, and now – more than ever – Lydecker didn't want to be around.

Lydecker was granted five days and opted for Saigon. He passed nearly all of his time in a Tu-Do bar brothel methodically working his way through the nine girls who serviced the clients. Out at the back of the bar there were three lean-to cabins with rickety iron beds. Lydecker spent the day drinking beer and every now and then would stagger up to one of the girls – comic-book whores with thickly mascaraed eyes, mini skirts and padded bras – and lurch outside to a cabin.

It was only on the third day that he noticed the young thin-shouldered girl who wiped and cleared the tables and periodically swept out the cabins. She was quiet and withdrawn and had slightly buck teeth. Unlike the others she wore an ao-dai and a thigh-length chemise. Her status in the bar was indeterminate. He never saw her with GIs and she never used the cabins. Sometimes she would go out to the back or into the toilets, but only with civilians or the occasional Vietnamese soldier, only spending the briefest time – about two minutes – away from her chores. She did not pout, flirt or posture like the other girls and never wore their cheap western clothes. Yet for all her quiet dignity and restraint she was the lowest creature in the bar. A quick-time girl – lower than the pimps and shoe-shine boys, lower even than the many cats and stray dogs that nosed around and were temporarily adopted and spoilt by the American servicemen. Why is she doing this? Lydecker found himself asking. What was it about her that kept her in this whores' city so calmly accepting the shitty jobs and compliantly carrying out the spurious sex-acts demanded of her? The paradox enraged and excited him and the girl gradually took a hold on his mind. Not having noticed her at first, he now seemed to see her everywhere. She hovered round the perimeter of his vision: taking the empty bottles from his table, slipping from a cabin as he entered, mopping up pools of vomit in the men's room. He discovered a disproportional irritation in this, and despite himself swore and shouted at her if she approached. Strengthened by his uniform in this city of obsequious servants, he befriended other servicemen who used the bar and in his noontide drunkenness wove obscene stories round the thin girl, flashing his eyes in her direction as he joined in the raucous guffaws.

She paid no attention to him, her frail body moving amongst the tables, her straight shiny hair framing her face.

At night Lydecker tossed in his bed and found his thoughts turning again and again to the thin girl. He stayed away from the bar a whole day before crashing in late at night in a beer-haze to seek her out. He found her in the corridor that led out to the cabins at the back, her arms full of dirty sheets. Lydecker bore down on her, maddened by her inscrutability and at the same time potently aroused. He wrenched the sheets from her hands and forced her against the wall drunkenly nuzzling her neck.

She made no move to resist him. He gazed into her eyes.

'Whassa fuckin matter with you? Damn you,' he implored slurringly, 'whyncha like the others? No good chicken-shit . . .' His voice tailed off into a wet whispering pant. He looked at her and saw why she wasn't like the others. Beneath the stretched oblique lids her brown eyes stared out defiantly in candid unalloyed hate.

Lydecker stepped back, suddenly dismayed and shocked. 'Ach, no good fuckin . . .' he grunted to himself and staggered off down the passage. The girl stood there, a grubby snowdrift of soiled sheets around her ankles, and watched him go.

During his last day of leave Lydecker took three cheery whores to bed. They giggled when he stared into their eyes.

'You like GI?' he would ask uncertainly.

'Sure, you number one,' they would smile. 'US number one.'

So no hooker fell in love with her John, Lydecker reasoned, but where did that little bit of skinny ass get the right to condemn him like that, to look at him in that way? It troubled and nagged at him, her contempt. It marred his swaggering progress through downtown Saigon; it sapped his confidence and aloof reserve as he pushed his way through the pimps and beggars; it made his hurried sex with the other prostitutes more grimy and unsatisfactory. Nobody, he declared, knew more about hate than him; surely no one had hated so intensely; but this chick . . . He was prepared, even willing to accept the scorn and despite of the peasant for the armed invader, but the look in that girl's eyes had seemed to mark him out personally for her wrath.

So on the last afternoon of his last day Lydecker sat in the bar and studied her, his mind a jostling crowd of vague tensions, obscure guilts and unresolved lusts. He was due to pick up a helicopter in a few hours that would ferry him back to the fleet on the Yankee station. He felt disturbed, hungover, sullen. Saigon had proved no release, no real solace. He felt immensely fatigued at the thought of returning to the catapult maintenance crew.

The bar was quiet in the afternoon's torpor. The whores lounged in groups around the wall, some ARVN soldiers played cards in a corner. Lydecker stared at the girl as she swept the floor. Her hair was tied up with a scrap of pink ribbon, her chemise shone crisply white. Once her gaze passed over him as he sat there but there was no flicker of recognition, no revulsion or even acknowledgement in her motionless face.

As the time drew nearer for his departure Lydecker was seized with a restless panic at the thought of leaving with so much uncertain and unfinished. He felt the sweat pool against his body and his uniform chafe. He drank beer after beer in an attempt to keep cool.

With an hour to go he beckoned one of the whores over. She had become something of a favourite with him and she now slid easily onto his knee. Her smile was wide and at once she started to whisper endearments and run her sharp fingers through his hair. Lydecker shrugged her hands away, for some reason the artifice and dishonesty repulsed him. He pointed to the thin girl.

'What about her?' he demanded hoarsely. 'How much?'

The whore looked archly offended, hurt. 'She no good. Not for GI. She number ten, Johnny, she quick-time girl. No ficky-fick.' She made a contemptuous jerking with her hand.

With a sudden movement Lydecker brutally tipped her from his lap and strode across the room towards the girl. He dropped a handful of notes on the bar in front of the startled *patron* and seizing the girl's hand dragged her out to the cabins at the back.

He pushed her into the first room. Solid slabs of sunlight beaming through the shutters sectioned the floor and the grubby coverlet on the bed. It was stiflingly hot. With a finger Lydecker sluiced perspiration from his forehead and upper lip. He stuffed the rest of his notes into the girl's unresponsive hand.

'Okay,' he croaked. 'Christ damn you. Let's really give you something to get riled over. Take 'em off.' He pulled off his own clothes in a hasty flurry of movement, leaving only his shorts.

The rough concrete of the floor cooled the soles of his feet. Sweat dampened the sparse black hairs on his pale chest. There was the distant sound of a Honda revving.

Very slowly the girl pocketed the money and tugged her hair free from the ribbon. She slipped the sandals from her feet and gently unwound the cloth from around her waist. The swish of material sent dust-motes spiralling among the sun-bars.

Without removing her chemise she went and lay on the bed. Lydecker stood, his chest heaving, his erection straining against his cotton undershorts.

'I said take it *all* off.' He spoke quietly, a tremble in his voice.

The girl did nothing, her hands clenched by her slim brown thighs.

'All of it, baby. That means the fuckin shirt.' Lydecker awkwardly slipped down his shorts and moved over to stand by the bed. The girl didn't look at him.

'I'm waiting,' Lydecker said harshly.

In response the girl raised the hem of her chemise to her waist and spread her legs. Lydecker gulped, a blob of sweat fell from the tip of his nose.

Suddenly he grabbed the girl's hand and jerked her roughly to her feet.

'Take it off!' he shouted. 'I fuckin *paid* you.'

'No,' the girl said evenly. 'No good.'

Lydecker seized her and crushed his mouth on hers, clashing their teeth together. Then Lydecker drew back. He had seen her eyes. On fire with disgust. Ashamed and angry, he wrenched at the chemise. It tore slightly at the shoulder. At the sound of the ripping cotton the girl's eyes registered alarm.

'No, Johnny,' she said as though only half remembering the unfamiliar whore's argot. 'No good.' She made vague passing movements with her hands in front of her face and soft explosion noises in the back of her throat. 'Number ten. No lie, GI. Not good for you, Johnny.'

What the fuck was she talking about? Lydecker wondered in desperation, her thin hands still swooping to and fro.

'Strip, damn you. Off. All of it,' he gasped.

She saw she could do nothing more. His purple swollen sex stood out from his belly like a clenched fist salute, an absurd symbol of his domination. Crossing her arms in front of her she swiftly pulled off the chemise.

Lydecker looked at the firm pubescent girl's body. 'That's more like it, baby,' he said, trying to sound kind. 'I ain't gonna hurt you.' His gaze cautiously returned once again to her eyes, hoping to find some more amicable response. 'What's all the trouble been about eh? C'mon, honey.' But then he was perturbed to see a look of almost contemptuous triumph cross her face. She turned abruptly to reveal her back. And as she turned Lydecker's beer-numbed mind grasped feebly at the reasons for her evasiveness. 'It's all right baby,' he said reflexively, but it was too late by then.

When he saw her back Lydecker's brain screamed in silent horror. His hands rose involuntarily to his mouth. The girl looked at him over her shoulder.

'Nay-pom,' she said quietly in explanation. 'Nay-pom, GI.'

Lydecker wrenched his bulging eyes away. Her back was a broad stripe, a swathe of purpled shiny skin where static waves of silvery scar tissue and blistered burn weals tossed in a horrifying flesh-sea.

Lydecker emptied his stomach into his cupped hands and his vomit splashed over his naked body.

On the Sea-King taking him back to the *Chester B.* Lydecker sat slumped in white-faced silent depression. The throb of the rotor's beat sounded remorselessly in his head. He considered his hatred and the girl's. Now he knew why he had been so fascinated by her. They were the same. Siblings. He looked into her eyes to find himself staring back. They were both burning up inside with their hate and it was wrong. Their hate had no consequences outside of themselves. It made them sick, ate them up. It accrued only inside of them, like a miser's hoard, poisoning everything. Their bodies couldn't nourish such a parasite for long. Lydecker saw that. He didn't want to end up like that girl. Infernal decades of grief and agony beamed out from those eyes. Perhaps what he needed was to cast it out into the world and let it flourish there. Like Pfitz did.

As the Sea-King approached the carrier, a great steel playing field ploughing through the choppy waters of the South China Sea, Lydecker was aware of a palpable change going through his body. He felt his breathing become shallower and perspiration break out on his forehead. It seemed as if his chest was hollow and filled with throbbing pulsating air.

Lydecker reported sick on landing and was found to be running a high temperature. The ship-board medics shot him full of penicillin and told him not to report for duty for two days. During that time Lydecker uneasily roved the corridors of the ship, a thinner and more consumptive figure than before, his mind obsessed with the violent images of his shore leave; of his casual unsatisfactory sex, fragments of obscene anecdotes he had heard, murmured accounts of battle-zone atrocities, and above them all, endlessly repeating itself like a video film loop, the vision of the young girl's ghastly pirouette to expose her ravaged back.

Even Lydecker's normally uninterested crew-mates commented on his yellowish pallor, the sheen of sweat forever on his forehead and upper lip, his staring red-rimmed eyes. They jokingly accused him of contracting some recondite strain of venereal disease and roared with laughter when he tried haltingly to tell them about the whore and her loathsome scars.

Gradually the nomadic circuit of Lydecker's thoughts began to focus once again on Pfitz and his Crusader. Covertly, he haunted the below-deck hangar, distantly supervised the fuelling and rearming of the plane, observed Pasquale and Huq trundle the fat napalm canisters from the magazine elevators. He even took to discreetly following Pfitz whenever he moved from the officers' quarters, studying the man's corridor-filling bulk, the contours of his large skull revealed by his razored crew cut, the pink fleshiness of his neck above the stiff collar of his flying suit. The glimmerings of an idea began to form in Lydecker's mind – he started to plot his revenge.

His nervous debility persisted, his temperature was regularly above normal and he collected sickness chits without problem.

Then, one afternoon he was lounging in a hatchway a few feet from the Crusader's arming bay. Pfitz was talking to Lee Otis as the mechanic checked a faulty shackle on a napalm canister. Lydecker strained to catch his words.

'. . . Yeah, there just ain't nothing to beat this jelly, man. It's gonna win us the woah. Shit, I can remember the original stuff. It wasn't so hot. If the dinks were quick enough they could scrape it off. So the scientists come up with a good idea. They started adding polystyrene – yeah, polystyrene. Hell man, now it sticks better 'n shit to a blanket.' He chortled. Lee Otis's eyes were glazed with boredom but Pfitz carried on, unaware in his enthusiasm. 'Trouble was, if the dinks were fast enough and jumped underwater it stopped burning. So some wise guy adds white phosphorous to the mix, and, get this boy, now it can burn *underwater*.' He reached down and patted the nose cone of the canister. 'That thing on okay, now? . . .'

Crouched in his hatchway Lydecker waited and watched until Pfitz hauled his bulky body into the narrow cockpit of the Crusader. He tasted acid bile in his throat, his fretting hands picked unconsciously at his olive green jacket and a slight shivering ran through his wasted body. It was clear now. Beyond doubt. He couldn't understand why he had waited so long. Pfitz was the guilty one. For that girl's sake Pfitz had to suffer too.

It didn't take Lydecker long to work out the technicalities of his revenge. The next day he was back on the catapult crew, silent and withdrawn, waiting for his time. In the evenings, with a rubber-based glue bought from the PX, and with sand from fire buckets and spare bolts and shards of metal from the machine rooms, he packed the beer can Pfitz had thrown at him with this glutinous hard-setting amalgam until it weighed heavy in his hand, a bright solid cylinder. To his fixated mind it had seemed only right that the beer can should be the agent of Pfitz's destruction. There was a kind of macabre symmetry in the way events were turning out that he found deeply satisfying.

Patiently Lydecker studied the mission rotas and the catapult launch schedules, waiting for the day when Pfitz was to be first in line.

It was a bright windy afternoon that day on the Yankee station. The mission was close support on some hostile ville on the Cambodian border. Pfitz was in a good mood. He had just heard that he was getting a new Phantom the day after tomorrow. First in the flight, he was towed into position on the catapult and waited with his canopy up for the *Chester B.* to get up steam and turn into the wind. He saw the rescue helicopters take off and assume their positions a hundred yards out from the sides of the carrier. Pfitz looked at the catapult crew hunched against the rush of wind with their thick goggles and macrocephalic helmets. He saw the thin figure of that shithead Lydecker staring up at him, the wire launch bridle dangling from his hand. Little bastard. He began to feel uncomfortable at the insistent way Lydecker was looking at him. He seemed to remember seeing too much of the little creep around lately. He'd have to kick his butt in when he got back, get the pill to keep his distance. He hauled down his canopy as he heard the crackle of instructions in his earphones preparing him for take-off and 'The Rose Train's' thirty-fifth mission. As he ran through the final cockpit checks he noticed the hunched, beetling figure of Lydecker scuttling up to the nose-wheel to secure the catapult bridle. As he moved out of his vision Pfitz reflected that he'd never really taught the little shit a proper lesson; he should have had him transferred right away.

Lydecker paused for a moment at the nose of the Crusader, out of Pfitz's line of sight, buffeted by the rush of wind. For an instant he rested his gloved hand on the side of the plane and felt it shuddering from the power of its engine. His ear-muffles dampened all noise to a muted sea-shell roar. Then he crouched down and fitted both ends of the cables to the shackles on the nose-wheel, looping the middle over the protruding shark's fin of the towing block. He knelt at the front of the plane for a second as if in supplication. And then, making sure his body obscured the view of the catapult officer, he swiftly withdrew the heavy beer can from his jacket and slotted it neatly into the recessed track, like a stubby bolt in a crossbow, just in front of the towing block.

Pfitz should have an unimpeded, normal take-off until the towing block reached the end of the catapult track. Then there would be a slight but vital check to the momentum imparted by the tons of steam pressure driving the block, as it obliterated the solid can jamming its clear run to the end of the track. It would be a slight, almost unnoticeable impediment but, Lydecker had calculated, a crucial one.

Lydecker ran back to his station and waved OK to the catapult officer. He barely acknowledged Lydecker's signal. It was just one launch among hundreds he had supervised, another routine mission. Nothing would happen. You were remote on the Yankee station, the battles were elsewhere, over the horizon. Nobody attacked you and you never saw the people you atomized, shattered and burned.

Lydecker saw Pfitz lock into full afterburn. The catapult officer swept his arm forward. The seaman across the deck punched the black rubber button on the console and the catapult's release sent the Crusader blasting down the track.

Only Lydecker observed the tiny explosion as the towing block ploughed through the can, grinding it into the end of the track. A minute inconsequential impact. But the effect on Pfitz's Crusader was dramatic. Instead of being thrown up at an angle into the skies the plane was flung down a shallow slope into the sea some two hundred yards in front and to the left of the carrier. It was over in a couple of seconds. With a huge gout of spray the Crusader was flipped into the sea, salt water flooding into the gaping intake, the screaming jets plunging the fully loaded aircraft deep under the surface.

There were shouts of alarm from the deck, but everything happened too quickly. Within moments they passed the spot where Pfitz had gone down; bubbling crazy water, a slick of oil, and men claimed to see the pale shape of the Crusader slipping ever deeper beneath the green surface of the sea.

Pfitz never came up and there was no further trace of the plane. The end of the catapult was found to be slightly warped and scarred and the accident was put down to yet another malfunction. The day's mission was aborted while the mechanism was taken apart.

Lydecker stood on the edge of the deck and looked out at where the rescue helicopters futilely hovered above the oil slick. Groups of men stood about and talked of the accident. Lydecker's heart was racing and his eyes were bright. Pfitz and his napalm somewhere at the bottom of the South China Sea. He felt good. No, he felt magnificent. He wanted to bite the stars.

Bat-Girl!

Arthur's got this amazing tongue. Very long and pointed, pale pink and thin as a knife. He can curl it right round my fingers – very flickery. And, it's wet and warm – not like a cat's which is rough and dry. I can tell you it doesn't half give me a funny feeling. I lie on my back and he licks away at my hands for hours. He seems quite happy and I get quite carried away sometimes. Shivers all through my body.

Arthur's my bat of course, and he and I do an 'act' together. My aunt Reen runs the show. There's me, Tracy, the bat-girl, and my younger sister Lorraine, snake-girl. I used to be snake-girl but that was when we only had one stall. Then someone gave Reen this big fruit bat and she thought, why not expand? She set up a new stall and here I am, having my fingers licked all day. SEE THE FABULOUS BAT-GIRL! £1000 IF ANIMAL NOT REAL!!

It sounds quite glamorous I know, but to be honest it's not much of a job. We do the summer fairground circuit all over England and in the winter go back to Yorkshire where my uncle Ted's got a battery-hen farm. I can tell you that after a few months with those bloody hens I'm aching to be out on the road again. You see, my big problem is that I always need some excitement in my life.

Above the pay-booth and running the length of the front of the stall there's a big picture of a blonde girl with no clothes on and there's a bat crawling across her body with its wings spread. The booth is new so the colours are still bright and not too badly chipped and also it's quite warm, which is just as well because it can get quite parky lying around inside a cage all day. I'm not nude, mind you. I wear a swimsuit, one piece, pink with a big bow that holds the two halves of the front together. Arthur hangs upside down from the top of the cage licking my fingers. I dip them in a pot of honey – which he absolutely loves – and he just licks it all off.

Lorraine's set-up is basically the same, except it's not quite so smart. Also the python does nothing but sleep and I think that what people like about the bat-girl is that they can see the bat is actually alive. He's quite big is Arthur; he's got a brown furry body about a foot long with nasty looking claws. And then of course there's his tongue, in and out, slipping all over my fingers. It seems to fascinate some people – they stare for ages. His wings remind me of a leather umbrella.

We'd been in Swindon for a week and had just come down to Oxford for St Giles fair. It was my second year in Oxford, though my first as bat-girl and I wasn't looking forward to it that much. Funny mixture of people you get in Oxford I always say. There's some right rough ones, don't you believe it. And then there are these student types, they think they're so bloody clever, with their tweed jackets and their haw-haw voices. I remember when I was snake-girl last year a whole crowd of them had stood and talked about me for twenty minutes as if I wasn't there. Really rude too: 'Eoh ai'm convinced she's not alive,' one of them says. 'Ai'm going to claim my thousand quid.' Gets on my wick that clever-clever lark. Give me the lads from Blackbird Leys any day.

The thing was I knew there would be extra trouble this year because of the painting Reen had put up of the naked girl. In Lorraine's snake-girl painting she's wearing a bikini, but for some reason Reen decided she'd make bat-girl nude. I said if they're all coming in thinking I'm starkers I want an extra fiver a day for all the aggro I'm going to get. Reen paid up so I'm not complaining but my God you should hear some of the things that get said to me: 'Take 'em off, darling' and 'Let's have a look then' and that's not half of it. The problem is this revealing swimsuit Reen makes me wear and the fact that I'm fairly big up top. It's a funny thing about being big-made – blokes seem to think they can say anything to you.

Still, it's water off a duck's back as far as I'm concerned. I'm used to it now so I just lie there and carry on reading my book. I always take a book into the cage because it's a long day and it can get very boring. I read mainly men's books: spies and thrillers, that's what I like. I like a bit of excitement as I said. That's really why I joined up with Reen soon as I left school. I'm eighteen now and I'm saving up for this dance course in London that I've seen advertised in a magazine. 'Felaine la Strade, Ecole de Dance'. £500 for two months of lessons. You get a diploma and at the bottom of their prospectus it says 'many of our graduettes have secured positions in West End shows'. Well, I've always been keen on dancing – quite good at it too – and as I say you've got to have some ambition and excitement in your life. I mean, look at Lorraine for e.g.; after this summer she's decided to go back to school and retake her 'O'-levels. I ask you, no spirit.

We'd set up in Oxford on the Sunday afternoon. The site's right in the middle of town on a wide street with trees which is the best thing about it. We had quite a brisk Monday and one woman had screamed when she'd seen Arthur's tongue. A couple of lads from Didcot who I'd met last year tried to chat me up in the evening. They claimed Trevor had said it was OK for me to come out with them. Trevor's my boyfriend, he works on the Whip taking money. I told them to push off. Trev would never let them do that. He's a very jealous sort of guy is Trev. Actually I'm not speaking to him at the moment. The last night we were in Swindon he showed up when we were taking down the stall with a big wad of cotton-wool sellotaped to his forearm. I had told him not to get any more tattoos and he'd just gone and done it. He's got enough of them as it is, all over his arms and shoulders and in any case I've gone right off tattoos. He'd promised not to, so I told him to shove it.

I know we'll get back together as Trev is really quite strong on me, but I am enjoying not having him hanging around. I'm getting on with my reading too. I finished a complete book on Monday and I've started a new one called *Hell Comes Tomorrow*. It's really exciting.

On Tuesday after lunch business really tailed off and I was racing through the book when I realized someone had crept into the booth on their own and was staring at me. I looked round and saw a thin bloke with round gold specs who was carrying a briefcase. Only a student I thought, and went back to my book. Arthur was asleep so I prodded him awake and he hooked his wing-claw over my thumb and gave it a good licking. I thought I'd better do that so's the guy could claim he'd got his money's worth. However, a few minutes later he was still there so I turned round again and gave him a look – as much to say that's your lot, mate – and he scurried out pretty sharpish.

But blow me if five minutes later he wasn't back. Just standing and staring. It was beginning to get on my nerves; I couldn't concentrate on my book at all. So I sat up and said:

'That's all there is you know. He doesn't do tricks or anything.'

He looked a bit startled. He had quite a nice face and shiny clean black hair with a middle parting.

'Oh I'm sorry,' he said. 'I . . . I find it fascinating, that's all.'

Well, I could tell by the way he kept touching the knot of his tie and the look he was giving me that 'it' didn't refer to Arthur. He kept on standing there all the same, as if he'd never seen a girl before.

To this day I don't know what made me do it. The heat perhaps – it was muggy and sunny outside. Maybe it was just plain boredom, and he looked so 'nice' and decent – the sort that wouldn't say boo to a goose.

When I got the idea I felt this excited feeling at the bottom of my spine – a sort of electric tingling. So, very slowly – not taking my eyes off him – I leant back on the cushions and pulled out the cord of the bow on my swimsuit. Well, the two front bits kind of fell away – not completely, but he wouldn't miss much. But then I went and laughed, I couldn't help it, the expression on his face, I swear his specs steamed up.

'This what you're after then?' I said between giggles.

You've *never* seen anyone move so fast. Out of the booth like a shot and I didn't stop laughing for ten minutes. Arthur didn't know what'd come over me.

Come five o'clock Reen shuts up the stall for half an hour to let me have a rest, a smoke and get to the lav. I pulled on my jersey and jeans (I keep them folded on a chair beside the cage) and went outside. I lit up a fag and had a good stretch. I normally meet Trev at this time but there was no sign of him on account of our row. But the student who'd been in the booth was there. I felt a bit embarrassed when he saw me and came over.

'Um, I was wondering if you'd like to come and have some tea with me,' he said.

Oh yes? I thought. But then he'd asked so politely so I said I would.

He took me to his college which wasn't very far away. They're nice these colleges that they live in – amazing lawns, not a weed in sight – and very quiet. We went up a little narrow stone staircase to his room. It was quite pleasant – a bit old-looking though and very untidy with lots of books and papers. I had a look through his bookshelves when he went out to make the tea but we obviously had different tastes in reading.

We had a few cups of tea and a piece of sponge cake ('Oh there goes me diet,' I said and would you believe it he blushed). He said his name was Gordon and he told me a bit about his work and asked me some questions about the fair. He was slim and about medium height was Gordon, and I quite liked him. I kept wondering when he would make his move.

It took him quite a while, but eventually he worked it so we were sitting side by side on the sofa. But then someone knocked on the door and stuck his head into the room. It was another guy with specs and he said,

'*Oh!* Jesus . . . sorry, Gord. Didn't know you had company,' and popped out again. Gordon had leapt to his feet and looked more embarrassed than ever. I've never known anyone quite like Gordon for going red, honestly. Anyway I put him out of his misery and told him I had to get back.

On the way to the booth he asked if he could meet me when the fair shut down. I told him we had to pack up tonight as we were setting up in Northampton tomorrow. He looked disappointed at this but said he'd still like to come and say goodbye. That was fine by me I said. He had nice manners had

Gordon. He hadn't once mentioned our little episode with the swimsuit.

Gordon was waiting for me at eleven o'clock when the fair began to shut down. I was carrying Arthur in a small parrot's cage. I was a bit worried in case Trev might have shown up but there was no sign of him. I told Gordon he could carry Arthur to Reen's car which was parked some way off. Gordon said he knew a short cut.

We walked through the fair. As usual Gordon wasn't saying much. Stalls were coming down and the big lorries were backing slowly along the street. A few groups of young kids hung around watching it all. The ground was covered in litter, tickets, squashed toffee apples and bits of coloured paper and burst balloons. It always makes me a bit sad when the fair comes down so I just walked along quietly beside Gordon.

We turned up this narrow alley that led between two of the old colleges. It was dark as there was only one street light and huge black chestnut trees hung over us. It felt a bit spooky so I linked my arm through Gordon's and you'd have thought I'd stabbed him in the back. His knee banged into Arthur's cage and I could hear Arthur scrabbling around trying to keep his grip.

'Hold on a sec, Gordon,' I said. 'Put Arthur down for a moment. Let him get settled.'

Gordon put the cage on the ground and I knelt down to peer in at Arthur. Gordon knelt down too and muttered something about Arthur being a fascinating creature.

We got up together and I thought poor sod and leant up against him ever so slightly. He put his arms round me and we sort of stood there for a while. I could feel him all shivery and excited and I ran my hands through his hair. It felt lovely.

The next thing I knew he wasn't there. He'd been torn out of my arms and I gave a little scream when I saw it was Trev. Trev, who had him by the back of his jacket and was spinning him round and around. Then he let him go and Gordon careered into the wall with an awful thump that sent his specs flying to the ground.

Trev stood in front of him swearing and spitting. 'Okay Trace,' he shouted over his shoulder at me. 'Where do I give it him first. You tell me, Trace.'

Christ, really, Trev looked amazing. He's a big lad and he had tight black jeans on and a white T-shirt with 'Kung-fu' written on it. His chest was heaving up and down and his hair was sort of wild.

Gordon leant up against the wall half crumpled, as if he'd been pinned on to it. He didn't stand a chance.

I didn't say anything though. Gordon must have seen me standing there all excited because he tried to get to his feet. Trev gave him a push and he fell onto the ground.

'Don't boot him, Trev,' I yelled, because I could see that was what he was about to do. 'Get his specs, go on, get his specs.'

Then Trev saw Gordon's specs on the ground and he just stamped on them. Bang. Once. Like he was squashing a beetle crawling across the floor. Then he kicked them up the alley.

He turned and looked at me. 'See you at the car, girl,' he says, all harsh and angry. 'Bloody pronto.' And he walks off just like that.

I felt my heart was going to punch itself out of my rib cage. My head felt all light. He can do that to me can Trev. Amazing sort of bloke.

I went and got Gordon's spectacles. There was no glass in them and they were badly bent. When I handed them back to him I could see the red marks they had made on his nose. His eyes were all watery and blank-looking.

'Sorry, Gordon,' I said. 'But it was better that he done your specs. He's mean is Trevor, and he's my boyfriend.'

Gordon nodded without saying anything and pushed his glasses into his pocket. I helped him up and straightened out his jacket. There didn't seem to be much to say. Trevor must have seen us at the stall and followed.

'I'd better go,' I said. Trev would be waiting, I knew. I picked up Arthur and began to walk off.

'Tracy,' I heard Gordon wheeze. 'Just a moment.'

I went back to him. He did look quite different without his glasses, sort of ordinary, not so intelligent.

'Next year,' he said. 'Will you be back next year?'

I was astonished. 'I don't know,' I said. 'Why?'

'I thought . . .' he began to say, then, 'It's just that I shall be here.' Then he gave a grim little laugh. 'In fact I shall probably die here.'

That made me feel all sorry for him – he had no excitement in his life apart from me – and so I decided not to tell him about Felaine la Strade and the Ecole de Dance. Better to let him dream a bit. *He* might be here still, but there was no way you'd catch me as bat-girl again next year, no chance. I'd be in London, the big smoke, a dancer or something.

But I reached out and patted Gordon's arm. 'Don't worry,' I said. 'Me and Arthur'll be back. We'll have tea again. See you next year.' Then I turned away and walked back up the alley to where I knew Trev would be waiting. Just before I turned the corner I looked back, and there was Gordon, standing there – he hadn't moved an inch – staring at me, just staring at me like the first time he had come into the booth. It still gave me the shivers. He was quite a nice guy, was Gordon. It was a pity really – yes, the whole thing was a pity.

Love Hurts

10 August 1973

It was sometime in the hot freedom of July that I introduced Cherylle to Lamar. I think it was at my delayed welcoming party that AOD were throwing. Cherylle was an out-of-work actress who rented the apartment below mine with two other girls. Quite spontaneously I had decided to invite one of them along – I had as yet made no friends since arriving here from England and felt I needed an ally of sorts at this gathering of off-duty American executives and their brittle, frosted wives. Cherylle was the only girl at home when I knocked on the apartment door. Such are the tricks time plays. She is marrying Lamar tomorrow.

Cherylle: tall, bony, a shock of wild blonde hair. Twenty-five years old? Typically Californian flawless skin. I find her an oddly attractive girl without really being able to say why – a product of the curious vectors of a face: the arc of an eyebrow, the prominence of a cheekbone. There is a simmering feral gleam in her gaze, a sense of coiled ticking energy within her which only truly strikes you on a third or fourth meeting.

Lamar, however, claims he spotted it instantly and it was this he found irresistibly attractive. I should say that Lamar has since become my closest friend out here on the coast. Looking back through my diary I see I first described him as 'a characteristically butch American businessman. Late thirties, handsome, tanned and stocky. Tough as a hill. Self-confidence surrounds him like a force field. The youngest vice-president in the company, responsible for sales and marketing. They say AOD will be his before the decade's out.' Now that I know him I would say that this is only partially true. Lamar still exudes this brash ease but it's something of a façade. He is no typical VP; he works hard at his job because that is all his background and education have trained him to do. He has his idiosyncracies and I find him both stimulating and sad.

For example the fact that I write – albeit commercially – for a living has prompted him to attack the cultural lacunae in his life with the same vigour he chases after contracts. He sees me as some sort of intellectual guru, a source to be tapped and exploited. Quite early on in our friendship he suggested we read through Shakespeare together 'because they say he's the best'. To feed this new enthusiasm I gave him reading lists and drew up programmes for his educational self-improvement. He proved to be a sensitive and intelligent student, surprisingly perceptive. He would question me so endlessly I felt exhausted, victim of some nightmare seminar, dizzy from the rapacity with which he plundered my brain.

His friendship with Cherylle did not affect the growth of our own. Indeed the three of us often went out together. And as the two of them became swiftly more infatuated my presence paradoxically seemed all the more essential. I became the talisman of their affair, as if they needed the constant reassuring presence of the catalyst that had started the reaction off.

I have, however, tried to talk to Lamar about the wisdom of this wedding – gently counselled delay. Cherylle is an incandescent but mercurial character, wayward, and I suspect, deeply uncertain of herself. But Lamar will not listen. He is in love, he insists, wholly in love for the first time in his life.

11 August 1973

The wedding. Lamar and Cherylle get riotously drunk. At the civic hall Cherylle arrived in thigh-length suede boots, jeans and a bright yellow windcheater. She dresses in a bizarre series of fashions – sometimes glaring lack of taste, sometimes shining with demure chicness. Hardly the wife for a rising vice-president I would have thought, but Lamar seems to accept her extravagances with a wide-eyed ingenuous thrill.

Now I know her better I take Cherylle's lurid anthology of fashion styles to be evidence of a chronic insecurity in her personality. She teeters on the brink of moods with the practised equilibrium of the perennially schizoid. Lamar, somehow, responds to this. His marriage to Cherylle is the one publicly irrational event in his entirely ordered life. He told me once he understood her perfectly, could predict her moves and responses with a Pavlovian confidence. He underestimates Cherylle, I think, and I am a little concerned. He has never displayed such verve and elation, but this is no Platonic union of opposites. Lamar's efficient diurnal parade has broken up to join Cherylle's Mardi Gras – and it likes the headlong pace.

14 August 1973

Working steadily for the last two days in the beach house. Windless, lustrous weather. Postcard from Lamar and Cherylle honeymooning in Mexico. Lamar's neat printed script overlaid at the foot of the card by some illegible felt-tip scrawl from Cherylle. Lamar says I would 'love the art'. Is he being ironic? I suspect it's a sop to our abandoned educational sessions – maybe he's feeling guilty – they didn't stand much chance against the potent lure of Cherylle's callow hard-edged embrace.

18 August 1973

Lamar and Cherylle returned this morning, tanned and restless, deeply bored by Mexico. They stayed for lunch. Their evident intoxication with each other is off-putting to say the least. Lamar was unshaven and in a T-shirt, there were bags under his eyes. I've never seen him like this.

Their self-absorption has its curious aspects too. Judging from the hints Lamar dropped about their days in Mexico it seems that it only functions non-destructively when observed by a third party. He alluded to uncouth nights of violent manic rows and equally violent and manic reconciliations. He calls it 'kamikaze love' and describes it as a mixture of 'laughter and pistol shots' – which is quite good for Lamar. He claims he finds it entirely invigorating.

I suspect I am to be enrolled as resident third party: token voyeur of their lambent encounters. I'm not sure I welcome the role; I sense this self-destruct mechanism poised inside Cherylle and it makes me uncomfortable. For example she was quiet and affectionate all afternoon, then she swam worryingly far out to sea. 'Trying for Catalina Island' was all she said when she returned exhausted. They left about eight in the evening heading for some dim bar on the Strip.

19 August 1973

To the downtown offices of AOD to present the first draft of my package. Looked in on Lamar but his office was empty. His secretary said you could never tell when he'd be in these days. Over lunch with some of his colleagues I found that Cherylle was the prime topic of conversation. There's a certain smug satisfaction evinced over the changes she's wrought in Lamar; normally the paradigm of the totally committed company man, he now delegates more and more and his faultless punctuality has degenerated to amnesiac randomness.

23 August 1973

Drove up the coast with Lamar and Cherylle in their new car, a preposterously large white Buick convertible. An unusual vernal, sappy feel to the day – all the colours seem unfledged and new. Cherylle was at her most entrancing, telling us stories of her attempts to break into the movies. Looking at Lamar I see devotion lodged in every feature. He seems not to listen to her words, rather watches her forming them – noting every smile, eye gleam, pout and hair-toss like some fervent anthropologist.

On the beach Cherylle changed into a skimpy scarlet bikini and we took photographs of each other. Lamar had given her an expensive camera as a present and we played with its delayed exposure device taking endless reels of the three of us in absurd vaudevillian poses, throughout which Cherylle flirted shamelessly with me. Lamar – a little subdued I thought – later moved up to the dunes with the telephoto lens. I saw him up there, obsessively sniping shots of her as she oiled herself and sunbathed.

When we got back home I found myself drained and exhausted from the sun and the fervid high spirits. Lamar and Cherylle wanted me to come and 'cruise bars'. Lately their favourite pastime, it lasts all night – an intoxicating carnival snaking through the seamier side of the city. I begged off – I scarcely had the energy for a shower – I don't know how they can keep this pace up.

4 September 1973

Lamar phoned and asked in a morose voice if he could come round and have a talk. Alone. I hadn't seen him or Cherylle since that day at the beach and I wondered what was going on. He looked something like his old self – neater, back in a suit. Apparently word had come down from the higher echelons that the honeymoon was over. The postures of his body, however, struck attitudes of despair and gloom. Things were not going well. Cherylle hated to be on her own now that he had to be regularly at work. On one of their bar-cruises they had met a young hippie-actor friend of Cherylle. He had stayed the night and was still there. 'He's a remarkable sort of guy,' Lamar insisted, unconvincingly. 'Only I wish he and Cherylle didn't laugh so much together.' Kick him out, I advised. No, Lamar said, no. Cherylle wouldn't like that. My heart went out to him. We sat on and talked a bit longer, Lamar feigning unconcern, but with his strong shoulders slumped, his kamikaze love in a screaming death dive, the end of his fabulous amours, his brief bright horizon dimmed by valedictory clouds.

11 September 1973

I arrived home at the beach house this evening to find Lamar there waiting. I knew from his blank eyes Cherylle had gone. 'Took the white Buick,' Lamar said, his voice numbly monotone, 'and everything in the house they could hock. No note, nothing.'

I poured him a drink. She was young, I said, headstrong. She'd be back soon, to apologize, wanting to be forgiven. As he left Lamar gripped my arm fiercely. 'You know,' he said evenly, 'I can't face it. If she doesn't come back.' I reassured him. I'd lay odds I said, five days, ten at the most. Wait until the money ran out, the binge was over.

29 September 1973

Lamar looks pale and sick. He hardly sleeps he says. He has hired a private detective to look for Cherylle. Apparently everyone at work has been most understanding. Now that Cherylle has been away for three weeks sympathetic consolation has turned to worldly reasoning. You're better off without her, his colleagues declare with firm logic. Think of your career – be objective – did she *really* fit in? Yeah, anyone could see there was something unstable there. Hell Lamar, they said, she's done you a *favour*.

But Lamar, it was obvious, would never agree. He spent more and more time at my place tirelessly rerunning the scenario of his brief courtship and marriage as if he were trying to unlock some code the memories contained. A bleak dawn often broke on these disconsolate monologues: me in a half-doze; Lamar, his head in his hands, eyes staring emptily out to sea as if searching the sombre distance for an answer.

5 October 1973

10.30 p.m. A call from Cherylle. Would I meet her in the forecourt of a filling station not far from my house. Ah, I thought, I am about to be enrolled as mediator. However Cherylle was proud and unrepentant. The Buick was parked at the kerb. Her boyfriend leaned against it just out of earshot. Cherylle looked more wild and unkempt. She gave me the keys to the car and an envelope of money. 'Tell him to keep away,' she said. 'I owe him nothing now.' I was puzzled and a little angry. 'What about an explanation?' I said. 'Why did you do it?' She laughed. 'Nobody could take that kind of a relationship,' she said. 'I was like some kind of dog, a pet dog. It would have killed me.'

When I got home I called Lamar and told him about our meeting. He came right over. When he saw the car and the money he broke down for the first time. I took him home, told him to get some sleep and said I'd be round the next day. He behaved like the victim of some appalling accident, a focal point for massive stresses.

14 October 1973

Much of my spare time over the last few days has been spent with Lamar. Our conversation on all other topics except Cherylle is desultory and half-hearted. There has been no further word from her.

Lamar is driven on remorselessly by his obsession. Now that her presence has been removed from him he hoards items of her clothing like religious treasures, the banal relics of a consumer saint. He carries around with him a cheap Zippo lighter engraved with her name and a disposable powder compact which he is forever touching and examining like some demented votary.

We drive around at night to the bars they visited in the vague hope of spotting her. Every distant blonde is excitedly approached until the lack of resemblance becomes clear. His moods on these occasions oscillate wildly, a leaping seismograph of elation and despair.

One day we drove back to the beach we had visited. Lamar sat in what he felt was the exact spot raking the sand with his fingers like an insane archaeologist, finding only the cellophane wrapper of a cigarette pack and the plastic top of a tube of sun-oil. Then two nights ago he asked me to come with him to Lake Folsom where he and Cherylle had spent a weekend. We wandered aimlessly through the resort complex and then went down to the marina. There Lamar stopped to talk to an old boatman who had rented them a cruiser for the day. He said he remembered Cherylle and asked for her. When Lamar told him what had happened he spat bitterly into the lake. He scrutinized the ripples he had caused for a few seconds and then said, 'Yeah. I seen 'em all.' Then he paused. 'I seen 'em all here,' he went on, 'fame, fornication and tears. That's all there is.'

Lamar seemed profoundly affected by this piece of folk-wisdom and repeated the remark approvingly to himself several times on the journey home.

17 October 1973

A surprise invitation to Lamar's for dinner. There were just the two of us. He tells me that after considerable thought he has eventually filed for divorce. He seems calmer but the brimming self-assurance that was there has not returned. The old solidity too seems a thing of the past; there is a slight lack of ease – a convalescent's awkwardness – in his movements. After dinner he brought out all the shiny photos he had taken of Cherylle. He flicked through them once and then burnt them. He pointed to a slowly curling kodachrome. 'Cherylle, that day at the beach . . . remember the swimsuit?' Then he smiled, embarrassed. 'I'm sorry,' he said. 'I know it's absurdly melodramatic, but at least I feel it's over now.'

We went out later to buy some cigarettes. On our way back we saw a girl in a yellow window crying over a typewriter. 'Think Cherylle's crying for me?' he asked harshly. I said that she might be. 'No she's not,' he said firmly. 'Not Cherylle.'

23 October 1973

I was woken early this morning by the police. They said Lamar wanted me. Outside he sat in the back seat of a police car. 'They've found her,' he said. 'They want me to identify. Will you come with me?'

Cherylle's decomposing body had been found in a shack at an abandoned dude ranch out in the desert near a place called Hi Vista. There was no sign of the hippie-actor friend. Apparently it had all the indications of a half-fulfilled suicide pact. There was a note with both their signatures but the police suspected that after Cherylle had pulled the trigger her lover had panicked, had second thoughts about joining her and had fled.

The deep irony was not lost on Lamar. He stood unmovingly as the policeman pulled back the blanket and there was only a slight huskiness in his voice as he identified her body.

2 November 1973

Lamar has just moved back to his flat. He has been staying with me since the inquest. The hippie has still not been tracked down. Lamar has been a moody and taciturn companion, not surprisingly, but he is not the broken man I expected him to be. There is a kind of fatalistic resignation about him, he talks less obsessively about Cherylle and I'm glad to say seems to have abandoned his mementoes. However, it has to be said that he is nothing like the person he was a few short months ago and he told me yesterday he planned to resign from the company. He keeps saying that Cherylle couldn't have been happy so it was just as well that she ended it all. 'She couldn't have been happy,' he will say. 'Not Cherylle. If she couldn't be happy with me how could she possibly be happy with anybody else?' To Lamar's numbed brain the logic of that statement appears incontrovertible.

8 November 1973

A dull smog-shrouded day of rain. By mistake the police forwarded on Cherylle's personal possessions to my house assuming Lamar was still staying here. A patrol car dropped them off early in the evening and I said I would make sure Lamar got them. There was a nylon suitcase full of crumpled clothes and a plastic bag of loose items. I laid them on the kitchen table and thought sadly of Cherylle. Cherylle, in her satin pants . . . her orange lips, her white blonde hair. And now? A few grubby clothes, a wooden hairbrush, sunglasses, a Mexican purse, a charm, a powder compact and a Zippo lighter with her name engraved on it . . .

I finally caught up with Lamar at a burger dinette down on the sea front not far from his apartment. It was still raining heavily. He sat at a table in the window surrounded by wax-paper wrappers and empty bottles of beer gazing out at the passing trucks on the coast highway. A red tail light glow lit his eyes.

I placed the Zippo and the compact in front of him on the table. 'Why did you do it?' I asked. He hardly looked surprised. He gave a momentary start before resuming his scrutiny of the passing traffic.

'They were hers,' he said dully. 'I didn't want them any more so I just put them back in her bag.'

'But why, Lamar? Why?' His woodenness infuriated me. 'Why Cherylle?'

He looked at me as though I'd asked a stupid question. 'She wasn't ever coming back, you know? But I found out where she was. I begged her on my knees to come home. But that hippie wouldn't let her go. I tried to buy him off, but he wasn't interested. And I couldn't let her leave me for someone like that – for anyone. I had to do it, so I set it up that way.'

'What about him? The hippie?'

'Oh, he's out there in the desert. No one's going to find him in a long time.'

Lamar smiled a bitter smile and traced a pattern in the wet Formica round his beer bottle. A young Hispanic waitress approached for my order, carrying her boredom like a rucksack. I waved her away. I wanted to get out of this melancholy bar with its flickering neon and clouded chrome.

I had reached the door when I felt his hand on my shoulder.

'You can tell them if you like. I don't care.' He looked at me tiredly.

I felt my voice thick in my throat. 'Just tell me one thing,' I said. 'I want to know how you feel now. Feel tough, Lamar? Feel noble? Come on, what's it like, Lamar?'

He shrugged. 'Remember that play we read once? "I'll sacrifice the lamb that I do love"? That's how it is, you know? It's like the song says – love hurts. It gets to hurt you so much you've got to do something about it.'

It was all the explanation I would ever get. He stood in the doorway and watched me walk to my car. Tyres swishing on the wet Tarmac, the road shiny like PVC, the rain slicking down his short hair. As I drove off I could see him in the rear mirror still standing there, a lurid burger sign smoking above his head. I never saw him again.

Extracts from the Journal of Flying Officer J.

Duke Senior: Stay, Jaques, stay.
Jaques: To see no pastime I: what you would have I'll stay to
know at your abandoned cave.

As You Like It, v.4

Ascension
'The hills round here are like a young girl's breasts.' Thus
Squadron Leader 'Duke' Verschoyle. Verbatim. 4.30 p.m., on
the lawn, loudly.

Rogation Sunday
Last night ladies were invited into the mess. I went alone.
'Duke' Verschoyle took a Miss Bald, a friend of Neves's. At
supper Verschoyle, who was sufficiently intoxicated, flipped a
piece of bread at Miss Bald. She replied with a fid of ham which
caught Verschoyle smack in his grinning face. A leg of chicken
was then aimed at the lady by our Squadron Leader, but it hit me,
leaving a large grease stain on my dress jacket. I promptly asked if
the mess fund covered the cost of cleaning. I was sconced for
talking shop.
Verschoyle liverish in morning.

4 June

Sortie at dawn. I took the monoplane. Flew south to the Chilterns. At 7,000 feet I felt I could see every trembling blade of grass. Monoplane solid as a hill. Low-level all the way home. No sign of activity anywhere.

Talked to Stone. Says he knew Phoebe at Melton in 1923. Swears she was a brunette then.

Friday, lunch-time

Verschoyle saunters up, wearing a raffish polka-dot cravat, a pipe clamped between his large teeth. Speaks without removing it. I transcribe exactly: 'Msay Jks, cd yizzim psibly siyerway tklah thnewmn, nyah?' *What?* He removes his loathsome teat, a loop of saliva stretching and gleaming momentarily between stem and lip. There's a new man, it appears. Randall something or something Randall. Verschoyle wants me to run a routine security clearance.

'Very well, sir,' I say.

'Call me Duke,' he suggests. Fatal influence of the cinema on the service. Must convey my thoughts on the matter to Reggie.

Stone is driving me mad. His shambling, loutish walk. His constant whistling of 'My Little Grey Home in the West'. The way he breathes through his mouth. As far as I can see he might as well not have a nose – he never uses it.

Sunday a.m.

French cricket by runway B. I slope off early down to The Sow & Farrow. The pub is dark and cool. Baking-hot day outside. Slice of joint on a pewter plate. Household bread and butter. A pint of turbid beer. All served up by the new barmaid,

Rose. Lanky, athletic girl, strong-looking. Blonde. We chatted amiably until the rest of the squadron – in their shouting blazers and tennis shoes – romped noisily in. I left a 4d. tip. Strangely attractive girl.

Memo. Randall's Interrogation
1. Where is the offside line in a rugby scrum?
2. Is Kettner's in Church Street or Poland Street?
3. What is 'squegging'? And who shouldn't do it?
4. How would you describe *Zéphire de Sole Paganini*?
5. Sing 'Hey, Johnny Cope'.
6. Which is the odd one out: BNC, SEH, CCC, LMH, SHC?
7. Complete this saying: 'Hope springs eternal in the –.'

Dominion Day (Canada)
Randall arrives. Like shaking hands with a marsh. Cheerful, round, young face. Prematurely bald. Tufts of hair deliberately left unshaved on cheekbones. Overwhelming urge to strike him. Why do I sense the man is not to be trusted?

Verschoyle greets him like a long-lost brother. It seems they went to the same prep school. Later, Verschoyle tells me to forget about the interrogation. I point out that it's mandatory under the terms of the draft constitution. 'Duke' reluctantly has to back down.

N.B. Verschoyle's breath smelling strongly of peppermint.

Wednesday night
Sagging, moist evening. Sat out on the lawn till late, writing to Reggie, telling him of Verschoyle's appalling influence on the squadron – the constant rags, high jinks, general refusal to take our task seriously. Started to write about the days with Phoebe at Melton, but kept thinking of Rose. Curious.

July –?

Sent to Coventry by no. 3 flight for putting their drunken Welsh mechanic on a charge. Today, Verschoyle declared the monoplane his own. I'm left with a lumbering old Ganymede II. It's like flying a turd. I'll have my work cut out in a dogfight.

p.m. Map-reading class: Randall, Stone, Guy and Bede. Stone hopeless; he'd get lost in a corridor. Randall surprisingly efficient. He seems to know the neighbourhood suspiciously well. Also annoyingly familiar. Asked me if I wanted to go down to The Sow & Farrow for a drink. I set his interrogation for Thursday, 15.00 hours.

Bank Holiday Monday

Drove down to the coast with Rose. Unpleasant day, scouring wind off the ice caps, grey-flannel sky. The pier was deserted, but Rose insisted on swimming. I stamped on the shingle beach while she changed in the dunes. Her dark-blue woollen bathing suit flashing by as she sprinted strongly into the breakers. A glimpse of white pounding thighs, then shrieks and flailing arms. Jovial shouts of encouragement from me. She emerged, shivering, her nose endearingly red, to be enfolded in the rough towel that I held. Her front teeth slightly askew. Made my heart cartwheel with love. She said it was frightfully cold but exhilarating. Her long nipples erect for a good five minutes.

21 July

Boring day. Verschoyle damaged the monoplane when he flew through a mob of starlings, so he's temporarily grounded himself. He and Randall as thick as thieves. I caught them leering across the bar at Rose. Cleverly, she disguised her feelings on seeing me, knowing how I value discretion.

Randall's Interrogation

Randall unable to complete final verse of 'Hey, Johnny Cope'. I report my findings to Verschoyle and recommend Randall's transfer to Movement Control. Verschoyle says he's never even heard of 'Hey, Johnny Cope'. He's a deplorable example to the men.

Note to Reggie: in 1914 we were fighting for our golf and our weekends.

Went to the zoological gardens and looked at the llama. Reminded me of Verschoyle. In the reptile house I saw a chameleon: repulsive bulging eyes – Randall. Peafowl – Guy. Civet cat – Miss Bald. Anteater – Stone. Gazelle – Rose. Bateleur eagle – me.

475th Day of the Struggle

Three battalions attacked today, north of Cheltenham. E. went down in one of the Griffins. Ground fire. A perfect arc. Crashed horribly not two miles from Melton.

Dawn patrol along the River Lugg. The Ganymede's crude engine is so loud I fly in a perpetual swooning migraine. Struts thrumming and quivering like palsied limbs. Told a disgruntled Fielding to decaulk cylinder heads before tomorrow's mission.

Randall returned late from a simple reconnaissance flight. He had some of us worried. Claimed a map-reading error. It was because of his skill with maps that he was put on reconnaissance in the first place. Verschoyle untypically subdued at the news from Cheltenham. Talk of moving to a new base in the Mendips.

Randall: Did you know that Rose was a promising young actress?

Stone: Oh, yes? What's she promised you, then?

As a result of this flash of wit, Stone was elected entertainments secretary for the mess. He plans a party before the autumn frosts set in.

63rd Wednesday

On the nature of love. There are two sorts of people you love. There are people you love steadily, unreflectingly: people who you know will never hurt you. Then there are people you love fiercely: people who you know can and will hurt you.

1 August. Monday

Tredgold tells me that Randall was known as a trophy maniac at college. Makes some kind of perverse sense.

7 August

Luncheon with Rose at The Compleat Angler, Marlow. Menu: *Oeufs* Magenta; Mock Turtle Soup; Turbot; Curried Mutton *au riz*; Orange Jelly. Not bad for these straitened times we live in. Wines: a half bottle of Gonzalez Coronation Sherry.

Sunday

Tea with the Padre. Bored rigid. He talked constantly of the bout of croupous pneumonia his sister had just endured.

Suddenly realized what it was that finally put me off Phoebe. It was the way she used to pronounce the word 'piano' with an Italian accent. 'Would you care for a tune on the *piano*?'

15 Aug., 17.05

Stone crash-landed on the links at Beddlesea. He was on the way back from a recce of the new base in the Mendips. Unharmed, luckily. But the old Gadfly is seriously damaged.

He trudged all the way back to the clubhouse from the 14th fairway, but they wouldn't let him use the phone because he wasn't a member.

Rose asked me today if it was true that Randall was the best pilot in the squadron. I said, don't be ridiculous.

Read Reggie's article, 'Air power and the modern guerrilla'.

500th Day of the Struggle

It's clear that Verschoyle is growing a beard. Broadmead and Collis-Sandes deserted. They stole Stone's Humber. It's worth noting, I think, that Collis-Sandes played wing three-quarter for Blackheath.

Wed. p.m.

Verschoyle's beard filmy and soft, with gaps. He looks like a bargee. The Padre seems to have taken something of a shine to yours truly. He invited me to his rooms for a drink yesterday evening. (One Madeira in a tiny clouded glass as big as my thumb and two *petit beurres*.) Croupous pneumonia again . . .

On the way home, stopped in my tracks by a vision of Rose. Pure and naked. Harmonious as a tree. *Rose!*

Mendip base unusable.

71st Monday

Verschoyle shaves off beard. Announcement today of an historic meeting between commands at Long Hanborough.

6th Sunday before Advent

Working late in the hangar with young Fielding (the boy is ruined with acne). Skirting through the laurels on a short cut back to the mess, I notice a torch flash three times from Randall's room.

Later, camped out on the fire escape and well bundled up, I see him scurry across the moonlit lawn in dressing-gown and pyjamas with what looks like a blanket (a radio? semaphore kit? maps?), heading for the summer-house.

The next morning I lay my accusations before Verschoyle and insist on action. He places me under arrest and confines me to quarters. I get the boy Fielding to smuggle a note to Rose.

Visit from Stone. Tells me the autogiro has broken down again. News of realignments and negotiations in the cities. Drafting of the new constitution halted. Prospects of Peace. No word from Rose.

3rd Day of Captivity

Interviewed by Scottish psychiatrist on Verschoyle's instructions. Dr Gilzean: strong Invernesshire accent. Patently deranged. The interview keeps being interrupted as we both pause to make copious notes. Simple ingenuous tests:

Word Association

DR GILZEAN		ME
lighthouse	—	a small aunt
cave	—	tolerant grass
cigar	—	the neat power station
mouth	—	mild
kay	—	kind
lock	—	speedy vans
cucumber	—	public baths
midden	—	the wrinkling wrists of gloves

Rorschach Blots
DR GILZEAN

ME
a queer nun   a new trug   a fucked hen

Dr Gilzean pronounces me entirely sane. Verschoyle apologizes.

First Day of Freedom
Stone's party in the mess. Verschoyle suggests the gymkhana game. A twisting course of beer bottles is laid out on the lawn. The women are blindfolded and driven in a harness of ribbons by the men. Stone steers Miss Bald into the briar hedge, trips and sprains his ankle. Randall and Rose are the winners. Rose trotting confidently, guided by Randall's gentle tugs and 'gee-ups!' Her head back, showing her pale throat, her knees rising and falling smartly beneath her fresh summer frock, reminding me painfully of days on the beach, plunging into breakers.

At midnight Verschoyle rattles a spoon in a beer mug. Important news, he cries. There is to be a peace conference in the Azores. The squadron is finally returning to base at Bath. Randall has just got engaged to Rose.

Saint Jude's Day
The squadron left today for the city. The mess cold and sad. Verschoyle, with uncharacteristic generosity, said I could keep

the monoplane. There's a 'drome near Tomintoul in the Cairn-gorms which sounds ideal. Instructed Fielding to fit long-range fuel tanks.

First snows of winter. The Sow & Farrow closed for the season. A shivering Fielding brings news that the monoplane has developed a leak in the glycol system. I order him to work on through the night. I must leave tomorrow.

p.m. Brooding in the mess about Rose, wondering where I went wrong. Stroll outside, find the snow has stopped. *Observation:* when you're alone for any length of time, you develop an annoying inclination to look in mirrors.

A cold sun shines through the empty beeches, casting a blue trellis of shadows on the immaculate white lawn.

Must write to Reggie about the strange temptation to stamp on smooth things. Snow on a lawn, sand at low tide. An overpowering urge to leave a mark?

I stand on the edge, overpoweringly tempted. It's all so perfect, it seems a shame to spoil it. With an obscure sense of pleasure, I yield to the temptation and stride boldly across the unreal surface, my huge footprints thrown into high relief by the candid winter sun . . .

The Coup

Isaac knocked at his door at half past three in the morning. It took Morgan a few minutes to wake up, then he washed, shaved and put on his light-weight tropical suit. He was going home.

The verandah was cluttered with the trunks and packing cases that were being shipped back to England separately by sea. Morgan ate his breakfast among them in a mood of quite pleasant melancholy. He gazed across the empty sitting room and at the bare walls of his bungalow and thought about the three years he had spent in this stinking sweaty country. Three rotting years. Christ.

He was still thinking about how much he wouldn't miss the place when the car from the High Commission arrived at half past four. Morgan registered a twinge of annoyance when he saw that, instead of the air-conditioned Mercedes he'd requested, he'd been issued with a cream Ford Consul. It was three-and-a-half hours from Nkongsamba to the capital by road; three-and-a-half hours of switchbacked, pot-holed hell through dense rainforest. It seemed that his last hours in this wretched country were destined to be spent in the same perspiring itching agony that so coloured his memories of the past three years. Typical of the bloody High Commissioner, thought Morgan, not bloody important enough for the Merc. Trust the little asthmatic bureaucrat to notice his transport application. He'd wanted the Merc desperately; to strap-hang in air-conditioned comfort, the Union Jack cracking on the bonnet. Go out in style, that had been the plan. He looked critically at the Consul; it needed a clean and one hub cap was missing, *and* they'd given him that imbecilic driver Peter. Morgan rolled his eyes heavenwards. He couldn't wait to leave.

He said good-bye to Isaac, and Moses his cook, and Moses's young wife Abigail, who helped with the washing and ironing. He'd given them all a sizeable farewell dash the previous evening and he noticed they were smiling hugely as they energetically pumped his hands. Bloody gang of Old Testament refugees, he thought, slightly put out at the absence of any sadness or solemnity, they'd never had it so good. He cast his eye fondly over Abigail's plump sleek body. Yes, he'd miss the women, he admitted, and the beer.

It was still quite black outside and a couple of toads burped at each other in the darkness of the garden as he eased himself on to the shiny plastic rear seat, gave a final wave, and told Peter to get going. They sped off through the deserted roads of the commercial reservation and passed quickly through the narrow empty streets of Nkongsamba before striking what was laughingly known as the trans-national highway.

This particular road was a crumbling, two-lane, Tarmacadam death trap that meandered through the jungle between Nkongsamba and the capital. A skilfully designed route of blind corners, uncambered Z-bends and savage gradients, it annually claimed hundreds of lives as the worst drivers in the world sought to negotiate its bizarre geometry. The small hours of the morning were the only time when it was anything like safe to travel – hence Morgan's early rise, even though his plane left at half past eleven.

As a citron light spread over the jungle Morgan reflected that they hadn't made such bad progress. With the windows wound full down the speeding car had been filled with a cool breeze and Morgan barely sweated at all. As expected, the roads had been quiet. They had passed the still-guttering remains of a crashed petrol tanker and once had been forced off the road by a criminally overloaded articulated lorry, its two huge trailers towering with sacks of groundnuts, as its bonus-hunting driver, high on kola-nuts, barrelled down the middle of the road en route for the capital and its busy port.

All in all a remarkably uneventful journey, thought Morgan as they raced through a town called Shagamu which marked the halfway stage. But then it was only a matter of a few miles further on, the sun's heat concentrating, Morgan's buttocks and the backs of his ample thighs beginning to chafe and fret on the plastic seats, that they had a puncture. The car veered suddenly, Morgan threw up his arms, Peter shouted 'Good Lord!', and he pulled on to the laterite verge.

After the steady rumble of their passage on the Tarmac it was very quiet. The road stretched empty before and behind them, the avenue of jungle rearing up on either side like high green walls.

Peter got out and looked at the tyre, sucking in air through the prodigious gaps in his teeth. He grinned.

'Dis be poncture, sah,' he explained through the window.

Morgan didn't budge. 'Well bloody fix it then,' he growled. 'I've got a plane to catch, you know.'

Peter went round to the back of the car and threw open the boot. Morgan sat scowling, the absence of breeze through the car windows reminding him pointedly of the high humidity and the unrelenting heat of the early morning sun. He had a sudden agonizing itch on his perineum. He scratched at it furiously.

Then Peter was back at the window.

'Ah-ah! Sah, dey never give us one spear.'

'Spear? Spear? What bloody spear?'

'Spear tyre, sah. Dere is no spear tyre for boot.'

Morgan climbed out of the car swearing. Sure enough, no spare. He felt an intolerable explosive frustration building up in him. This bloody country just wasn't going to give up, was it? Oh no, far too much to expect to catch a plane unhindered. He gazed wildly around at the green jungle before telling himself to calm down.

'You'd better take the wheel back to Shagamu.' He thrust some notes into Peter's hand. 'Try and get it fixed. And hurry!'

Peter jacked up the Consul, removed the wheel and trundled it back down the road to Shagamu. It was too hot to sit in the car so Morgan crouched on the verge in what little shade it offered and watched the sun climb the sky.

A few cars whizzed past but nobody stopped. The highway, Morgan grimly noted, was particularly quiet today.

Two-and-a-half hours later Peter returned with a repaired and newly inflated tyre. It took another ten minutes to replace it before they were on their way once more. Morgan's plane was due to leave in just over an hour. They would never make it. His face was taut and expressionless as they roared down the road to the airport.

The airport was situated on flat land about ten miles from the capital and was quite cut off, surrounded by a large light-industrial estate. As they drove past the small factories, freight depots and vehicle pools, Morgan again commented on the lack of traffic, everybody seemed to be staying away. Small groups of people gathered in the villages at the roadside and stared curiously at the cream Consul as it went by. Probably some bloody holiday, reasoned Morgan thankfully, as he saw the sign posts directing them to the airport, at least something was working in his favour.

Soon he saw the familiar roadside billboards advertising airlines and the exotic places they visited, and Morgan felt the first thrill of excitement at the thought of flying off home; the well-modulated chill of the aircraft, the crisp stewardesses and the duty-free liquor. He was straightening his tie as they rounded a corner and almost ran down a road-block.

The road-block consisted of three fifty-gallon oil drums surmounted by planks of wood. Parked to one side was a chubby armoured car, surrounded by at least two dozen soldiers wearing camouflaged uniforms and armed with sub-machine guns with sickle-shaped magazines.

Morgan stared in open-mouthed astonishment about him and at the airport buildings 200 yards ahead. Four huge tanks were parked in front of the arrivals hall. Morgan noticed with alarm that several of the soldiers had levelled their guns at the car. Peter's face was positively grey with fear. A young officer approached with a red cockade in his peaked cap. He politely asked Morgan to get out and produce his documents.

'What's going on?' Morgan asked impatiently. 'Is this some kind of an exercise? Terrorists? Or what? Look here,' he pointed to his identity card, 'I'm a member of the British Diplomatic Corps and I've got a plane to catch.'

The young officer returned the documents.

'This airport is now under the command of the military government . . .' he began, as if reading prompt-cards behind Morgan's head.

'What military government?' Morgan interrupted, then, as realization dawned, 'Oh no, oh my God no. A coup, it's a coup. Don't tell me. That's all I need, a bloody *coup*.' He raised his right hand to his forehead in an unconsciously dramatic gesture of despair. He felt he was getting a migraine. A bad one.

Just then a BOAC staff car drove up from the airport buildings and a harassed official got out. After some conferring with the young officer he hurried over to Morgan.

'What on earth are you doing here, man?' he asked irritatedly. 'Haven't you heard about the coup? This place has been like an armed camp since six o'clock this morning.'

Morgan explained about his early start and the puncture. 'Listen;' he went on agitatedly, 'my plane. Have I missed my plane? When can I get out of here?'

'Sorry, old chap. The last plane left here at midnight. The airport's closed to civil traffic. As you can see there's not a thing here. This is what usually happens I believe. Nobody flies in or out for a few days until things have sorted themselves out. You know, until the radio blackout's lifted, the fighting stops and the new government's officially recognized.'

'But look here,' Morgan insisted, 'I'm from the Commission at Nkongsamba. I've got diplomatic immunity, all that sort of stuff.'

'I'm afraid that doesn't carry any weight at all at the moment,' said the airlines official in an annoyingly good-humoured manner. 'Britain hasn't recognized the new government yet. I'd hang on for a few days before you start claiming any privileges.'

'Hang on! Good God, man, where do you suggest I hang on?'

'Well you can't get back to Nkongsamba. They'll have roadblocks on the highway now for sure. And there's a twenty-four-hour curfew on in the capital as well. So if I were you I'd go to the airport hotel down the road. Show them your ticket. I suppose you're in our care now, after a fashion, and they'll bill the airline. I should think they'll be glad of the custom. Everyone else has kept well away, stayed at home. In fact you're the only person who's turned up to catch a flight today. I suppose you were just unlucky.'

Morgan turned away. Unlucky. Just unlucky. Story of his life. He climbed morosely into the car and told Peter to take him to the airport hotel. Peter backed up with alacrity and they drove off.

The airport hotel was a mile away. They were stopped by a patrol on the road and Morgan again explained his predicament flourishing his passport and ticket. He was sunk in a profound depression; the final bizarre revenge of a hostile country. The magnitude of his ill-fortune left him feeling weak and exhausted.

Morgan had stayed at the airport hotel several times before. He remembered it as a lively cosmopolitan place with two restaurants, several bars, an Olympic-sized swimming pool and a small casino. It was usually populated by a mixed crowd of jet-lagged transit passengers, air-crew and stewardesses and a somewhat raffish and frontier collection of bush-charter pilots, oil company troubleshooters and indeterminate tanned and brassy females whom Morgan imaginatively took to be the mistresses of African politicians, part-time nightclub singers, croupiers, hostesses, expensive whores and bored wives. It was as close as Morgan ever came to being a member of the jet-set and a stay there always made him feel vaguely mysterious and highly sexed. As they approached, he recalled how only last year he had almost successfully bedded a strong-shouldered female helicopter pilot and his heart thumped in anticipation. Every cloud, he reminded himself, silver lining and all that. This had to be the one consolation of a truly awful day.

The airport hotel was large. A low-slung old colonial edifice at the centre was lined by shaded concrete pathways to more modern bedroom blocks, the pool, the hair-dressing salon and other amenities. As they swept up the drive Morgan looked about him with something approaching eagerness.

The large car park, however, was unsettlingly empty and Morgan noticed that the familiar troupe of hawkers who spread their thorn carvings, their ithyphallic ebony statuary and ropes of ceramic beads on the steps up to the front door were absent. Also there was an unnatural hush and tranquillity in the foyer, as if Morgan had arrived at the dead of night rather than midday. Sitting on squeaky cane chairs in front of the reception desk were two bored soldiers with small aluminium machine pistols in their laps. The clerk behind the long desk was asleep, his head resting on the register. One of the soldiers shook him awake and as Morgan signed in he noticed that only a few names were registered along with his own.

'Are you busy?' he asked with faint hope.

The receptionist smiled. 'Oh no, sah. Everybody gone. Only eight people staying since last night. No planes,' he added, 'no guests.'

An aged bellhop with bare feet and a faded blue uniform showed Morgan to his room in one of the new blocks. Morgan was glad to find the air-conditioning still functioned.

The day's frustrations were not over. Morgan tried to phone the Commission in Nkongsamba but was informed that all the lines had been closed down by the army. He then went back outside and instructed Peter – who had elected to stay and live in the car in the car park – to drive to the embassy in the capital and report Morgan's plight.

Peter shook his head with a convincing display of bitter disappointment.

'You can never go dere,' he lamented. 'Dey done build one big road-block for here,' he gestured at a point a few yards up from the end of the hotel drive. 'Plenty soldier. Dey are never lettin' you pass.'

So that was it. Morgan looked at his watch. By rights he should be high over Europe now, a stewardess handing him his meal on a tray, an hour or so from an early evening touchdown at Heathrow airport. Instead he was marooned in a deserted hotel complex while a military coup raged outside the gate.

He walked sadly back to his room through the afternoon heat. Lizards basked on stones in the sun, idly doing press-ups as he approached, reverting to glazed immobility once more as he walked on by. To his left he saw the tall diving board of the swimming pool and some asterisks of light flashed off the blue water he could glimpse through the perforated concrete screen that surrounded the pool area. Normally it would be lively with bathers, the bars crowded with sun-reddened guests, the nearby tennis courts resounding to the pock-pock of couples knocking up. Where were the other people who were staying here? Morgan wondered. What were they like? He felt like some mad dictator, or eccentric millionaire recluse, alone in an entire multi-bedroomed block with only his taciturn guards for company.

His second question was answered that evening when he went down to the restaurant. There was a table of four Syrians or Lebanese men, and an ancient wrinkled American couple. The Lebanese ignored him; the Americans said 'Hello there' and looked anxious to exchange grumbles about their common predicament. Morgan sat as far away as he could. Pretend nothing has happened, he told himself; as soon as we start behaving like victims of a siege – sharing resources, privations and anecdotes – this enforced stay really will become a nightmare.

He was well in to his rather firm avocado when the eighth guest arrived. If he had been asked to speculate, unseen, on his or her identity, Morgan – knowing his luck – would have laid long odds on the eighth guest being a nun, an overweight salesman or moustachioed spinster. He was surprised then, and almost enchanted when a young woman entered wearing the dark blue skirt and white blouse of BOAC. She was quite pretty too, Morgan assessed, his avocado untended, as he watched her sway through the empty tables to her seat close to the Americans.

For a minute or so Morgan's heartbeat seemed to echo rather loudly in his chest as, more surreptitiously, he scrutinized the girl. 'Girl' was perhaps a little too kind. She looked to be well into her thirties, that short blonde hair certainly dyed, a slightly predatory air about her features due to the rather hooked nose, the liberally applied cosmetics and lines that ran from the corner of her nostrils to the ends of her thin orange lips. She had amazingly long painted nails that matched the colour of her lipstick.

For the first time that day Morgan's spirits were lifted. Something about her – the dark eye-shadow, her tan against the white cotton of her blouse – reminded him of the brisk sexual allure of the helicopter pilot of the year before. He passed the rest of the meal in a pleasantly absorbing miasma of sexual fantasy.

Fantasy was all he had to content himself with however, as the girl appeared to return to her room directly after dinner. Morgan drank a couple of whiskies in the bar but was driven out by the increasingly clamorous garrulity of the four Lebanese who played bridge with a quite un-English fervour and intensity. The American couple tried to befriend him once again but Morgan repelled their polite 'Say, do you have any idea where we can change some dollars?' with a rush of eyebrow-jerking, shoulder-shrugging pseudo French: '*Ah desolé, haw . . . euh je vous ne comprendre non? Oui? Disdonc, eur, bof, vous savez haha parler pas Anglais. Mmm?*' They wandered off with an air of baffled resignation.

The next morning Morgan looked out of his fifth-floor window. From this height he commanded a considerable view of the hotel area. He could see Peter pissing into a bush on the edge of the car park. A military jeep was pulled up in front of the central building. Over to his left and partially obscured by a clump of trees he could see the swimming pool: a static blue slab surrounded by grey concrete and ranks of empty lounging chairs. Then as he watched a small figure came into his line of vision. It was the stewardess, wearing what looked like a tiny yellow bikini. She jumped into the pool and swam around. Morgan watched dry-mouthed as she clambered dripping up the steps and fingered free the sodden material of her briefs that had become wedged in the cleft between her buttocks. Morgan turned from the window and rummaged in his suitcase for his swimming trunks.

Morgan was not proud of the state he had allowed his body to get into. Always what his mother had called 'a big lad', the beer-gut he had assiduously developed at university never disappeared and indeed had since expanded like some soft subcutaneous parasite around the sides of his torso, padding his back and swelling his already considerable buttocks and thighs. He could have done something about it once, he supposed, as he stood in front of the full-length bathroom mirror; there was nothing he could do about his balding head, but the recent addition of a thick Zapata moustache had effected some positive transformation of his appearance. A straggling line of pale brown hair ran straight down from his throat, between his worryingly plump breasts to disappear beneath the waist band of his capacious trunks. 'Not a pretty sight,' a girlfriend had once remarked on observing him as he stumbled – soap-blind – from the shower, groping for a towel. Well, it was too late now, he concluded, inflating his chest and trying to suck in his stomach. In a suit he fancied he looked merely beefy; but this was another trouble with tropical climes: the terrible exposure that resulted through the regular need to shed as much clothing as possible.

Still, he felt quite good as he strolled down the walkway towards the pool, a carefully slung towel modestly covering his shuddering paps. A few more soldiers lounged by the hotel entrance, and the sun beat down from a perfectly blue sky. The enforced unreal isolation and the unsettling threat of casually sported arms he found strangely invigorating; as if the deserted hotel complex was infused with a lurking wayward sexuality only waiting to be sprung from cover.

Morgan spread his towel a polite few chairs away from the girl. She was lying on her front, bikini top unclipped. He was perturbed to see the Lebanese encamped on the other side of the pool playing bridge. There was a fat one, far fatter than Morgan, in a white shirt and bermuda shorts. The others wore tiny swimming suits like jock straps: two thin weaselly men – one of whom had a face pitted like a peach stone – and the fourth, gratingly handsome in a lounge-lizard kind of way, with a thin moustache and a thick springy rug of hair over a lean and muscly chest. Morgan worried rather about him; he kept looking over at the girl.

There was a persistent roaring in his head, furious red static grumbled and flushed behind his eyes, slabs of heat burned his thighs and belly. Morgan was sunbathing. It was agony. He sat up, rockets and anti-aircraft shells pulsating and exploding everywhere he looked, and reached behind him for the bottle of beer he'd ordered and kept in the shade beneath a lounger. The bottle was still cool, the green glass slippy with beads of condensation. Morgan took great juddering pulls at it, beer spilling from the upended bottle over his chin, dripping onto his chest. His brain seemed to soar and cartwheel with the alcohol.

He let out a silent satisfying belch and stood up ready to plunge into the pool.

The first thing he noticed was the girl's striped towel, occupied only by the damp imprint of her body. Then he heard a ripple of laughter from the shallow end of the pool and he saw her chatting to the hairy Lebanese who, as Morgan gazed, stood on his hands and walked around with his brown legs waving comically above the water to the delighted laughter of the girl.

It can only have been this flirtatious display of agility, coupled with the dizzying effects of the cold beer, that drove Morgan to the diving board. As he climbed laboriously to the top he grew increasingly aware of the absurdity of the position he had committed himself to, and of all its hackneyed connotations. He sensed, as he emerged on the highest board, the attention of the others below turn to him. He had only seconds to decide. Beyond the lip of the board he saw the girl looking up at him, and the frank interest of her gaze inspired him and yet was somehow depressing. Depressing to think that he had stooped to these despised macho techniques to gain the girl's absorption, and inspiring to find that they actually worked. He hitched up the waistband of his trunks. He would compromise: he wouldn't dive – he wasn't sure if he could remember how – and he wouldn't climb back down. No, he would jump. He tried to saunter casually to the edge of the board. The pool slowly revealed itself beneath him. He thought: good God, it seems higher from up here. Bloody high. Shouldn't there be some kind of legal limit . . . His doubts were cut off in mid-stream as he realized with a gulp of horror that he had missed his step and clownishly fallen forward off the board, not in an elegant vertical jump, but at a gradually diminishing angle of forty-five degrees to the water. And as the glinting shimmering surface rushed up to meet him Morgan spread his arms in a grotesque parody of a swallow-dive and belly flopped full force with a ghastly echoing smack.

Everything was white. White and fizzing as if he was immersed in a glass of Andrew's Liver Salts. He felt strong arms pulling him to the side. He felt his hands on the tiled edge of the pool. He took great gasping mouthfuls of air. His vision cleared. The hairy Lebanese was by his side, an arm protectively round his shoulders. Morgan shrugged him off and looked up. The stewardess crouched on the pool edge above him, concern filling her eyes.

'Are you all right?' she asked. 'It made an awful sound.'

'Mmmm. Sure,' Morgan wheezed. 'I'm . . . fine.'

He rested in his room all afternoon. The entire front of his body flushed and tingling for at least two hours. The girl had gathered up his stuff, draped a towel across his winded shoulders and led him back to his block. He felt as if he had just swum the Channel; his lungs heaved, his body creaked with pain and he could barely gasp replies to the girl's worried solicitations. And when the pain and the agony subsided it was replaced with an equally cruel shame. Morgan writhed with embarrassment on his bed, cursing his ridiculous pretensions, his preposterous lifeguard conceit and his absurd gigolo rivalry.

He ate his evening meal as soon as the restaurant opened. Only the Americans accompanied him but they maintained a frosty indifference. He inquired at the desk if there had been any word about the coup or news of the airport opening. The reception clerk told him that there was nothing but martial music on the radio but he planned to listen to the BBC World Service news at nine. Perhaps that would give them some reliable information.

Morgan found a dark corner of the bar and flicked through old magazines for a while. No one interrupted him. There was no sign of the stewardess or the Lebanese. He ordered a large whisky. To hell with everyone, he thought.

Shortly after nine Morgan went out to look for the receptionist but the desk was empty. He waited for a few minutes and then decided to turn in early. He was walking down the passageway that led out to his block when he heard noises coming from behind a door marked 'Games Room'. He stopped. He could hear a man's voice; an indistinct seductive bass. He then heard some feminine giggles. He was about to walk on when he heard the girl say 'No. Stop it. Come on now.' He listened again. She grew more insistent. 'Look. *Stop it*. Really. Come on, it's your serve.' She was still giggling but it seemed to Morgan that a worried tone had entered her voice. Then: '*Ow!* – Honestly, cut it out! No. Stop it, please.'

Morgan pushed open the door. The girl stood there in the hairy Lebanese's arms. He seemed to be biting her shoulder. As Morgan entered they broke apart and the girl, blushing, quickly readjusted the strap of her cream dress that had slipped down her arm. Morgan felt supremely foolish for the second time that day. He wasn't at all clear about what one was meant to say in situations like this. The girl smiled, he felt slightly reassured. She seemed pleased to see him and backed away from the Lebanese. He smiled too, white and gold teeth beneath his moustache.

'How you feel?' he asked Morgan confidently, tapping his stomach. 'The belly. Is good?'

They were standing in front of a ping-pong table. Morgan walked over to it and picked up a bat. He swished it menacingly about.

'My turn to serve, I think,' he said pointedly, in as clipped and cool a tone as he could summon. 'Why don't you push off, Abdul? Eh?'

The Lebanese looked at the girl, who earnestly studied her fingernails. He gave a snort of laughter and pushed past Morgan out of the room, saying something harsh and guttural in Arabic, as if he had a forest of fish bones stuck in his throat. An expressive language, Morgan admitted to himself, hugely relieved.

Morgan and the stewardess went to the bar and had a quiet mature laugh about it all. There had been no real problem the girl insisted, he was just getting a little fresh. Still, she was glad Morgan had walked in. They had a few drinks. The stewardess said her name was Jayne Darnley. She'd come down with a touch of upset tummy and had to be left behind when the last plane took off. Morgan bought some more drinks. She was wearing a loose satin dress and Morgan admired the roll of her heavy breasts beneath the bodice as she reached down into her bag for a menthol cigarette. They got on famously; Morgan even laughed about his ill-fated dive. 'It was terribly brave of you,' stated Jayne. She came, it transpired, from Tottenham and had worked on 'promotions' before becoming a stewardess. The whisky made Morgan feel virile and capable; he could smell the pungent scent she used and the click of the sentry's boots in the foyer lent a frisson of exotic danger to the atmosphere. He started to lie grandly. Yes, he admitted, he was leaving this country for a new posting: Paris. He was going to be Defence Attaché at the Paris embassy. 'Ooh Paree,' enthused Jayne. 'I *love* Paris.' And from there, Morgan confided, a spot of work at the UN perhaps. After that, who knows? Although his first loyalty had always been to the Service he'd always had a secret yearning for the cut and thrust of political life, and, with his experience, maybe . . . Morgan went on to conjure up a large, interesting and cultured family, a trendy public school, a starred first. He created a modest private income, a chic *pied-à-terre* in Chelsea; he fabricated costly hobbies and recondite enthusiasms, and spoke knowingly of half-

famous intellectuals, minor royalty, television show compères. As
the whisky and his rising sexual excitement fuelled his imagination so Jayne grew more entranced, edging forward on her chair,
lips set apart in a ready smile of anticipation. Her eyes gleamed;
what a good time she was having. Morgan concurred, and called
for another Pernod and blackcurrant.

At midnight, both a little unsteady on their feet, they walked
arm in arm up the pathway towards the residential blocks.
Crickets telephoned endlessly all around. The path bifurcated.
'Well,' Jayne sighed, raising her face to his. 'I go this way.'

Morgan was quite satisfied with their lovemaking. It hadn't
exactly made the earth move for him but Jayne had produced a
flattering tocsin of appreciative yips and mews as he had humped
away in the dark heat of the room. He lay back now, his chest
and belly heaving and thought how perhaps events had not
turned out so badly.

Jayne smoked a cigarette and whispered compliments to him.
Then she propped herself on one elbow and gazed down at his
face tracing its contours with a sharp red fingernail.

'I can't believe my luck,' she confided softly. 'To . . . well, to
meet you like this.' Her thin lips pecked at his face like a dabbing
fish. 'I'd just never have thought it possible. Someone like you.
You know?'

Morgan wasn't sure that he did, and for the first time he found
the ambiguity somewhat unsettling.

Jayne still maintained the same vein of ingenuous lyricism in the
morning before she returned to her own room. Strangely, and
against his better judgement, she elicited similar vague responses
from Morgan. He was half asleep and unused to finding a warm
naked woman in his bed on waking up. The associated sensations
of comfort and cosy eroticism were agreeably complementary.

They admitted that, yes, they both really liked each other; and it was funny how people like them – from such different backgrounds – got along so tremendously easily. It was almost, almost like fate really, wasn't it? What with her illness, his puncture and of course the coup. Didn't he think so? Jayne prompted, searching beneath the sheet. A squirming Morgan felt bound to agree, suggesting, almost before he realized what he was saying, that once this thing was over they really ought to see some more of each other. Miraculously, it seemed, Jayne had two weeks of leave coming up and nothing in particular planned for them. If Morgan had some time to spare before his Paris posting came through it would be fun to see each other in London. Of course, Morgan whispered, nuzzling her neck, of course.

But then Jayne was out of bed and swiftly into her cream dress, patting her face with powder and applying fresh lipstick. She kissed him on the cheek.

'See you downstairs,' she said. 'Let's go to the pool again.'

Alone, Morgan dressed slowly. Post-coital tristesse, not an ailment he was usually afflicted with, weighed heavy on him today. He moved like a man deep in thought, like a hasty investor who's just had the dubious ramifications of his latest deal explained. His early swaggering confidence, his locker-room bravado, his smug self-congratulations had mysteriously dissipated, leaving a querulous nagging tone of rebuke and stale second thoughts.

He walked distractedly into the hotel lobby, his mind preoccupied, and was surprised to find it full of the guests, their luggage and the same flustered BOAC official who had met him at the airport gates two days previously.

'Ah, Mr Leafy,' he said to Morgan. 'Here at last. You'll be glad to know that the airport has reopened, diplomatic relations have

been established, and you're flying out on,' he consulted his clip-
board, 'the third plane. 11.45 this morning. We're getting you all
along to the airport as quickly as possible as things are a bit
chaotic, to put it mildly. If you could report back to me here in
fifteen minutes?' He turned to answer a phone ringing on the
reception desk.

Jayne came up to Morgan. She was wearing a lurid print dress
and large round sunglasses.

'We're on the same plane,' she said. 'Isn't that a stroke of luck?
Don't worry, I'll see we get seats beside each other. I've a friend
at the airport.'

Morgan smiled wanly, muttered something about having to
pack, and returned to his room.

As he laid his clothes in his suitcase he felt unfamiliar symptoms
of panic sweep over him as if he was some inefficient refugee too
late to flee the advance of an invading army. He felt like a
crapulous sailor who's overstayed his shore leave, watching his
ship steam out of harbour. Things were moving far too quickly
he realized; he no longer felt in control. Suddenly they were
leaving for home and he found himself teamed up with this
Jayne, thinking of themselves as a couple, without really understanding how it had all come about. He felt mystified, bemused.
Who was this woman? Why was she making assumptions about
him, organizing his life?

The mini-bus that was to take them to the airport contained only
two of the Lebanese and Jayne, who had kept Morgan a seat. As
he settled in beside her, studiously avoiding the hostile looks of
the others, she squeezed his hand and smiled at him. Morgan felt
sick, queasy; like a man on a tossing ship who realizes he should
have refused those second helpings. God, he hadn't envisaged
anything like this at *all*, he reflected, as Jayne explained about her

friend at the airport. No, by Christ, it was getting terribly out of hand. Why had he lied so convincingly; as if he was short-listed for Foreign Secretary? Why hadn't he been callous and knowing, taken his pleasure like the chance acquaintances they were? Then he felt foolish and sad as he reasoned that it had only been the lies and false grandeur that had attracted the woman to him at all; and that without the fake glitter and borrowed glory, Morgan Leafy was of little consequence as a person, a minor district official leaving for a boring desk job in central London; and that without the stories and the make-believe he could have stared and lusted at the side of the pool or fantasized in the bar for days, and she would probably never have noticed he was there.

The low pre-fab shacks of the airport building heaved and pulsed with hot irate travellers like some immense festering yeast culture. Queues intertwined and doubled back on themselves before makeshift desks, where airline clerks mindlessly flipped through damp sheets of passenger manifests and ticket counter-foils in a futile attempt to match names to seats and parties to destinations. Beyond customs control gangs of green-suited porters hurled bags on to lorries and starched impassive military police forced everyone to hand over their local currency.

After a two-hour struggle Morgan and Jayne arrived in the departure lounge, their clothes mussed and sticky with perspiration, clutching handfuls of official departure forms and exchange control declarations to be filled out in triplicate. Normally the blatant inefficiency and wanton lack of automation fixed Morgan in a towering rage but today he was merely sullen and leaden-hearted. Jayne had clung to his arm throughout the obstacle course of the check-in and, dashing his last faint hope, had successfully arranged with her friend behind the desk for the two of them to have adjacent seats.

As she went up to the bar Morgan gazed blindly at the ancient photographs of long-out-of-commission aircraft and thought of the appalling chain of events the coup had unwittingly set in motion. He mentally compared his parents' semi-detached in Pinner, where he would be staying, with the Chelsea mews flat he had described to Jayne in such detail. He anguishedly contrasted his menial job off Whitehall in a grimy office block, with the post of Defence Attaché at the Paris embassy. He sighed in frustration as he considered how he had meekly accepted Jayne's invitation to meet her Mum and Dad the following Sunday. It was pathetic. He felt like weeping.

Jayne returned with two warm bottles of Fanta orange. 'All they had,' she explained. 'Come on, dear, move up. Make room for little me.'

Dear! Morgan's spirit finally collapsed. He felt he couldn't simply tell her to go away as he himself had so deliberately contrived to deceive her. Perhaps when she found out the truth she'd reject him. But he looked at the tight lips sucking on a straw, the shrewd eyes with their delta of discreet lines, the coruscating talons gripping the Fanta bottle and he thought no, Jayne was running out of time, and there wasn't much hope of that.

At eleven o'clock their plane was called and they assembled at the departure lounge door. None of the airport buses was functioning and they had to walk across the shimmering apron to the plane. Morgan plodded across the hot tarmac, his eyes on the heels of the couple in front of him. The sun beat down on his exposed head causing runnels of perspiration to drip from his brow. Jayne's hand was latched firmly in the crook of his elbow.

They paused at the foot of the steps. Morgan looked up. Stewardesses beamed at the entrance to the plane. He'd never trust those smiles again. He felt he was about to climb the gallows. He looked at Jayne. Her eyes were invisible behind the opaque lenses of her sunglasses. She squeezed his arm and smiled revealing patches of orange on her teeth that had smudged from her lips.

'Oh look,' she said, gesturing beyond Morgan's shoulder. 'Must be someone important. Bet he tries to barge the queue.'

Morgan turned and saw an olive green Mercedes driving across the tarmac from the airport buildings at some speed. A pennant cracked above the radiator grille. The car stopped and a young man got out. He held a piece of paper in his hand. He was tall and sunburnt and wore a well-pressed white tropical suit similar to the one Morgan had on. He was like the Platonic incarnation of everything Morgan had tried to create in his conversations with Jayne. And for Jayne, he was the misty image, the vague ideal of the man she fancied she had met in the airport hotel. They both stared uncomfortably at him for a brief moment then simultaneously turned away, for his presence made reality a little hard to bear.

The young man walked up the line of waiting passengers.

'Mr Leafy?' he called in a surprisingly high, piping voice. 'Is there a Mr Morgan Leafy here?'

At first, absurdly, Morgan didn't react to the sound of his own name. What could this vision want with him? Then he put up his hand like a schoolkid who's been asked to own up.

'Telex,' the young man said handing Morgan the piece of paper. 'I'm from the embassy here,' he added, 'frightfully sorry we didn't get to you before this. Hope it wasn't too bad in the hotel . . .' He went on, but Morgan was reading the telex.

'LEAFY,' he read, 'RETURN SOONEST NKONGSAM-BA. YOU ARE URGENTLY REQD. RE. LIAISING WITH NEW MILITARY GOVT. ALL CLEAR LONDON. CART-WRIGHT.'

Cartwright was the High Commissioner at Nkongsamba. Morgan looked at the young man. He couldn't speak, his throat was choked with emotion. He handed the telex to Jayne. She frowned with incomprehension.

'What does this mean?' she asked harshly, the poise cracking for an instant as Morgan stepped out of the queue.

'Duty calls, darling.' There seemed to be waves crashing and surging behind his ribcage. He felt dazed, abstracted from events. He waved his hands about meaninglessly, like a demented conductor. 'Absolutely nothing I can do.' He had reached the Mercedes, the young man held the back door open for him. The embarking passengers looked on curiously. He saw the Americans. 'Hey!' the woman shouted angrily, 'You're British!' He suppressed a whoop of gleeful laughter. 'Sorry, darling,' he called again to Jayne, 'I'll write, soon. I'll explain everything,' trying desperately to keep the elation from his voice. A final shrug of his shoulders and he ducked into the car. It was deliciously cool, the air-conditioning whirred softly.

'I'll come as far as the airport buildings,' the young man said deferentially. 'Then this'll take you straight back up the road to Nkongsamba if that's okay with you.'

'Oh that's fine,' said Morgan loosening his tie and waving to Jayne as the car moved off. 'Oh yes. That's absolutely fine.'

Long Story Short

Part One

Louella and I stood alone in the darkening garden. There was the first hint of autumn frost in the evening. The soft light from the drawing-room windows set shimmers glowing in her thick auburn hair. Louella hugged herself, crushing her full breasts with her forearms. I felt an almost physical pain of love and desire in my gut.

'I think they're lovely,' she said, turning to face the house.

'So do I . . . oh, you mean Ma and Pa?'

'Of course. I'm so glad I've met them.'

'They like you too, you know, very much.' I moved beside her and put my arms round her slim waist. I rested my forehead on hers. 'I like you too,' I said whimsically. She laughed, showing her pale throat, and we hugged each other. I stared past her at the trees and bushes slowly relinquishing their forms to the night. Then I felt her posture change slightly.

'Well, hello little brother,' came a deep, sardonic voice. 'What have we got here?'

It was Gareth. And somehow I knew everything would be spoilt.

★　　★　　★

Actually it wasn't Gareth at all. It was Frank. God I'm tired of this relentless artifice. Let's start again, shall we?

Part Two

Louella and William stood alone in the darkening garden. There was the first hint of autumn frost in the evening . . . drawing-room windows, yes, . . . crushing her full breasts etc., . . . almost physical pain and so on.

'I don't see why you're so upset,' Louella said. 'I mean, he is your brother. If I'm going to be one of the family I might as well meet him.'

'But he's such a shit. A fat smarmy shit and a mean little sod to boot. I know you won't like him. He's just not our type,' William said petulantly, conscious of the fact that he was only stimulating Louella's interest.

They heard the sound of a car in the drive. William felt his throat tighten. Louella tried to appear nonchalant – with only partial success.

Frank opened the drawing-room windows and sauntered into the garden to join them. He was wearing a maroon cord suit with unfashionably flared trousers and a yellow nylon shirt. A heavy gold ingot swung at his throat. His once even features, William noticed, had become thickened and distorted with fat. He was almost completely bald now.

No, it's no good. It keeps getting in the way, this dreadful compulsion to tell lies (you write fiction and what are you doing? You're telling lies, pal, that's all). And besides, it's very unfair to Frank, who was very good-looking, exceptionally well-dressed and had as thick and glossy a head of hair as Louella in part one. Louella – the real Louella – in fact had dyed blonde hair, but I've always had a hankering for auburn. (Come to that she doesn't have full breasts either.)

To get rid of the fiction element perhaps I should begin by distinguishing myself from the 'I' in part one. I – now – am the author (you know my name – check it out). The 'I' in part one is fictional, *not* me. Neither is the 'William' in part two. It's just a device. No doubt, in any case, you thought to yourself 'hold on a second', as you read part two. 'Little bit odd this,' you probably thought, 'character's got the same name as the author. Something fishy here.' But you must watch out for that sort of thing, it's an error readers are prone to fall into. There are a lot of Williams about. Lots. It doesn't need to be me.

But now, having got rid of all this obfuscation, I am speaking to you directly. The author talking to the reader – whoever you are. Imagine me as a voice in your ear, unmediated by any notions or theories you may have heard about books and stories, textuality and reading, that sort of thing. I was, as it so happens, in actual fact, really engaged to a girl called Louella once, and I did have a brother called Frank. And certain factual events to do with the three of us inspired, were at the back of, the two beginnings I attempted. Louella was an American girl. I'd met her in New York, fallen in love, got engaged and had brought her back to England to meet my parents. She also met Frank.

Frank. Frank was the sort of older brother nobody needs. Tall, socially at ease, rich, good job (journalist on an up-market Sunday). Very attractive too. He had a polished superficial charm which, to my surprise, managed to take in one hell of a lot of people. But he was a smug self-satisfied bastard and we never really liked each other. He always needed to feel superior to me.

'Pleased to meet you,' Frank said to Louella, holding on to her hand far longer than William thought necessary.

'Hi,' said Louella. 'William's told me so much about you.'

Frank laughed. 'Listen,' he said. 'You don't want to believe anything he says.'

He didn't say that, in fact. But it's typical of the sort of thing I can imagine him saying. Anyway I only did that just to show you how easy it is – and how diffcrent. I can make Frank bald, add four inches to Louella's bust, supply William with a flat in Belgravia. But it's not going to solve anything. Because – to cut a long story short (quite a good title, yes?) – I really did love Louella (we'll still call her that, if you don't mind – saves possible embarrassment). I wanted to marry her. And that bastard Frank steadily and deliberately took her away from me.

At the time we were staying with my parents. We hadn't fixed a date for the wedding as we were waiting until we had a house first. However, plans were being made, Louella's mother was going to fly over, a guest list was being drawn up. Frank was very subtle. He contented himself with being incredibly *nice*. He was around a lot and spent a great deal of time with Louella – just chatting. I was away in London (my parents live near Witney, Oxfordshire) trying to get a job. I can still remember – quite vividly – sitting on the London train, rigid with a kind of frustrated rage. I knew exactly what was happening. I could sense Louella's increasing fascination with Frank, but there was nothing I could do about it, no accusation I could level, without being accused in turn of chronic paranoia. Nothing physical had happened between Louella and Frank, yet in a way she was more intimate with him than she'd ever been with me.

I couldn't stand it any longer. The house seemed to brim with their complicity. I felt pinioned by their innuendoes, webbed in by their covert glances. It was impossible. Yet the whole relationship was occurring at such a subliminal, cerebral level that any apportioning of blame on my part would look like an act of near insanity. So I went away. I said I had to be in London for an entire week job-hunting and having interviews. I entrusted Louella to my parents' care, but I knew Frank wouldn't be far away.

I took up an uncomfortable post in the wood behind my parents' house armed with a pair of powerful binoculars and watched the comings and goings. I saw Frank arrive the next day, homing in unerringly. Saw them walk in the garden, go out for drives. Saw Frank take my place at the family dinner table pouring wine, recounting anecdotes that I should have been telling.

In fact William hated Frank with all the energy he could summon. Hated his lean, permanently tanned face, his fake self-deprecating smile. Despised his short fingernails, his modishly scruffy clothes. Loathed his intimate knowledge of current affairs, his casual travelogues. And he ached when Louella touched his arm in admiring disbelief as Official Secrets were dropped, off-the-record confidences disclosed. Suffered when she showed her pale pulsing throat as she laughed at his smart in-jokes.

Sorry. Sorry. It's a lapse, I know. I promised. But fiction is so safe, so easy to hide behind. It won't happen again.

It was a Sunday afternoon when I became really alarmed. My vigil in the wood had lasted three days (sleeping in my car: extremely uncomfortable) and I was beginning to wonder if I'd overdramatized things rather. Mother and Father had gone out on some interminable Sunday ramble in the car (I sense that I haven't really done my parents justice – not that they're all that interesting really – but they play no significant part in the following events). Then Frank came round in his car – a Triumph Stag: pure Frank, that. There was some activity in the house. Frank appeared briefly in the sitting room with two suitcases. I scampered through the garden and peered around the corner of the house. Frank was rearranging luggage in the boot. I saw him take out a fishing rod and repack it. Then Louella appeared, she seemed quite calm. She said,

'Have you left a note for them?'

Frank: 'Yes, on the hall table.'

Louella: 'What about William?'

Frank: 'Oh don't worry about him. Ma and Pa will break the news.'

Reader, imagine how I felt.

They drove off. I knew where they were going. I went inside and read the note Frank had written to my parents. It went something like this.

> Louella and I have gone away for a few days. We have fallen very much in love and want to think things over. Please break this to William as gently as possible. Back sometime next week. Love Frank.

The family have a small cottage on the west coast of Scotland. We have spent many summers there. I knew that was where Frank was heading. The fishing rod gave it away. Fly fishing is his great 'passion'. He thinks it somehow both intellectual – respectable literature on the sport – and gentlemanly – Alec Douglas Home and the Queen Mother do it. I filled my car up with petrol and went to London. There I dropped in on a few friends and made some calls. Then, that night, I followed them north.

The family cottage – more of a house to be honest – lies off the main road near the village of A —. (Funny how this is meant to make it more realistic. It seems so obvious. Why not give the name? It's Achranich, not far from Oban. I'm not interested in misleading you.) Behind the house is one of those typical Scottish hills, khaki green, shaded with brown and purple, covered in a thick, moss-sprung grass. An energetic hike over this and you find one of the best stretches of Highland salmon-river in Scotland. That was why Frank brought his fishing rod. He can never resist it.

Picture the scene. Me huddling chilled in a damp clump of bracken, exhausted after an overnight drive. Waiting for Frank to appear. And, sure enough, he does, after a late breakfast (porridge, kippers, toast and marmalade. That's just a guess. How could I know what he'd had for breakfast?). He looks disgustingly pleased with himself as he strides up the hill with his rod and his bags and his tackle, passing – oh – within thirty yards of my hiding place. I keep still. After all, I know where he's going.

Thirty minutes later I catch up with him. He's at the big pool. The river hurtles and elbows its way down the hillside. It's the colour of unmilked tea and is shallow with a bed of rounded pebbles and stones. Except at one point. Here there is a cascade that froths into a large, deep, chill pool. A great angled slab of rock juts out into the pool setting up eddies and deflecting currents. Beneath this the fish lurk. Stand on the lip of the cascade (thigh waders obligatory) leaning back against the nudge and pressure of the water, cast down into the pool below the rock and you can't go wrong. Frank was positioned exactly so. Two small creaming waves where his green rubber waders broke the solid parabola of the falling water.

I enter the stream twenty yards above and slosh down. Frank can't hear me because of the noise of the falling water. I stand behind him. I tap his shoulder. He looks round. His eyes widen in wordless surprise. He instinctively jerks back as though expecting a blow. It is enough. He loses his balance and with a despairing, grabbing whirl of arms is flipped over the edge into the pool. I don't even wait to see what happens. Waders filled with water, heavy clothes sodden, freezing water. He'd go down like . . . like a stone.

I was in London by late evening. I was summoned home by a phone call just before lunch the next day. Dreadful news. I have to take the twin blows of my fiancée's infidelity and my brother's accidental death. My parents are grim and unforgiving; they think Louella is in some way responsible. I am shocked and stunned. But poor Louella. She has to turn somewhere. I am deeply hurt, but relent under the shared burden of grief. We go for drives and talk and, to cut a long story short, we . . .

But I've lost you, haven't I? Where was it? That bit about me hiding in the wood? Or setting up my alibi and following them to Scotland? It wasn't a question of continuing to suspend disbelief, but rather the belief beginning to crumble away of its own accord. You were saying: if he wants us to believe him, if he wants us to think we're reading something true, then surely confessing to a murder in cold print is, well, a bit implausible?

You're right of course. I got carried away. Fiction took over once again. Anyway, I could never do a thing like that, could I?

PS:

Frank and 'Louella', wherever you are, if you should happen to read this – no hard feelings? It's just a joke.

The Destiny of Nathalie 'X'

MAN'S VOICE (OVER)

I once heard a theory about this
town, this place where we work
and wrangle, where we swindle and
swive. It was told to me by this
writer I knew. He said: 'It's only a
dance, but then again, it's the *only*
dance.' I'm not so sure he's right but,
anyway, he's dead now . . .

FADE UP

Once upon a time – actually, not so very long ago at all, come to
think of it – in east central West Africa, on one enervating May
morning Aurélien No sat on the stoop of his father's house
staring aimlessly at the road that led to Murkina Leto, state capital
of the People's Republic of Kiq. The sun's force seemed to press
upon the brown dusty landscape with redundant intensity,
Aurélien thought idly, there was surely no moisture left out
there to evaporate and it seemed . . . He searched for a word for

a second or two: it seemed 'stupid' that all that calorific energy should go to waste.

He called for his little brother Marius to fetch him another beer but no reply came from inside the house. He scratched his cheek; he thought he could taste metal in his mouth – that new filling. He shifted his weight on his cane chair and wondered vaguely why cane made that curious squeaking sound. Then his eye was caught by the sight of a small blue van that was making its way up the middle of the road with what seemed like undue celerity, tooting its horn at the occasional roadside pedestrian and browsing cow not so much to scare them out of the way as to announce the importance of this errand it was on.

To Aurélien's mild astonishment the blue van turned abruptly into his father's driveway and stopped equally abruptly before the front door. As the laterite dust thrown up by the tyres slowly dispersed the postman emerged from the auburn cloud like a messenger from the gods carrying before him a stiff envelope blazoned with an important-looking crest.

Marius No For sure, I remember that day when he won the prize. Personally, I was glad of the distraction. He had been emmerding me all morning. 'Get this', 'Get that', 'Fetch me a beer'. I just knew it had gone quiet for ten minutes. When I came out on to the stoop he was sitting there, looking even more vacant than normal, just staring at this paper in his hands. 'Hey, Coco,' I said to him. 'Military service, mm? Poor *salaud*. Wait till those bastard sergeants give you one up the *cul*.' He said nothing, so I took the paper from his hands and read it. It was the hundred thousand francs that had shocked him, struck him dumb.

When *Le Destin de Nathalie 'X'* (*metteur en scène* Aurélien No) won the Prix d'Or at the *concours général* in Paris of *L'Ecole*

Supérieur des Etudes Cinématographiques (ESEC), the Kiq Minister of Culture (Aurélien's brother-in-law) laid on a reception for two hundred guests at the Ministry. After a long speech the Minister called Aurélien on to the podium to shake him publicly by the hand. Aurélien had gathered his small tight dreadlocks into a loose sheaf on the top of his head and the photographs of that special evening show him startled and blinking in the silvery wash of the flash bulbs, some natural flinch causing the fronds of his dreadlock sheaf to toss simultaneously in one direction as if blown by a stiff breeze.

The Minister asked him what he planned to do with the prize money.

'Good question,' Aurélien said and thought for ten seconds or so before replying. 'It's a condition of the prize that I put the money towards another film.'

'Here in Kiq?' the Minister said, smiling knowingly.

'Of course.'

Delphine Drelle 'It's impossible,' I said when he called me. 'Completely out of the question. Are you mad? What kind of film could you make in Kiq?' He came to my apartment in Paris, he said he wanted me to be in his new film. I say I don't want to be an actress. Well, as soon as I started explaining Aurélien saw I was making sense. That's what I like about Aurélien, by the way, he is responsive to the powers of reason. Absolutely not, I said to Aurélien, never in my life. He said he had an idea, but only I could do it. I said, Look what happened the last time, do you think I'm crazy? I've only been out of the clinic one month. He just smile at me. He said, What do you think if we go to Hollywood?

Aurélien No turned out of the rental park at LAX and wondered which direction to take. Delphine Drelle sat beside him studying her face intently in the mirror of her compact and moaning about the dehydrating effect of international air travel. In the back seat of the car sat Bertrand Holbish, a photographer, and ex-boyfriend of Delphine, squashed in the cramped space left by the two large scratched and dented silver aluminium boxes that held the camera and the sound equipment.

Aurélien turned left, drove four hundred metres and turned left again. He saw a sign directing him to the freeway and followed it until he reached a hotel. DOLLARWIZE INN, he saw it was called as he pulled carefully into the forecourt. The hotel was a six-storey rectangle. The orange plastic cladding on the balconies had been bleached salmon pink by the sun.

'Here we are,' Aurélien said. 'This is perfect.'

'Where's Hollywood?' Bertrand Holbish asked.

'Can't be far away,' Aurélien said.

Bertrand Holbish Immediately, when he asked me, I said to Aurélien that I didn't know much about sound. He said, You switch it on, you point the volume. No, you check the volume and you point the, ah, what's the word? . . . What? Ah, yes, 'boom'. I said, You pay my ticket? You buy me drugs? He said, Of course, only don't touch Delphine. [Laughs, coughs.] That's Aurélien for you, one crazy guy.

Delphine Drelle Did I tell you that he is a very attractive man, Aurélien? Yes? He's a real African, you know, strong face, strong African face . . . and his lips, they're like they're carved. He's tall, slim. He has this hair, it's like that tennis player, Noah, like little braids hanging down over his forehead. Sometimes he puts beads on the end of them. I don't like it so much. I want him to shave his head. Completely. He speaks real good English, Aurélien. I never knew this about him. I ask him once how he pronounced his name and he said something like 'Ngoh'. He says it is a common name in Kiq. But everybody pronounces it differently. He doesn't mind.

When Aurélien went out the next day to scout for locations he discovered that the area they were staying in was called West-chester. He drove through the featureless streets – unusually wide, he thought, for such an inactive neighbourhood – the air charged and thunderous with landing jetliners, until he found a small cluster of shops beneath a revolving sign declaiming 'Brogan's Mini-Mall'. There was a deli, a pharmacy, a novelty store, a Korean grocery and a pizzeria-cum-coffee shop that had most of the features he was looking for: half a dozen tables on the sidewalk, a predominantly male staff, a licence to sell alcoholic beverages. He went inside, ordered a *cappuccino*, and asked how long they stayed open in the evenings. Late, came the answer. For the first time since he had suggested coming to Los Angeles Aurélien sensed a small tremor of excitement. Perhaps it would be possible after all. He looked at the expressionless tawny faces of the men behind the counter and the cheerful youths serving food and drink. He felt sure these gentlemen would allow him to film in their establishment – for a modest fee, of course.

Michael Scott Gehn Have you ever seen *Le Destin de Nathalie 'X'*? Extraordinary film, extraordinary. No, I tell you, I'd put it right up there with *Un Chien Andalou*, Todd's *Last Walk, Chelsea Girls*, Downey's *Chafed Elbows*. That category of film. Surreal, bizarre . . . Let's not beat about the bush, sometimes downright incomprehensible, but it gets to you. Somehow, subcutaneously. You know, I spend more time thinking about certain scenes in *Nathalie 'X'* than I do about Warner's annual slate. And it's my business, what more can I say? Do you smoke? Do you have any non-violent objections if I do? Thank you, you're very gracious. I'm not kidding, you can't be too careful here. *Nathalie 'X'* . . . OK. It's very simple and outstandingly clever. A girl wakes up in her bed in her room –

Aurélien looked at his map. Delphine and Bertrand stood at his shoulder, sunglassed, fractious.

'We have to go from here . . . to here.'

'Aurélien, when are we going to film?'

'Tomorrow. Maybe. First we walk it through.'

Delphine let her shoulders slump. 'But we have the stock. Why don't we start?'

'I don't know. I need an idea. Let's walk it through.'

He took Bertrand's elbow and guided him across the road to the other side. He made an oblong with his thumbs and his forefingers and framed Delphine in it as she lounged against the Exit sign of the Dollarwize Inn.

'Turn right,' Aurélien shouted across the road. 'I'll tell you which way to go.'

Michael Scott Gehn – a girl wakes up in her own bed in her own room, somewhere in Paris. She gets out of bed and puts on her make-up, very slowly, very deliberately. No score, just the noises she makes, as she goes about her business. You know, paints her nails, mascara on eyelashes. She hums a bit, she starts to sing a song to herself, snatches of a song in English. Beatles song, from the 'White Album', what's it called? Oh yeah, 'Rocky Raccoon'. This girl's French, right, and she's singing in English with a French accent, just quietly to herself. The song sounds totally different. Totally. Extraordinary effect. Bodywide goose-bumps. This takes about twenty, thirty minutes. You are completely, but *completely*, held. You do not notice the time passing.

That something so totally – let's not beat about the bush – banal can hold you that way. Extraordinary. We're talking mundanity, here, absolute diurnal minutiae. I see, what, two hundred and fifty movies a year in my business, not counting TV. I am replete with film. Sated. But I am held. No, mesmerized would be fair. (Pause.) Did I tell you the girl was naked?

'Turn left,' Aurélien called.

Delphine obliged and walked past the mirror-glass façade of an office building.

'Stop.'

Aurélien made a note on the map and turned to Bertrand.

'What could she do here, Bertrand? She needs to do something.'

'I don't know. How should I know?'

'Something makes her stop.'

'She could step in some dog shit.'

Aurélien reflected for a while. He looked around him: at the cracked parched concrete of the street, the dusty burnish on the few parked cars. There was a bleached, fumy quality to the light that day, a softened glare that hurt the eyes. The air reverberated as another jumbo hauled itself out of LAX.

'Not a bad idea,' he said. 'Thanks, Bertrand.' He called to Delphine. 'OK, go up to the end of the road and turn left.'

Michael Scott Gehn I've written a lot about this movie, analysed the hell out of it, the way it's shot, the way it manipulates mood, but it only struck me the other day how it works. Essentially, basically. It's all in the title, you see. '*Le Destin*'. *The Destiny of Nathalie 'X'*. Destiny. What does destiny have in store for this girl, I should say, this astoundingly attractive girl? She gets up, she puts on her make-up, she sings a song, she gets dressed. She leaves her apartment building and walks through the streets of Paris to a café. It's night-time. She sits in this café and orders a beer. We're watching her, we're waiting. She drinks more beers, she seems to be getting drunk. People come and go. We wait. We wonder: What is the destiny of Nathalie 'X'? (It's pronounced 'eeeks' in French. Not 'ecks', 'eeeks'.) And then? But I don't want to spoil the movie for you.

They started filming on their sixth day in Los Angeles. It was late afternoon – almost magic hour – and the orange sun basted the city in a thick viscous light. Aurélien shot the sequence of the walk in front of the mirror-glass building. The moving clouds-cape on the mirror-glass curtain wall was disturbingly beautiful. Aurélien had a moment's regret that he was filming in black and white.

Delphine wore a short black skirt and a loose, V-neck taupe cashmere sweater (no bra). On her feet she wore skin-coloured kid loafers, so fine you could roll them into a ball. She had a fringed suede bag over her shoulder. Her long hair was dyed a light sandy blonde and – after much debate – was down.

Aurélien set up the camera across the road for the first take. Bertrand stood beside him and pointed his microphone in the general direction of Delphine.

Aurélien switched on the camera, chalked 'Scene One' on the clapperboard, walked into frame, clicked it and said, '*Vas-y, Delphine.*'

Nathalie 'X' walked along the sidewalk. When she reached the middle of the mirror-glass wall she stopped. She took off one of her shoes and peeled the coin of chewing-gum from its sole. She stuck the gum to the glass wall, refitted her shoe and walked on.

Michael Scott Gehn I have to say, as a gesture of contempt for Western materialism, the capitalist macrostructure that we function in, that takes some beating. And it's not in the French version. Aurélien No has been six days in Los Angeles and he comes up with something as succinct, as moodily epiphanic, as that. That's what I call talent. Not raw talent, talent of the highest sophistication.

Bertrand Holbish The way Delphine cut her hair, you know, is the clue, I think. It's blonde, right? Long and she has a fringe, OK? But not like anybody else's fringe. It's just too long. It hangs to her lower eyelash. To here [gestures], to the middle of her nose. So she shakes her head all the time to clear her vision a little. She pulls it aside – like this – with one finger when she wants to see something a little better . . . You know, many many people look at Delphine and find this very exciting, sexually, I mean. She's a pretty girl, for sure, nice body, nice face. But I see these girls everywhere. Especially in Los Angeles. It's something about this fringe business that makes her different. People look at her all the time. When we were waiting for Aurélien we – Delphine and me – used to play backgammon. For hours. The fringe, hanging there, over her eyes. It drove me fucking crazy. I offered her five hundred dollars to cut it one centimetre, just one centimetre. She refused. She knew, Delphine, she knew.

Aurélien filmed the walk to the café first. It took four days, starting late afternoon, always approaching the café at dusk. He filmed Nathalie's *levée* in one sustained twelve-hour burst. Delphine woke, made up, sang and dressed eight times that day in a series of long takes, cuts only coming when the film ran out. The song changed: Delphine sang Bob Dylan's 'She Belongs to Me' with the pronoun changed to 'He'. This was Delphine's idea, and a good one Aurélien thought; the only problem was she kept forgetting. 'He's an artist, she don't look back,' Delphine sang in her flat breathy voice as she combed her hair, 'He never stumbles, she's got no place to fall.'

Every evening they would go to the pizzeria and eat. Aurélien insisted that Delphine get drunk, not knee-walking drunk, but as far as woozy inebriation. Of course the waiters came to know them and conversation ensued. 'What you guys doin' here anyway? Making a movie? Great. Another beer for the lady? No problemo.'

After a week's regular visiting Aurélien asked the owner, a small nervy man called George Malinverno, if they could film at the pizzeria, outside on the 'terrace', for one night only. They agreed on a remuneration of two hundred dollars.

Michael Scott Gehn Have you ever heard of the Topeka Film Festival? That's Topeka, Kansas? No? Neither have I. So you can understand that I was kind of pissed when my editor assigned me to cover it. It ran a week, the theme was 'Kansas in the Western 1970–1980'. It's not my subject, my last book was on Murnau, for Christ's sake, but let's not get embroiled in office politics. The point is I'm on my way to the airport and I realize I've left my razor and shaving foam behind. I pull into this mini-mall where there's a drugstore. I'm coming out of the shop and I see there's a film crew setting up a shot at the pizzeria. Normally I see a film crew and chronic catatonia sets in. But there's something about this one: the guy holding the boom mike looks like he's stoned – even I can see that it keeps dropping into shot. So I wander over. The camera is set up behind these plants, kind of poking through a gap, like it's hidden or something. And there's this black guy behind the camera with this great hair with beads on it. I see he's D.P. and clapperboy and director. He calls out into the darkness and this sensational-looking girl walks into the pizzeria terrace thing. She sits down and orders a beer and they just keep filming. After about two minutes the sound man drops the boom and they have to start over. I hear them talking – French. I couldn't believe it. I had this guy figured for some wannabe homeboy director out of South Central LA. But they're talking French to each other. When was the last time a French crew shot a movie in this town? I introduced myself and that's when he told me about *Nathalie 'X'* and the Prix d'Or. I bought them all some drinks and he told me his story and gave me a video cassette of the movie. Fuck Topeka, I thought, I knew this was too good to miss. French underground movies shooting next door to LAX. Are you kidding me? They were all staying in some fleabag hotel under the flightpath, for God's sake. I called my editor and threatened to take the feature to *American Film*. He reassigned me.

The night's shooting at the pizzeria did not go well. Bertrand proved incapable of holding the boom aloft for more than two minutes and this was one sequence where Aurélien knew he needed sound. He spent half an hour taping a mike under Delphine's table and snaking the wires round behind the potted plants. Then this man who said he was a film critic turned up and offered to buy them a drink. While Aurélien was talking to him Delphine drank three margaritas and a Negroni. When they tried to restart, her reflexes had slowed to such an extent that when she remembered she had to throw the glass of beer the waiter had turned away and she missed completely. Aurélien wrapped it up for the night. Holbish wandered off and Aurélien drove Delphine back to the hotel. She was sick in the parking lot and started to cry and that's when Aurélien thought about the gun.

Kaiser Prevost I rarely read *film/e*. It's way too pretentious. Ditto that creep Michael Scott Gehn. Any guy with three names and I get irrationally angry. What's wrong with plain old Michael Gehn? Are there so many Michael Gehns out there that he has to distinguish himself? 'Oh, you mean Michael *Scott* Gehn, I got you now.' I'd like a Teacher's, straight up, with three ice cubes. Three. Thank you. Anyway for some reason I bought it that week – it was the issue with that great shot of Jessica, no, Lanier on the cover – and I read the piece about this French director Aurélien No and this remake *Seeing Through Nathalie* he was shooting in town. Gehn – sorry, Michael Scott Gehn – is going on like this guy is sitting there holding God's hand and I read about the Prix d'Or and this *Nathalie 'X'* film and I think, hmmm, has Aurélien got representation? This is Haig. This is not Teacher's.

Michael Scott Gehn I knew, I just knew when this young guy Kaiser Prevost calls me up, things would change. 'Hi, Michael,' he says, 'Kaiser Prevost here.' I don't know jack shit about any Kaiser Prevost but I do know I hate it when someone uses my Christian name from the get-go – what's wrong with Mr Gehn? Also his tone just assumes, just oozes the assumption, that I'm going to know who he is. I mean, I am a film critic of some reputation, if I may be immodest for a moment, and these young guys in the agencies . . . There's a problem of perspectives, that's what it comes down to, that's what bedevils us. I have a theory about this town: there is no overview, nobody steps back, no one stands on the mountain looking down on the valley. Imagine an army composed entirely of officers. Let me put it another way: imagine an army where everyone *thinks* they're an officer. That's Hollywood, that's the film business. No one wants to accept the hierarchy, no one will admit they are a foot soldier. And I'm sorry, a young agent in a boutique agency is just a GI Joe to me. Still, he was a persuasive fellow and he had some astute and flattering things to say about the article. I told him where Aurélien was staying.

Aurélien No met Kaiser Prevost for breakfast in the coffee shop of the Dollarwize. Prevost looked around him as if he had just emerged from some prolonged comatose sleep.

'You know, I've lived in this town for all my life and I don't think I've ever even driven through here. And as for shooting a movie . . . . It's a first.'

'Well, it was right for me.'

'Oh no. I appreciate that. I think it's fresh, original. Gehn certainly thinks a lot of you.'

'Who?'

Prevost showed him the article in *film/e*. Aurélien flicked through it. 'He has written a lot.'

'Have you got a rough assembly of the new movie? Anything I could see?'

'No.'

'Any dailies? Maybe you call them rushes.'

'There are no dailies on this film. None of us see anything until it is finished.'

'The ultimate *auteur*, huh? That is impressive. More than that it's cool.'

Aurélien chuckled. 'No, it's a question of – what do you say? – *faute de mieux*.'

'I couldn't have put it better myself. Look, Aurélien, I'd like you to meet somebody, a friend of mine at a studio. Can I fix that up? I think it would be mutually beneficial.'

'Sure. If you like.'

Kaiser Prevost I have a theory about this town, this place, about the way it works: it operates best when people go beyond the bounds of acceptable behaviour. You reach a position, a course of action suggests itself, and you say, 'This makes me morally uncomfortable,' or 'This will constitute a betrayal of friendship.' In any other walk of life you withdraw, you rethink. But my theory instead goes like this: make it your working maxim. *When you find yourself in a position of normative doubt then that is the sign to commit.* My variation on this theory is that the really successful people go one step further. They find themselves in this moral grey area, they move right on into the black. Look at Vincent Bandine.

I knew I was doing the right thing with Aurélien No because I had determined not to tell my boss. Sheldon started ArtFocus after ten years at ICM. It was going well but it's clear that the foundations are giving. Two months ago we lost Larry Swiftsure. Last Saturday I get a call from Sheldon: Donata Vail has walked to CAA. His own Donata. He was weeping and was looking for consolation, which I hope I provided. Under these circumstances it seemed to me at best morally dubious that I should go behind his back and try and set up a deal for Aurélien at Alcazar. I was confident it was the only route to take.

The gun idea persisted, it nagged at Aurélien. He talked about it with Bertrand, who thought it was an amusing notion.

'A gun, why not? Pam-pam-pam-pam.'

'Could you get me one? A hand-gun?' Aurélien asked. 'Maybe one of those guys you know . . .'

'A prop gun? Or a real one?'

'Oh, I think it should be real. Don't tell Delphine, though.'

The next day Bertrand showed Aurélien a small scarred

automatic. It cost five hundred dollars. Aurélien did not question him about its provenance.

He reshot the end of Nathalie's *levée*. Nathalie, dressed, is about to leave her room, her hand is on the doorknob. She pauses, turns and goes to a dresser, from the top drawer of which she removes the gun. She checks the clip and places it in her fringed suede shoulder bag. She leaves.

He and Delphine had a prolonged debate about whether they should reshoot the entire walk to the restaurant. Delphine thought it was pointless. How, she argued, would the audience know if the gun were in her shoulder bag or not? But *you* would know, Aurélien countered, and everything might change. Delphine maintained that she would walk the same way whether she had a gun in her bag or not; also they had been in Los Angeles for three weeks and she was growing bored; *Le Destin* had been filmed in five days. A compromise was agreed: they would only reshoot the pizzeria sequence. Aurélien went off to negotiate another night's filming.

Bob Berger I hate to admit it but I was grateful to Kaiser Prevost when he brought the *Nathalie 'X'* project to me. As I told him, I had admired Aurélien No's work for some years and was excited and honoured at the possibility of setting up his first English-language film. More to the point the last two films I exec-ed at Alcazar had done me no favours: *Disintegrator* had only grossed thirteen before they stopped tracking and *Sophomore Nite II* had gone straight to video. I liked the idea of doing something with more art quality and with a European kind of angle. I asked Kaiser to get a script to me soonest and I raised the project at our Monday morning staff meeting. I said I thought it would be a perfect vehicle for Lanier Cross. Boy, did that make Vincent sit up. Dirty old toad (he's my uncle).

Kaiser Prevost I'll tell you one fact about Vincent Bandine. He has the cleanest teeth and the healthiest gums in Holly- wood. Every morning a dental nurse comes to his house and flosses and cleans his teeth for him. Every morning, 365 days a year. That's what I call class. Have you any idea how much that must cost?

Kaiser Prevost thought he detected an unsettled quality about Aurélien as he drove him to the meeting at Alcazar. Aurélien was frowning as he looked about him. The day was perfect, the air clear, the colours ideally bright; more than that he was going to a deal meeting at a major minor studio, or minor major depending on who you were talking to. Usually in these cases the anticipa- tion in the car would be heady, palpable. Aurélien just made clicking noises in his mouth and fiddled with the beads on the end of his dreadlocks. Prevost told him about Alcazar Films, their money base, their ten-picture slate, their deals or potential deals with Goldie, Franklin Dean, Joel, Demi, Carlo Sancarlo and ItalFilm. The names seemed to make no impact.

As they turned up Coldwater to go over into the valley Prevost finally had to ask if everything was all right.

'There's a slight problem,' Aurélien admitted. 'Delphine has left.'

'That's too bad,' Prevost said, trying to keep the excitement out of his voice. 'Gone back to France?'

'I don't know. She's left with Bertrand.'

'Bitch, man.'

'We still have the whole last scene to reshoot.'

'Listen, Aurélien, relax. One thing you learn about working in this town. Everything can be fixed. Everything.'

'How can I finish without Delphine?'

'Have you ever heard of Lanier Cross?'

Vincent Bandine My nephew has two sterling qualities: he's dumb and he's eager to please. He's a good-looking kid too and that helps, no doubt about it. Sometimes, sometimes, he gets it right. Sometimes he has a sense for the popular mood. When he started talking about this *Destiny of Nathalie* film I thought he was way out of his depth until he mentioned the fact that Lanier Cross would be buck naked for the first thirty minutes. I said, Get the French guy in, tie him up, get him together with Lanier. She'll go for that. She'll go for the French part. If the No fellow won't play get the Englishman in, what's his name, Tim Pascal, he'll do it. He'll do anything I tell him.

I have a theory about this town: there's too much respect for art. That's where we make all our mistakes, all of them. But if that's a given then I'm prepared to work with it once in a while. Especially if it'll get me Lanier Cross nekkid.

Michael Scott Gehn When I heard that Aurélien No was doing a deal with Vincent Bandine at Alcazar I was both suicidal and oddly proud. If you'd asked me where was the worst home possible for a remake of *Nathalie 'X'* I'd have said Alcazar straight off. But that's what heartens me about this burg, this place we fret and fight in. I have a theory about this town: they all talk about the 'business', the 'industry', how hard-nosed and bottom-line obsessed they are but it's not true. Or, rather, not the whole truth. Films of worth are made and I respect the place for it. God, I even respected Vincent Bandine for it and I never thought those words would ever issue from my mouth. We shouldn't say: look at all the crap that gets churned out; instead we should be amazed at the good films that do emerge from time to time. There is a heart here and it's still beating even though the pulse is kind of thready.

★   ★   ★

Aurélien was impressed with the brutal economy of Bob Berger's office. A black ebony desk sat in the middle of a charcoal-grey carpet. Two large black leather sofas were separated by a thick sheet of glass resting on three sharp cones. On one wall were two black-and-white photographs of lily trumpets and on another was an African mask. There was no evidence of work or the tools of work apart from the long flattened telephone on his desk. Berger himself was wearing crushed banana linen; he was in his mid twenties, tall and deeply tanned.

Berger shook Aurélien's hand warmly, his left hand gripping Aurélien's forearm firmly as if he were a drowning man about to be hauled from a watery grave. He drew Aurélien to one of the leather sofas and sat him upon it. Prevost slid down beside him. A great variety of drinks was offered though Aurélien's choice of beer caused some consternation. Berger's assistant was despatched in search of one. Prevost and Berger's decaff espressos arrived promptly.

Prevost gestured at the mask. 'Home sweet home, eh, Aurélien?'

'Excuse me?'

'I love African art,' Berger said. 'What part of Africa are you from?'

'Kiq.'

'Right,' Berger said.

There was a short silence.

'Oh. Congratulations,' Berger said.

'Excuse me?'

'On the prize. Prix d'Or. Well deserved. Kaiser, have we got a print of *Nathalie 'X'*?

'We're shipping it over from Paris. It'll be here tomorrow.'

'It will?' Aurélien said, a little bemused.

'Everything can be fixed, Aurélien.'

'I want Lanier to see it. And Vincent.'

'Bob, I don't know if it's really Vincent's scene.'

'He has to see it. OK, after we sign Lanier.'

'I think that would be wise, Bob.'

'I want to see it again, I must say. Extraordinary piece.'

'You've seen it?' Aurélien said.

'Yeah. At Cannes, I think. Or possibly Berlin. Have we got a script yet, Kaiser?'

'There is no script. Extant.'

'We've got to get a synopsis. A treatment at least. Mike'll want to see something on paper. He'll never let Lanier go otherwise.'

'Shit. We need a goddam writer, then,' Prevost said.

'Davide?' Berger said into the speaker phone. 'We need a writer. Get Matt Friedrich.' He turned to Aurélien. 'You'll like him. One of the old school. What?' He listened to the phone again and sighed. 'Aurélien, we're having some trouble tracking down your beer. What do you say to a Dr Pepper?'

Bob Berger I have a theory about this town, this place. You have people in powerful executive positions who are, to put it kindly, very ordinary-looking types. I'm not talking about intellect, I'm talking about looks. The problem is these ordinary-looking people control the lives of individuals with sensational genetic advantages. That's an unbelievably volatile mix, I can tell you. And it cuts both ways; it can be very uncomfortable. It's fine for me, I'm a handsome guy, I'm in good shape. But for most of my colleagues . . . It's the source of many of our problems. That's why I took up golf.

Lanier Cross Tolstoy said: 'Life is a *tartine de merde* that we are obliged to consume daily.'

★   ★   ★

'This is for me?' Aurélien said, looking at the house, its land-scaped, multilevelled sprawl, the wide maw of its vast garage.

'You can't stay down by the airport,' Prevost said. 'Not any more. You can shoot in Westchester but you can't *live* there.'

A young woman emerged from the front door. She had short chestnut hair, a wide white smile and was wearing a spandex leotard and heavy climbing boots.

'This is Nancy, your assistant.'

'Hi. Good to meet you, Aurélien. Did I say that right?'

'Aurélien.'

'Aurélien?'

'It's not important.'

'The office is in back of the tennis court. It's in good shape.'

'Look, I got to fly, Aurélien. You're meeting Lanier Cross 7.30 a.m. at the Hamburger Haven on the Shore. Nancy'll fix everything up.'

To his surprise Kaiser Prevost then embraced him. When they broke apart Aurélien thought he saw tears in his eyes.

'We'll fucking show them, man, we'll fucking show them. Onward and upward, way to fucking go.'

'Any news of Delphine?'

'Who? No. Nothing yet. Any problems, call me, Aurélien. Twenty-four hours a day.'

Matt Friedrich *Le Destin de Nathalie 'X'* was not as boring as I had expected but then I was expecting terminal boredom. I was bored, sure, but it was nice to see Paris again. That's the great thing they've got going for them, French films, they carry this wonderful cargo of nostalgic francophilia for all non-French audiences. Pretty girl too, easy on the eye. I never thought I could happily watch a girl drink herself drunk on beer in a French café, but I did. It was not a wasted hour and a half.

It sure freaked out Prevost and Berger, though. 'Extraordinary,' Prevost said, clearly moved, 'extraordinary piece.' Berger mused awhile before announcing, 'That girl is a fox.' 'Michael Scott Gehn thinks it's a masterpiece,' I said. They agreed, vehemently. It's one of my tricks: when you don't know what to say, when you hated it or you're really stuck and anything qualified won't pass muster, use someone else's praise. Make it up if you have to. It's infallible, I promise.

I asked them how long they wanted the synopsis to be: sentence length or half a page. Berger said it had to be over forty pages, closely spaced, so people would be reluctant to read it. 'We already have coverage,' he said, 'but we need a document.' 'Make it as surreal and weird as you like,' Prevost said, handing me the video cassette, 'that's the whole point.'

We walked out into the Alcazar lot and went in search of our automobiles. 'When's he meeting Lanier?' Berger said. 'Tomorrow morning. She'll love him, Bob,' Prevost said. 'It's a done deal.' Berger gestured at the heavens. 'Bountiful Jehovah,' he said. 'Get me Lanier.'

I looked at these two guys, young enough to be my sons, as they crouched into their sleek, haunchy cars under a tallow moon, fantasizing loudly, belligerently, about this notional film, the deals, the stars, and I felt enormous pity for them. I have a theory about this town: our trouble is we are at once the most confident and the most insecure people in the world. We seem bulging with self-assurance, full of loud-voiced swagger, but in reality we're terrified, or we hate ourselves, or we're all taking happy pills of some order or another, or seeing shrinks, or getting counselled by fakirs and shamans, or fleeced by a whole gallimaufry of frauds and mountebanks. This is the Faustian pact — or should I say this is the Faust deal — you have to make in order to live and work here: you get it all, sure, but you get royally fucked up in the process. That's the price you pay. It's in the contract.

Aurélien No was directed to Lanier Cross's table in the dark rear angles of the Hamburger Haven. Another man and a woman were sitting with her. Aurélien shook her thin hand. She was beautiful, he saw, but so small, a child-woman, the musculature of a twelve-year-old with the sexual features of an adult.

She introduced the others, an amiable, grinning, broad-shouldered youngster and a lean, crop-haired woman in her forties with a fierce, strong face.

'This is my husband,' she said, 'Kit Vermeer. And this is Naomi Tashourian. She's a writer we work with.'

'We love your work,' Kit said.

'Beautiful film,' echoed Lanier.

'You've seen it?' Aurélien said.

'We saw it two hours ago,' Lanier said.

Aurélien looked at his watch: Nancy had made sure he was punctual – 7.30 a.m.

'I called Berger, said I had to see it before we met.'

'We tend to sleep in the day,' Kit said. 'Like bats.'

'Like lemurs,' Lanier said. 'I don't like bats.'

'– like lemurs.'

'It's a beautiful film,' Lanier said, 'that's why we wanted to meet with you.' She reached up and unfastened a large plastic bulldog clip on the top of her head and uncoiled a great dark glossy hank of hair a yard long. She pulled and tightened it, screwing it up, winding it around her right hand, piling it back on the top of her head before she refastened it in position with the clip. Everyone remained silent during this operation.

'That's why we wanted you to meet with Naomi.'

'This is a remake, right?' Naomi said.

'Yes. I think so.'

'Excellent,' Lanier said. 'I know Kit wants to put something to you. Kit?'

Kit leaned across the table. 'I want to play the waiter,' he said.

Aurélien thought before answering. 'The waiter is only in the film for about two minutes, right at the end.'

'Which is why we thought you should meet with Naomi.'

'The way I see it,' Naomi said, 'is that Nathalie has been in a relationship with the waiter. That's why she goes to the restaurant. And we could see, in flashback, you know, their relationship.'

'I think it could be extraordinary, Aurélien,' Lanier said.

'And I know that because of our situation, I and Lanier, our marital situation,' Kit added, 'we could bring something extraordinary to that relationship. And beautiful.'

Lanier and Kit kissed each other, briefly but with some passion, before resuming the argument in favour of the flashback. Aurélien ordered some steak and French fries as they fleshed out the relationship between Nathalie 'X' and her waiter-lover.

'And Naomi would write this?' Aurélien asked.

'Yes,' Lanier said. 'I'm not ready to work with another writer just yet.'

'I think Bob Berger has another writer – Matt Friedrich.'

'What's he done?' Kit said.

'We have to let Matt go, Aurélien,' Lanier said. 'You shouldn't drink beer this early in the morning.'

'Why not?'

'I'm an alcoholic,' Kit said. 'It's the thin end of the wedge, believe me.'

'Could you guys leave me alone with Aurélien?' Lanier said. They left.

Lanier Cross I have a theory about this town: the money doesn't matter. THE MONEY DOESN'T MATTER. Everybody thinks it's about the money but they're wrong. They think it's only because of the money that people put up with the godawful shit that's dumped on them. That there can be only one possible reason why people are prepared to be so desperately unhappy. Money. Not so. Consider this: everybody who matters in this town has more than enough money. They don't need any more money. And I'm not talking about the studio heads, the top directors, the big stars, the people with obscene amounts. There are thousands of people in this town, possibly tens of thousands, who are involved in movies who have more money than is reasonably acceptable. So it's not about money, it can't be, it's about something else. It's about being at the centre of the world.

'She loved you,' Kaiser Prevost said. 'She's all over you like a rash.'

'Any news of Delphine?'

'Who? Ah, no. What did you say to her, to Lanier? Bob called, she'll do it for nothing. Well, half her normal fee. Sensational idea about Kit Vermeer. Excellent. Why didn't I think of that? Maybe that's what swung it.'

'No, it was her idea. How are we going to finish the film without Delphine?'

'Aurélien. Please. Forget Delphine Drelle. We have Lanier Cross. We fired Friedrich, we got Tashourian writing the flashback. We're in business, my son, in business.'

Naomi Tashourian I have a theory about this town, this place. Don't be a woman.

★   ★   ★

Aurélien sat in the cutting room with Barker Lear, an editor, as they ran what existed of *Seeing Through Nathalie* on the Moviola.

Barker, a hefty man with a grizzled ginger goatee, watched Delphine sit down at the pizzeria and order a beer. She drank it down and ordered another, then the sound boom, which had been bobbing erratically in and out of frame for the last few minutes, fell fully into view and the screen went black.

Barker turned and looked at Aurélien who was frowning and tapping his teeth with the end of a pencil.

'That's some film,' Barker said. 'Who's the girl, she's extra-ordinary.'

'Delphine Drelle.'

'She a big star in France?'

'No.'

'Sorta hypnotic effect, she has . . .' He shrugged. 'Shame about the boom.'

'Oh, I don't worry about that sort of thing,' Aurélien said. 'It adds to the verisimilitude.'

'I don't follow.'

'You're meant to know it's a film. That's why the end works so well.'

'So what happens in the end? You've still got to shoot it, right?'

'Yes. I don't know what happens. Neither does Delphine.'

'You don't say?'

'She gets drunk, you see. We watch her getting drunk. We don't cut away. We don't know what she might do. That's what makes it so exciting – that's the "Destiny of Nathalie 'X' ".'

'I see . . . So, ah, what happened at the end of the first film?'

'She goes to the café, she drinks six or seven beers very quickly, and I can see she's quite drunk. She orders another drink and when the waiter brings it she throws it in his face.'

'You don't say? Then what?'

'They have a fight. Delphine and the waiter. They really hit each other. It's fantastic. Delphine, she's had this training, self-defence. She knees this guy in the *couilles*. Boff!'

'Fascinating.'

'He falls over. She collapses, crying, she turns to me, swears at me. Runs off into the night. The end. It's amazing.'

Barker rubbed his beard, thinking. He glanced at Aurélien covertly.

'Going to do the same thing here?'

'No, no. It's got to be different for the USA, for Hollywood. That's why I gave her the gun.'

'Is it a real gun?'

'Oh yes. Otherwise what would be the point?'

Barker Lear I definitely had him for a wacko at first, but after I spent an afternoon with him, talking to him, it seemed to me he really knew what he was doing. He was a real calm guy, Aurélien. He had his own vision, didn't worry about other people, what other people might think about him. And it was the easiest editing job I ever did. Long long takes. Lot of hand-held stuff. The walk had a few reverses, a few mid shots, dolly shots. And the film was kind of exciting, I have to admit, and I was really quite disappointed that he still hadn't shot the end. This girl Delphine, with this crazy blonde fringe over her eyes, there was definitely something wild about her. I mean, who knows, once she got loaded, what she might have done. Maybe Aurélien wasn't a wacko, but she definitely was.

You know I have a theory about this town, this place. I've been working here for twenty-five years and I've seen them all. In this town you have very, very clever people and very, very wacko people, and the problem is, and that's what makes this place different, our special problem is the very clever people *have* to work with the very wacko people. They have to, they can't help it, it's the nature of the job. That doesn't happen other places for one simple reason – clever and wacko don't mix.

Aurélien stood by the pool with Nancy enjoying the subdued play of morning light on the water. Today Nancy's hair was white blonde and she wore a tutu over her leotard and cowboy boots with spurs. She handed him a pair of car keys and an envelope with a thousand dollars in it.

'That's the new rental car. Celica, OK? And there's your *per diem*. And you've got dinner at Lanier Cross's at 6.30.'

'6.30 p.m.?'

'Ah, yeah . . . She can make it 6.00 if you prefer? She asked me to tell you it will be vegetarian.'

'What are all those men doing? Is it some kind of military exercise?'

'Those are the gardeners. Shall I make them go away?'

'No, it's fine.'

'And Tim Pascal called.'

'Who's he?'

'He's an English film director. He has several projects in development at Alcazar. He wanted to know if you wanted to lunch or drink or whatever.'

The doorbell rang. Aurélien strode across the several levels of his cool white living-room to answer it. As he did so the bell rang twice again. It was Delphine.

Kaiser Prevost I have a theory about this town: it doesn't represent the fulfilment of the American dream, it represents the fulfilment of an American reality. It rewards relentless persistence, massive stamina, ruthlessness and the ability to live with grotesque failure. Look at me: I am a smallish guy, 138 pounds, with pretty severe myopia, and near-average academic qualifications. But I have a personable manner and an excellent memory and a good head of hair. I will work hard and I will take hard decisions and I have developed the thickest of thick skins. With these attributes in this town nothing can stop me. Or those like me. We are legion. We know what they call us but we don't care. We don't need contacts, we don't need influence, we don't need talent, we don't need cosmetic surgery. That's why I love this place. It allows us to thrive. That's why when I heard Aurélien had never showed for dinner with Lanier Cross I didn't panic. People like me take that kind of awful crisis in their stride.

Aurélien turned over and gently kissed Delphine's right breast. She stubbed out her cigarette and hunched into him.

'This house is incredible, Aurélien. I like it here.'

'Where's Holbish?'

'You promised you wouldn't mention him again. I'm sorry, Aurélien, I don't know what made me do it.'

'No, I'm just curious.'

'He's gone to Seattle.'

'Well, we can manage without him. Are you ready?'

'Of course, it's the least I can do. What about the pizzeria?'

'I was given a thousand dollars cash today. I knew it would come in useful.'

Matt Friedrich I have to admit I was hoping for the *Seeing Through Nathalie* rewrite. When Bob Berger fired me and said that Naomi Tashourian was the new writer it hurt for a while. It always does, no matter how successful you are. But in my case I was due a break and I thought *Nathalie* was it. I've missed out on my last three Guild arbitrations and a Lanier Cross film would have helped, however half-baked, however art-house. Berger said they would honour the fee for the synopsis I did (obfuscation takes on new meaning) but I guess the check is still in the post. But, I do not repine, as a great English novelist once said, I just get on with the job.

I have a theory about this town, this place, this *spielraum* where we dream and dawdle: one of our problems – perhaps it's *the* problem – is that here ego always outstrips ability. Always. That applies to everyone: writers, directors, actors, heads of production, d-boys and unit runners. It's our disease, our mark of Cain. When you have success here you think you can do anything and that's the great error. The success diet is too rich for our digestive systems: it poisons us, addles the brain. It makes us blind. We lose our self-knowledge. My advice to all those who make it is this: *take the job you would have done if the film had been a flop.* Don't go for the big one, don't let those horizons recede. Do the commercial, the TV pilot, the documentary, the three-week rewrite, the character role or whatever it was you had lined up first. Do that job and then maybe you can reach for the forbidden fruit, but at least you'll have your feet on the ground.

'Kaiser?'
  'Bob?'
  'He's not at the house, Kaiser.'
  'Shit.'
  'He's got to phone her. He's got to apologize.'
  'No. He's got to lie.'
  'She called Vincent.'
  'Fuck. The bitch.'
  'That's how bad she wants to do it. I think it's a good sign.'
  'Where is that African bastard? I'll kill him.'
  'Nancy says the French babe showed.'

'Oh, no. No, fuckin' no!'

'It gets worse, Kaiser. Vincent told me to call Tim Pascal.'

'Who the fuck's he?'

'Some English director. Lanier wants to meet with him.'

'Who's his agent?'

'Sheldon . . . Hello? Kaiser?'

George Malinverno I got a theory about this town, this place: everybody likes pizza. Even the French. We got to know them real well, I guess. They came back every night, the French. The tall black guy, the ratty one and the blonde girl. Real pretty girl. Every night they come. Every night they eat pizza. Every night she ties one on. Everybody likes pizza. [Bitter laugh.] Everybody. Too bad I didn't think of it first, huh?

They film one night. And the girl, she's steaming. Then, I don't know, something goes wrong and we don't see them for a while. Then he comes back. Just the black guy, Aurélien, and the girl. He says can they film, one night, thousand bucks. I say for sure. So he sets up the sound and he sets up the camera behind the bushes. You know, it's not a disturbance, exactly. I never see anybody make a film like this before. A thousand bucks, it's very generous. So the girl, she walks up, she takes a seat, she orders beer and keeps on drinking. Soon she's pretty stewed. Aurélien sits behind the bushes, just keeps filming. Some guy tries to pick her up, puts his hand on the table, like, leans over, she takes a book of matches, like that one, and does something to the back of his hand with the corner. I couldn't see what she did but the guy gasps with pain, shudders like this, just backs off.

Then we get a big party in, birthday party, they'd already booked, fourteen people. She sits there drinking and smoking, Aurélien's filming. Then we bring the cake out of the kitchen, candles all lit. Whenever there's a birthday we get Chico to sing.

Chico, the little waiter, tubby guy, wanted to be an opera singer. Got a fine strong voice. He's singing 'Happy Birthday to You' – he's got a kind of drawn-out, elaborate way of singing it. Top of his voice, *molto vibrato*, you know. Next thing I know the girl's on her feet with a fuckin' gun in her hand, screaming in French. Nobody can hear because Chico's singing his balls off. I tear out from behind the bar, but I'm too late. POW. First shot blows the cake away. BAM. Second one gets Chico in the thigh. Flesh wound, thanks God. I charge her to the ground, Roberto jumps on top. We wrestle the gun away. She put up quite a fight for a little thing. Did something to my shoulder too, she twisted it in some way, never been the same since. Aurélien got the whole thing on film. I hear it looks great.

Aurélien sat outside the Alcazar screening room with Kaiser Prevost and Bob Berger. Berger combed and recombed his hair, he kept smelling his comb, smelling his fingertips. He asked Prevost to smell his hair. Prevost said it smelt of shampoo. Prevost went to the lavatory for the fourth time.

'Relax,' Aurélien said to them both. 'I'm really pleased with the film. I couldn't be more pleased.'

Berger groaned. 'Don't say that, don't say that.'

'If he likes it,' Kaiser said, 'we're in business. Lanier will like it, for sure, and Aurélien will apologize. Won't you, Aurélien? Of course you will. No problem. Lanier loved him. Lanier loved you, didn't she, Aurélien?'

'Why are we worried about Lanier?' Aurélien said. 'Delphine came back. We finished the film.'

'Jesus Christ,' said Bob Berger.

'Don't worry, Bob,' Kaiser said. 'Everything can be fixed.'

Vincent Bandine emerged from the screening room.

Aurélien stood up. 'What do you think?'

Vincent Bandine I believe in candour. I have a theory about this town, this place: we don't put enough stock in candour. I am into candour in a big way. So I take Aurélien aside, gently, and I say: 'Aurélien, or whatever your name is, I think your film is goatshit. I think it's a disgusting, boring piece of grade "A" manure. I wouldn't give the sweat off my balls for your goatshit film.' That's what I said, verbatim. And, I have to give it to the kid, he just stood there and looked at me, sort of slight smile on his face. Usually when I'm this candid they're in deep shock, or weeping, or vomiting by now. And he looks at me and says, 'I can't blame you for thinking like this. You're not a man of culture, so I can't blame you for thinking like this.' And he walks. He walks out jauntily. I should have had his fucking legs broken. I've got the biggest collection of Vuillard paintings on the west coast of America. I should have had his fucking legs broken. We had to pay the waiter fifty grand not to press charges, keep the Alcazar name out of things. The girl went to a clinic for three weeks to dry out . . . Aurélien No. Not a man of culture, eh?

Kit Vermeer Ah, Lanier took it badly. I don't think that. Do you mind? Thank you. Bats and lemurs, man, wow, they didn't get a look-in. Bats and lemurs. Story of my life. *Weltanschauung*, that's what I'm up for. No, *Weltschmerz*. That's my bag. Bats and lemurs. Why not owls and armadillos? No, I'm not looking at you, sir, or talking to you. Forsooth. Fuckin' nerd. Wank in a bath, that's what an English friend of mine calls them. What a wank in a bath. Owls and armadillos.

Matt Friedrich Aurélien came to see me before he left, which was gracious of him, I thought, especially for a film director, and he told me what had happened. I commiserated and told him other sorry stories about this town, this place. But he needed no consoling. 'I enjoyed my visit,' he said. 'No, I did. And I made the film. It was a curious but interesting experience.'

'It's just a dance,' I think I remember saying to him. 'It's just a dance we have to do.'

He laughed. He found that funny.

END ROLLER

Bob Berger
is working from home,
where he is writing several screenplays

Delphine Drelle
plays the character Suzi de la Tour
in NBC's *Till Darkness Falls*

Kaiser Prevost
works for the investment bank
Harbinger Cohen in New York City

Marius No
is in his first year at L'Ecole Supérieur
des Etudes Cinématographiques

Bertrand Holbish
manages the Seattle band Morbid Anatomy

Naomi Tashourian
has written her first novel, *Credits Not Contractual*

Michael Scott Gehn
is chief executive critic
and on the editorial board of *film/e*

Kit Vermeer
is a practising Sikh and wishes
to be known as Khalsa Hari Atmar

Lanier Cross
is scheduled to star in Lucy Wang's film
Charles Baudelaire's Les Fleurs du mal

George Malinverno
has opened a third pizzeria in Pacific Palisades

Vincent Bandine
has announced Alcazar Films'
eighteen-picture slate for the coming year

Barker Lear
lives in San Luis Obispo

Matt Friedrich
has taken his own life

Nathalie 'X' aux Etats-Unis
has been nominated for an Academy Award
in the 'Best Foreign Film' category

Aurélien No
is not returning your calls

Transfigured Night

'From my 10th or 11th year I
remember the following incident:
     box on the ear
     looking for a gymnasium
Aryan origin
     Gymnasium   love for Erich
        fight
     relation to Paul
        to Gretl
        to Rudi   good
memories
Wolfrum   I attempt to win him over
and entice him away from my
brother
     being in love   Paul a mischief
maker
        innocent expression
          lewdness
Latin exercises for Papa   thoughts of
suicide'

     The private papers of Ludwig Wittgenstein

Selbstmord

In this city, and at this time, you should understand that suicide was a completely acceptable option, an entirely understandable, rational course of action to take. And I speak as one who knows its temptations intimately: three of my elder brothers took their own lives – Hans, Rudi and Kurt. That left Paul, me, and my three older sisters. My sisters, I am sure, were immune to suicide's powerful contagion. I cannot speak for Paul. As for myself, I can only say that its clean resolution of all my problems – intellectual and emotional – was always most appealing; that open door to oblivion always beckoned to me and, odd though it may seem, suicide – the idea of suicide – lies at the very foundations of all my work in ethics and logic.

The Benefactor

I came down from the Hochreith, our house in the country, to Vienna especially to meet Herr Ficker. The big white villa in the park of Neuwaldegg was closed up for the summer. I had one of the gardeners prepare my room and make up a bed and his wife laid the table on the terrace and helped me cook dinner. We were to have *Naturschnitzel* with *Kochsalat* with a cold bottle of Zöbinger. Simple, honest food. I hoped Ficker would notice.

I shaved and dressed and went out on to the terrace to wait for him to arrive. I was wearing a banana-yellow, soft-collared shirt with no tie and a light tweed jacket that I had bought years before in Manchester. Its fraying cuffs had been repaired, in the English way, with a dun green leather. My hair was clean and still damp, my face was cool, scraped smooth. I drank a glass of sherbet-water as I waited for Ficker. The evening light was milky and diffused, as if hung with dust. I could hear the faint noise of motors and carriages on the roads of Neuwaldegg and in the gathering dusk I could make out the figure of the gardener moving about in the Allee of pleached limes. A fleeting but palpable peace descended on me and I thought for some minutes of David and our holidays together in Iceland and Norway. I missed him.

Ficker was an earnest young man, taller than me (mind you, I am not particularly tall), with fine thinning hair brushed back off his brow. He wore spectacles with crooked wire frames, as if he had accidently sat upon them and had hastily straightened them out himself. He was neatly and soberly dressed, wore no hat and was clean-shaven. His lopsided spectacles suggested a spirit of frivolity and facetiousness which, I soon found out, was entirely inaccurate.

I had already explained to him, by letter, about my father's death, my legacy and how I wished to dispose of a proportion of it. He had agreed to my conditions and promised to respect my demand for total anonymity. We talked, in business-like fashion, about the details but I could sense, as he expressed his gratitude, strong currents of astonishment and curiosity.

Eventually he had to ask. 'But why me? Why my magazine . . . in particular?'

I shrugged. 'It seems to be exemplary, of its sort. I like its attitude, its, its seriousness. And besides, your writers seem the most needy.'

'Yes . . . That's true.' He was none the wiser.

'It's a family trait. My father was a great benefactor – to musicians mainly. We just like to do it.'

Ficker then produced a list of writers and painters he thought were the most deserving. I glanced through it: very few of the names were familiar to me, and beside each one Ficker had written an appropriate sum of money. Two names, at the top of the list, were to receive by far the largest amounts.

'I know of Rilke, of course,' I said, 'and I'm delighted you chose him. But who's *he*?' I pointed to the other name. 'Why should he get so much? What does he do?'

'He's a poet,' Ficker said. 'I think . . . well, no man on this list will benefit more from your generosity. To be completely frank, I think it might just save his life.'

Schubert

My brother Hans drowned himself in Chesapeake Bay. He was a musical prodigy who gave his first concert in Vienna at the age of nine. I never really knew him. My surviving brother, Paul, was also musically gifted, a brilliant pianist who was a pupil of Leschetitzky and made his début in 1913. I remember Paul saying to me once that of all musical tastes the love of Schubert required the least explanation. When one thinks of the huge misery of his life and sees in his work no trace of it at all – the complete absence in his music of all bitterness.

The Bank

I had arranged with Ficker that I would be in the Österreichische Nationalbank on Schwarzspanier Strasse at three o'clock. I was there early and sat down at a writing desk in a far corner. It was quiet and peaceful: the afternoon rush had yet to begin and the occasional sound of heels on the marble floor as clients crossed from the entrance foyer to the rows of counters was soothing, like the background click of ivory dominoes or the ceramic kiss of billiard balls in the gaming-room of my favourite café near the art schools.

Ficker was on time and accompanied by our poet. Ficker caught my eye and I gave a slight nod and then bent my head over the spectral papers on my desk. Ficker went to a teller's *guichet* to enquire about the banker's draft, leaving the poet standing momentarily alone in the middle of the marble floor, gazing around him like a peasant at the high dim vaults of the ceiling and the dazzle of afternoon sunshine on the ornamental brasswork of the chandeliers.

Georg, as I shall refer to him, was a young man, twenty-seven years old — two years older than me — small and quite sturdily built, and, like many small men, he seemed to have been provided with a head designed for a bigger body altogether. His head was crude and heavy-looking, its proportions exaggerated by his bristly, close-cropped hair. He was clean-shaven. He had a weak mouth, the upper lip overhung the bottom one slightly, and a thick triangular nose. He had low brows and slightly oriental-looking, almond-shaped eyes. He was what my mother would have called 'an ugly customer'.

He stood now, looking expressionlessly about him, swaying slightly, as if buffeted by an invisible crowd. He appeared at once ill and strong — pale-faced, ugly, dark-eyed, but with something about the set of his shoulders, the way his feet were planted on the ground, that suggested reserves of strength. Indeed the year before, Ficker had told me, he had almost died from an overdose of Veronal that should have killed an ordinary man in an hour or two. Since his schooldays, it transpired, he had been a compulsive user of narcotic drugs and was also an immoderate drinker. At school he used chloroform to intoxicate himself. He was now a qualified dispensing chemist, a career he had taken up, so Ficker informed me, solely because it gave him access to more effective drugs. I found this single-mindedness oddly impressive. To train for two years at the University of Vienna as a pharmacist, to pass the necessary exams to qualify, testified to an uncommon dedication. Ficker had given me some of his poems to read. I could not understand them at all; their images for me were strangely haunting and evocative but finally entirely opaque. But I liked their *tone*; their tone seemed to me to be quite remarkable.

I watched him now, discreetly, as Ficker completed the preliminary documentation and signalled him over to endorse the banker's draft. Ficker — I think this was a mistake — presented the cheque to him with a small flourish and shook him by the hand, as if he had just won first prize in a lottery. I could sense that Georg knew very little of what was going on. I saw him turn the cheque over immediately so as to hide the amount from his own eyes. He exchanged a few urgent words with Ficker, who smiled encouragingly and patted him on the arm. Ficker was very happy, almost gleeful — in his role as the philanthropist's go-between he was vicariously enjoying what he imagined would be Georg's astonished surprise. But he was wrong. I knew it the instant Georg turned over the cheque and read the amount. Twenty thousand crowns. A thriving dispensing chemist would have to work six or seven years to earn a similar sum. I saw the cheque flutter and tremble in his fingers. I saw Georg blanch and swallow violently several times. He put the back of his hand to his lips and his shoulders heaved. He reached out to a pillar for support, bending over from the waist. His body convulsed in a spasm as he tried to control his writhing stomach. I knew then that he was an honest man for he had the honest man's profound fear of extreme good fortune. Ficker snatched the cheque from his shaking fingers as Georg appeared to totter. He uttered a faint cry as warm bile and vomit shot from his mouth to splash and splatter on the cool marble of the Nationalbank's flagged floor.

A Good Life – A Good Death

I came to know Ficker quite well during our various meetings about the division and disposal of my benefaction. Once in our discussions the subject of suicide came up and he seemed genuinely surprised when I told him that scarcely a day went by when I did not think about it. But I explained to him that if I could not get along with life and the world then to commit suicide would be the ultimate admission of failure. I pointed out that this notion was the very essence of ethics and morality. For, if anything is not to be allowed, then surely that must be suicide. For if suicide is allowed, then anything is allowed.

Sometimes I think that a good life should end in a death that one could welcome. Perhaps, even, it is only a good death that allows us to call a life 'good'.

Georg, I believe, has nearly died many times. For example, shortly before the Veronal incident he almost eliminated himself by accident. Georg lived for a time in Innsbruck. One night, after a drinking bout in a small village near the city he decided to walk home. At some stage on his journey back, overcome with tiredness, he decided to lie down in the snow and sleep. When he awoke in the morning the world had been replaced by a white turbid void. For a moment he thought . . . but almost immediately he realized he had been covered in the night by a new fall of snow. In fact it was about forty centimetres deep. He heaved himself to his feet, brushed off his clothes and, with a clanging, gonging headache, completed his journey to Innsbruck. Ficker related all this to me.

How I wish I had been passing that morning! The first sleepy traveller along that road when Georg awoke. In the still, crepuscular light, that large hump on the verge begins to stir, some cracks and declivities suddenly deform the smooth contours, then a fist punches free and finally that crude ugly face emerges, with its frosty beret of snow, staring stupidly, blinking, spitting . . .

The War

The war saved my life. I really do not know what I would have done without it. On 7 August, the day war was declared on Russia, I enlisted as a volunteer gunner in the artillery for the duration and was instructed to report to a garrison artillery regiment in Cracow. In my elation I was reluctant to go straight home to pack my bags (my family had by now all returned to Vienna) so I took a taxi to the Café Museum.

I should say that I joined the army because it was my civic duty, yet I was even more glad to enlist because I knew at that time I had to *do* something, I had to subject myself to the rigours of a harsh routine that would divert me from my intellectual work. I had reached an impasse and the impossibility of ever proceeding further filled me with morbid despair.

By the time I reached the Café Museum it was about six o'clock in the evening (I liked this café because its interior was modern: its square rooms were lined with square, honey-coloured oak panelling, hung with prints of the drawings of Charles Dana Gibson). Inside it was busy, the air noisy with speculation about the war. It was warm and muggy, the atmosphere suffused with the reek of beer and cigar smoke. The patrons were mostly young men, students from the nearby art schools, clean-shaven, casually and unaffectedly dressed. So I was a little surprised to catch a glimpse in one corner of a uniform. I pushed through the crowd to see who it was.

Georg, it was obvious, was already fairly drunk. He sat strangely hunched over, staring intently at the table top. His posture and the ferocious concentration of his gaze clearly put people off as the three other seats around his table remained unoccupied. I told a waiter to bring a half-litre of *Heuniger Wein* to the table and then sat down opposite him.

Georg was wearing the uniform of an officer, a lieutenant, in the Medical Corps. He looked at me candidly and without resentment, and of course without recognition. He seemed much the same as the last time I had seen him, at once ill-looking and possessed of a sinewy energy. I introduced myself and told him I was pleased to see a fellow soldier as I myself had just enlisted.

'It's your civic duty,' he said, his voice strong and unslurred. 'Have a cigar.'

He offered me a Trabuco, those ones that have a straw mouthpiece because they are so strong. I declined – at that time I did not smoke. When the wine arrived he insisted on paying for it.

'I'm a rich man,' he explained as he filled our glasses. 'Where're you posted?'

'Galicia.'

'Ah, the Russians are coming.' He paused. 'I want to go somewhere cold and dark. I detest this sun, and this city. Why aren't we fighting the Eskimos? I hate daylight. Maybe I could declare war on the Lapps. One-man army.'

'Bit lonely, no?'

'I want to be lonely. All I do is pollute my mind talking to people . . . I want a dark cold lonely war. Please.'

'People will think you're mad.'

He raised his glass. 'God preserve me from sanity.'

I thought of something Nietzsche had said: 'Our life, our happiness, is beyond the north, beyond ice, beyond death.' I looked into Georg's ugly face, his thin eyes and glossy lips, and felt a kind of love for him and his honesty. I clinked my glass against his and asked God to preserve me from sanity as well.

Tagebuch: 15 August. Cracow. . . . If your wife, for example, continually puts too much sugar in your tea it is not because she has too much sugar in her cupboard, it is because she is not educated in the ways of handling sweetness. Similarly, the problem of how to live a good life cannot ever be solved by continually assaulting it with the intellect. Certain things can only be shown, not stated.

The Searchlight

I enlisted in the artillery to fire howitzers but instead found myself manning a searchlight on a small, heavily armed paddle-steamer called the *Goplana*. We cruised up and down the Vistula, ostensibly looking for Russians but also to provide support for any river crossings by our own forces.

I enjoyed my role in charge of the searchlight. I took its mounting apart and oiled and greased its bearings. Reassembled, it moved effortlessly under the touch of my fingers. Its strong beam shone straight and true in the blurry semi-darkness of those late summer nights. However, I soon found the living conditions on the *Goplana* intolerable because of the stink, the proximity and the vulgarity of my fellow soldiers. And because we were constantly in motion life below decks was dominated by the thrum and grind of the *Goplana*'s churning paddles. I spent long hours in my corner of the bridge-house needlessly overhauling the mechanism of the searchlight – anything to escape the torrent of filth and viciousness that poured from the men. But despite these periods of solitude and isolation I found my old despair began to creep through me again, like a stain.

One day we disembarked at Sandomierz and were sent to a bath-house. As we washed I looked at my naked companions, their brown faces and forearms, their grey-white bodies and dark dripping genitals, as they soaped and sluiced themselves with garrulous ostentation. I felt only loathing for them, my fellow men. It was both impossible to work with them and have nothing to do with them. I was glad that I felt no stirrings of sensuality as I contemplated their naked bodies. I saw that they were men but I could not see they were human beings.

Tagebuch: 8 September. Sawichost. . . . The news is worse. All the talk is of Cracow being besieged. Last night there was an alarm. I ran up on deck to man the searchlight. It was raining and I wore only a shirt and trousers. I played the beam of the searchlight to and fro on the opposite bank of the river for hours, my feet and hands slowly becoming numb. Then we heard the sound of gunfire and I at once became convinced I was going to die that night. The beam of the searchlight was a lucent arrow pointing directly at me. And for the first time I felt, being face to face with my own death, with possibly only an hour or two of life remaining to me, that I had in those few hours the chance to be a good man, if only because of this uniquely potent consciousness of myself. And, as ever, my attempts to articulate my experience as I understood and *felt* it, and to seize intellectually its profound implications, slipped beyond the power of language. 'I did my duty and stayed at my post.' That is all I can say about that tremendous night.

The Amputee

Of course I did not die and of course I fell back into more abject moods of self-disgust and loathing. Perhaps the only consolation was that my enormous fatigue made it impossible for me to think about my work.

It was about this time – in September or October – that I heard the news about my brother Paul. He was a quite different personality from me – fierce and somewhat dominating – and he had tackled his vocation as concert pianist with uncompromising dedication. Since his début his future seemed assured, an avenue of bright tomorrows. To receive the news, then, that he had been captured by the Russians and had had his right arm amputated at the elbow, as the result of wounds he had sustained, was devastating. For days my thoughts were of Paul and of what I would do in his situation. Poor Paul, I thought, if only there were some other solution than suicide. What philosophy it will take to get over this!

Tagebuch: 13 October. Nadbrzesze. . . . We have sailed here, waited for twelve hours, and have now been ordered to return to Sawichost. All day we can hear the mumble of artillery in the east. I find myself drawn down into dark depression again, remorselessly. Why? What is the real basis of this malaise? . . . I see one of my fellow soldiers pissing over the side of the boat in full view of the few citizens of Nadbrzesze who have gathered on the quayside to stare at us. The long pale arc of his urine sparkles in the thin autumn sunshine. Another soldier leans on his elbows staring candidly at the man's white flaccid penis, held daintily between two fingers like a titbit. This is shaken, its tip squeezed and then tucked away in the coarse serge of his trousers. I think if I was standing at a machine-gun rather than a searchlight I could kill them both without a qualm . . . Why do I detest these simple foolish men so? Why can I not be impassive? I despise my own weakness, my inability to distance myself from the common-place.

The Battle of Grodek

On our return from Sawichost I received mail. A long letter from David – I wonder if he thinks of me half as much as I think of him? – and a most distressing communication from Ficker – to whom I had written asking for some books to be sent to me. I quote:

. . . I see from your letter that you are not far from Cracow. I wonder if you get the opportunity you could attempt to find and visit [Georg]. You may have heard of the heavy fighting at Grodek some two weeks ago. Georg was there and, owing to the chaos and disorganization that prevailed at the time, was mistakenly placed in charge of a field hospital not far behind our lines. Apparently he protested vigorously that he was merely a dispensing chemist and not a doctor, but resources were so stretched he was told to do the best he could.

Thus Georg found himself, with two orderlies (Czechs, who spoke little German), in charge of a fifty-bed field hospital. As the battle wore on more than ninety severely wounded casualties were delivered during the day. Repeatedly, Georg signalled for a doctor to be sent as he could do nothing for these men except inject them with morphine and attempt to dress their wounds. In fact it became clear that through some oversight these casualties had been sent to the wrong hospital. The ambulance crews that transported them had been erroneously informed that there was a field surgery and a team of surgeons operating there.

By nine in the evening all of Georg's supplies of morphine were exhausted. Shortly thereafter men began to scream from the resurgent pain. Finally, one officer, who had lost his left leg at the hip, shot himself in the head.

At this point Georg ran away. Two kilometres from the field hospital was a small wood, which at the start of the battle had been a battalion headquarters. Georg went there for help, or at least to report the ghastly condition of the wounded in his charge. When he arrived there he found that an impromptu military tribunal had just executed twenty deserters by hanging.

I do not know exactly what happened next. I believe that at the sight of these fresh corpses Georg tried to seize a revolver from an officer and shoot himself. Whatever happened, he behaved in a demented manner, was subdued and was arrested himself for desertion in the face of the enemy. I managed to visit him briefly in the mental hospital at Cracow ten days ago. He is in a very bad way, but at least, thank God, the charges of desertion have been dropped and he is being treated for dementia praecox. For some reason Georg is convinced he will be prosecuted for cowardice. He is sure he is going to hang.

The Asylum at Cracow

Georg's cell was very cold, and dark, the only illumination coming from an oil-lamp in the corridor. Georg needed a shave but otherwise he looked much the same as he had on my two previous encounters with him. He was wearing a curious oatmeal canvas uniform, the jacket secured with strings instead of buttons. With his big head and thin eyes he looked strangely Chinese. There was one other patient in his cell with him, a major in the cavalry who was suffering from *delerium tremens*. This man remained hunched on a truckle bed in the corner of the room, sobbing quietly to himself while Georg and I spoke. Georg did not recognize me. I merely introduced myself as a friend of Ficker.

'Ludwig asked me to visit you,' I said. 'How are you?'

'Well, I'm . . .' He stopped and gestured at the major. 'I used to think I was a heavy drinker.' He smiled. 'Actually, he's being quite good now.' Georg rubbed his short hair with both hands.

'I heard about what happened,' I said. 'It must have been terrible.'

He looked at me intently, and then seemed to think for a while.

'Yes,' he said. 'Yes, yes, yes. All that sort of thing.'

'I completely understand.'

He shrugged uselessly. Certain things can only be shown, not stated.

He smiled. 'You don't have any cigars on you, by any chance? They haven't brought me my kit. One longs for a decent cigar.'

'Let me get some for you.'

'I smoke Trabucos – the ones with the straw holder.'

'They're very strong, I believe. I don't smoke, but I heard they can burn your throat.'

'It's a small price to pay.'

We sat on in silence for a moment, listening to the major's snufflings.

'It's very cold here,' George began slowly, 'and very dark, and if they got rid of the major the conditions would be perfect.'

'I know what you mean.'

'Actually, I have several boxes of Trabucos in my kit,' he went on. 'If you could get a message to my orderly perhaps he could bring me a couple.'

'Of course.'

'Oh, and would you ask him to bring me my green leather case.'

'Green leather case.'

'Yes.' He paused. 'That is essential . . .' He rubbed his face, as if his features were tired of being eternally composed.

'I think with a good cigar I could even tolerate the major.'

★   ★   ★

I found Georg's orderly in the Medical Corps' billet in a small village on the outskirts of Cracow. The city was clearly visible across the flat cropped meadows where some piebald ponies grazed; a low attenuated silhouette punctuated by a few domes and spires and the odd factory chimney. In the indistinct grainy light of the late afternoon the bulk of the Marienkirche had the look of a vast warehouse. I passed on Georg's instructions: two boxes of Trabuco cigars and his green leather case.

'How is the lieutenant?' the orderly asked.

'He's very well,' I said. 'Considering . . . very well indeed.'

Georg died that night from a heart seizure brought on by a massive intravenous injection of cocaine. According to his orderly, who was the last person to speak to him, he was 'in a state of acute distress' and must have misjudged the dose.

Tagebuch: 10 November. Sawichost. . . . The simplest way to describe the book of moral philosophy that I am writing is that it concerns what can and cannot be said. In fact it will be only half a book. The most interesting half will be the one that I cannot write. That half will be the most eloquent.

Tea at Neuwaldegg

It is springtime. After a shower of rain we take tea on the terrace of the big house at Neuwaldegg. Me, my mother, my sisters Hélène and Hermine – and Paul. I am on leave; Paul has just been returned from captivity as part of an exchange of wounded prisoners. He sits with his right sleeve neatly pinned up, awkwardly squeezing lemon into his tea with his left hand. I think of Georg and I look at Paul. His hair is greying, his clothes are immaculate.

Quite suddenly he announces that he is going to continue with his career as a concert pianist and teach himself to play with the left hand only. He proposes to commission pieces for the left hand from Richard Strauss and Ravel. There is silence, and then I say, 'Bravo, Paul. Bravo.' And, spontaneously, we all clap him.

The modest sound of our applause carries out over the huge garden. A faint breeze shifts the new spring foliage of the chestnut trees, glistening after the rain, and the gardener, who has just planted out a bed of geraniums, looks up from his work for a moment, smiles bemusedly at us, clambers to his feet and bows.

Hôtel des Voyageurs

Hôtel de la Louisiane. Me for good
talk, wet evenings, intimacy, *vins
rouges en carafe*, reading, relative
solitude, street worship . . . shop
gazing, alley sloping, café
crawling . . . I am for the intricacy of
Europe, the discreet and many
folded strata of the old world, the
past, the North, the world of ideas.
I am for the Hôtel de la Louisiane.
    Cyril Connolly, *Journal 1928–1937*

Monday, 26 July 1928

Paris. Boat-train from London strangely quiet, I had a whole
compartment to myself. Fine drizzle at the Gare du Nord. After
breakfast I spent two hours trying to telephone Louise in
London. I finally got through and a man's voice answered.
'Who's calling?' he said, very abruptly. 'Tell Louise it's Logan
Mountstewart,' I said, equally brusquely. Longish silence. Then
the man said Louise was in Hampshire. I kept telling him that

Louise was never in Hampshire during the week. Eventually I realised it was Robbie. He refused to admit it so I called him every foul name I could think of and hung up.

Lonely bitter evening, drank too much. A protracted street prowl through the Marais. The thought of Louise with Robbie made me want to vomit. Robbie: *faux bonhomme* and fascist shit.

Tuesday

More rain. I cabled Douglas and Sylvia in Bayonne and told them I was driving down. I then hired the biggest car I could find in Paris, a vast American thing called a Packard, a great beast of a vehicle, with huge bulbous headlamps. I set off after lunch in a thunderstorm resolved to drive through the night. The south, the south, at last. That's where I will find my peace. Intense disgust at the banality of my English life. How I detest London and all my friends. Except Sholto, perhaps. And Hermione. And Sophie.

Wednesday

Crossed the Loire and everything changed. Blue skies, a mineral flinty sun hammering down. *Beau ciel, vrai ciel, regarde-moi qui change.* Opened every window in the Packard and drove in a warm buffeting breeze.

Lunch in Angoulême. Ham and Moselle. I had a sudden urge to take Douglas and Sylvia some sweet Monbazillac as a present. Drove on to Libourne and then up the river to St Foy. I turned off the main road, trying to remember the little château we had visited before, in '26, near a place called Pomport.

I must have missed a sign because I found myself in a part of the countryside I did not recognize, in a narrow valley with dark woods at its rim. Blond wind-combed wheat fields stirred silently on either side, the road no longer metalled. And that was when the clanking started in the Packard's engine.

I stopped and raised the bonnet. A hot, oily smell, a wisp of something. Smoke? Steam? I stood there in the gathered, broiling heat of the afternoon wondering what to do.

A goatish farmer in a pony and trap understood my request for a 'garage' and directed me up a dusty lane. There was a village, he said, St Bartélemy.

St Bartélemy: one street of ancient shuttered houses, with pocked, honey-coloured walls. A church with a hideous new spire, quite out of proportion. I found the garage by a bridge over the torpid stream that wound round the village. The *garagiste*, a genial young man in horn-rimmed spectacles, looked at the Packard in frank amazement and said he would have to send to Bergerac for the part he needed. How long would that take? I asked. He shrugged. A day, two days, who knows? And besides, he said, pointing to a glossy limousine up on blocks, he had to finish Monsieur le Comte's car first. There was a hotel I could stay in, he said, at the other end of the village. The Hôtel des Voyageurs.

Thursday

Dinner in the hotel last night. Stringy roast chicken and a rough red wine. I was alone in the dining-room, served by an ancient wheezing man, when the hotel's other guest arrived. A woman. She was tall and slim, her dark brown hair cut in a fashionable bob. She wore a dress of cobalt-blue crêpe de Chine, with a short skirt gathered at the hips. She barely glanced at me and treated the old waiter with brutal abruptness. She was French, or else completely bilingual, and everything about her was redolent of wealth and prestige. At first glance her face seemed not pretty, a little hard, with a slightly hooked nose, but as I covertly gazed at her across the dining-room, studying her features as she picked at her meal, her face's shadowed planes and angles, the slight pout of the upper lip, the perfect plucked arcs of her eyebrows began to assume a fascinating worldly beauty. She ordered a coffee and smoked a cigarette, never once looking in my direction. I was about to invite her to join me for a *digestif*, when she stood up and left the room. As she passed my table she looked at me for the first time, squarely, with a casual candid curiosity.

Slept well. For the first time since leaving London did not dream of Louise.

Friday

Encountered the woman in the hotel's small garden. I was sitting at a tin table beneath a chestnut tree, spreading fig jam on a croissant, when I heard her call.

'Thierry?'

I turned, and her face fell. She apologized for interrupting me; she said she thought I was someone else, the linen jacket I was wearing had made her think I was her husband. He had one very similar, the same hair colour too. I introduced myself. She said she was La Comtesse de Benoit-Voulon.

'Your husband is staying here?' I asked. She was tall, her eyes were almost on the same level as mine. I could not help noticing the way the taupe silk singlet she wore clung to her breasts. Her eyes were very pale brown; they seemed to look at me with unusual curiosity.

She told me her husband was visiting his mother. The arc of an eyebrow lifted. 'The old lady and I . . .' she paused diplomatically, 'we do not enjoy each other's company, so . . . so I prefer to wait in the hotel. And, besides, our car is being repaired.'

'So is mine,' I said, with a silly laugh, which I instantly regretted. 'Quite a coincidence.'

'Yes,' she said thoughtfully, frowning. That curious glance again. 'It is, isn't it?'

To fill my empty day I walked to the next village, called Argenson, and lunched on a tough steak and a delicious tangy *vin rouge en carafe*. On the way back I was given a lift in a lorry piled high with sappy pine logs. My nose prickled with resin all the way back to St Bartélemy.

The hotel was quiet, no one was in the lobby. My key was missing from its hook behind the desk so I assumed the maid was still cleaning the room. Upstairs, the door was very slightly ajar, the room beyond dark and shuttered against the sun. I stepped inside. La Comtesse de Benoit-Voulon was lifting a book from my open suitcase.

'Mr Mountstewart,' she said, the guilt and surprise absent from her face within a second. 'I'm so glad you decided to come back early.'

Friday

I must make sure I have this right. Must make sure I forget nothing.

We made love in the cool afternoon darkness of my room. There was a strange relaxed confidence about it all, as if it had been prefigured in some way, in the unhurried, tolerant manner our bodies moved to accommodate each other. And afterwards we chatted, like old friends. Her name, she said, was Giselle. They were going to Hyères, they had a house there. They always spent August in Hyères, she and her husband.

Then she turned to face me and said, 'Logan? . . . Have we ever met before?'

I laughed. 'I think I would have remembered.'

'Perhaps you know Thierry? Perhaps I've seen you with Thierry.'

'Definitely not.'

She cradled my face in her hands and stared fiercely at me. She said in a quiet voice, 'He didn't send you, did he? If he did you must tell me now.' Then she laughed herself, when she saw my baffled look, heard my baffled protestations. 'Forget it,' she said. 'I always think he's playing tricks on me. He's like that, Thierry, with his games.'

I slept that afternoon, and when I woke she had gone. Downstairs the old waiter had set only one table for dinner. I asked where the lady was and he said she had paid her bill and left the hotel.

At the garage the limousine had gone. The young *garagiste* proudly brandished the spare part for my Packard and said it would be ready for tomorrow. I pointed at the empty blocks where the count's car had been.

'Did he come for his car?'

'Two hours ago.'

'With his wife?'

'Who?'

'Was there a woman with him, a lady?'

'Oh yes.' The *garagiste* smiled at me and offered me one of his yellow cigarettes, which I accepted. 'Every year he spends two days with his mother, on his way South. Every year there's a different one.'

'Different wife?'

He looked at me knowingly. He drew heavily on his cigarette, his eyes wistfully distant. 'They're from Paris these girls. Amazing.' He shook his head in frustrated admiration. Once a year St Bartélemy had a visit from one of these astonishing women, he said, these radiant visitors. They stayed in the Hôtel des Voyageurs . . . One day, one day he was going to go to Paris and see them for himself.

Saturday

At the Café Riche et des Sports in Bergerac, finish my article on Sainte-Beuve. I pour a cognac into my coffee and compose a telegram to Douglas cancelling my visit. *O qu'ils sont pittoresques les trains manqués!* That will not be my fate. I unfold my road map and plot a route to Hyères.

Never Saw Brazil

On one of the sunniest of bright May mornings Senator Dom Liceu Maximiliano Lobo needlessly ran his comb through his neat goatee and ordered his chauffeur to pull into the side of the road. On mornings like these he liked to walk the remaining five hundred metres to his office, which he maintained, out of sentiment's sake, and because of the sea breezes, in Salvador's *Cidade Alta*. He sauntered along the side-walks, debating pleasantly whether to linger a moment with a coffee and a newspaper on the terrace of the hotel, or whether to stop off at Olimpia's little apartment, which he kept for her, at very reasonable expense, in an old colonial building in a square near the cathedral. She would not be expecting him, and it might be an amusing, not to say sensuous, experience to dally an hour or so this early before the day's work called. How bright the sun was, this fine morning, Senator Dom Liceu Maximiliano Lobo thought as he turned towards the cathedral, his heels ringing on the cobbles, and how very vivid the solar benefaction made the geraniums. Life was indeed good.

The name was the problem, he saw. The problem lay there, definitely. Because . . . Because if you were not happy with your name, he realized, then a small but sustained lifelong stress was imposed on your psyche, your sense of self. It was like being condemned to wear too-small shoes all the time: you could still get about but there would always be a pinching, a corn or two aching, something unnaturally hobbled about your gait.

Wesley Bright. Wesley. Bright.

The trouble with his name was that it wasn't *quite* stupid enough – he was not a Wesley Bilderbeest or a Wesley Bugger; in fact, it was *almost* a good name. If he had been Wesley Blade, say, or Wesley Beauregard he would have no complaints.

'Wesley?'

Janice passed him the docket. He clicked the switch on the mike.

'Four–seven? Four–seven?'

Silence. Just the permanent death rattle of the ether.

Four–seven answered. 'Four–seven.'

'Parcel, Four–seven. Pick up at Track-Track. Going to Putney, as directed.'

'Account?'

Wesley sighed. 'Yes, Four–seven. We do not do cash.' These new drivers. God.

'Oh, yeah. Roger, Rog.'

He could always change his name, he supposed. Roger, perhaps. Roger Bright. Wesley Roger . . . No. There was that option, though: choose a new moniker, a new handle. But he wondered about that too: hard to shake off an old name, he would guess. It was the way you thought of yourself, after all, your tag on the pigeon-hole. And when you were young you never thought your name was odd – it was a dissatisfaction that came with ageing, a realization that one didn't really like being a 'Wesley Bright' sort of person at all. In his case it had started at college, this chafing, this discomfort. He wondered about these fellows, actors and rock musicians, who called themselves Tsar, or Zane Zorro, or D. J. Sofaman . . . He was sure that, to themselves, they were always Norman Sidcup or Wilbur Dongdorfer in their private moments.

'Wesley?'

Janice handed him the phone receiver. 'It's your Pauline. Wants a word.'

Colonel Liceu 'o Falcao' Lobo opened his eyes and he saw the sun had risen sharp and green through the leafmass outside his bedroom. He shifted and stretched and felt the warm flank of Nilda brush his thigh. He eased himself out of bed and stood naked in the greenbright gloom. He freed his sweaty balls, tugging delicately at his scrotum. He rubbed his face and chest, inhaled, walked quietly out on to the balcony and felt the cool morning on his nakedness. He stood there, the wooden planks rough beneath his bare feet, and leaned on the balustrade looking at the beaten earth parade-ground his battalion had spent two weeks clearing out of the virgin jungle. There was nothing like a new parade-ground, Colonel Liceu Lobo thought, with a thin smile of satisfaction, to signal you were here to stay.

He saw Sergeant Elias Galvao emerge from the latrines and amble across the square towards the battalion mess, tightening his belt as he went. A good man, Galvao, a professional, up this early too.

'Morning, Sergeant,' Colonel Liceu Lobo called from his balcony. Sergeant Elias Galvao came abruptly to attention, swivelled to face his naked colonel and saluted.

'Carry on,' Colonel Liceu Lobo instructed. Not a flicker on his impassive face, excellent. Sergeant Galvao's lieutenant's pips could not be long away.

'Liceu?' Nilda's husky sleepy voice came from the bedroom. 'Where are you?' The colonel felt his manhood stir, as if of its own accord. Yes, he thought, there were some compensations to be had from a provincial command.

Wesley, trying not to inhale, walked with his business partner, Gerald Brockway, co-owner of B. B. Radio Cars, through the humid fug of the 'bullpen' towards the front door. There were three drivers there waiting for jobs and they were naturally talking about cars.

'How's the Carlton, Tone?' Gerald asked.

'Magic.'

'Brilliant.'

'Cheers.'

Outside, Wesley opened the passenger door of his Rover for Gerald.

'You happy with this?' Gerald asked. 'I thought you wanted a Scorpio.'

'It's fine,' Wesley said.

'Noel got five grand for his Granada.'

'Really?'

'They hold their value, the old ones. Amazing. Years later. It's well rubbish what they did, restyling like that.'

Wesley couldn't think of what to say. He thought a shrill ringing had started in his inner ear. Tinnitus. He lived in constant fear of tinnitus.

'Change for the sake of change,' Gerald said, slowly, sadly, shaking his head.

Wesley started the engine and pulled away.

'Look at Saab.'

'Sorry?'

'They've had to bring back the 900. You can't give away a 9000.'

'Can we talk about something else, Ger?'

Gerald looked at him. 'You all right?'

'Of course. Just, you know.'

'No prob, my son. Where are we going to eat?'

'Everyone has heard of samba and bossa nova, sure,' Wesley said. 'But this is another type of music called *chorinho* – not many people know about it. Love it. Play it all the time. I can lend you some CDs.'

'I'd like to give him a break, Wes. But something in me says fire the bastard. Why should we, why should we help him, Wes? Why? Big error. "No good deed goes unpunished", that's my personal philosophy. Is there any way we can turn this down? What the hell is it?'

'*Chorinho*.'

'You cannot diddle major account customers. Two hours' waiting time? I mean, what does he take us for? Couple of merchant bankers?'

'It means "little cry".'

'What is this stuff, Wesley? You got any English music?'

Wesley watched Gerald mash his egg mayonnaise into a creamy pulp. He dribbled thin streams of olive oil and vinegar on to the mixture, which he stirred, and then freely sprinkled on pepper and salt.

'That's disgusting,' Wesley said. 'How am I meant to eat this?' He pointed his knife at his steak.

'I haven't had a steak for two years. You should have my teeth problems, Wesley. You should feel sorry for me, mate.'

'I do feel sorry for you. I'd feel more sorry for you if you'd been to a dentist. You *can* be helped, you know. You don't have to suffer. A man of your age. Jesus.'

'Dentists and me, Wes. Not on. Actually, it's very tasty.'

He ate some of his mixture. Wesley looked round for a waitress and saw Elizabetta, the plump one. She came over, beaming.

'Pint of lager, please. Ger?'

'Large gin and tonic.'

Wesley lowered his voice. 'Is, um, Margarita in today?' he asked Elizabetta.

'This afternoon she come.'

He shifted his shoulders round. Gerald was not listening. 'Tell her I'll phone. Say Wesley will phone. Wesley.'

'Wesley. OK.'

Gerald pulped his apple crumble with the back of his spoon.

'Nice little place this, Wes. Worth the drive. What is it, Italian?'

'Sort of. Bit of everything.'

' "International cuisine", then.'

Wesley looked around the Caravelle. There was no nautical theme visible in its pragmatic décor, unless you counted the one seascape amongst its five reproductions on the wall. He and Gerald sat in a row of booths reminiscent more of – what was the word? Seating arrangements in libraries . . . – carrels, yes. Maybe the name was a malapropism, he thought. An asparagus on the banks of the Nile. Someone had blundered: it should have been called the the Carrel Café & Restaurant. Names, again . . . He stopped thinking about it and thought instead about Margarita.

Mar-gar-it-a. Not Margaret.

He rolled the 'r's. Marrrrgarrritha.

She was dark of course, very Latin, with a severe thin face that possessed, he thought, what you might call a strong beauty. Not pretty, exactly, but there was a look about her that attracted him, although, he realized, she was one of these southern European

273

women who would not age well. But now she was young and slim and her hair was long and, most important of all, she was Portuguese. *Uma moca bonita.*

Gerald offered him one of his small cigars.

Doctor Liceu Lobo put down his coffee cup and relit his *real excelente*. He drew, with pedantic and practised care, a steady thin stream of smoke from the neatly docked and already nicely moist end and held it in his mouth, savouring the tobacco's dry tang before pluming it at the small sunbird that pecked at the crumbs of his pastry on the patio table. The bird flew off with a shrill *shgrreakakak* and Doctor Liceu Lobo chuckled. It was time to return to the clinic, Senhora Fontenova was due for her vitamin D injections.

He felt Adalgisa's hand on his shoulder and he leaned his head back against her firm midriff; her finger trickled down over his collar bone and tangled and twirled the dense grey hairs on his chest.

'Your mother wants to see you.'

Wesley swung open the gate to his small and scruffy garden and reminded himself yet again to do something about the clematis that overburdened the trellis on either side of his front door. Pauline was bloody meant to be i/c garden, he told himself, irritated at her, but then he also remembered he had contrived to keep her away from the house the last month or so, prepared to spend weekends and the odd night at her small flat rather than have her in his home. As he hooked his door keys out of his tight pocket with one hand he tugged with the other at a frond of clematis that dangled annoyingly close to his face and a fine confetti of dust and dead leaves fell quickly on his hair and shoulders.

After he had showered he lay naked on his bed, his hand on his cock, and thought about masturbating but decided against. He felt clean and, for the first time that day, almost relaxed. He thought about Margarita and wondered what she looked like with her clothes off. She was thin, perhaps a little on the thin side for his taste, if he were honest, but she did have a distinct bust and her long straight hair was always clean, though he wished she wouldn't tuck it behind her ears and drag it taut into a lank, swishing ponytail. Restaurant regulations, he supposed. He realized then that he had never even seen her with her hair down and felt, for a moment, a sharp intense sorrow for himself and his lot in life. He sat up and swung his legs off the bed, amazed that there was a shimmer of tears in his eyes.

'God. Jesus!' he said mockingly to himself, out loud. 'Poor little chap.'

He dressed himself brusquely.

Downstairs, he poured himself a large rum and Coke and put Milton Nascimento on the CD player and hummed along to the great man's ethereal falsetto. Never failed to cheer him up. Never failed. He took a great gulp of the chilled drink and felt the alcohol surge. He swayed over to the drinks cabinet and added another slug. It was only four-thirty in the afternoon. Fuck it, he thought. Fuck it.

He should have parked somewhere else, he realised crossly, as unexpected sun warmed the Rover as he waited outside Pauline's bank. He didn't have a headache but his palate was dry and stretched and his sinuses were responding unhappily to the rum. He flared his nostrils and exhaled into his cupped hand. His breath felt unnaturally hot on his palm. He sneezed, three times, violently. Come on, Pauline. Jesus.

She emerged from the stout teak doors of the bank, waved, and skittered over towards the car. High heels, he saw. She *has* got nice legs. Definitely, he thought. Thin ankles. They must be three-inch heels, he reckoned, she'll be taller than me. Was it his imagination or was that the sun flashing off the small diamond cluster of her engagement ring?

He leant across the seat and flung the door open for her.

'Wesley! You going to a funeral or something? Gaw!'

'It's just a suit. Jesus.'

'It's a black suit. Black. Really.'

'Charcoal grey.'

'Where's your Prince of Wales check? I love that one.'

'Cleaners.'

'You don't wear a black suit to a christening, Wesley. Honestly.'

Professor Liceu Lobo kissed the top of his mother's head and sat down at her feet.

'Hey, little Mama, how are you today?'

'Oh, I'm fine. A little closer to God.'

'Nah, little Mama, He needs you here, to look after me.'

She laughed softly and smoothed the hair back from his forehead in gentle combing motions.

'Are you going to the university today?'

'Tomorrow. Today is for you, little Mama.'

He felt her small rough hands on his skin at the hairline and closed his eyes. His mother had been doing this to him ever since he could remember. Soothing, like waves on the shore. 'Like waves on the shore your hands on my hair' . . . The line came to him and with it, elusively, a hint of something more. Don't force it, he told himself, it will come. The rhythm was fixed already. Like waves on the shore. The mother figure, mother earth . . .

Maybe there was an idea to investigate. He would work on it in the study, after dinner. Perhaps a poem? Or maybe the title of a novel? *As ondas em la praia.* It had a serene yet epic ring to it.

He heard a sound and looked up, opening his eyes to see Marialva carrying a tray. The muffled belling of ice in a glass jug filled with a clear fruit punch. Seven glasses. The children must be back from school.

Wesley looked across the room at Pauline trying vainly to calm the puce, wailing baby, Daniel-Ian Young, his nephew. It was a better name than Wesley Bright, he thought – just – though he had never come across the two Christian names thus conjoined before. Bit of a mouthful. He wondered if he dared point out to his brother-in-law the good decade of remorseless bullying that lay ahead for the youngster once his peers discovered what his initials spelled. He decided to store it away in his grudge-bunker as potential retaliation. Sometimes Dermot really got on his wick.

He watched his brother-in-law, Dermot Young, approach, two pint-tankards in hand. Wesley accepted his gladly. He had a terrible thirst.

'Fine pair of lungs on him, any road,' Dermot said. 'You were saying, Wesley.'

'– no, it's a state called Minas Geraes, quite remote, but with this amazing musical tradition. I mean, you've got Beto Guedes, Toninho Horta, the one and only Milton Nascimento, of course, Lo Borges, Wagner Tiso. All these incredible talents who –'

'– HELEN! Can you put him down, or something? We can't hear ourselves think, here.'

Wesley gulped fizzy beer. Pauline, relieved of Daniel-Ian, was coming over with a slice of christening cake on a plate, his mother in tow.

'All right, all right,' Pauline said, with an unpleasant leering tone to her voice, Wesley thought. 'What are you two plotting? Mmm?'

'Where did you get that suit, Wesley?' his mother asked, guilelessly. 'Is it one of your dad's?'

There was merry laughter at this. Wesley kept a smile on his face.

'No,' Dermot said, 'Wes was telling me about this bunch of musicians from –'

'– Brazil.' Pauline's shoulders sagged and she turned wearily to Wesley's mother. 'Told you, didn't I, Isobel? Brazil. Brazil. Told you. Honestly.'

'You and Brazil,' his mother admonished. 'It's not as if we've got any Brazilians in the family.'

'Not as if you've even been there,' Pauline said, a distinct hostility in her voice. 'Never even set foot.'

Wesley silently hummed the melody from a João Gilberto samba to himself. Gilberto had taken the traditional form and distilled it through a cool jazz filter. It was João who had stripped away the excess of percussion in Brazilian music and brought bossa nova to the –

'Yeah, what is it with you and Brazil, Wes?' Dermot asked, a thin line of beer suds on his top lip. 'What gives?'

WHUCHINNNNNNG! WHACHANNNNGGG!! Liceu Lobo put down his guitar and before selecting the mandolin he tied his dreadlocks back behind his head in a slack bun. Gibson Piacava played a dull roll on the *zabumba* and Liceu Lobo began slowly to strum the musical phrase that seemed to be dominating 'The Waves on the Shore' at this stage in its extemporized composition. Joel Carlos Brandt automatically started to echo the mandolin phrases on his guitar and Bola da Rocha plaintively picked up the melody on his saxophone.

Behind the glass of the recording studio Albertina swayed her hips to and fro to the sinuous rhythm that was slowly building. Pure *chorinho*, she thought, sensuous yet melancholic, only Liceu is capable of this, of all the great *choroes* in Brazil, he was the greatest. At that moment he looked round and caught her eye and he smiled at her as he played. She kissed the tip of her forefinger and pressed it against the warm glass of the window that separated them. Once Liceu and his fellow musicians started a session like this it could last for days, weeks even. She would wait patiently for him, though, wait until he was finished and take him home to their wide bed.

Wesley stepped out into the back garden and flipped open his mobile phone.

'Café Caravelle, may I help you, please?'

'Ah. Could I speak to, ah, Margarita?'

'MARGARITA! Telefono.'

In the chilly dusk of a back garden in Hounslow Wesley Bright listened to the gabble of foreign voices, the erratic percussion of silverware and china, and felt he was calling some distant land, far overseas. A warmth located itself in his body, a spreading coin of heat, deep in his bowels.

'Hello?' That slight guttural catch on the 'h' . . .

'Margarita, it's Wesley.'

'Ghello?'

'Wesley. It's me – Wesley?'

'Please?'

'WESLEY!' He caught himself from shouting louder, and repeated his name in a throat-tearing whisper several times, glancing round at the yellow windows of Dermot's house. He saw someone peering at him, a silhouette.

'Ah, Weseley,' Margarita said. 'Yes?'

279

'I'll pick you up at ten, outside the café.'

Pauline stood at the kitchen door frowning out into the thickening dusk of the garden. Wesley advanced into the rectangle of light the open door had thrown on the grass.

'What're you up to, Wesley?'

Wesley slid his thin phone into his hip pocket.

'Needed a breath of fresh air,' he said. 'I'm feeling a bit off, to tell the truth. Those vol-au-vents tasted dodgy to me.'

Pauline was upset, she had been expecting a meal out after the christening, but she was also concerned for him and his health. 'I thought you looked a bit sort of pallid,' she said when he dropped her at her flat. She made him wait while she went inside and re-emerged with two sachets of mint infusion, 'to help settle your stomach', she said. She took them whenever she felt bilious, she told him, and they worked wonders.

As he drove off he smelt strongly the pungent impress of her perfume, or powder or make-up, on his cheek where she had kissed him and he felt a squirm of guilt at his duplicity – if something so easily accomplished merited the description – and a small pelt of shame covered him for a minute or two as he headed east towards the Café Caravelle and the waiting Margarita.

Her hair was down. Her hair was down and he was both rapt and astonished at the change it wrought in her. And to see her out of black, too, he thought, it was almost too much. He carried their drinks through the jostling noisy pub to the back where she sat, on a high stool, elbow resting on a narrow shelf designed to take glasses. She was drinking double vodka and water, no ice and no slice, a fact he found exciting and vaguely troubling. He had smelt her drink as the barmaid had served up his rum and Coke and it had seemed redolent of heavy industry, some strange fuel or new lubricant, something one would pour into a machine rather than down one's throat. It seemed, also, definitely not a drink of the warm south either, not at all apt for his taciturn Latin beauty, more suited to the bleak cravings of a sheet-metal worker in Smolensk. Still, it was gratifying to observe how she put it away, shudderless, in three pragmatic draughts. Then she spoke briefly, brutally, of how much she hated her job. It was a familiar theme, one Wesley recognized from his two previous social encounters with Margarita — the first a snatched coffee in a hamburger franchise before her evening shift began, and then a more leisurely autumnal Sunday lunch at a brash pub on the river at Richmond.

On that last occasion she had seemed out of sorts, cowed perhaps by the strapping conviviality of the tall noisy lads and their feisty, jolly girls. But tonight she had returned to the same tiresome plaint — the mendacious and rebarbative qualities of the Caravelle's manager, João — so Wesley had to concede it was clearly something of an obsession.

They had kissed briefly and not very satisfactorily after their Sunday pub tryst and Wesley felt this allowed him now to take her free hand (her other held her cigarette) and squeeze it. She stopped talking and, he thought, half smiled at him.

'Weseley,' she said, and stubbed out her cigarette. Then she grinned. 'Tonight, I thin' I wan' to be drunk . . .'

There you had it, he thought. There. That was it. That moment held the gigantic difference between a Pauline and a Margarita. A mint infusion and an iceless vodka. He felt his bowels weaken with shocking desire.

He returned to the bar to fetch another drink for her and ordered the same for himself. The tepid alcohol seemed all the more powerful for the absence of chill. His nasal passages burned, he wrinkled his tear-flooded eyes. Made from potatoes, hard to believe. Or is it potato peelings? His teeth felt loose. He stood beside her. Someone had taken his stool.

Margarita sipped her drink with more decorum this time. 'I hate that fackin' job,' she said.

He raised her knuckles to his lips and dabbed at them.

'God, I've missed you,' he said, then took a deep breath. 'Margarita,' he said softly, '*tenho muito atração para tu.*' He hoped to God he had it right, with the correct slushing and nasal sounds. He found Portuguese farcically difficult to pronounce, no matter the hours he spent listening to his tapes.

She frowned. Too fast you fool, you bloody fool.

'What?' Her lips half formed a word. 'I, I don't —'

More slowly, more carefully: '*Tenho muito atração — muito, muito — para tu.*'

He slipped his hand round her thin back, fingers snagging momentarily on the buckle of her bra, and drew her to him. He kissed her, there in the hot pub, boldly, with noticeable teeth clash, but no recoil from Margarita.

He moved his head back, his palm still resting on her body, warm above her hip.

She touched her lips with the palp of her thumb, scrutinizing him, not hostile, he was glad to see, not even surprised. She drank some more of her grey flat drink, still looking at him over the rim of her glass.

'*Sempre para tu, Margarita, sempre.*' Huskily, this. Sincere.

'Weseley. What you saying? *Sempre*, I know. But the rest . . .'

'I . . . I am speaking Portuguese.'

'For why?'

'Because, I . . . Because I want to speak your language to you. I love your language, you must understand. I love it. I hear it in my head, in your music.'

'Well . . .' She shrugged and reached for her cigarettes. 'Then you must not speak Portuguese at me, Weseley. I am Italian.'

Marta shucked off her brassière and had hooked down her panties with her thumbs within seconds, Liceu Lobo thought, of his entering her room in the bordello. He caught a glimpse of her plump fanny from the light cast by the bathroom cubicle. She was hot tonight, on fire, he thought, as he hauled off his T-shirt and allowed his shorts to fall to the floor. As he reached the bedside he felt her hands reaching for his engorged member. He was a pretty boy and even the oldest hooker liked a pretty boy with a precocious and impatient tool. He felt Marta's hands all over his *pepino* as if she were assessing it for some strumpet's inventory. *Maldito seja!* Liceu Lobo thought, violently clenching his sphincter muscles as Marta settled him between her generous and welcoming thighs, he should definitely have jerked off before coming here tonight. Marta always had that effect on him. *Deus!* He hurled himself into the fray.

It had not gone well. No. He had to face up to that, acknowledge it squarely. As love-making went it was indubitably B minus. B double-minus, possibly. And it was his fault. But could he put it down to the fact that he had been in bed with an Italian girl and *not* a Portuguese one? Or perhaps it had something to do with the half-dozen vodkas and water he had consumed as he kept pace with Margarita? . . .

But the mood had changed, subtly, when he had learned the truth, a kind of keening sadness, a thin draught of melancholy seemed to enter the boisterous pub, depressing him. An unmistakable sense of being let down by Margarita's nationality. She was meant to be Portuguese, that was the whole point, anything else was wrong.

He turned over in his bed and stared at the faint silhouette of Margarita's profile as she slept beside him. Did it matter? he urged himself. This was the first non-British girl he had kissed, let alone made love to, so why had he been unable to shake off that sense of distraction? It was a sullenness of spirit that had possessed him, as if he were a spoilt child who had been promised and then denied a present. It was hardly Margarita's fault, after all, but an irrational side of him still blamed her for not being Portuguese, for unconsciously raising his hopes by not warning him from their first encounter that she didn't fit his national bill. Somehow she had to share the responsibility.

He turned away and dozed, and half dreamed of Liceu Lobo in a white suit. On a mountain top with Leonor or Branca or Caterina or Joana. A balcony with two cane chairs. Mangoes big as rugby balls. Liceu, blond hair flying, putting down his sunglasses, offering his hand, saying, 'My deal is my smile.' Joana's slim mulatto body. The sound of distant water falling.

He half sat, blinking stupidly.

'Joana?'

The naked figure in his doorway froze.

'Joana?'

The figure moved.

'*Vaffanculo*,' Margarita said, weariness making her voice harsh. She switched on the light and began to get dressed, still talking, but more to herself than to him. Wesley's meagre Portuguese was no help here, but he could tell her words were unkind. He hadn't fully awakened from his dream. How could he explain that to her? She was dressed in a moment and did not shut the door as she left.

After she had gone, Wesley pulled on his dressing-gown and walked slowly down the stairs. He sat for a while in his unlit sitting-room swigging directly from the rum bottle, resting it on his knee between mouthfuls, coughing and breathing deeply, wiping his mouth with the back of his hand. Eventually he rose to his feet and slid Elis Regina into his CD player. The strange and almost insupportable plangency of the woman's voice filled the shadowy space around him. '*Nem Uma Lagrima*'. 'Not one tear,' Wesley said to himself. Out loud. His voice sounded peculiar to him, a stranger's. Poor tragic Elis, Elis Regina, who died in 1982, aged thirty-seven, tragically, of an unwise cocktail of drugs and alcohol. 'Drink 'n' drugs' the CD's sleeve notes had said. Tragic. A tragic loss to Brazilian music. Fucking tragic. He would call Pauline in the morning, that's what he would do. In the meantime he had his *chorinho* to console him. He would make it up with Pauline, she deserved a treat, some sort of treat, definitely, a weekend somewhere. Definitely. Not one tear, Elis Regina sang for him. He would be all right. There was always Brazil. Not one tear.

The Dream Lover

'None of these girls is French, right?'

'No. But they're European.'

'Not the same thing, man. French is crucial.'

'Of course . . .' I don't know what he is talking about but it seems politic to agree.

'You know any French girls?'

'Of course,' I say again. This is almost a lie, but it doesn't matter at this stage.

'But *well*?' I mean well enough to ask out?'

'I don't see why not.' Now this time we are into mendacity, but I am unconcerned. I feel good, adult, quite confident today. This lie can germinate and grow for a while.

I am standing in a pale parallelogram of March sunshine, leaning against a wall, talking to my American friend, Preston. The wall belongs to the *Centre Universitaire Méditerranéen*, a large stuccoed villa on the front at Nice. In front of us is a small cobbled courtyard bounded by a balustrade. Beyond is the Promenade des Anglais, its four lanes busy with Nice's traffic. Over the burnished roofs of the cars I can see the Mediterranean. The Baie des Anges looks grey and grim in this season: old, tired water − ashy, cindery.

'We got to do something . . .' Preston says, a hint of petulant desperation in his voice. I like the 'we'. Preston scratches his short hard hair noisily. 'What with the new apartment, and all.'

'You moved out of the hotel?'

'Yeah. Want to come by tonight?' He shifts his big frame as if troubled by a fugitive itch, and pats his pockets – breast, hip, thigh – looking for his cigarettes. 'We got a bar on the roof.'

I am intrigued, but I explain that the invitation has to be turned down as it is a Monday, and every Monday night I have a dinner appointment with a French family – friends of friends of my mother.

Preston shrugs, then finds and sets fire to a cigarette. He smokes an American brand called 'Picayune' which is made in New Orleans. When he came to France he brought two thousand with him. He has never smoked anything else since he was fourteen, he insists.

We watch our fellow students saunter into the building. They are nearly all strangers to me, these bright boys and girls, as I have only been in Nice a few weeks, and, so far, Preston is the only friend I have made. Slightly envious of their easy conviviality, I watch the others chatter and mingle – Germans, Scandinavians, Italians, Tunisians, Nigerians . . . We are all foreigners, trying hard to learn French and win our diplomas . . . Except for Preston, who makes no effort at all and seems quite content to remain monoglot.

A young guy with long hair rides his motorbike into the courtyard. He is wearing no shirt. He is English and, apart from me, the only other English person in the place. He revs his motorbike unnecessarily a few times before parking it and switching it off. He takes a T-shirt out of a saddle-bag and nonchalantly pulls it on. I think how I too would like to own a motorbike and do exactly what he has done . . . His name is Tim. One day, I imagine, we might be friends. We'll see.

Monsieur Cambrai welcomes me with his usual exhausting, impossible geniality. He shakes my hand fervently and shouts to his wife over his shoulder.

'*Ne bouge pas. C'est l'habitué!*'

That's what he calls me – *l'habitué*. *L'habitué de lundi*, to give the appellation in full, so called because I am invited to dinner every Monday night without fail. He almost never uses my proper name and sometimes I find this perpetual alias a little wearing, a little stressful. '*Salut, l'habitué*', '*Bien mangé, l'habitué?* '*Encore du vin, l'habitué?*' and so on. But I like him and the entire Cambrai family; in fact I like them so much that it makes me feel weak, insufficient, cowed.

Monsieur and Madame are small people, fit, sophisticated and nimble, with neat spry figures. Both of them are dentists, it so happens, who teach at the big medical school here in Nice. A significant portion of my affection for them owes to the fact that they have three daughters – Delphine, Stéphanie and Annique – all older than me and all possessed of – to my fogged and blurry eyes – an incandescent, almost supernatural beauty. Stéphanie and Annique still live with their parents, Delphine has a flat somewhere in the city, but she often dines at home. These are the French girls that I claimed to know, though 'know' is far too inadequate a word to sum up the complexity of my feelings for them. I come to their house on Monday nights as a supplicant and votary, both frightened and in awe of them. I sit in their luminous presence, quiet and eager, for two hours or so, unmanned by my astonishing good fortune.

I am humbled further when I consider the family's disarming, disinterested kindness. When I arrived in Nice they were the only contacts I had in the city and, on my mother's urging, I duly wrote to them citing our tenuous connection via my mother's friend. To my surprise I was promptly invited to dinner and then invited back every Monday night. What shamed me was that I knew I myself could never be so hospitable so quickly, not even to a close friend, and what was more I knew no one else who would be, either. So I cross the Cambrai threshold each Monday with a rich cocktail of emotions gurgling inside me: shame, guilt, gratitude, admiration and – it goes without saying – lust.

Preston's new address is on the Promenade des Anglais itself – the 'Résidence Les Anges'. I stand outside the building, looking up, impressed. I have passed it many times before, a distressing and vulgar edifice on this celebrated boulevard, an unadorned rectangle of coppery, smoked glass with stacked ranks of gilded aluminium balconies.

I press a buzzer in a slim, free-standing concrete post and speak into a crackling wire grille. When I mention the name 'Mr Fairfield' glass doors part softly and I am admitted to a bare granite lobby where a taciturn man in a tight suit shows me to the lift.

Preston rents a small studio apartment with a bathroom and kitchenette. It is a neat, pastel-coloured and efficient module. On the wall are a series of prints of exotic birds: a toucan, a bateleur eagle, something called a blue shrike. As I stand there looking round I think of my own temporary home, my thin room in Madame d'Amico's ancient, dim apartment, and the inefficient and bathless bathroom I have to share with her other lodgers, and a sudden hot envy rinses through me. I half hear Preston enumerating various financial consequences of his tenancy: how much this studio costs a month; the outrageous supplement he had to pay even to rent it in the first place; and how he had been obliged to cash in his return fare to the States (first class) in order to meet it. He says he has called his father for more money.

We ride up to the roof, six storeys above the Promenade. To my vague alarm there is a small swimming-pool up here and a large glassed-in cabana – furnished with a bamboo bar and some rattan seats – labelled 'Club Les Anges' in neon copperplate. A barman in a short cerise jacket runs this place, a portly, pale-faced fellow with a poor moustache whose name is Serge. Although Preston jokes patronizingly with him it is immediately quite clear to me both that Serge loathes Preston and that Preston is completely unaware of this powerful animus directed against him.

I order a large gin and tonic from Serge and for a shrill palpitating minute I loathe Preston too. I know there are many better examples on offer, of course, but for the time being this shiny building and its accoutrements will do nicely as an approximation of The Good Life for me. And as I sip my sour drink a sour sense of the world's huge unfairness crowds ruthlessly in. Why should this guileless, big American, barely older than me, with his two thousand Louisiana cigarettes, and his cashable first-class air tickets, have all *this* . . . while I live in a narrow frowsty room in an old woman's decrepit apartment? My straightened circumstances are caused by a seemingly interminable postal strike in Britain that means money cannot be transferred to my Nice account and I have to husband my financial resources like a neurotic peasant conscious of a hard winter lowering ahead. Where is *my* money, I want to know, my exotic bird prints, *my* club, *my* pool? How long will I have to wait before these artefacts become the commonplace of my life? . . . I allow this unpleasant voice to whine and whinge on in my head as we stand on the terrace and admire the view of the long bay. One habit I have already learnt, even at my age, is not to resist these fervent grudges – give them a loose rein, let them run themselves out, it is always better in the longer run.

In fact I am drawn to Preston, and want him to be my friend. He is tall and powerfully built – the word 'rangy' comes to mind – affable and not particularly intelligent. To my eyes his clothes are so parodically American as to be be beyond caricature: pale-blue baggy shirts with button–down collars, old khaki trousers short enough to reveal his white-socked ankles and big brown loafers. He has fair, short hair and even, unexceptionable features. He has a gold watch, a Zippo lighter and an ugly ring with a red stone set in it. He told me once, in all candour, in all modesty, that he 'played tennis to Davis Cup standard'.

I always wondered what he was doing in Nice, studying at the *Centre*. At first I thought he might be a draftee avoiding the war in Vietnam but I now suspect – based on some hints he has dropped – that he has been sent off to France as an obscure punishment of some sort. His family don't want him at home: he has done something wrong and these months in Nice are his penance.

But hardly an onerous one, that's for sure: he has no interest in his classes – those he can be bothered to take – nor in the language and culture of France. He simply has to endure this exile and he will be allowed home where, I imagine, he will resume his soft life of casual privilege and unreflecting ease once more. He talks a good deal about his eventual return to the States where he plans to impose his own particular punishment, or extract his own special reward. He says he will force his father to buy him an Aston Martin. His father will have no say in the matter, he remarks with untypical vehemence and determination. He will have his Aston Martin, and it is the bright promise of this glossy English car that really seems to sustain him through these dog days on the Mediterranean littoral.

*   *   *

Soon I find I am a regular visitor at the Résidence Les Anges, where I go most afternoons after my classes are over. Preston and I sit in the club, or by the pool if it is sunny, and drink. We consume substantial amounts (it all goes on his tab) and consequently I am usually fairly drunk by sunset. Our conversation ranges far and wide but at some point in every discussion Preston reiterates his desire to meet French girls. If I do indeed know some French girls, he says, why don't I ask them to the club? I reply that I am working on it, and coolly change the subject.

Steadily, over the days, I learn more about my American friend. He is an only child. His father (who has not responded to his requests for money) is a millionaire – real estate. His mother divorced him recently to marry another, richer, millionaire. Between his two sets of millionaire parents Preston has a choice of eight homes to visit in and around the USA: in Miami, New York, Palm Springs and a ranch in Montana. Preston dropped out of college after two semesters and does not work.

'Why should I?' he argues reasonably. 'They've got more than enough money for me too. Why should I bust my ass working trying to earn more?'

'But isn't it . . . What do you do all day?'

'All kinds of shit . . . But mostly I like to play tennis a lot. And I like to fuck, of course.'

'So why did you come to Nice?'

He grins. 'I was a bad boy.' He slaps his wrist and laughs. 'Naughty, naughty Preston.'

He won't tell me what he did.

It is spring in Nice. Each day we start to enjoy a little more sunshine and whenever it appears within ten minutes there is a particular girl, lying on the *plage publique* in front of the *Centre*, sunbathing. Often I stand and watch her spread out there, still, supine, on the cool pebbles – the only sunbather along the entire bay. It turns out she is well known, that this is a phenomenon that occurs every year. By early summer her tan is solidly established and she is very brown indeed. By August she is virtually black, with that kind of dense, matt tan, the life burned out of the skin, her pores brimming with melanin. Her ambition each year, they say, is to be the brownest girl on the Côte d'Azur . . .

I watch her lying there, immobile beneath the iridescent rain of ultraviolet. It is definitely not warm – even in my jacket and scarf I shiver slightly in the fresh breeze. How can she be bothered? I wonder, but at the same time I have to admit there is something admirable in such single-mindedness, such ludicrous dedication.

Eventually I take my first girl to the club to meet Preston. Her name is Ingrid, she is in my class, a Norwegian, but with dark auburn hair. I don't know her well but she seems a friendly, uncomplicated soul. She speaks perfect English and German.

'Are you French?' Preston asks, almost immediately.

Ingrid is very amused by this. 'I'm Norwegian,' she explains. 'Is it important?'

I apologize to Preston when Ingrid goes off to change into her swimming costume, but he waves it away, not to worry, he says, she's cute. Ingrid returns and we sit in the sun and order the first of our many drinks. Ingrid, after some prompting, smokes one of Preston's Picayune cigarettes. The small flaw that emerges to mar our pleasant afternoon is that, the more Ingrid drinks, so does her conversation become dominated by references to a French boy she is seeing called Jean-Jacques. Preston hides his disappointment; he is the acme of good manners.

Later, we play poker using cheese biscuits as chips. Ingrid sits opposite me in her multicoloured swimsuit. She is plumper than I had imagined, and I decide that if I had to sum her up in one word it would be 'homely'. Except for one detail: she has very hairy armpits. On one occasion she sits back in her chair, studying her cards for a full minute, her free hand idly scratching a bite on the back of her neck. Both Preston's and my eyes are drawn to the thick divot of auburn hair that is revealed by this gesture: we stare at it, fascinated, as Ingrid deliberates whether to call or raise. (After she has gone Preston confesses that he found her un-shavenness quite erotic. I am not so sure.)

That evening we sit on in the club long into the night, as usual the place's sole customers, with Serge unsmilingly replenishing our drinks as Preston calls for them. Ingrid's presence, the unwitting erotic charge that she has detonated in our normally tranquil, bibulous afternoons; seems to have unsettled and troubled Preston somewhat and without any serious prompting on my part he tells me why he has come to Nice. He informs me that the man his mother remarried was a widower, an older man, with four children already in their twenties. When Preston dropped out of college he went to stay with his mother and new stepfather.

He exhales, he eats several olives, his face goes serious and solemn for a moment.

'This man, Michael, had three daughters – and a son, who was already married – and, man, you should have seen those girls.' He grins, a stupid, gormless grin. 'I was eighteen years old and I got three beautiful girls sleeping down the corridor from me. What am I supposed to do?'

The answer, unvoiced, seemed to slip into the club like a draught of air. I felt my spine tauten.

'You mean –?'

'Yeah, sure. All three of them. Eventually.'

I don't want to speak, so I think through this. I imagine a big silent house, night, long dark corridors, closed doors. Three bored blonde tanned stepsisters. Suddenly there's a tall young man in the house, a virtual stranger, who plays tennis to Davis Cup standard.

'What went wrong?' I manage.

'Oldest one, Janie, got pregnant, didn't she? Last year.'

'Abortion?'

'Are you kidding? She just married her fiancé real fast.'

'You mean she was engaged when –'

'He doesn't know a thing. But she told my mother.'

'The . . . the child was –'

'Haven't seen him yet.' He turns and calls for Serge. 'No one knows, no one suspects . . .' He grins again. 'Until the kid starts smoking Picayunes.' He reflects on his life a moment, and turns his big mild face to me. 'That's why I'm here. Keeping my head down. Not exactly flavour of the month back home.'

The next girl I take to the club is also a Scandinavian – we have eight in our class – but this time a Swede, called Danni. Danni is very attractive and vivacious, in my opinion, with straight white-blonde hair. She's a tall girl, and she would be perfect but for the fact that she has one slightly withered leg, noticeably thinner than the other, which causes her to limp. She is admirably unselfconscious about her disability.

'Hi,' Preston says, 'are you French?'

Danni hides her incredulity. '*Mais, oui, monsieur. Bien sûr.*' Like Ingrid, she finds this presumption highly amusing. Preston soon realizes his mistake, and makes light of his disappointment.

Danni wears a small cobalt bikini and even swims in the pool, which is freezing. (Serge says there is something wrong with the heating mechanism but we don't believe him.) Danni's fortitude impresses Preston: I can see it in his eyes, as he watches her dry herself. He asks her what happened to her leg and she tells him she had polio as a child.

'Shit, you were lucky you don't need a caliper.'

This breaks the ice and we soon get noisily drunk, much to Serge's irritation. But there is little he can do as there is no one else in the club who might complain. Danni produces some grass and we blatantly smoke a joint. Typically, apart from faint nausea, the drug has not the slightest effect on me, but it affords Serge a chance to be officious and as he clears away a round of empty glasses he says to Preston, '*Ça va pas, monsieur, non, non, ça va pas.*'

'Fuck you, Serge,' he says amiably and Danni's unstoppable blurt of laughter sets us all off. I sense Serge's humiliation and realize the relationship with Preston is changing fast: the truculent deference has gone; the dislike is now overt, almost a challenge.

After Danni has left Preston tells me about his latest money problems. His bar bill at the club now stands at over $400 and the management is insisting it be settled. His father won't return his calls or acknowledge telegrams and Preston has no credit cards. He is contemplating pawning his watch in order to pay something into the account and defer suspicion. I buy it off him for 500 francs.

I look around my class counting the girls I know. I know most of them by now, well enough to talk to. Both Ingrid and Danni have been back to the club and have enthused about their afternoons there, and I realize that to my fellow students I have become an object of some curiosity as a result of my unexpected ability to dispense these small doses of luxury and decadence: the exclusive address, the privacy of the club, the pool on the roof, the endless flow of free drinks . . .

Preston decided to abandon his French classes a while ago and I am now his sole link with the *Centre*. It is with some mixed emotions — I feel vaguely pimp-like, oddly smirched — that I realize how simple it is to attract girls to the Club Les Anges.

Annique Cambrai is the youngest of the Cambrai daughters and the closest to me in age. She is only two years older than me but seems considerably more than that. I was, I confess, oddly daunted by her mature good looks, dark with a lean attractive face, and because of this at first I think she found me rather aloof, but now, after many Monday dinners, we have become more relaxed and friendly. She is studying law at the University of Nice and speaks good English with a marked American accent. When I comment on this she explains that most French universities now offer you a choice of accents when you study English and, like ninety per cent of students, she has chosen American.

I see my opportunity and take it immediately: would she, I diffidently enquire, like to come to the Résidence Les Anges to meet an American friend of mine and perhaps try her new accent out on him?

The next morning, on my way down the rue de France to the *Centre* I see Preston standing outside a pharmacy reading the *Herald Tribune*. I call his name and cross the road to tell him the excellent news about Annique.

'You won't believe this,' I say, 'but I finally got a real French girl.'

Preston's face looks odd: half a smile, half a morose grimace of disappointment.

'That's great,' he says, dully, 'wonderful.'

A tall, slim girl steps out of the pharmacy and hands him a plastic bag.

'This is Lois,' he says. We shake hands.

I know who Lois is, Preston has often spoken of her: my damn-near fiancée, he calls her. It transpires that Lois has flown over, spontaneously and unannounced, to visit him.

'And, boy, are my Mom and Dad mad as hell,' she laughs.

Lois is a pretty girl, with a round, innocent face quite free of make-up. She is tall, even in her sneakers she is as tall as me, with a head of incredibly thick, dense brown hair which, for some reason, I associate particularly with American girls. I feel sure also, though as yet I have no evidence, that she is a very clean person – physically clean, I mean to say – someone who showers and washes regularly, redolent of soap and the lingering farinaceous odour of talcum powder.

I stroll back with them to the Résidence. Lois's arrival has temporarily solved Preston's money problems: they have cashed in her return ticket and paid off the bar bill and the next quarter's rent which had come due. Preston feels rich enough to buy back his watch from me.

Annique looks less mature and daunting in her swimsuit, I'm pleased to say, though I was disappointed that she favoured a demure apple-green one-piece. The pool's heater has been 'fixed' and for the first time we all swim in the small azure rectangle – Preston and Lois, Annique and me. It is both strange and exciting for me to see Annique so comparatively unclothed and even stranger to lie side by side, thigh by thigh, inches apart, sunbathing.

Lois obviously assumes Annique and I are a couple – a quite natural assumption under the circumstances, I suppose – she would never imagine I had brought her for Preston. I keep catching him gazing at Annique, and a mood of frustration and intense sadness seems to emanate from him – a mood of which only I am aware. And in turn a peculiar exhilaration builds inside me, not just because of Lois's innocent assumption about my relation to Annique, but also because I know now that I have succeeded. I have brought Preston the perfect French girl: Annique, by his standards, represents the paradigm, the Platonic ideal for this American male. Here she is, unclothed, lying by his pool, in his club, drinking his drinks, but he can do nothing – and what makes my own excitement grow is the realization that for the first time in our friendship – perhaps for the first time in his life – Preston envies another person. Me.

As this knowledge dawns so too does my impossible love for Annique. Impossible, because nothing will ever happen. I know that – but Preston doesn't – and somehow the ghostly love affair, our love affair, between Annique and me, that will exist in Preston's mind, in his hot and tormented imagination, embellished and elaborated by his disappointment and lost opportunity, will be more than enough for me, more than I could have ever hoped for.

Now that Lois has arrived I stay away from the Résidence Les Anges. It won't be the same again and, despite my secret delight, I don't want to taunt Preston with the spectre of Annique. But I find that without the spur of his envy the tender fantasy inevitably dims; because in order for my dream life, my dream love, to flourish I need to share it with Preston. I decide to pay a visit. Preston opens the door of his studio.

'Hi, stranger,' he says, with some enthusiasm. 'Am I glad to see you.' He seems sincere. I follow him into the apartment. The small room is untidy, the bed unmade, the floor strewn with female clothes. I hear the noise of the shower from the bathroom: Lois may be a clean person but it is clear she is also something of a slut.

'How are things with Annique?' he asks, almost at once, as casually as he can manage. He has to ask, I know it.

I look at him. 'Good.' I let the pause develop, pregnant with innuendo. 'No, they're good.'

His nostrils flare and he shakes his head.

'God, you're one lucky . . .'

Lois comes in from the bathroom in a dressing-gown, towelling her thick hair dry.

'Hi, Edward,' she says, 'what's new?' Then she sits down on the bed and begins to weep.

We stand and look at her as she sobs quietly.

'It's nothing,' Preston says. 'She just wants to go home.' He tells me that neither of them has left the building for eight days. They are completely, literally, penniless. Lois's parents have cancelled her credit cards and collect calls home have failed to produce any response. Preston has been unable to locate his father and now his stepfather refuses to speak to him (a worrying sign) and although his mother would like to help she is powerless for the moment, given Preston's fall from grace. Preston and Lois have been living on a diet of olives, peanuts and cheese biscuits served up in the bar and, of course, copious alcohol.

'Yeah, but now we're even banned from there,' Lois says, with an unfamiliar edge to her voice.

'Last night I beat up on that fuckwit, Serge,' Preston explains with a shrug. 'Something I had to do.'

He goes on to enumerate their other problems: their bar bill stands at over $300; Serge is threatening to go to the police unless he is compensated; the management has grown hostile and suspicious.

'We got to get out of here,' Lois says miserably. 'I hate it here, I hate it.'

Preston turns to me. 'Can you help us out?' he says. I feel the laugh erupt within me.

I stand in Nice station and hand Preston two train tickets to Luxembourg and two one-way Iceland Air tickets to New York. Lois reaches out to touch them as if they were sacred relics.

'You've got a six-hour wait in Reykjavik for your connection,' I tell him, 'but, believe me, there is no cheaper way to fly.'

I bask in their voluble gratitude for a while. They have no luggage with them as they could not be seen to be quitting the Résidence. Preston says his father is now in New York and assures me I will be reimbursed the day they arrive. I have spent almost everything I possess on these tickets, but I don't care – I am intoxicated with my own generosity and the strange power it has conferred on me. Lois leaves us to go in search of a *toilette* and Preston embraces me in a clumsy hug. 'I won't forget this, man,' he says many times. We celebrate our short but intense friendship and affirm its continuance, but all the while I am waiting for him to ask me – I can feel the question growing in his head like a tumour. Through the crowds of passengers we see Lois making her way back. He doesn't have much time left.

'Listen,' he begins, his voice low, 'did you and Annique . . .? I mean, are you –'

'We've been looking for an apartment. That's why you haven't seen much of me.'

'Jesus . . .'

Lois calls out something about the train timetable, but we are not listening. Preston seems to be trembling, he turns away, and when he turns back I see the pale fires of impotent resentment light his eyes.

'Are you fucking her?'

I look at him in that way men look at each other. And then I say, 'Why else would we be looking for an apartment?'

Lois arrives and immediately notices Preston's taut face, oddly pinched. 'What's going on?' Lois asks. 'Are you OK?'

Preston gestures at me, as if he can't pronounce my name. 'Annique . . . They're moving in together.'

Lois squeals. She's so pleased, she really is, she really really likes Annique.

By the time I see them on to the train Preston has calmed down and our final farewells are sincere. He looks around the modest station intently as if trying to record its essence, as if now he wished to preserve something of this city he inhabited so complacently, with such absence of curiosity.

'God, it's too bad,' he says with an exquisite fervour. 'I know I could have liked Nice. I *know*. I really could.'

I back off, wordless; this is too good, this is too generous of him. This is perfect.

'Give my love to Annique,' Preston says quietly, as Lois calls loud goodbyes. He grins. 'Lucky bastard.'

'Don't worry,' I say, looking at Preston. 'I will.'

Alpes Maritimes

Anneliese, Ulricke and I go into Steve's sitting-room. Steve is sitting at a table writing a letter. 'Hi,' he says, not looking up. 'Won't be a second.' He scribbles his name and seals the letter in an envelope as the three of us watch him, wordlessly. He stands and turns to face us. His long clean hair, brushed straight back from his forehead, falls to his shoulders. Perhaps it's something to do with the dimness of the room but, against the pale ghost of his swimming trunks, his cock seems oddly pigmented – almost brown.

'Make yourselves at home,' he says. 'I'll just go put some clothes on.'

I have a girl now – Ulricke – and so everything should be all right. And it is, I suppose, except that I want Anneliese, her twin sister. I look closely at Anneliese to see her reaction to Steve's nakedness (Steve wants Anneliese too). She and Ulricke smile at each other. They both press their lips together with a hand, their eyes thin with delighted amusement at Steve's eccentricity. Automatically I smile too, but in fact I am covered in a hot shawl of irritation as I recall Steve's long-stride saunter from the room, his calmness, his unconcern.

★   ★   ★

Bent comes in. He is Steve's flat-mate, a ruddy Swede, bespectacled, with a square bulging face and unfortunate frizzy hair.

'Does he always do that?' Anneliese asks.

'I'm afraid so,' Bent says, ruefully. 'He comes in – he removes his clothes.'

The girls surrender themselves to their laughter. I ask for a soft drink.

It wasn't easy to meet Ulricke. She and Anneliese were doing a more advanced course than me at the *Centre* and so our classes seldom coincided. I remember being struck by rare glimpses of this rather strong-looking fashionable girl. I think it was Anneliese that I saw first, but I can't be sure. But the fact is that the one I met was Ulricke. How was I meant to know they were twins? By the time I discovered that those glimpses were not of one and the same person it was too late.

One lunchtime I was walking up to the university restaurant by the *Faculté de Droit* (the *restauru* by the *fac* as the French have it) when I heard my name called.

'Edward!' I turned.

It was Henni, a Finnish girl I knew, with Anneliese. At least I thought it was Anneliese but it turned out to be Ulricke. Until you know them both it's very hard to spot the difference.

We had lunch together. Then Ulricke and I went for coffee to a bar called Le Pub Latin. We spoke French, I with some difficulty. There was no mention of a twin sister, that first day, no Anneliese. I talked about my father; I lied modestly about my age, with more élan about my ambitions. Soon Ulricke interrupted to tell me that she spoke very good English. After that it was much easier.

Ulricke: tall, broad-shouldered, with a round, good-complexioned face – though her cheeks and nose tend to develop a shine as the day wears on – thick straight peanut-coloured hair parted in the middle . . . She and Anneliese are not-quite-identical twins. To be candid, Anneliese is prettier, though by compensation Ulricke has the sweeter temperament, as they say. Recently, Anneliese has streaked her hair blonde, which, as well as distinguishing her from her sister (too late, too late), adds, in my opinion, dramatically to her attractiveness. In Bremen, where they live (father a police inspector), they were both prize-winning gymnasts as youngesters. Ulricke told me that they ceased entering competitions 'after our bosoms grew', but the strenuous training has left them with the legacy of sturdy well-developed frames. They are thin-hipped and broad-shouldered, with abnormally powerful deltoid muscles which give their figures a tapered manly look.

Steve returns, in pale jeans, sandals and a cheesecloth smock-shirt he brought back from his last trip to Morocco. He pours wine for everyone. Steve is an American, somewhat older than the rest of us – late twenties, possibly even thirty. He is very clean, almost obsessive with his cleanliness, always showering, always attending to the edges of his body – the calluses on his toes, his teeth, his cuticles. He has a moustache, a neat blond General Custer affair, which curls up at the ends. It's a similarity – to General Custer – which is amplified by his wavy shoulder-length brown hair. He has spent several years travelling the Mediterranean – Rhodes, Turkey, Ibiza, Hammamet. It's quite likely that he sells drugs to support himself. He's not rich, but he's not poor either. None of us knows where he gets his money. On his return from his last Moroccan trip he had also purchased a mid-calf, butter-coloured Afghan coat, which I covet. I've known him vaguely since I arrived in Nice, but lately, because of his interest in Anneliese, I tend to see him rather more often than I would wish. Whenever

I get the chance I criticize Steve for Anneliese's benefit, but subtly, as if my reservations are merely the result of a disinterested study of human nature. Just before we arrived at the flat I managed to get Anneliese to accept that there was something unappealingly sinister about Steve. Now, when he's out of earshot, we exchange remarks about his nudism. I don't believe the girls find it as offensive as I do.

'I think it's the height of selfishness,' I say. 'I didn't ask to see his penis.'

The girls and Bent laugh.

'I think he's strange,' Anneliese says, with a curious expression on her face. I can't tell if she finds this alluring or not.

Ulricke and I continued to see each other. Soon I learned about the existence of Anneliese, duly met her and realized my mistake. But by then I was 'associated' with Ulricke. To switch attention to Anneliese would have hurt and offended her sister, and with Ulricke hurt and offended, Anneliese would be bound to take her side. I found myself trapped; both irked and tantalized. I came to see Anneliese almost as often as I saw Ulricke. She appeared to like me – to my deep chagrin we became 'friends'.

I forced myself to concentrate on Ulricke – to whom I was genuinely attracted – but she was only the shadow on the cave wall, so to speak. Of course I was discreet and tactful: Ulricke – and Anneliese at first – knew nothing of my real desires. But as the bonds between the three of us developed I came to think of other solutions. I realised I could never 'possess' Anneliese in the way I did her twin; I could never colonize or settle my real affections in her person with her approval . . . And so I resolved to make her instead a sphere of influence – unilaterally, and without permission, to extend my stewardship and protection over her. If I couldn't have her, then I would do my best to make sure no one else should.

'When ought we to go to Cherry's, do you think?' Bent asks in his precise grammar.

We discuss the matter. Cherry is an American girl of iridescent, unreal – and therefore perfectly inert – beauty. She lives in a villa high above the coast at Villefranche which she shares with some other girl students from a college in Ann Arbor, Michigan. They stick closely and rather chastely together, these American girls, as their guileless amiability landed them in trouble when they first arrived in Nice. The Tunisian boys at the *Centre* would ask them back to their rooms for a cup of coffee, and the girls, being friendly, intrigued to meet foreigners and welcoming the opportunity to practise their execrable French, happily accepted. And then when the Tunisian boys tried to fuck them they were outraged. The baffled Tunisians couldn't understand the tears, the slaps, the threats. Surely, they reasoned, if a girl agrees to have a cup of coffee in your room there is only one thing on her mind? As a result, the girls moved out of Nice to their high villa in Villefranche, where – apart from their classes at the *Centre* – they spent most of their time and their French deteriorated beyond redemption. Soon they could only associate with Anglophones and all yearned to return to the USA. They were strange gloomy exiles, these girls, like passengers permanently in transit. The present moment – always the most important – held nothing for them. Their tenses were either past or future; their moods nostalgia or anticipation. And now one of their number – Cherry – was breaking out, her experiences in Nice having confirmed her in her desire to be a wife. She was returning to marry her bemused beau, and tonight was her farewell party.

We decide to go along, to make our way to Villefranche. Mild

Bent has a car – a VW – but he says he has to detour to pick up his girlfriend. Ulricke announces that she and I will hitchhike. Steve and Anneliese can go with Bent, she says. I want to protest, but say nothing.

Ulricke and Anneliese live in a large converted villa, pre-war, up by the *Fac de Lettres* at Magnan. They rent a large room in a ground-floor flat which belongs to a Uruguayan poet (he teaches Spanish literature at the university) called César.

One night – not long after our first meetings – I'm walking Ulricke home. It's quite late. I promise myself that if we get to the villa after midnight I'll ask if I can stay, as it's a long walk back to my room in the rue Dante down in the city. Dependable Ulricke invites me in for a cup of coffee. At the back of the flat the windows are at ground level and overlook a garden. Ulricke and Anneliese use them as doors to avoid passing through the communal hall. We clamber through the window and into the room. It is big, bare and clean. There are two beds, a bright divan and some wooden chairs which have recently been painted a shiny new red. A few cute drawings have been pinned on the wall and there is a single houseplant, flourishing almost indecently from all the attention it receives – the leaves always dark green and glossy, the earth in the pot moist and levelled. The rest of the flat is composed of César's bedroom, his study, a kitchen and bathroom.

We drink our coffee, we talk – idly, amicably. Anneliese is late, out at the cinema with friends. I look at my watch: it is after midnight. I make my request and Ulricke offers me the divan. There is a moment, after we have stripped off the coverlet and tucked in an extra blanket, when we both stand quite close to each other. I lean in her direction, a hand weakly touches her shoulder, we kiss. We sit down on the bed. It is all pleasantly uncomplicated and straightforward.

When Anneliese returns she seems pleased to see me. After more coffee and conversation, the girls change discreetly into their pyjamas in the bathroom. While they're gone I undress to my underpants and socks and slide into bed. The girls come back, the lights go out and we exchange cheery *bonsoirs*.

On the hard small divan I lie awake in the dark, Ulricke and Anneliese sleeping in their beds a few feet away. I feel warm, content, secure – like the member of a close and happy family, as if Ulricke and Anneliese are my sisters and beyond the door in the quiet house lie our tender parents . . .

In the morning I meet César. He is thin and febrile, with tousled dry hair. He speaks fast but badly flawed English. We talk about London, where he lived for two years before coming to Nice. Ulricke tells me that as a poet he is really quite famous in Uruguay. Also she tells me that he had an affair with Anneliese when the girls first moved in – but now they're just friends. Unfortunately this forces a change in my attitude towards César: I like him, but resentment will always distance us now. Whenever he and Anneliese talk I find myself searching for vestiges of their former intimacy – but there seems nothing there any more.

We all possess, like it or not, the people we know, and are possessed by them in turn. We all own and forge an image of others in our minds that is inviolable and private. We make those private images public at our peril. Revelation is an audacious move to be long pondered. Unfortunately, this impulse occurs when we are least able to control it, when we're distracted by love – or hate . . .

But we can possess others without their ever being truly aware of it. For example, I possess Steve and Anneliese in ways they would never imagine.

★   ★   ★

I often wonder what Anneliese thinks about while Ulricke and I are fucking across the room from her. Is she irritated? Curious? Happy? The intimacy of our domestic set-up causes me some embarrassment at first, but the girls seem quite unperturbed. I affect a similar insouciance. But although we live in such proximity we maintain a bizarrely prim decorum. We don't wander around naked. Ulricke and I undress while Anneliese is in the bathroom or else with the lights out. I have yet to see Anneliese naked. And she's always with us too − Ulricke and I have never spent a night alone. Since her affair with César she has had no boyfriend. My vague embarrassment swiftly departs and I begin to enjoy Anneliese's presence during the night − like some mute and unbelievably lax chaperone. One day, to my regret, she tells me how happy she is that Ulricke 'has' me; how pleased she is that we are together. The twin sisters are typically close: Anneliese is the more self-composed and assured and she feels protective towards Ulricke, who's more vulnerable and easily hurt. I reassure her of my sincerity and try not to let the strain show on my face.

With some dismay I watch Steve − an exotic figure, in his Afghan coat and flowing hair − join Anneliese in the back of Bent's VW. Ulricke and I wave them on their way, then we walk down the road from the apartment block towards the Promenade des Anglais. Although it is after nine o'clock the night air is not unpleasantly cool. For the first time the spring chill has left the air − a presage of the bright summer to come. We walk down rue de la Buffa and cut over to the rue de France. The whores in the boutique doorways seem pleased at the clemency of the weather. They call across the street to each other in clear voices; some of them even wear hotpants.

It's not that warm. Ulricke wears a white PVC raincoat and a scarf. I put my arm round her shoulders and hear the crackle of the plastic material. The glow from the street lamps sets highlights in the shine on her nose and cheeks . . . I worry about Steve and Anneliese in the back of Bent's car.

I begin to spend more and more nights at Ulricke's. Madame d'Amico, my landlady, makes no comment on my prolonged absences. I visit my small room in her flat regularly to change my clothes but I find myself increasingly loath to spend nights alone there. Its fusty smell, its dismal view of the interior courtyard, the dull conversations with my fellow lodger, depress me. I am happy to have exchanged lonely independence for the huggermugger intimacy of the villa. Indeed, for a week or so life there becomes even more cramped. The twins are joined by a girlfriend from Bremen, called Clara – twenty-two, sharp-faced, candid – in disgrace from her parents and spending a month or two visiting friends while waiting for tempers back home to cool. I ask her what she has done. She says she had an affair with her father's business partner and oldest friend. This was discovered, and the ramifications of the scandal spread to the boardroom: suits are being filed, resignations demanded, takeover bids plotted. Clara seems quite calm about it all, her only regret being that her lover's daughter – who hitherto had been her constant companion since childhood – now refuses to see or speak to her. Whole lives are irreparably askew.

Clara occupies the divan. She sleeps naked and is less concerned with privacy than the other girls. I find I relish the dormitory-like aspect of our living arrangements even more. At night I lie docilely beside Ulricke listening to the three girls talking in German. I can't understand a word – they could be talking about me, for all I know. Clara smokes French cigarettes and their pleasant sour smell lingers in the air after the lights are switched out. Ulricke and I wait for a diplomatic five minutes or so before making love. That fragrance of Gauloise or Gitanes is forever associated with those tense palpitating moments of darkness: Ulricke's warm strong body, the carnal anticipation, the sounds of Clara and Anneliese settling themselves in their beds, their fake yawns.

On the Promenade des Anglais the shiny cars sweep by. Ulricke and I stick out our thumbs, goosing the air. We always get lifts immediately and have freely hitched, usually with Anneliese, the length of the Côte d'Azur, from San Raphael to Menton, at all hours of the day or night. One warmish evening, near Aix-en-Provence, the three of us decided spontaneously to sleep out in a wood. We huddled up in blankets and woke at dawn to find ourselves quite soaked with dew.

A car stops. The driver – a man – is going to Monte Carlo. We ask him to take the *haute corniche*. Cherry's villa is perched so high above the town that the walk up from the coast road is exhausting. Ulricke sits in the front – the sex of the driver determines our position. To our surprise we have found that very often single women will stop for the three of us. They are much more generous than the men as a rule: in our travels the women frequently buy us drinks and meals, and once we were given 100 francs. Something about the three of us prompts this largess. There is, I feel, something charmed about us as a trio, Ulricke, Anneliese and me. This is why – quite apart from his rebarbative personal habits – I so resent Steve. He is an interloper, an intruder: his presence, his interest in Anneliese, threatens me, us. The trio becomes a banal foursome, or – even worse – two couples.

★　★　★

From the small terrace at Cherry's villa there is a perfect view of Villefranche and its bay, edged by the bright beads of the harbour lights and the headlamps of cars on the coast road. The dim noise of traffic, the sonic rip of some lout's motorbike, drift upward to the villa, competing with the thump and chords of music from inside. *Crosby, Stills, Nash and Young — Live, The Yes Album, Hunky Dory* . . . curious how these LPs pin and fix humdrum moments of our lives — precise as almanacs. An *ars brevis* for the quotidian.

The exquisite Cherry patrols her guests, enveloped in a fug of genial envy from her girlfriends. It's not her impending marriage that prompts this emotion so much as the prospect of the 'real' Coca Cola, 'real' milk and 'real' meat she will be able to consume a few days hence. The girls from Ann Arbor reminisce indefatigably about American meals they have known. To them, France, Nice, is a period of abstention, a penance for which they will be rewarded in calories and carbohydrates when they return home.

I stroll back inside to check on Steve and Anneliese. My mistake was to have allowed them to travel together in Bent's car. It conferred an implicit acknowledgement of their 'coupledom' on them without Steve having to do anything about it. Indeed he seems oddly passive with regard to Anneliese, as if content to bide his time. Perhaps he is a little frightened of her? Perhaps it's his immense vanity: time itself will impress upon her the logic and inevitability of their union . . .? Now I see him sitting as close to Anneliese as possible, as if adjacency alone is sufficient to possess her.

Ulricke talks to Bent's girlfriend, Gudrun, another Scandinavian. We are a polyglot crew at the *Centre* — almost every European country represented. Tonight you can hear six distinct languages . . . I pour myself a glass of wine from an unlabelled bottle. There is plenty to drink. I had brought a bottle of Martini

Rosso as my farewell present to Cherry but left it in my coat pocket when I saw the quantity of wine on offer.

The wine is cold and rough. Decanted no doubt from some huge barrel in the local *cave*. It is cheap and not very potent. We were drinking this wine the night of my audacity.

César had a party for some of his students on the Spanish Lit. course. After strenuous consumption most people had managed to get very drunk. César sang Uruguayan folk songs – perhaps they were his poems, for all I know – to his own inept accompaniment on the guitar. I saw Anneliese collect some empty bottles and leave the room. Moments later I followed. The kitchen was empty. Then from the hall I saw the bathroom door ajar. I pushed it open. Anneliese was reapplying her lipstick.

'I won't be long,' she said.

I went up behind her and put my arms round her. The gesture was friendly, fraternal. She leant back, pursing, pouting and repursing her lips to spread the orange lipstick. We talked at our reflections.

'Good party,' I said.

'César may be a poet but he cannot sing.'

We laughed, I squeezed. It was all good fun. Then I covered her breasts with my hands. I looked at our reflection: our faces side by side, my hands claws on her chest.

'Anneliese . . .' I began, revealing everything in one word, watching her expression register, interpret, change.

'Hey, tipsy boy,' she laughed, clever girl, reaching round to slap my side, 'I'm not Ulricke.'

We broke apart, I heeled a little, drunkenly. We grinned, friends again. But the moment lay between us, like a secret. Now she knew.

★　　★　　★

The party is breaking up. People drift away. I look at Steve; he seems to have his arm round Anneliese. Ulricke joins me.

'What's happening?' I ask Steve.

'Cliff's taking us down to the town. He says they may be at the café tonight.'

I confirm this with Cliff who, improbably, is French. He's a dull, inoffensive person who – we have discovered to our surprise – runs drug errands for the many tax-exiled rock musicians who while away their time on the Côte d'Azur. Every now and then these stars and their retinue emerge from the reclusive licence of their wired-off villas and patronize a café on the harbour front at Villefranche. People sit around and gawp at the personalities and speculate about the hangers-on – the eerie thugs, the haggard, pale women, the brawling kids.

A dozen of us set off. We stroll down the sloping road as it meanders in a sequence of hairpins down the steep face of the hills to the bright town spangling below. Steve, I notice, is holding hands with Anneliese. I hate the look on his face: king leer. I feel a sudden unbearable anger. What *right* has he got to do this, to sidle into our lives, to take possession of Anneliese's hand in that way?

The four of us and Cliff have dropped back from the others. Cliff, in fractured English, is telling us of his last visit to the rock star's villa. I'm barely listening – something to do with a man and a chicken . . . I look back. Anneliese and Steve have stopped. He removes his Afghan coat and places it cape-like round Anneliese's shoulders. He gives a mock-chivalric bow and Anneliese curtsies. These gestures, I recognize with alarm, are the early foundations of a couple's private language – actions, words and shared memories whose meaning and significance only they can interpret and which exclude the world at large. But at the same time they tell me that nothing intimate – no kiss, no caress – has yet passed between them. I have only moments left to me.

The other members of our party have left the road and entered a narrow gap between houses that is the entrance to a thin defile of steps – some hundred yards long – that cuts down the hill directly to the town below. The steps are steep and dark with many an illogical angle and turn. From below I hear the clatter of descending feet and excited cries. Cliff goes first, Ulricke follows. I crouch to tie a shoelace. Anneliese passes. I jump up and with the slightest of tussles insinuate myself between her and Steve.

In the dark cleft of the steps there is just room for two people to pass. I put my hands on the rough iron handrails and slow my pace. Anneliese skips down behind Ulricke. Steve bumps at my back. Soon I can barely make out Anneliese's blonde hair.

'Can I get by, please?'

I ignore Steve, although he's treading on my heels. Below me Anneliese turns a bend out of sight.

'Come *on*, for God's sake.'

'Bit tricky in the dark.'

Roughly, Steve attempts to wrest my arm from the handrail. He swears. I stop dead, lock my elbows and brace myself against his shoving.

'You English fuck!' He punches me quite hard in the back. I run down the steps to a narrow landing where they make a turn. I face Steve. He is lean and slightly taller than me, but I'm not interested in physical prowess, only delay. Further down the flights of steps the sound of footfalls grows ever fainter. I hold the bridge. Steve is panting.

'What do you think you're doing?' he says. 'Who do you think you are? Her father? You don't own these girls, you know.'

He takes a swing at me. I duck my head and his knuckles jar painfully on my skull. Steve lets out a yip of pain. Through photomatic violet light I lunge at him as he massages blood into his numbed fist. With surprising ease I manage to throw him heavily to the ground. At once I turn and spring down the steps. I take them five at a time, my fingertips brushing the handrails like outriggers.

Ulricke and Anneliese are waiting at the bottom. The others have gone on to the harbour front. I seize their hands.

'Quickly,' I say. 'This way!'

Astonished, the girls run with me, laughing and questioning. We run down back streets. Eventually we stop.

'What happened?' Anneliese asks.

'Steve attacked me,' I say. 'Suddenly – tried to hit me. I don't know why.'

Our feet crunch on the pebbles as we walk along Villefranche's *plage publique*. I pass the Martini bottle to Ulricke, who stops to take a swig. We have discussed Steve and his neuroses for a pleasant hour. At the end of the bay's curve a small green hut is set on the edge of the coast road. It juts out over the beach where it is supported by thick wooden piles. We settle down here, sheltered by the overhang, spreading Steve's Afghan coat on the pebbles. We huddle up for warmth, pass the bottle to and fro and decide to watch the dawn rise over Ventimiglia.

The three of us stretch out, me in the middle, on Steve's convenient coat. Soon Ulricke falls asleep. Anneliese and I talk on quietly. I pass her the Martini. Carefully she brings it to her mouth. I notice how, like many women, she drinks awkwardly from the bottle. She fits her lips round the opening and tilts head and bottle simultaneously. When you drink from the bottle like this some of the fluid in your mouth, as you lower your head after your gulp, runs back into the bottle.

'Ow. I think I'm drunk,' she says, handing it back.

I press my lips to the bottle's warm snout, try to taste her lipstick, raise the bottle, try to hold that first mouthful in my throat, swilling it round my teeth and tongue . . .

Ulricke gives a little snore, hunches herself into my left side, pressing my right side against Anneliese. Despite what you may think I want nothing more from Anneliese than what I possess now. I look out over the Mediterranean, hear the plash and rattle of the tiny sluggish waves on the pebbles, sense an ephemeral lunar greyness – a lightening – in the air.

N is for N

Nguyen N, Laotian belle-lettrist and amateur philosopher. Born in Vientiane, Laos, 1883; died Paris, France, 22 February 1942. N's family was of bourgeois stock, comparatively wealthy, francophone and francophile. Nguyen, a precocious but somewhat unhealthy youth, yearned for Paris, but World War I delayed his arrival there until he was twenty-four.

But after humid Vientiane Paris proved noisome and frustrating. The severe winter of 1920 caused his health to fail (something cardiovascular) and he went south to recuperate, to the Côte d'Azur. Strengthened, he decided to settle there. He earned his living as a maths tutor and semi-professional table-tennis player, participating in the short-lived ping-pong leagues that briefly flourished on that sunny littoral in the 1920s.

And it was there that he wrote his little masterpiece, *Les Analectes de Nguyen N* (Monnier, Toulon, 1928), a copy of which I found last year in Hyères, its cerise wrapper dusty and sun-bleached, its pages uncut. A sequence of epiphanic images and apophthegms, its tone fragile and nervy, balancing perilously between the profound and the banal. 'Somewhere snow is gently falling,' Nguyen writes amidst the mimosa and the umbrella pines, 'and I still feel pain.' English cannot do their tender sincerity full justice.

After the book's success Nguyen was taken up by the cultural salons of Paris, where he returned permanently in 1931. He is a tenant of the footnotes of literary history; the unidentified face at the café table; a shadowy figure on the perimeter of many a memoir and biography.

He wrote once to André Gide, who had taxed him on his unusual surname, which is not uncommon in Laos '. . . It is properly pronounced *unnnnhhhh*, effectively three syllables, the final "h"s being as plosive as possible, if you can imagine that. Ideally, after introducing me, you should be very slightly out of breath.'

The war brought penury. Nguyen went to work in the kitchens of Paris's largest Vietnamese restaurant, where he discovered a talent for the decorative garnish. His lacy carrot carnations, scallion lilies and translucent turnip roses were miniature works of art. In between shifts he wrote his short autobiography, *Comment ciseler les legumes* (Plon et Noël, Paris, 1943 – very rare), which was published posthumously.

Nguyen N was run over in the blackout one gloomy February night by a *gendarme* on a bicycle. He died instantly.

The Persistence of Vision

Persistence of vision is a trick of the
eye, an ability the eye possesses to fill
in the gaps between discrete images
and make them appear perfectly
contiguous. This is what makes
animation work.
Murray and Ginsberg's Dictionary of Cinema (1949)

4.05 a.m. The island. Seated on the terrace in front of my house. This is what I tried to retain. This is what I wanted to come to me unbidden from those three years. The soft explosion of a pile of leaves. A bare-breasted gypsy girl dancing for some native soldiers. Orange snakes uncoiling in the glossy panels of an antique automobile. Big papery blue blossoms of hydrangea. A red printed smile on a square of tissue. A honeyed triangle of toast on a faience plate. Tennis in Sausalito. The huge pewtery light of the salt pans. The bleached teak decks of a motor yacht. A rare cloud trapped in a cloud-reflecting pool.

It was in the gusty autumnal pathways of the park that I first saw her. Her small dog had nosed its way into a crackling and shifting drift of plane leaves and she was tugging crossly at the lead, shouting 'Mimi, no, come on, really, you impossible beast!' in her surprisingly deep voice. But it was her wrists that held my attention first and provoked that curious breathlessness which I always associate with moments of intense irritation or intense desire. They were very thin, with the bony nodule of the wrist bone, the ulna, particularly prominent as she tugged and heaved on recalcitrant Mimi's crocodile-skin leash. She was bundled up against the astringent frostiness of the day in an old ankle-length apple-green tweed coat, a black cashmere shawl and a soft felt hat that concealed her figure, but the length and slimness of her pale wrists and swift computations and assessments thereafter – a slightly hooked nose, sunglasses of an opaque ultramarine hue, a corkscrew of auburn hair – were enough for me to lose concentration totally and allow Gilbert, my adored but ineffably stupid labrador pup, to gallop by me, unchecked, from whatever shubbery or tree bole he was dousing, and hurl himself into Mimi's leaf-drift.

The soft explosion of dry leaves, the terrified yips and idiot barkings, the cuffs administered to Gilbert's golden rump, the apologies, the pacifying of Mimi, the crouchings down, the straightenings up, the removal of sunglasses, the removal of a calfskin glove from my right hand, the briefest gripping of those thin cold ringless (ringless!) fingers were achieved in a kind of roaring silence as if one half of my brain were registering the full tapestry of sounds available (the dogs, our voices, and above the traffic the querulous 'where-the-hell-are-you?' toot of an impatient motorist, blocked in by a delivery van or waiting for someone) while the other half, as if in some dust-free, shadowless laboratory, were pedantically analysing and observing. Noting: the ability to raise one eyebrow (the left) without any change in expression; the depth of the blue hollows in the undulations of bone and skin where the clavicle joined the manubrium below her throat; the wide mouth and the perfect unevenness of her teeth. Assessing: the exact moment when to affect the introduction; the exchange of doggy arcana ('A Norfolk terrier? Quite rare, I think.' 'Norwich, actually.' 'Really?'); the casual invitation absent-mindedly offered just as one was saying goodbye, about to set off: 'Look, I don't suppose you'd fancy . . .?' The observable pause, the flick of the eye towards the east gate of the park, the decisive, independent jut of the chin and the tautening of the lips to suppress a smile as she accepted.

We sat at a small table and she rubbed a small circle, tugging her coat sleeve down over the heel of her hand, in the bleary condensation of the window to peer out at the motor cars speeding past. She chose hot chocolate and smoked a French cigarette. I had an apple juice and tried not to sneeze. Her name was − is − Golo.

Even at the wedding her father did not trouble to disguise his candid dislike for me. That he had a handsome, young, parent-less, independently wealthy son-in-law whose devotion to his daughter was both profound and unequivocal seemed to make no difference at all. I asked Golo why he hated me. 'Oh, Daddy's like that,' she said. 'He hates everybody. It's nothing to do with the fact that I'm marrying you.' I asked my best friend, and best man, Max. Doctor Max thought for a while and then said: 'It's obvious. He's jealous.'

Of course that made it worse. We married in a small rural church stacked with the tombs and effigies of Golo's ancestors, a short canter from the family home. I had a flaming sword of indigestion rammed down my oesophagus for three days preceding the ceremony that miraculously disappeared the moment I said 'I do' and I knew that the old man had lost his power to frighten me any more. I could look at his seamed, haughty face, the thinning, oiled hair and the debonair hidalgo's sideburns that he affected and feel no fear. I was not at ease, true, but I was no longer scared. 'You may call me Avery, now,' he said, as we shook hands after the ceremony, but I never did.

At the reception the relief made me drink too much and feeling myself unsteady I sought a distant lavatory in which to vomit. I tickled my throat with the thin end of my tie and emptied my stomach. Patting my lips with a hand towel and feeling markedly better I realized I had wandered into Golo's father's apartments. The bathroom was panelled in a knotty and brooding oxblood cherrywood. Many stern, blazered, cross-armed young men sitting in rows gazed proudly out from sepia photographs. Here and there amongst the cased memorabilia were samples of discreet erotica: breast-baring gypsy maidens playing the tambourine for languid *zouaves*; loose *peignoirs* slipping off shoulders at midday *levées*. And a picture of Golo, a thin and pubescent fourteen.

The room was redolent of expensive hair oils and sandalwood soaps. It was a private shrine to the sort of clubby yet perverse masculinity that I loathed – the beery sexuality of the first-fifteen locker room or the officers' mess after the port has gone round. Max's observation now seemed alarmingly apt. I crumpled my face towel and threw it in the wastepaper basket. I had to get out. I opened the door.

'What the hell are you doing in here?' Her father – Avery – said. He held a long cigar, ash down, in his five fingers.

'Came to say goodbye, sir.' I offered my hand. 'I was told you were in your sitting-room.'

Avery was not convinced, but, transferring his cigar, he shook my hand all the same. 'They've only just started the ball, for Christ's sake.'

'Ferry to catch.'

I stood in the misted blue dusk with Max, waiting for Golo, standing beside the old burnished Malvern some uncle had given us as a present, our cases strapped into the boot. Fitful orange snakes danced in the glossy bodywork from the flares burning down the drive.

'I've got to get her out of here,' I said, a little hysterically. 'That man is a monster. No wonder her sisters went to live with the mother.'

'Stepsisters,' Max said. 'Golo's from the first wife.'

'Oh? I didn't see her here.'

'She committed suicide when Golo was five.'

'Jesus. How do you know?'

'I was talking to a cousin, inside.'

Max offered me a small silver box. I lifted its lid: it was full of small round unmarked pills. 'My wedding present,' Max said. 'I rarely prescribe them. One has to have an exceptionally healthy heart, but they're guaranteed to make your honeymoon go with a zing.'

We embraced and I caught a scent of the menthol jujubes Max used to suck to sweeten his breath.

'Where is that girl?' I said, my voice thick with emotion.

Max reached into the Malvern and tooted a brisk cadenza on the horn, redundantly, as Golo, dressed as far as my blurry eyes could tell in a matador's spangled suit of light, emerged through the front door and seemed to flow luminously down the stairs into my arms.

We honeymooned at my little house on the island. I had had its clapboard exterior repainted a lemony cream the better to offset the regulation bottle-green demanded by the mayor's office. Big cloudy blue blossoms of hydrangea lined the sandy path down to the beach. Across the silver bay I could see the dark stripe of the mainland. A lone yacht slowly edged its way east. In a minute the composition would be perfect. I ached for my sketchpad.

Image. Golo sitting on the lavatory, her skirt hitched up to her thighs, her ankles footcuffed by her impossibly sheer panties. Her long pale thighs angled upwards, knees meeting, her satin evening shoes just clinging to her heels as she sits on tiptoes, like a jockey straddling a thoroughbred. Except this jockey is simultaneously painting her lips vermilion without the aid of a mirror. She purses her lips, pouts, and turns to offer me her best false smile.

'Mmm?'

'Perfect. I don't know how you do it.'

She tears off a square of lavatory paper and prints her lips on it. Neatly folded once, it does the work it was intended for down below, before the panties are hoicked to the knee and then Golo rises in a swoop and rustle of crêpe. There is a millisecond of buttock-cleft on view before the dressing is complete and the chrome knob is pressed and the cistern voids itself.

'Why did you quit medical school?' she asks, apropos of nothing, checking her impassive face in the mirror. Her little finger lightly touches each corner of her mouth.

'What? Because I wanted to be a painter.'

'Can't you be a doctor and a painter at the same time?'

'I can't.'

'What about your friend? He's a doctor and other things.'

'Max? But Max is Renaissance Man. I can't compete with Max, for heaven's sake.'

'Can we get a yacht?'

'Of course. But why on earth?'
'I think I want to learn to sail. Where are we going tonight?'
'The Maharani's.'
'How dreary.'

I watched Max dicing the garlic cloves. Each clove was peeled, halved lengthways and then laid flat and held with a fingertip on the chopping board, where, with a small fine knife, the clove was sliced vertically into a fan, turned through ninety degrees and sliced across again, tiny neat cubes resulting. The residue left under the finger was discarded.

'Why don't you use a press?'
'It doesn't taste the same.'

We were in his garden flat in Kensington, not far from one of the hospitals where he had consulting rooms. He was cooking me supper—scallops. In oil and tomatoes. His kitchen was both efficient and picturesque. Big cleared areas for working, many pan-crowded shelves and racks, and, hung here and there, hams and sausage, pimentoes, chillies and garlic. Needless to say, Max was a highly accomplished cook and he liked his cuisine flavoursome.

'Thank you for my picture,' he said.
'It's the view from the sitting-room.'
'I know.' He wandered over to peer at the picture where he had placed it on a pine dresser. 'You've changed the hydrangeas, or is that artistic licence?'
'Well remembered. When were we there?'
'Thanks. Two summers ago. Is that the *Heliotrope*?'
'What's that?'
'The yacht I used to sail at university. You remember, you met us once at Juan les Pins. Something about the spinnaker. That's a nice thought. Thank you.'
'It's just a yacht, I'm afraid. Isn't that enough garlic?'

He held up his knife in warning. 'You can never have enough garlic.'

He slid the garlic off the board into a pan, where it spat and sizzled in the hot oil.

'How's Golo?' he said.

'Wonderful.'

Later, over the cheese, he said: 'Don't mind me saying this, old friend, but don't leave a woman on her own for long.'

'God, I'm only away for one night. I had to see the trustees.'

'I'm not talking about now. Women get bored much faster than men.'

'Says who?'

'It's a well-known medical fact. Try some of this quince jelly with the cheese. Just something an old lothario told me once.'

Golo is lying on her side, on the bed, naked. I stand in the doorway of the bathroom, showered, spent, happy. Propped on one elbow, she is reading a trashy Sunday paper and laughing to herself at its idiocies. At her elbow, on a faience plate I bought at St Martin, is a triangle of honeyed toast. Through the window I see the sun on the bay and that obliging yacht attended by two or three sea gulls. Without looking up Golo searches the bed with her right foot for the square of sunshine that was warming her flank a moment ago. She finds it and allows her foot a sun bath while she reads, reaches for her toast and bites.

'Why do you buy this rubbish? The stuff they say.'

'I only get it for the funnies.' I think I must be the happiest fellow in the world.

'A likely story.'

We travelled that first year. I let the house in Carlyle Square to a Brazilian diplomat and we went east to India, Ceylon, Thailand.

We saw out the winter with Golo's schoolchum Charlotte and her husband, Didier Van Breuer, in Sydney, Australia. Spring found us in a little house in Sausalito, on another, larger bay. The exhibition of my Indian gouaches in a Broome Street gallery was a modest success. Golo developed a surprisingly effective kicking second serve. We were never a night apart.

I felt a physical presence in my gut, like a stone lodged between my liver and my pancreas. I looked out over the dark trees of Carlyle Square and made all sorts of bargains with any number of deities.

Max came through from the bedroom, running his hands through his hair, which was greying remarkably fast, I noticed, for some odd reason. He looks more tired than me, I thought.

'Relax,' he said. 'I'm not a gynaecologist, but I would say your wife is pregnant.'

I have a son. His name is Dominic. He bellows with rage, he screams, he howls. Odette, his nurse, takes him to his room. I touch Golo's face with my knuckles.

'Welcome home,' I say and from my pocket remove the ring I have had made from an emerald I bought in Bangkok. Golo slips it on her finger.

'She manages to say "I love you" before she dissolves in tears,' I gently mock her.

She hugs me to her. 'You're so sweet,' she says, 'and I do love you.'

Didier Van Breuer to dinner at Carlyle Square. He tells us he is divorcing Charlotte. I leave the room when a messenger comes to the front door and when I return Van Breuer is sitting hunched over his food, sobbing. It is all too terribly sad.

★   ★   ★

Summer came round again and we open up the house on the island. The new annexe for Odette and Dominic blended perfectly with the rest of the house. Odette – a strong raw-boned girl, with many moles – proved to be a capable cook as well as a capable nurse. In one week we were served bouillabaisse, *oursins à la provençale*, marinated veal chops with ratatouille, *poulet* stuffed with roast garlic, *pied de porc Lyonnais*, liver and onions. It was delicious but too rich for me. I found myself feeling overstuffed and bilious, my throat salt and my sinus passages pungent and herby even the next morning. I fasted for twenty-four hours, drinking only distilled water, and endured a night sweat which drove Golo from the bed.

'We must smell like a tinker's camp,' I said to her the day I began to feel better. 'Tell Odette it's salads for the rest of the summer.' By and large she complied, though from time to time a reeking stew or casserole would arrive at the table and the place would smell like a Neapolitan trattoria once again.

I found it hard to paint in the house now that its routines revolved around Dominic's noisy needs rather than my own. I was trying to complete enough work for an exhibition that a friend, who owned a little gallery in the rue Jacob, was kindly arranging for me and so, most days, I would load the panniers on my bicycle with my paints and brushes and set off for various parts of the island that were not pestered with tourists or summer residents, returning home as the evening began to approach. I found a place overlooking the salt pans that promised great refulgent expanses of sky and water. I loved the salt pans with their strange poetry of desiccation, though the series of water-colours I produced there, well enough done, had a lonely simplicity that seemed a little repetitive.

So it was in search of some contrasting bustle and busyness that I reluctantly ventured into one of the little ports and set up my easel by the marina. But after the serenity of the salt pans I found the presence of curious sightseers peering over my shoulder off-putting and, to be frank, my technique was found wanting when I came to render the bobbing mass of yachts and powerboats, dinghies and cruisers that were crowded in amongst the piers and the jetties.

I was sitting there one mid-morning, having torn up my first attempt, wondering vaguely if it would be worth looking at some Dufys that I knew hung in a provincial gallery not more than half a day's drive away, when my peripheral attention was caught by a half-glimpsed figure, male, slim in white khakis and a navy sweater, that I was convinced was familiar. You know the way your instinctive apprehension is often more sure and certain than something studied and sought for: the glance is often more accurate than the stare. I was oddly positive that I had seen someone I knew and, having nothing on the easel to detain me, I sauntered off to find out who it was.

Didier Van Breuer sat in the sunshine of the restaurant terrace with a small glass of brandy and a *caffe latte* on the table in front of him, shirtless with a navy-blue cotton sweater. He had a small red bandanna at his throat. He looked changed since we had last seen him, older and more gaunt. He did not seem too surprised to see me (he knew I summered on the island, he said) but I was glad to discover that my instincts and my eyesight were as sharp and shrewd as they had always been. He was cordial, with none of that reserve that I had always associated with him.

'Where are you staying?' I asked.

He pointed to the harbour, at a vast gin-palace of a motor yacht with a single tall funnel (yellow with a magenta stripe). Crew members swabbed down bleached teak decks, brown water was being pumped from bilges. He was alone, he told me, on an endless meandering summer cruise trying to forget Charlotte and her grotesque betrayal (she was living with Didier's estranged son). I asked him to dinner that night (I had seen Odette empty almost an entire tin of cumin into a lobster stew) but he declined, saying they were setting sail for the Azores later. He finished his drink and we wandered round the quay to his boat (his trousers were pale blue, I noted with a private smile; however vigilant, the corner of your eye cannot achieve 20:20 vision). He had changed the name from *Charlotte III* to *Clymene*, who, he told me, with harsh irony, was the mistress of the sun. He invited me on board and we strolled through the empty state rooms smoking cigars, the warm buttock of a brandy goblet cupped in my right palm. I felt sad for him, with his pointless wealth and the cheerless luxury of his life, and felt sad myself as the boat reminded me of Pappi's old schooner, the *Vergissmein-nicht*, and my lost childhood. He had a rather fine Dufy in the dining-room and I took the opportunity of making a few quick notes and sketches while he went upstairs to make a telephone call.

Nota bene. To be remembered: the serene roseate beauty of the summer dusk as I cycled homeward, a little drunk, a rare cloud trapped in a cloud-reflecting puddle at the side of the road. To be remembered: my almost insupportable feeling of happiness.

4 a.m. I am alone on the terrace of my small house, looking east beyond my blue hydrangeas towards the mainland waiting for the sun to rise. I wonder how many people there are on that mainland as miserable as I am.

Golo's note was terse. She had left me and our child. She was no longer in love with me. There was another man in her life whose identity she would not reveal at this moment. I must not look for her. She would be in touch with me in due course. This was the only way. She needed none of my money. She asked my forgiveness and understanding and hoped, for the sake of Dominic, that we could remain friends.

Odette said simply that during the day Madame had received and made numerous phone calls, had packed one suitcase and then, at about four o'clock, she had heard the taxi klaxonning for her in the lane. She was going to visit her family, she had told Odette; she had left a note for me and was gone.

I wasted no time. I drove at once back to the port, where of course there was no sign of the *Clymene. En route* for the Azores or God knew where. I returned to my house (not *our* house any more) and cried a few hot tears of rage and frustration over my son's cot (*my* son, not *our* son any more) until I woke him and he began to bawl as well. I drank half a bottle of Pernod then drove the car to the ferry and was transported to the mainland. I spent a fruitless hour searching for a 'Venus of the Crossroads', as Pappi used to refer to them, feeling the urge for revenge slowly ebb from me. At around midnight in an overlit dockside bar I half-heartedly bought a large woman with bobbed hair and a tight jersey a few drinks but then lost my nerve. On the last ferry back to the island a bearded youngster played some form of Hawaiian music on a guitar.

The sky is lightening, a pale cornflower-blue shading into lemon, my dead eyes watch the beautiful transformation, unmarvelling. I must think, I must clarify my thoughts. The betrayed husband is always the last to know, they say. Didier Van Breuer. Were our friends in Sydney, Australia, all laughing behind my back that winter? What had made Didier come to our house to announce his separation? What had made him break down that way over the meal? What had been said while I was out of the room? To end this stream of answerless questions I force myself to think of Encarnacion, a Mexican girl I had briefly loved and to whom I had once thought of proposing. Dear, lissom Encarna, some kind of ex-athlete, a hurdler or swimmer. So different from Golo. I think of a meal we shared in New York, that little restaurant in New York, south of Greenwich Village, where she cajoled me into eating a pungent shouting salsa from her native province that made my eyes water, obliging me to suck peppermints for days . . .

This is what I must retain. These are the fragments I must hoard from these last three years. The soft explosion of a pile of leaves. The querulous where-the-hell-are-you tooting of a waiting motorist. The scent of menthol jujubes. A lone yacht on a silver bay. The immaculate dicing of a garlic clove. The dark trees of Carlyle Square. *Oursins à la provençale*. A slim male figure in white khakis and a navy sweater. A tin of cumin. A taxi klaxonning in the lane. A pungent shouting salsa that obliged me to suck peppermints for days.

Cork

O homem não é um animal
É uma carne inteligente
Embora às vezes doente.
(A man is not an animal;
Is intelligent flesh,
Although sometimes ill.)
                    Fernando Pessoa

My name is Lily Campendonc. A long time ago I used to live in Lisbon. I lived in Lisbon between 1929 and 1935. A beautiful city, but melancholy.

Agostinho Boscán, Christmas 1934: 'We never love anyone. Not really. We only love our idea of another person. It is some conception of our own that we love. We love ourselves, in fact.'

'Mrs Campendonc?'
    'Yes?'
    'May I be permitted to have a discreet word with you? Discreetly?'
    'Of course.'

He did not want this word to take place in the office so we left
the building and walked down the rua Serpa towards the Arsenal.
It was dark, we had been working late, but the night was warm.

'Here, please. I think this café will suit.'

I agreed. We entered and sat at a small table in the rear. I asked
for a coffee and he for a glass of *vinho verde*. Then he decided to
collect the order himself and went to the bar to do so. While he
was there I noticed him drink a brandy standing at the bar,
quickly, in one swift gulp.

He brought the drinks and sat down.

'Mrs Campendonc, I'm afraid I have some bad news.' His thin
taut features remained impassive. Needlessly he restraightened his
straight bow tie.

'And what would that be?' I resolved to be equally calm.

He cleared his throat, looked up at the mottled ceiling and
smiled vaguely.

'I am obliged to resign,' he said; 'I hereby offer you one
month's notice.'

I tried to keep the surprise off my face. I frowned. 'That is bad
news, Senhor Boscán.'

'I am afraid I had no choice.'

'May I ask why?'

'Of course, of course, you have every right.' He thought for a
while, saying nothing, printing neat circles of condensation on the
tan scrubbed wood of the table with the bottom of his wineglass.

'The reason is . . .' he began, 'and if you will forgive me I will
be entirely candid – the reason is,' and at this he looked me in the
eye, 'that I am very much in love with you, Mrs Campendonc.'

'Cork'

The material of which this monograph treats has become of
double interest because of its shrouded mystery, which has

never been pierced to the extent of giving the world a complete and comprehensive story. The mysticism is not associated with its utility and general uses, as these are well known, but rather with its chemical makeup, composition and its fascinating and extraordinary character.

Consul Schenk's Report on the
Manufacture of Cork, Leipzig, 1890

After my husband, John Campendonc, died in 1932 I decided to stay on in Lisbon. I knew enough about the business, I told myself, and in any event could not bear the thought of returning to England and his family. In his will he left the company – the Campendonc Cork Co. Ltd – to me with instructions that it should continue as a going concern under the family name or else be sold. I made my decision and reassured those members of John's family who tried earnestly to dissuade me that I knew exactly what I was doing, and besides there was Senhor Boscán who would always be there to help.

I should tell you a little about John Campendonc first, I suppose, before I go on to Boscán.

John Campendonc was twelve years older than me, a small strong Englishman, very fair in colouring, with fine blond hair that was receding from his forehead. His body was well muscled with a tendency to run to fat. I was attracted to him on our first meeting. He was not handsome – his features were oddly lopsided – but there was a vigour about him that was contagious and that characterized his every movement and preoccupation. He read vigorously, for example, leaning forward over his book or newspaper, frowning, turning and smoothing down the pages with a flick and crack and a brisk stroke of his palm. He walked everywhere at high speed and his habitual pose was to thrust his left hand in the pocket of his coat – thrust strongly down – and, with his right hand, to smooth his hair back in a series of rapid caresses. Consequently his coats were always distorted on the left, the pocket bulged and baggy, sometimes torn, the constant strain on the seams inevitably proving too great. In this manner he wore out three or four suits a year. Shortly before he died I found a tailor in the rua Garrett who would make him a suit with three identical coats. So for John's fortieth birthday I presented him with an assortment of suits − flannel, tweed and cotton drill − consisting of three pairs of trousers and nine coats. He was very amused.

I retain a strong and moving image of him. It was about two weeks before his death and we had gone down to Cascaes for a picnic and a bathe in the sea. It was late afternoon and the beach was deserted. John stripped off his clothes and ran naked into the sea, diving easily through the breakers. I could not − and still cannot − swim and so sat on the running-board of our motor car, smoked a cigarette and watched him splash about in the waves. Eventually he emerged and strode up the beach towards me, flicking water from his hands.

'Freezing,' he shouted from some way off. 'Freezing freezing freezing!'

This is how I remember him, confident, ruddy and noisy in his nakedness. The wide slab of his chest, his fair, open face, his thick legs darkened with slick wet hair, his balls clenched and shrunken with cold, his penis a tense white stub. I laughed at him and pointed at his groin. Such a tiny thing, I said, laughing. He stood there, hands on his hips, trying to look offended. Big enough for you, Lily Campendonc, he said, grinning, you wait and see.

Two weeks and two days later his heart failed him and he was dead and gone for ever.

Why do I tell you so much about John Campendonc? It will help explain Boscán, I think.

CORK

The cork tree has in no wise escaped from disease and infections; on the contrary it has its full allotted share which worries the growers more than the acquiring of a perfect texture. Unless great care is taken all manner of ailments can corrupt and weaken fine cork and prevent this remarkable material from attaining its full potential.

Consul Schenk's Report

Agostinho da Silva Boscán kissed me one week after he had resigned. He worked out his month's notice scrupulously and dutifully. Every evening he came to my office to report on the day's business and present me with letters and contracts to sign. On this particular evening, I recall, we were going over a letter of complaint to a cork grower in Elvas – hitherto reliable – whose cork planks proved to be riddled with ant borings. Boscán was standing beside my chair, his right hand flat on the leather top of the desk, his forefinger slid beneath the upper page of the letter ready to turn it over. Slowly and steadily he translated the Portuguese into his impeccable English. It was hot and I was a little tired. I found I was not concentrating on the sonorous monotone of his voice. My gaze left the page of the letter and focused on his hand, flat on the desktop. I saw its even, pale brownness, like milky coffee, the dark glossy hairs that grew between the knuckles and the first joint of the fingers, the nacreous shine of his fingernails . . . the pithy edge of his white cuffs, beginning to fray . . . I could smell a faint musky perfume coming off him – farinaceous and sweet – from the lotion he put on his hair, and mingled with that his own scent, sour and salt . . . His suit was too heavy, his only suit, a worn shiny blue serge, made in Madrid he had told me, too hot for a summer night in Lisbon . . . Quietly, I inhaled and my nostrils filled with the smell of Agostinho Boscán.

'If you say you love me, Senhor Boscán,' I interrupted him, 'why don't you do something about it?'

'I am,' he said, after a pause. 'I'm leaving.'

He straightened. I did not turn, keeping my eyes on the letter. 'Isn't that a bit cowardly?'

'Well,' he said. 'It's true. I would like to be a bit less . . . cowardly. But there is a problem. Rather a serious problem.'

Now I turned. 'What's that?'

'I think I'm going mad.'

My name is Lily Campendonc, née Jordan. I was born in Cairo in 1908. In 1914 my family moved to London. I was educated there and in Paris and Geneva. I married John Campendonc in 1929 and we moved to Lisbon where he ran the family's cork-processing factory. He died of a coronary attack in October 1931. I had been a widow for nine months before I kissed another man, my late husband's office manager. I was twenty-four years old when I spent my first Christmas with Agostinho da Silva Boscán.

The invitation came, typewritten on a lined sheet of cheap writing paper.

My dear Lily,

I invite you to spend Christmas with me. For three days – 24, 25, 26 December – I will be residing in the village of Manjedoura. Take the train to Cintra and then a taxi from the station.

My house is at the east end of the village, painted white with green shutters. It would make me very happy if you could come, even for a day. There are only two conditions.

One, you must address me only as Balthazar Cabral. Two, please do not depilate yourself – anywhere.

Your good friend,
Agostinho Boscán

'Balthazar Cabral' stood naked beside the bed I was lying in. His penis hung long and thin, but slowly fattening, shifting. Uncircumcised. I watched him pour a little olive oil into the palm of his hand and grip himself gently. He pulled at his penis, smearing it with oil, watching it grow erect under his touch. Then he pulled the sheet off me and sat down. He wet his fingers with the oil again and reached to feel me.

'What's happening?' I could barely sense his moving fingers.

'It's an old trick,' he said. 'Roman centurions discovered it in Egypt.' He grinned. 'Or so they say.'

I felt oil running off my inner thighs on to the bed-clothes. Boscán clambered over me and spread my legs. He was thin and wiry, his flat chest shadowed with fine hairs, his nipples almost black. The beard he had grown made him look strangely younger.

He knelt in front of me. He closed his eyes.

'Say my name, Lily, say my name.'

I said it. Balthazar Cabral. Balthazar Cabral. Balthazar Cabral . . .

After the first stripping the cork tree is left in the juvenescent state to regenerate. Great care must be taken in the stripping not to injure the inner skin or epidermis at any stage in the process, for the life of the tree depends on its proper preservation. If injured at any point growth there ceases and the spot remains for ever afterward scarred and uncovered.

Consul Schenk's Report

I decided not to leave the house that first day. I spent most of the time in bed, reading or sleeping. Balthazar brought me food – small cakes and coffee. In the afternoon he went out for several hours. The house we were in was square and simple and set in a tangled uncultivated garden. The ground floor consisted of a sitting-room and a kitchen and above that were three bedrooms. There was no lavatory or bathroom. We used chamber pots to relieve ourselves. We did not wash.

Balthazar returned in the early evening bringing with him some clothes which he asked me to put on. There was a small short maroon jacket with epaulettes but no lapels – it looked vaguely German or Swiss – a simple white shirt and some black cotton trousers with a drawstring at the waist. The jacket was small, even for me, tight across my shoulders, the sleeves short at my wrists. I wondered if it belonged to a boy.

I dressed in the clothes he had brought and stood before him as he looked at me intently, concentrating. After a while he asked me to pin my hair up.

'Whose jacket is this?' I asked as I did so.

'Mine,' he said.

We sat down to dinner. Balthazar had cooked the food. Tough stringy lamb in an oily gravy. A plate of beans the colour of pistachio. Chunks of greyish spongy bread torn from a flat crusty loaf.

On Christmas Day we went out and walked for several miles along unpaved country roads. It was a cool morning with a fresh breeze. On our way back home we were caught in a shower of rain and took shelter under an olive tree, waiting for it to pass. I sat with my back against the trunk and smoked a cigarette. Balthazar sat cross-legged on the ground and scratched designs in the earth with a twig. He wore heavy boots and coarse woollen trousers. His new beard was uneven – dense around his mouth and throat, skimpy on his cheeks. His hair was uncombed and greasy. The smell of the rain falling on the dry earth was strong – sour and ferrous, like old cellars.

That night we lay side by side in bed, hot and exhausted. I slipped my hands in the creases beneath my breasts and drew them out, my fingers moist and slick. I scratched my neck. I could smell the sweat on my body. I turned. Balthazar was sitting up, one knee raised, the sheet flung off him, his shoulders against the wooden headboard. On his side of the bed was an oil-lamp set on a stool. A small brown moth fluttered crazily around it, its big shadow bumping on the ceiling. I felt a sudden huge contentment spill through me. My bladder was full and was aching slightly, but with the happiness came a profound lethargy that made the effort required to reach below the bed for the enamel chamber pot prodigious.

I touched Balthazar's thigh.

'You can go tomorrow,' he said. 'If you want.'

'No, I'll stay on,' I said instantly, without thinking. 'I'm enjoying myself. I'm glad I'm here.' I hauled myself up to sit beside him.

'I want to see you in Lisbon,' I said, taking his hand.

'No, I'm afraid not.'

'Why?'

'Because after tomorrow you will never see Balthazar Cabral again.'

From this meagre description we now at least have some idea of what 'corkwood' is and have some indication of the constant care necessary to ensure a successful gathering or harvest, while admitting that the narration in no wise does justice to this most interesting material. We shall now turn to

examine it more closely and see what it really is, how this particular formation comes about and its peculiarities.

Consul Schenk's Report

Boscán: 'One of my problems, one of my mental problems, rather – and how can I convince you of its effect? – horrible, horrible beyond words – is my deep and abiding fear of insanity . . . Of course, it goes without saying: such a deep fear of insanity is insanity itself.'

I saw nothing of Boscán for a full year. Having left my employ he then, I believe, became a freelance translator, working for any firm that would give him a job and not necessarily in the cork industry. Then came Christmas 1933 and another invitation arrived, written on a thick buff card with deckle-edges in a precise italic hand, in violet ink:

Senhora Campendonc, do me the honour of spending the festive season in my company. I shall be staying at the Avenida Palace hotel, rooms 35–38, from the 22nd–26th December inclusive.

Your devoted admirer,

J. Melchior Vasconcelles

PS Bring many expensive clothes and scents. I have jewels.

Boscán's suite in the Avenida Palace was on the fourth floor. The bellhop referred to me as Senhora Vasconcelles. Boscán greeted me in the small vestibule and made the bellhop leave my cases there.

Boscán was dressed in a pale grey suit. His face was thinner, clean-shaven and his hair was sleek, plastered down on his head with Macassar. In his shiny hair I could see the stiff furrows made by the teeth of the comb.

When the bellhop had gone we kissed. I could taste the mint from his mouthwash on his lips.

Boscán opened a small leather suitcase. It was full of jewels, paste jewels, rhinestones, strings of artificial pearls, *diamanté* brooches and marcasite baubles. This was his plan, he said: this Christmas our gift to each other would be a day. I would dedicate a day to him, and he to me.

'Today you must do everything I tell you,' he said. 'Tomorrow is yours.'

'All right,' I said. 'But I won't do everything you tell me to, I warn you.'

'Don't worry, Lily, I will ask nothing indelicate of you.'

'Agreed. What shall I do?'

'All I want you to do is to wear these jewels.'

The suite was large: a bathroom, two bedrooms and a capacious sitting-room. Boscán/Vasconcelles kept the curtains drawn, day and night. In one corner was a freestanding cast-iron stove which one fed from a wooden box full of coal. It was warm and dark in the suite; we were closed off from the noise of the city; we could have been anywhere.

We did nothing. Absolutely nothing. I wore as many of his cheap trinkets as my neck, blouse, wrists and fingers could carry. We ordered food and wine from the hotel kitchen which was brought up at regular intervals, Vasconcelles himself collecting everything in the vestibule. I sat and read in the electric gloom, my jewels winking and flashing merrily at the slightest shift of position. Vasconcelles smoked short stubby cigars and offered me fragrant oval cigarettes. The hours crawled by. We smoked, we ate, we drank. For want of anything better to do I consumed most of a bottle of champagne and dozed off. I woke, fuzzy and irritated, to find Vasconcelles had drawn a chair up to the sofa I was slumped on and was sitting there, elbows on knees, chin on fists, staring at me. He asked me questions about the business, what I had been doing in the last year, had I enjoyed my trip home to England, had the supply of cork from Elvas improved and so on. He was loquacious, we talked a great deal but I could think of nothing to ask him in return. J. Melchior Vasconcelles was, after all, a complete stranger to me and I sensed it would put his tender personality under too much strain to inquire about his circumstances and the fantastical life he led. All the same, I was very curious, knowing Boscán as I did.

'This suite must be very expensive,' I said.

'Oh yes. But I can afford it. I have a car outside too. And a driver. We could go for a drive.'

'If you like.'

'It's an American car. A Cadillac.'

'Wonderful.'

That night when we made love in the fetid bedroom he asked me to keep my jewels on.

'It's your day today.'

'Thank you. Merry Christmas.'

'And the same to you . . . What do you want me to do?'

'Take all your clothes off.'

I made Vasconcelles remain naked for the entire day. It was at first amusing and then intriguing to watch his mood slowly change. Initially he was excited, sexually, and regularly aroused.

But then, little by little, he became self-conscious and awkward. At one stage in the day I watched him filling the stove with coal, one-handed, the other cupped reflexively around his genitals, like adolescent boys I had once seen jumping into the sea off a breakwater at Cidadella. Later still he grew irritable and restless, pacing up and down, not content to sit and talk out the hours as we had done the day before.

In mid-afternoon I put on a coat and went out for a drive, leaving him behind in the suite. The big Cadillac was there, as he had said, and a driver. I had him drive me down to Estoril and back. I was gone for almost three hours.

When I returned Vasconcelles was asleep, lying on top of the bed in the hot bedroom. He was deeply asleep, his mouth open, his arms and legs spread. His chest rose and fell slowly and I saw how very thin he was, his skin stretched tight over his ribs. When I looked closely I could see the shiver and bump of his palpitating heart.

Before dinner he asked me if he could put on his clothes. When I refused his request it seemed to make him angry. I reminded him of our gifts and their rules. But to compensate him I wore a tight sequinned gown, placed his flashy rings on my fingers and roped imitation pearls round my neck. My wrists ticked and clattered with preposterous rhinestone bangles. So we sat and ate: me, Lily Campendonc, splendid in my luminous jewels and, across the table, J. Melchior Vasconcelles, surly and morose, picking at his Christmas dinner, a crisp linen napkin spread modestly across his thighs.

The various applications of cork that we are now going to consider are worthy of description as each application has its *raison d'être* in one or more of the physical or chemical properties of this marvellous material. Cork possesses three key properties that are unique in a natural substance. They are: impermeability, elasticity and lightness.

Consul Schenk's Report

I missed Boscán after this second Christmas with him, much more – strangely – than I had after the first. I was very busy in the factory that year – 1934 – as we were installing machinery to manufacture Kamptulicon, a soft, unresounding cork carpet made from cork powder and indiarubber and much favoured by hospitals and the reading-rooms of libraries. My new manager – a dour, reasonably efficient fellow called Pimentel – saw capably to most of the problems that arose but refused to accept any responsibility for all but the most minor decisions. As a result I was required to be present whenever anything of significance had to be decided, as if I functioned as a symbol of delegatory power, a kind of managerial chaperone.

I thought of Boscán often, and many nights I wanted to be with him. On those occasions, as I lay in bed dreaming of Christmasses past and, I hoped, Christmasses to come, I thought I would do anything he asked of me – or so I told myself.

One evening at the end of April I was leaving a shop on the rua Conceição, where I had been buying a christening present for my sister's second child, when I saw Boscán entering a café, the Trinidade. I walked slowly past the door and looked inside. It was cramped and gloomy and there were no women clients. In my glimpse I saw Boscán leaning eagerly across a table, around which sat half a dozen men, showing them a photograph, which they at first peered at, frowning, and then broke into wide smiles. I walked on, agitated, this moment frozen in my mind's eye. It was the first time I had seen Boscán, and Boscán's life, separate from myself. I felt unsettled and oddly envious. Who were these men? Friends or colleagues? I wanted suddenly and absurdly to share in that moment of the offered photograph, to frown and then grin conspiratorially like the others.

I waited outside the Trinidade sitting in the back seat of my motor car with the windows open and the blinds down. I made Julião, my old chauffeur, take off his peaked cap. Boscán eventually emerged at about 7.45 and walked briskly to the tramway centre at the Rocio. He climbed aboard a no.2 which we duly followed until he stepped down from it near São Vicente. He set off down the steep alleyways into the Mouraria. Julião and I left the car and followed him discreetly down a series of *boqueirão* – dim and noisome streets that led down to the Tagus. Occasionally there would be a sharp bend and we would catch a glimpse of the wide sprawling river shining below in the moonlight, and beyond, the scatter of lights from Almada on the southern bank.

Boscán entered the door of a small decrepit house. The steps up to the threshold were worn and concave, the tiles above the porch were cracked and slipping. A blurry yellow light shone from behind drab lace curtains. Julião stopped a passer-by and asked who lived there. Senhor Boscán, he was told, with his mother and three sisters.

'Mrs Campendonc!'

'Mr Boscán.' I sat down opposite him. When the surprise and shock began to leave his face I saw that he looked pale and tired. His fingers touched his bow tie, his lips, his ear lobes. He was smoking a small cigar, chocolate brown, and wearing his old blue suit.

'Mrs Campendonc, this is not really a suitable establishment for a lady.'

'I wanted to see you.' I touched his hand, but he jerked it away as if my fingers burned him.

'It's impossible. I'm expecting some friends.'

'Are you well? You look tired. I miss you.'

His gaze flicked around the café. 'How is the Kamptulicon going? Pimentel is a good man.'

'Come to my house. This weekend.'

'Mrs Campendonc . . .' His tone was despairing.

'Call me Lily.'

He steepled his fingers. 'I'm a busy man. I live with my mother and three sisters. They expect me home in the evening.'

'Take a holiday. Say you're going to . . . to Spain for a few days.'

'I only take one holiday a year.'

'Christmas.'

'They go to my aunt in Coimbra. I stay behind to look after the house.'

A young man approached the table. He wore a ludicrous yellow overcoat that reached down to his ankles. He was astonished to see me sitting there. Boscán looked even iller as he introduced us. I have forgotten his name.

I said goodbye and went towards the door. Boscán caught up with me.

'At Christmas,' he said quietly. 'I'll see you at Christmas.'

A postcard. A sepia view of the Palace of Queen Maria Pia, Cintra:

'I will be one kilometre west of the main beach at Paco d'Arcos. I have rented a room in the Casa de Bizoma. Please arrive at dawn on 25th December and depart at sunset.

I am your friend,

Gaspar Barbosa

The bark of the cork tree is removed every 8–10 years, the quality of the cork improving with each successive stripping. Once the section of cork is removed from the tree the outer surface is scraped and cleaned. The sections – wide curved planks – are flattened by heating them over a fire and submitting them to pressure on a flat surface. In the heating operation the surface is charred, and thereby the pores are closed up. It is this process that the industry terms the 'nerve' of cork. This is cork at its most valuable. A cork possesses 'nerve' when its significant properties – lightness, imperme-ability, elasticity – are sealed in the material for ever.

Consul Schenk's Report

In the serene, urinous light of dawn the beach at Paco d'Arcos looked slate grey. The seaside cafés were closed up and conveyed sensations of dejection and decrepitude as only out-of-season holiday resorts can. To add to this melancholy scene a fine cold rain blew off the Atlantic. I stood beneath my umbrella on the coast road and looked about me. To the left I could just make out the tower of Belem. To the right the hills of Cintra were shrouded in a heavy opaque mist. I turned and walked up the road toward the Casa de Bizoma. As I drew near I could see Boscán sitting on a balcony on the second floor. All other windows on this side of the hotel were firmly shuttered.

A young girl, of about sixteen years, let me in and led me up to his room.

Boscán was wearing a monocle. On a table behind him were two bottles of brandy. We kissed, we broke apart.

'Lise,' he said. 'I want to call you Lise.'

Even then, even that day, I said no. 'That's the whole point,' I reminded him. 'I'm me – Lily – whoever you are.'

351

He inclined his body forward in a mock bow. 'Gaspar Barbosa . . . Would you like something to drink?'

I drank some brandy and then allowed Barbosa to undress me, which he did with pedantic diligence and great delicacy. When I was naked he knelt before me and pressed his lips against my groin, burying his nose in my pubic hair. He hugged me, still kneeling, his arms strong around the backs of my thighs, his head turned sideways in my lap. When he began to cry softly I raised him up and led him over to the narrow bed. He undressed and we climbed in, huddling up together, our legs interlocking. I reached down to touch him.

'I don't know what's wrong,' he said. 'I don't know.'

'We'll wait.'

'Don't forget you have to go at sunset, remember.'

'I won't.'

We made love later but it was not very satisfactory. He seemed listless and tired – nothing like Balthazar Cabral and Melchior Vasconcelles.

At noon – the hotel restaurant was closed – we ate a simple lunch he had brought himself: some bread, some olives, some tart sheep's-milk cheese, some oranges and almonds. By then he was on to the second bottle of brandy. After lunch I smoked a cigarette. I offered him one – I had noticed he had not smoked all day – which he accepted but which he extinguished after a couple of puffs.

'I have developed a mysterious distaste for tobacco,' he said, pouring himself some more brandy.

In the afternoon we tried to make love again but failed.

'It's my fault,' he said. 'I'm not well.'

I asked him why I had had to arrive at dawn and why I had to leave at sunset. He told me it was because of a poem he had written, called 'The Roses of the Gardens of the God Adonis'.

'You wrote? Boscán?'

'No, no. Boscán has only written one book of poems. Years ago. These are mine, Gaspar Barbosa's.'

'What's it about?' The light was going; it was time for me to leave.

'Oh . . .' He thought. 'Living and dying.'

He quoted me the line which explained the truncated nature of my third Christmas with Agostinho Boscán. He sat at the table before the window, wearing a dirty white shirt and the trousers of his blue serge suit, and poured himself a tumblerful of brandy.

'It goes like this – roughly. I'm translating: "Let us make our lives last one day," ' he said. ' "So there is night before and night after the little that we last." '

The uses to which corkwood may be put are unlimited. And yet when we speak of uses it is only those that have developed by reason of the corkwood's own peculiarity and not the great number it has been adapted to, for perhaps its utility will have no end and, in my estimation, its particular qualities are but little appreciated. At any rate it is the most wonderful bark of its kind, its service has been a long one and its benefits, even as a stopper, have been many. A wonderful material truly, and of interest, so full that it seems I have failed to do it justice in my humble endeavour to describe the Quercus Suber of Linnaeus – Cork.

Consul Schenk's Report

Boscán, during, I think, that last Christmas: 'You see, because I am nothing, I can imagine *anything* . . . If I were something, I would be unable to imagine.'

★   ★   ★

It was early December 1935 that I received my last communication from Agostinho Boscán. I was waiting to hear from him as I had received an offer for the company from the Armstrong Cork Co. and was contemplating a sale and, possibly, a return to England.

I was in my office one morning when Pimentel knocked on the door and said there was a Senhora Boscán to see me. For an absurd, exquisite moment I thought this might prove to be Agostinho's most singular disguise, but remembered he had three sisters and a mother still living. I knew before she was shown in that she came with news of Boscán's death.

Senhora Boscán was small and tubby with a meek pale face. She wore black and fiddled constantly with the handle of her umbrella as she spoke. Her brother had requested specifically that I be informed of his death when it arrived. He had passed away two nights ago.

'What did he die of?'

'Cirrhosis of the liver . . . He was . . . My brother had become an increasingly heavy drinker. He was very unhappy.'

'Was there anything else for me, that he said? Any message?'

Senhora Boscán cleared her throat and blinked. 'There is no message.'

'I'm sorry?'

'That is what he asked me to say: "There is no message." '

'Ah.' I managed to disguise my smile by offering Senhora Boscán a cup of coffee. She accepted.

'We will all miss him,' she said. 'Such a good quiet man.'

From an obituary of Agostinho da Silva Boscán:

    . . . Boscán was born in 1888, in Durban, South Africa, where his father was Portuguese consul. He was the youngest of four

354

children, the three elder being sisters. It was in South Africa that he received a British education and where he learned to speak English. Boscán's father died when he was seventeen and the family returned to Lisbon, where Boscán was to reside for the rest of his life. He worked primarily as a commercial translator and office manager for various industrial concerns, but mainly in the cork business. In 1916 he published a small collection of poems, *Insensivel*, written in English. The one Portuguese critic who noticed them, and who wrote a short review, described them as 'a sad waste'. Boscán was active for a while in Lisbon literary circles and would occasionally publish poems, translations and articles in the magazine *Sombra*. The death of his closest friend, Xavier Quevedo, who committed suicide in Paris in 1924, provoked a marked and sudden change in his personality which became increasingly melancholic and irrational from then on. He never married. His life can only be described as uneventful.

A NOTE ON THE AUTHOR

William Boyd is the author of nine novels, many of which have won prizes. *A Good Man in Africa* won the Whitbread Literary Award for Best First Novel; *An Ice-Cream War* won the John Llewellyn Rhys Memorial Prize and was shortlisted for the Booker Prize; *Brazzaville Beach* won the James Tait Black Memorial Prize; *The Blue Afternoon* was the winner of the *Los Angeles Times* Book Prize for Fiction; and most recently *Restless* won the 2006 Costa Novel Award. In addition, some thirteen of his screenplays have been filmed and in 1998 he both wrote and directed the feature film *The Trench*.

A NOTE ON THE TYPE

The text of this book is set in Bembo. This type
was first used in 1495 by the Venetian printer
Aldus Manutius for Cardinal Bembo's *De Aetna*,
and was cut for Manutius by Francesco Griffo.
It was one of the types used by Claude Garamond
(1480–1561) as a model for his Romain de
L'Université, and so it was the forerunner of what
became standard European type for the following
two centuries. Its modern form follows the original
types and was designed for Monotype in 1929.